GIFT

OF

BLOOD

The Miranda Chronicles: Book III

GIFT OF BLOOD

Susan Old

Zairesue Books Arlington,
Washington 2021

I want to thank you for taking time to read my book and hope you enjoy it. When you have finished it, I would love if you took a moment to leave a review of the book on Amazon. Reviews are enormously helpful to independent authors, not only to find out what readers think but also for other reads to find the book and help decide whether to read it. It is the best way for independent authors to get the word out.

You can go to my website for more about Miranda, the nocturnal maniacs and me. If you like you can also sign up for my newsletter.

www.susanold.com
www.amazon.com

Copyright

Cast of Characters
Vampires

Historically Sir and Lady denote the ruling class Haute Caste vampires with HH blood. After brave and exemplary service to the Magus during Alexander's failed coup attempt several Common Caste were elevated to Haute Caste who did not possess HH blood. To the chagrin of many of the Haute Caste Miranda often refers to them without using their titles.

The Magus aka Desmon Dontinae, the first vampire, rules over world vampire society from his mansion in L.A. Born in Mesopotamia.

Baron Tristan Mordecai, 2nd most powerful vampire. Born in what is currently Lithuania. Ex-husband of Miranda and father of Tomas, Marie and Desmon. Wealthy publishing mogul who lives in L.A.

Baroness Miranda Ortega-Mordecai, the first half-vampire, raised in Rossville, Illinois by Pete and Connie Ortega. Only as an adult found out that she is the biological daughter of Sir Omar Sedaghi. She was secretly watched over by various members of vampire society. She moved to L.A. to attend UCLA and to pursue a writing career. Was pursued and seduced by Tristan Mordecai. Mother of Tomas, Desmon, Marie and Jacques.

Sir Angel, House of Plows, Lives in L.A. Serves the Magus.

Lady Anastasia Romanov aka The High Priestess, significant other of Sir Omar and the only "surviving" member of Tsar Nicholas' family.

Antoinella, aide to Sir Borgia, House of Pentacles

Sir Bartholomew aka The Hierophant prefers to be called Bart. Lived at Miranda's Rossville, IL. estate to watch over Miranda and her offspring.

Sir Billy aka Billy the Kid – motorcycle riding member of the House of Plows and traveling companion to Sir Robert.

Sir Cesare Borgia, Head of The House of Pentacles, London, England

Chang – Common Caste, transformed by Scheherazade. He was duped by Scheherazade to join with her in Alexander's coup attempt. He then swore allegiance to the Magus and was allowed to join the House of Cups.

Sir Franco, Knight to Sir Jorge, House of Arrows

Guillaume born in France, transformed by the Magus, guardian to Miranda and her offspring at the Granite Falls estate.

Sir Henry – One of the ancients but not affiliated with any established House. He was Cleopatra's lover and was transformed after her death.

Sir Jorge, Head of The House of Arrows, Caracas, Venezuela

Lady Kabedi, Knight to Lady Kananga, House of Wands

Lady Kananga, Head of The House of Wands, Kinshasa, Democratic Republic of the Congo

Lady (Princess) Khunbish Head of the House of Cups, Mongolia. Replaced Kyoto after being disgraced for participating in Alexander's coup attempt.

Sir (Dr.) Kyoto, disgraced former Head of The House of Cups, Tokyo, Japan. Was once the trusted physician to Miranda and her children. He had grave concerns about the effect of vampire/mortal hybrids on vampire society. He secretly conducted research that resulted in Jacque's conception without Miranda's consent. Was reduced in status to Common Caste and banished to a Mongolian monastery.

Lena was the 2nd most powerful vampire destroyed by the Magus for an attempted coup.

Lady (Dr.) Lily, former knight and longtime love interest of Kyoto.

Sir Omar Sedaghi Head of The House of Swords, Doha, Qatar, biological father to Miranda.

Lady Pauline, House of Plows

Raf – rogue Haute Caste who loosely leads the Common Caste in Portland. He is not affiliated with any established House.

Sir Robert Johnson – blues guitarist, singer, and songwriter. Recognized as a master of the Delta blues. A legend says that Johnson at a crossroad in the south met a large black man (the Devil) who took the guitar and tuned it then played a few songs and returned the guitar to Johnson, giving him mastery of the instrument.

Sir Ruben, brother and Knight to Lady Sarah, House of Plows

Lady Sarah, Head of The House of Plows, Toronto, Canada

Scheherazade, Common Caste, The House of Pentacles a very ambitious vampiress

Sir Steve, House of Plows

Mortals

Al psychiatrist, Lolly's significant other, F.O.V.

Batu, bodyguard from Mongolia, assigned to protect Miranda and the offspring in Rossville, IL.

Camo, a biker friend of Sir Ruben bodyguard to the Mordecai family

Clive, Tristan's longtime chauffeur and aide

Connie Ortega, Miranda's mother, Rossville, IL

Danuta, Miranda's housekeeper in Rossville, IL

Grigoryi, a reformed vampire hunter, former monk, who owes a debt to Miranda for sparing him during attempted coup by Lena.

Hulagu – named after Hulagu Khan, a Mongol ruler who conquered much of Western Asia. He was a grandson of Genghis Khan

James, dentist from Montana, F.O.V. Had dated Miranda before she married Tristan.

Leif – Goat keeper, bass player in Henry's band and daytime security for Miranda and her family in Granite Falls.

Lolly longtime friend of Miranda, F.O.V.

Teri Park, a martial arts expert and bodyguard to the Mordechai family

Glossary

Bien sur (French) – certainly, of course

Bon Soir (French) – Good evening

Common Caste – Vampires with blood other than HH. Have lesser rights and power in vampire society. In book I, *Rare Blood,* vampiress Lena organized some of the Common Caste to attempt a coup against the Magus

Dobber - a dobber is a penis. Used in Glasgow and the surrounding places instead of saying 'Ya cock', ya dick etc.

D'Artagnan – In history, a French Musketeer who served Louis XIV as captain of the Musketeers of the Guard. In Dumas' novel The Three Musketeers a young, foolhardy, brave and clever man seeking to become a musketeer.

Daughter of Kali – Descendant of Kali who is a Hindu goddess. Kali's earliest appearance is that of a destroyer of evil forces.

Du sang-froid - coolness of mind; calmness; composure:

Emerald City – Seattle, WA

Eye of Horus - The Eye of Horus is an ancient Egyptian symbol of protection, royal power, and good health.

F.O.V. – Friends of Vampires. A term coined by James as a way of referring to mortal friends of Miranda who are aware of the existence of vampire society. Because of their relationship to Miranda, they have protected status.

Fleur-de-lys - A stylized lily that is used as a decorative design or symbol. The fleur-de-lis associated with France

Hannibal ante portas - (Latin) – Hannibal is at the gates

Haute Caste – Elite ruling caste of vampire society. Only those with HH blood can be Haute Caste

Hierophant - A priest in ancient Greece, who interprets sacred mysteries or esoteric principles. His task is to pass down his spiritual wisdom and maintain the balance between the conscious and subconscious minds and the unlocking of mysteries, which only he can teach.

HH Blood - Called Bombay Blood, it is the rarest of blood It was first discovered by human science in Bombay in 1952. Only 0.0004% (about 4 per million) of the total human population have this blood type. Haute Caste vampires all have HH blood.

K-Pop - Mainstream South Korean popular music

Kali – A Hindu goddess, a destroyer of evil forces, protector of the innocent.

Kufiya – A traditional Arabian headdress that originated in the Arabian Peninsula It is fashioned from a square scarf, and is usually made of cotton.

Knight – An aide-de-camp to the Head of a vampire House, highly trusted and performs important and confidential tasks. A Knight may be a personal representative to the Head of a House at important vampire society functions.

Mangia bene (Italian) – Enjoy your meal, similar to bon Appetit in French.

Menudo - A traditional Mexican soup made with beef stomach (tripe) in broth with a red chili pepper base.

Rohypnol – A tranquilizer sometimes used to commit sexual assaults because it renders the victim incapable of resisting, giving it the reputation of a "date-rape" drug.

PED - A performance-enhancing drug

Pikes Place Market - 108-year-old farmers' market draws in more than 10 million visitors annually—is justly famous for fishmongers, produce stalls, craft stands and specialty food shops

Sang-froid (French) – Calmness and composure

Shorts – Term used in the vampire society for mortals or short-lived.

Solar urticaria – An allergy to sunlight that causes hives to form on skin exposed to the sun

Throwing shade - A subtle, sneering expression of contempt for or disgust with someone

Vive le Roi (French) – Long Live the King

Acknowledgements

Gratitude to my husband/editor Joel who orchestrates the final version of all my books.

Thanks to my kids and their significant others for their love, inspiration, and sense of humor.

Thanks to Trevor for his help getting Detective Takeda and the police scenes right.

Shout-out to Shannon Kennedy for her equine knowledge. She is the author of Shamrock Stable Series and others. Find her on Amazon and her website https://www.shannonkennedybooks.com/home/

Special thanks to my friends Annette and Laurie for taking on the task of Beta Readers and doing it amazingly well. You both rock big time!

The sincerest thanks to all the members of the Writers Cooperative of the Pacific Northwest for your support. Special thanks to Matt Buza, marketing and tech guru, Toni Kief, Susan Brown and Linda Jordan for sharing their experience and knowledge about writing, editing and publishing. All these people are indie authors with a wide array of genres. Check out their books on Amazon and http://www.writers-coop.com/

To my friends, readers who have stayed with Miranda through some crazy and difficult times I am grateful for your kind appreciation of my work.

May your coffee mugs never be empty, and may your imaginations keep you sane.

Dedication

For my darling grandchildren.

You can read this when you are all grown up, to encourage you to become writers.

"Never trust a vampire...unless you have no other option...and maybe not even then."

-Baroness Miranda Ortega-Mordecai

Chapter 1

The Undead Highway Patrol

Vampires secretly desire to be loved, and that is their hidden Achilles' heel. Since my birth, I have turned their world upside down. My life has taken many unexpected turns. After growing up in a small rural Illinois town, I went to seek fame and fortune as a writer in L.A. Little did I know my life would become much more complicated.

I wrote my first book, and as they say I was swept off my feet by my publisher, who was charming, seductive, and unbelievably handsome. It turned out he was Baron Tristan Mordecai, the second most powerful vampire in the world. He was second only to the Magus, the first vampire who ruled the undead society with iron fangs, disguised behind a velvet smile. In months, I found myself married to Tristan and pregnant with triplets. Soon after they were born, I was pregnant again with a son.

Only after we were married did I learn that I was a descendant of Jacques de Molay, a Knight Templar. He had given the Templar gold to the undead in exchange for the protection of his heirs shortly before the eve of Friday, October 13, 1307, when the Templars were tortured and killed by King Philip. I was shocked to learn that my biological father was not Pete Ortega, who raised me, but Sir Omar Sedaghi, the Head of the vampire House of Swords. Even after learning that, I would always think of Pete as Dad. Being half vampire, a descendant of de Molay, and my rare HH blood type put the kids and me in the center of all the insanity of the vampire world.

For fifteen years, I tried to make it work with my Thor look-alike husband. Still, his arrogance, chauvinism, and infidelity became intolerable. He thought it was enough to be faithful, only when I was around. Since being married into the nocturnal clan, I had survived two vampire caste wars. I decided I had had enough and divorced him. The kids and I were on the way to a new home near Seattle to get away from the undead circus before we got pulled into another really weird, dangerous situation. Even though we were now divorced, I was still considered a Baroness. I would never be totally divorced from the nocturnal society as they still protected and watched over my children and me.

"Miranda?" Teri, our ninja bodyguard, interrupted my thoughts. "We are heading to Seattle from Vegas. Wouldn't it have been much quicker just going straight north instead of west through California?'

"I suppose, but I love the ocean and thought the kids would enjoy going up the coast on Route One."

"Makes sense, just wondered." She nodded to the back of the vehicle. "Are they asleep?"

I looked behind me in the Range Rover I had borrowed from my biological father, Sir Omar. My fourteen-year-old son, Jacques, had made a bed out of backpacks in the back. He had curled up with the Black Lab puppy we had rescued at a gas station not long after leaving Vegas. His siblings, the fifteen-year-old triplets going on forty, had their heads resting on each other's shoulders, blissfully quiet.

"Yes," I answered.

"Batu will return to you," she said softly.

I sighed and thought about our bodyguard in Rossville, Illinois. I had grown up there and moved back to raise the kids away from the vampire insanity. Or so I thought. I had developed deep feelings for him. I whispered, "When he does, he'll be a vampire like the others. He's a hot, intelligent, and charming Mongol warrior now. Can you imagine what he'll be like then? What will stop him from being another arrogant bastard like my ex-husband?"

"You!" she smiled.

It was the first time I had called Tristan, my ex. We had been divorced for 36 hours.

A groggy voice from the backseat mumbled, "Dad's not a bastard."

"His parents weren't married, so yes, he is. Go back to sleep Tomas."

"Whatever..."

I waited a few minutes until he seemed to have gone back to sleep. "I've never been with anyone besides Tristan. I was waiting for the 'right' one. I found out later Tristan had kept anyone who might have been interested away from me. Batu and I talked a lot during the time he protected us, but that was all."

"Seriously?" Teri responded.

"Yep!" I had to chuckle."

"You had no idea that vampires were watching over you your whole life?"

"None. Not until Tristan told me after we were married."

"So, what's it like to have sex with a vampire?"

"I've got nothing to compare it with. I never asked you about this before, but don't you have HH blood?"

16

She got quiet for a moment, just stared at the highway. "Yeah. How did you know?"

"Being half vampire, I can smell blood type."

"And you're not even one of them yet. My doctor introduced me to Lady Pauline because we had this rare blood type. He told me that if I ever needed a transfusion, I would be out of luck unless I knew someone else who was HH because it is so rare."

"How did you just "happen" to have a doctor that sees vamps?"

"I donated blood, and the blood bank called me to talk about my blood type and referred me to a hematologist."

"How much do you want to bet the Magus arranged the whole thing. He keeps tabs on people with HH and probably had someone connected to the vamp world working at the blood bank. He told me the computer age made it much easier to find people with HH blood." I looked at her. "Have they pressured you to transform?"

"No. Pauline just talks about how great it is. They never age, never get sick, and live outside of society's petty rules."

"Don't forget Pauline was transformed only a few years ago by Lady Sarah and hasn't become blasé or jaded yet. They always leave out ripping apart some unlucky soul's throat. Though I have to admit, they are pretty good about not getting blood on their designer threads."

Teri said softly, "I try not to think about Angel that way."

"Angel? Did you know he was a Common Caste vampire from L.A. who recently got promoted to the Haute Caste? So, you've got a thing for him?"

"Kinda, he makes me laugh and doesn't take himself too seriously. You know, like your ex."

I chuckled, "Baron Tristan Mordecai has actually laughed twice in the last fifteen years. I guess women don't like him for his sense of humor."

"Is he that good?"

"If I ever have sex with anyone else, I'll let you know."

"Mom, stop it! We're trying to sleep!" Des complained from the back seat.

"Now, we're traumatized for life," Tomas added.

Marie called out, "I'm hungry!"

I turned around and saw that they were all awake now. "If you're traumatized, it's not because of my side of the family," I responded. Long ago, I knew I was out of the running for a mother of the year award.

Jacques pointed, "Look! Tacos! Up ahead. There's a Mexican restaurant."

We were just north of Salinas and came upon a couple of gas stations, a hotel, and a Mexican restaurant. I saw a "Menudo on Sundays" sign in the window and knew the food would not disappoint. We were saved.

We checked into the Starlight Hotel, which was three stars if you were feeling generous. It was clean, and we were able to get one room with two king-sized beds and a rollaway.

The restaurant was a bit like the café in Illinois that my mom Connie and my dad Pete had opened and operated for years. He was killed in a botched kidnapping attempt as part of an aborted coup by some members of the Common

Caste. Sitting in the café got us all a little nostalgic. The food was good. Tamales and barbacoa tacos were our comfort food. Des tried to flirt with the waitress, who looked about sixteen, while Tomas hit him in the face with a straw wrapper. Marie just rolled her eyes at her siblings. Jacques put a piece of leftover tamale in a napkin as a treat for his new pup, Lugosi. With full bellies, we went to our room. Teri did a security check around the hotel.

About midnight, out of sheer exhaustion, we all settled into bed. Marie slept with me, Des and Tomas shared the other bed. Jacques had the roll-away bed shared with Lug. Teri insisted on doing her bodyguard thing, sleeping on a bedroll beside the door. I sent a text message to Tristan to let him know his offspring were fine, then fell fast asleep.

About two in the morning, I was jarred awake by Teri. She placed one hand over my mouth and, with the other hand, pointed to the hotel room window. I could see a shadow through the curtains. I mentally reached out with my ability to sense people's emotions and felt concern from them. Lug began to growl. I crept up to the window, and even though it was closed, I could smell her Haute Caste vampire scent.

There was a quiet knock on the door. "Miranda, Teri, it's me, Pauline."

She was one of the few that I trusted, so I let her in. The sleepy kids all sat up. "Lady Pauline?" Des muttered, "We don't have any more beds."

"You can have my bed," Jacques offered gallantly.

The blonde, former surfer-queen, smiled at the kids. "I'm glad you're all safe. Teri, how could you let them stay here? There is an approved five-star hotel less than an hour away."

"There's an approved hotel list for vamps?" I asked. I had never heard about that.

"Of course. The Magus didn't tell you?" Pauline responded.

I noticed Teri had started petting Lug to avoid looking at me. "No, but apparently everyone else knew."

"They have heavy drapes that block out sunlight, concierge on duty all night...."

Someone thumped on the wall next door. "Shut up! We're trying to sleep!"

"...and security." Pauline got an evil look. The kid's eyes got big.

I whispered, "No. Leave them alone." "It's my decision where we stay. This place is Miranda approved. Are we going to be watched the whole trip?"

"The network has been alerted to your route. It's just to be sure that no one bothers you."

"The undead highway patrol, nice! We need to get some more sleep before we hit the road. Thanks, but we're staying put till morning. I don't mean to be rude, but good night Pauline."

She left in a huff. Teri walked outside to have a few words with her. I got in bed and turned off all the lights except the bathroom, "Go to sleep, all of you. We have a long drive tomorrow." I whispered.

After a few minutes, Teri returned, turned off the bathroom light, and lay down beside the door. I hated to admit it but knowing the undead were keeping track of us actually made me feel safer.

18

Lady Pauline was irritated and was not looking forward to reporting on the travels of the Royal family to the Magus and the Baron. She climbed into a Range Rover identical to the one Miranda was using, also borrowed from Sir Omar. She decided that she needed some vampire "comfort food," pulled out her phone, and checked a file titled "Worthy Targets." The target list included child pornographers, rapists, drug dealers, and other reprehensible members of society that the justice system had failed to deal with but that the Haute Caste thought humanity would be better without. On the list were child pornographers, rapists, drug dealers, and other reprehensible members of society never dealt with by the justice system. At the top of the list was Philip Emerson, aka The Pill King, who recently had a case against him thrown out when the key witness disappeared. She read his detailed file and thought. "This will be a nice distraction!"

About thirty minutes later, she parked across the street from a seedy bar that Phil frequented off Soledad St. She saw his red Cadillac parked in front of the bar. Checking the area, Pauline noticed a couple of homeless people looking for a safe place to sleep and a prostitute walking off with a man who could have been her grandfather. She wasn't worried about them, knowing they would never talk to the police. Despite Phil's money, he still spent most of his time in this shady neighborhood, where he started as a street drug runner.

Inside the bar, Phil was having a slow night. He knew he had to stay away from his regular business contacts for a few months until the cops stopped their active investigations. He was forty and afraid some young punk would take his business. The lack of action was driving him nuts. He downed a shot of tequila and threw the glass against the wall behind the bar, then left a hundred dollars on the counter. "These bitches are too ugly to Rufi," he exclaimed, referring to drugging a woman's drink with Rohypnol.

The chubby, bald bartender grabbed the money and said, "Outta here Phil!"

Phil muttered some obscenities as he left. The drug kingpin was a small man who carried a Glock in his waistband under his jacket but knew better than to start a fight without his crew. Phil stumbled as he walked towards his car. "Fucking cops!" Then he saw her, a beautiful, tall blonde in skintight jeans and heels, leaning against the hood of his car. He physically responded to her, and his eyes grew wide.

"Hey Phil," Pauline purred. "I'm thirsty."

"How do you know my name?" He looked around, afraid that a rival was setting him up, but the street was deserted. He stood a little straighter and pulled in his paunch. She just smiled seductively. He got excited. "I got a bottle of Jack in the car." He unlocked the doors and climbed in the driver's side. With his ego, he never doubted she would join him. He never opened doors for women.

She got in and moved close to him. Phil tried to put his hand on her thigh. She grabbed his wrist and jerked his hand back so hard a bone cracked, causing him to cry out in pain. Pauline wasted no time, reached up, and snapped his neck like a pencil to silence him. She tore into his throat with her fangs. Unlike some vampires, Pauline never played with her food. She gorged herself on his warm blood, causing a surge of energy and a sensation of heat from head to toe. It felt like the rush of riding a perfect wave. She pushed away his drained body with some blood left. She had learned to leave something for the medical examiners so as not to raise suspicions. Pauline pulled a knife from her boot and slashed his neck to disguise the puncture wounds. She took a packet of wipes out of her pocket and carefully cleaned up any trace of her, and said, "Thanks Phil." She checked her watch and, with a small smile, and thought, "The quickest assassination yet."

The street was still deserted when she got back to the Range Rover, and she knew there were no security cameras in this part of town to worry about. Pauline drove away thinking of the admonition of Lady Sarah, her undead mentor, to let the Worthy Target know which crimes had led to the decision to execute them. Pauline had wanted to be the perfect Haute Caste vampire, but she had no patience. She would never take the time to remind a scumbag of all the damage he had wreaked on others. She took comfort in knowing she had removed the wealthy lowlife criminal from society. A few miles away, she pulled into a gas station and checked her black blouse for any telltale bloodstains. There were a few spots of blood. Although her excellent assassin skills had been a factor in her being transformed, she still had much to learn about taking out Worthy Targets discreetly. "Damn!" Pauline ducked down and changed into a clean t-shirt. The gas station attendant walked by and pretended he had not seen her. She got out and filled the tank for the trip back to Vegas.

At four in the morning, Manny Takeda's phone woke him from a heavy sleep. Another murder in the quiet agricultural city of Salinas. He was the youngest and most junior detective on the force, so he always got the shit calls. Another drug dealer taken out in Chinatown. He wondered why no one in Salinas ever got murdered at ten o'clock in the morning. When he heard it was Phil the "Pill King" Emerson, he was not surprised. He grabbed a coffee and a breakfast burrito from a 24-hour convenience store on the way to the crime scene. Manny parked behind the coroner's van and looked around the area. Due to the early hour, there were only a few curious onlookers being held back by the crime scene tape cordoning off the area around Phil's car. The coroner was standing next to the car watching the crime scene techs finishing up their work. All the doors were open, and the body was still in the front seat. Manny had the remains of the burrito in his hand as he ducked under the crime scene tape and walked over to the coroner. She turned to him, then frowned at the burrito in his hand. "Really?" she exclaimed. He shoved the rest of the burrito in his mouth and shrugged. She appeared a little rattled by the murder. Eula Brock never looked rattled. She usually had things wrapped up by the time he arrived.

"What's the deal, Eula?"

They stood next to the car, looking in at Phil. The drug dealer was pale, and his eyes reminded Manny of a dead fish. His throat wound was wide with bruising but not deep.

"I've never seen a body left like this. The throat is slashed open, but there's barely any blood on the body or the seats. Where did it go?"

"Are you sure he was killed in the car?" Manny asked.

Eula stared at him and just said: "Yes, I'm sure!"

"Sorry. Anything else?" Manny replied, properly chastised.

"No! Nothing! No prints! No hair besides the vic's. Nothing! It's like a ghost killed him." She shook her head.

"I know Emerson had a lot of enemies, but I would have expected a gun, not a knife. Any other injuries?"

"All that I could find without an autopsy was a broken wrist, so I think he briefly struggled with the killer. He still has his wallet with eight hundred dollars cash, and his gun is still in his waistband. Nothing seems to be missing."

A uniformed officer walked up to Manny and said, "I was the first on the scene. Fred Chaney owns the bar Emerson was in last night and saw him dead in the car when he was taking out the trash."

"Appropriate," the detective commented.

The officer continued, "We got his initial statement, and my partner is holding him for you to talk to."

"Thanks, I'll do that now." Manny walked across the street and up to Fred. "I'm Detective Takeda. Did you see anyone on the street Mr. Chaney?"

"No, except a black late-model SUV driving away. I'm pretty sure it was a Range Rover. I didn't see who was driving it or notice the license plates. None of my regulars, none of them can afford a car like that."

"Did Phil have any problems with anyone tonight?"

"Hell, Phil had a problem with everyone, every night, but he always paid his tab and then some."

"Did he didn't leave with anyone?"

"No, not his lucky night I guess."

Manny went back to look at the body before it was moved. "Where is all the blood?" he asked no one in particular.

A young officer shook her head. "You got me. Professional cartel hit?"

"Probably not. They would have done it with a clean shot to the head." He did not think Emerson was important enough for the drug cartel to go to all that trouble. Emerson had stayed in his lane selling pharmaceuticals and did not get involved with pot, cocaine, heroin, or meth. His pharmaceuticals provided the cartel with new customers when his clients graduated to cheaper opiates. Manny went back to the station to see if there were any other murders with a similar M.O. Something was bugging him about this case. He was sure he had read about a couple of unsolved murders with the same lack of blood at the scene.

By eight o'clock in the morning, the kids had eaten a million pancakes and way too much maple syrup to be stuck in a car for hours, but Teri and I were game. She and Jacques took Lug over to a small patch of grass by the hotel office while the triplets and I loaded the car.

"Ms. Ortega?"

I turned to see a plainclothes policeman flashing a badge. He looked about thirty, sweet-faced, with kind eyes.

"She's Ms. Mordecai," Tomas stated loudly.

"I'm divorced. Ortega is fine. How do you know my name, and who are you?" I asked.

"I'm Detective Takeda. I'm sorry to bother you, but your car matches the description of one seen leaving a crime scene. A patrol officer driving past the hotel saw your car and called it in. I asked the clerk in the office whose car it is, and she said it was yours. Can you tell me where you were at three this morning?"

"Trying to get some sleep in this marvelous hotel with four children, a puppy, and my friend over there," pointing over at Teri. "I sent a text message to my ex-husband about midnight, then fell asleep till the puppy woke us around six."

"Did anyone other than you drive the car last night?" Manny asked.

"Nope, it has been parked here all night," I replied.

Teri and Jacques joined us. "What's going on?" Teri asked.

"This is Detective Takeda. He says someone driving a Range Rover, like ours, broke the law last night while we were sound asleep." I gave the kids a "this is serious" look. I didn't want them complicating things by bringing up our late-night visitor.

"I'm Teri Park, a friend of the family. We had a boring night, not much to do around here. We drove all day and were pretty tired. What happened?" she asked, giving Takeda a charming smile. This was a side of Teri I had not seen before.

"A murder," he replied, watching our reactions closely.

Lug walked up to the detective, and with perfect timing, started to raise a leg. "Lug!" I exclaimed as Manny jumped out of the way. "I'm sorry." I picked up the pup.

"That's okay," he patted Lug on the head. "Are you going to be staying in the area?"

"No, we just stopped here for the night," Teri told him.

"Where are you headed now?"

Teri answered in, "We're on our way to Washington. I'll give you my number if you want to ask us anything else."

"C'mon kids." I opened the car door and started loading my family.

The young detective wrote down our names, the car license number, and Teri's cell number. "Before you go, would you mind if I took a look inside the car?"

"We really have to hit the road so, I'll have to say no," I answered.

"Thank you, Ms. Park, Ms. Ortega." He turned to leave then stopped and turned back. "Oh, by the way, Ms. Ortega, have you ever lived in Los Angeles?"

I thought that was a weird question for a cop in Salinas to ask, but I answered, "I was born in Illinois, got a scholarship to go to U.C.L.A., met my ex, had the triplets, and moved back to Illinois. I don't have time to tell you my life history, but it's fascinating. Are we free to go?"

Detective Takeda nodded and watched as we drove away. I glanced at Teri. "Damn Pauline! What did she tell you?"

"Not to put the local news on this morning," Teri said sheepishly. Somehow, I knew we would be hearing from Detective Takeda again.

It took us a couple of days to get to our new home in Washington. Much to Teri's disappointment and my relief, the detective did not call. It bothered me that our stop in Salinas had resulted in someone becoming a snack for Pauline. I knew the victim was not an innocent soul, but now he or she would never have a chance to change their ways.

The undead highway patrol kept their distance, but I could sometimes smell faint traces of their scent in the night along the way. The drive up to Seattle gave me a lot of time to think about the vampire species. Proud, seductive, confident, attractive, passionate, and intelligent were traits that helped them survive in vampire culture and the greater world. They needed to work on their sense of humor and dial down the vanity. Their charisma allowed them to get close to and manipulate any mortal. Their assassin skills made it easy for them to remove those they deemed Worthy Targets from the gene pool. I was half-vampire, and my kids were three-quarters vampire, but that side of our natures would hopefully stay recessive unless we decided to transform and join the nocturnal maniac world.

My kids had lots of time before they might feel compelled to join the bloodsucker club. I was thirty-eight, which made me nine years past the normal cut-off age for the transformation ceremony. The Magus gave me a Transform Anytime Card because my mother, Connie Ortega, became the first mortal impregnated by a vampire, which gave me my unique status. My female ancestors had a lot of "contact" with male vampires over the centuries.

I was only the second mortal to be impregnated by a vampire. Apparently, four kids later, I was still really compatible with male vampires in the procreation sense. My ex tried to convince me that when you live forever, sex is just another form of exercise. Here's the kicker, he did not want me to have any exercise companions but him because I might get pregnant. To his shock and mine, our vampire family physician, Dr. Kyoto, had artificially inseminated me during an exam after my first pregnancy with the semen of Alexander the Great, one of the ancient vampires. I became pregnant and gave birth to my son Jacques. Dr. Kyoto said it was just an experiment and that he was amazed it worked. Not as amazed, shocked, and angered as the rest of our family. To Tristan's credit, he rallied to support our youngest child, but he could not change the truth.

We stopped for the night in a small town in Oregon. Tomorrow we would make it to Seattle. Then we could spend our last day and night on the road as tourists. Our new home, Granite Falls, was just north of Emerald City, and I wanted the kids to have some normal fun. After everything else we had been through, how weird could Seattle be?

Chapter 2

Batu's Last Meal

My parents owned a small diner in our little town, so I did not grow up in luxury. Getting millions in financial support from my ex-husband was a little unreal but an appreciated safety net. I worried about how it might affect the kids, so I tried to scale down our lifestyle. When we arrived in Seattle, I put my socialist tendencies aside and got a suite at the top of a hotel near Pike's Place Market with an amazing view of the Puget Sound.

After we checked in, we walked over to a Korean restaurant that Teri had found near our hotel. The kids didn't seem too happy about it, and she told them that there was more to life than tacos. Growing up in Rossville, they had limited exposure to international cuisine though they liked the Mongolian dumplings Batu used to make for us. Even though I tried to be vegetarian, I was aware that the kids and I tended to need a lot of iron in our diets, apparently because of our vampire genes. Once we were seated and got our menus, I told the kids they could order whatever they wanted.

The server brought appetizers to the table, and Des started eating from a bowl of Kimchi like it was an entree. The restaurant owner came over to our table to see him eating the spicy pickled cabbage by the spoonful. She smiled. "On the house." And she placed a platter of Kimchi pancakes on the table. They were delicious.

We had steaming clay bowls of noodle soup with assorted veggies, meats, and a poached egg on top. In varying degrees of spiciness, several smaller bowls of various condiments came with the main dishes and perfectly round mounds of rice. By the end of the meal, we were stuffed. Teri surprised us all when she gave compliments to the chef in Korean. Who knew? She always said she was just a SoCal person.

After dinner, we went back to the hotel. The kids were lying on their beds watching TV, and Teri and I sat in the kitchenette area having coffee. I asked Teri, "When did your family come to this country?"

"After the Korean War, my grandparents were able to immigrate here. They came to Los Angeles because they had seen movies that showed how beautiful and warm it was in California. It was rough finding jobs here because of the language. They both had been doctors in Korea but weren't able to get medical licenses here, so they worked as nurse's aides. Eventually, they opened a restaurant serving comfort food for other Koreans. Some GIs who had served in

Korea would come by too. My mom was their only kid, and she got pregnant by a professor of Asian Studies while attending USC. Go Trojans!"

I hugged Teri. "I'm sorry I never asked you about your family when we were in Rossville. I knew that you and Batu would sometimes go hang out with his Asian friends at the U of I in Champaign." With all the chaos brought on by the attempted Common Caste coup, the crazy monk vampire hunters, and my dad's murder, I never had the chance to get to know Teri better.

"They were into K-pop, which helped my social standing. Anyway, you know Batu never took any of those women seriously." She made sure the kids were all watching Jumanji, then she whispered, "He was intimate with a few of them, but I always knew he only really cared about you."

I sat quietly for a minute, thinking about Batu. The Magus had assigned him to watch over the kids and me in Rossville. We had developed strong feelings for each other but had never acted on them. He was now back in Mongolia, preparing to be transformed and become another of the undead. I guess I should never have expected him to remain celibate. "He and Tristan should form a club," I shook my head. "I hope he stays in Mongolia."

"I'm sorry I said anything. I just wanted you to know how much you mean to him."

"Teri, it's not your fault. Please do me a favor. Just don't talk about him anymore."

Near Choibalsan, Mongolia, Batu was about to meet with Princess Khunbish to discuss his desire to transform. She was the new head of the House of Cups after the Magus stripped Dr. Kyoto of his position and Haute Caste status for having impregnated Miranda without her knowledge. Her headquarters was a compound with a palace, befitting her rank, surrounded by several large stone yurts, incorporating the traditional nomadic dwelling design with more permanent luxury. She was a Little Person of great strength, a descendent of the Khans. She wore a tunic with beautiful beadwork, and her hair was swept up with jeweled combs. The Princess turned to Chang, one of her aides. "You may let Sir Batu enter."

Batu's long, arduous trip from Las Vegas involved two flights, taxis, trains, and a rickety bus over rough roads to get to the Princess's residence. Despite his exhaustion, the anticipation of being transformed energized him. The tall, handsome Mongol had taken care to pull his thick, long black hair back in traditional fashion. He wore an embroidered shirt and dark pants. He bowed, then kneeled before the Princess on a Persian rug. Lit candles, fragrant incense, and eastern furnishings created an exotic ambiance. Batu expected the audience to be short as it was near dawn.

She looked pleased. "Welcome, Sir Batu."

"Thank you for considering me for transformation. I am not worthy."

She smiled. "You were a valued and obedient servant in the past. The Magus told me that you protected the Baroness and her children with courage and devotion. I expect the same loyalty to our House in your new position."

"Of course," Batu replied.

"You do not mind being away from the Baroness?" Princess Khunbish watched his response closely.

He lowered his eyes before responding. "She is amazing, but my destiny and goal have always been to be transformed, and the Magus has granted me Haute Caste status. Transformation is an honor I would never turn down."

"And...?" She prompted.

"After transformation and learning the proper conduct of a Haute Caste vampire, I hope to some night be worthy of her."

"What do you think, Sir Steve?"

At four feet, ten inches, Sir Steve was the shortest member of the House of Plows but was slightly taller than the Princess. He was an accomplished assassin and consort to her highness. Sir Steve and the Princess had "known" each other briefly in Los Angeles. Because of their relationship, it was no shock to the vampire world that he had recently been granted a dual membership in the House of Cups. Steve was Irish American, but as far as the Princess was concerned, he was now a Mongol.

He stepped out of a dark alcove at the back of the room and bowed to her. His shoulder-length blonde hair fell forward, and he wore a leather belt carrying two knives with ornately carved handles. He brushed his hair back and smiled. "Well said, Sir Batu. I feel the same way about the Head of the House of Cups."

"You'll have to get better at riding a horse for that to happen," she replied with a small smile.

Batu tried not to chuckle. He had spent years improving his riding skills to be able to impress the Princess. He could hang sideways from his horse and hit targets with a bow and arrow while at full gallop, but his knife skills could use some improvement. "Sir Steve, I hope to improve my ability with a blade while spending time with you."

The Princess had heard enough. "Let us talk about the transformation. I shall perform it with the assistance of Dr. Kyoto. He is staying in the nearby monastery doing research as a penance for his rebellious acts."

"You trust him?" Batu asked.

Sir Steve responded, "He is remorseful and hopeful that some century he will regain his Haute Caste status. He will do anything to get back in the good graces of the Magus. He is researching why the Baroness' blood has developed an antigen to vampire DNA. He will meet with you shortly."

"Of course, though the Baroness would not approve of his research. She is a mystery within a mystery," Batu said. "She is still very angry with Kyoto about Jacques."

The Princess responded, "Her outrage is justified, but he is not a villain. He was misguided and acted without permission of the Magus. Even so, you will find much to be learned from an ancient member of our society like Dr. Kyoto. We will have the transformation ceremony tomorrow night. You need to rest from your journey before the event." She clapped her hands. Chang entered with a large tray of Mongolian delicacies. "Your last taste of a mortal diet."

26

Chang set the tray of Mutton, meat-filled dumplings, a bowl of stew, a large cup of airag, an alcoholic beverage of fermented mare's milk before him. Without a word, he began to eat. Batu realized how much he loved food and knew that he would no longer be able to indulge in it after tomorrow night. "Small price to pay," he thought.

Sir Steve was amused as he watched Batu eat like a condemned man given a last meal. A hundred and fifty years ago, he had gorged himself on roast chicken, potatoes, and half a chocolate cake the night before he became immortal. No food would be allowed during the day, much like fasting before some medical procedure. It would be bad form to throw up on a member of the Haute Caste, especially a Princess.

Princess Khunbish stood, which caused Batu to stop eating while she left the room. Sir Steve turned to Batu. "Dr. Kyoto has arrived. We will leave you alone to discuss the transformation process. Good night Sir Batu."

"Thanks to you and the Princess," Batu responded, then bit into the mutton.

A few minutes later Kyoto entered. He wore a monk's drab robes, though he had carefully styled his hair into a samurai topknot. After his attempt to transform the Baroness against her will, she had asked the Magus not to kill him, that there had been enough violence already. The Magus agreed, removed Kyoto's Haute Caste status, and exiled him to the monastery. He sat on the cushion facing Batu. "You desire the burdens and pleasures of the gift of immortality?"

"Yes," Batu responded, pushing the almost empty tray of food away from him.

Kyoto glanced at the few scraps left on the plates and observed. "Your appetite will change."

"These delicacies are a small sacrifice," Batu claimed.

"But what of the Baroness?"

He did not want to discuss her, but Batu realized the Haute Caste saw Miranda as his Achille's heel. He wondered if the Baron was behind this line of questioning, or even the Magus. "I hope that in time she will approve of my choice to transform. It was solely based on my desire to become immortal and to be of service to the Magus."

Kyoto smiled. "Well said. Due to your bravery during the battle with Alexander, the Magus has made you one of the few with Common Caste blood to be granted Haute Caste status. Do you truly deserve that privilege?"

"Since you betrayed the Magus and the Baroness, did you think you deserved to have your status removed despite your HH blood?"

"I can see why the Baroness likes you." He adjusted his robes. "I am an outcast due to my folly. I intended to persuade the Baroness to transform to protect her from those who resented a mortal having Haute Caste status."

Batu bristled. "I might understand you were thinking that transforming her, even by force, could protect her, but artificial insemination without her consent? How did that protect her?"

"It was an ill-advised research experiment. Ultimately, though, I believe Jacques was destined to be. I also believe that it is not healthy to have all vampires/mortals sired by a single genetic vampire donor. Not healthy at all. Now it will be interesting to study their differences."

"They are children, not horses, not a breeding experiment," Batu protested.

Kyoto smiled. It was obvious how much Batu cared for the children as well as the Baroness. "I agree to help with your transformation. I'll tell the Princess and the Magus that you will make a fine vampire. You are honest, with just enough arrogant righteousness to be an excellent assassin." He stood.

"I didn't know I needed your approval."

"The Magus always consults with some of the ancients before giving the final approval. He still trusts my judgment in this matter. I don't know why he thought Alexander was a good candidate, but that was a bit before my time."

Batu stood and bowed. "Sir Kyoto, I am in your debt."

Kyoto merely nodded in return. He got to his feet and left without another word.

Batu went back to his room and collapsed on the low bed with silk sheets and fur throws. He wished Miranda could be there to share his last mortal day with him. Batu sent a text message to Teri,

All is well. I will be transformed tomorrow night.

He fell asleep and dreamt of nights when he would be able to hold Miranda in his arms.

"Have you finished your report?" the grizzled old police captain glared at Manny over a cup of coffee strong enough to kill a cockroach.

"No," Manny closed the file and turned away from his computer. "I've been trying to get a lead from the car the bartender saw leaving the scene. I questioned a woman at a motel who drove the same model. She claimed they were in their room all night. Another guest said there was a lot of noise from the room next door, about two in the morning, but it quieted down after he pounded on the wall. The woman is Miranda Ortega-Mordecai. She's a writer. I looked her up, not much on social media except information about her books."

"So, you got nothing," Jenkins said, "Another dope dealer dead in Chinatown, don't waste too much time on it."

"There is just one thing that's bugging me. The vic lost a lot of blood, which the M.E. can't account for, and this Ms. Mordecai writes vampire books. Weird coincidence?"

"You really must not want a promotion. Takeda, just finish the report. Vampires in Salinas? You won't be able to close the case. Get over it. It happens to all of us." He walked back to his office, muttering under his breath.

Manny felt in his gut that he was on to something big. He had a sense that Miranda Mordecai was more than just a novel writer. She just did not seem capable of killing a drug dealer and draining the body of blood, but murderers had surprised him before. The lead detective was probably right, but he hated to lose. He did not want a killer to get away with a murder, even if the vic was a dope dealer. Manny believed everyone deserved justice. He opened the file he had been

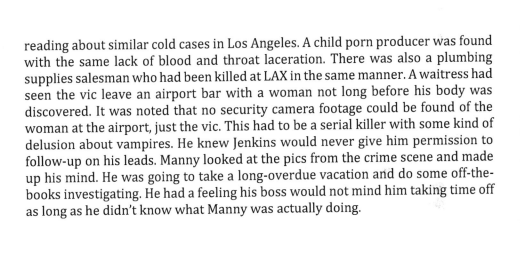

reading about similar cold cases in Los Angeles. A child porn producer was found with the same lack of blood and throat laceration. There was also a plumbing supplies salesman who had been killed at LAX in the same manner. A waitress had seen the vic leave an airport bar with a woman not long before his body was discovered. It was noted that no security camera footage could be found of the woman at the airport, just the vic. This had to be a serial killer with some kind of delusion about vampires. He knew Jenkins would never give him permission to follow-up on his leads. Manny looked at the pics from the crime scene and made up his mind. He was going to take a long-overdue vacation and do some off-the-books investigating. He had a feeling his boss would not mind him taking time off as long as he didn't know what Manny was actually doing.

Chapter 3

The Emerald City

I stood at the floor-to-ceiling window in our hotel suite and looked out across Puget Sound. I could see the ferries going to and from the many beautiful islands and across to the Olympic Peninsula's lush green mountains. It was breathtaking! Late Summer was spoiling us with a warm, clear, sunny day. The hotel staff told me that the rains were coming soon. While the kids decided what they wanted to see, I called my mom.

"Hi Mom, how are you? Did Scheherazade arrive?"

"Randie! Sheri got here with Billy and Robert two nights ago. My goodness is she something! How are the kids?"

I thought it was hilarious that Mom was calling Scheherazade Sheri. "Fine. We're spending a day in Seattle, and then tomorrow, we'll head up to our new house. It's about an hour north of the city. Do you think it will work out with Sheri?" Scheherazade was sent to Rossville by the Magus to work in my mom's café as a punishment for aiding Alexander in his attempted coup.

"There's been an increase in eye-rolling around here. Danuta didn't like the way Sheri flirts with every man in sight. Jeanne took her behind the barn, and they had a "talk" last night. They both looked pretty rough afterward, but Sheri seemed to have gotten the message."

I had been concerned about how Scheherazade would behave in Rossville, a very conservative farming town. It was good to know that Jeanne, aka Joan of Arc, had explained the facts of life on the prairie to "Sheri." I hoped that now she wouldn't even think about seducing any of the mortals in town.

"How is Bart dealing with this?" Sir Bartholomew was a brilliant, spiritual, talented monk-vampire who liked caring for horses and adored Jeanne. They had been a couple on and off for centuries.

"You know Bart, he just gets that little smile and goes back to the barn. Guess he figures Jeanne can handle Sheri. We can always use help for the dinner rush. I don't think the farmers will mind having that gal pour their coffee."

"Their wives might. How are Billy and Robert? Are they going to stick around?"

"They said they'll stay for a while to make sure Sheri is behaving. Billy has decided to teach Robert how to ride. He has been snooping around since Pete was killed. I think we're just the most interesting thing going on in Vermilion County."

What the young Sheriff didn't know was that a crazed vampire-hunter monk had killed my dad in an attempted kidnapping gone wrong. Vampire justice took care of him, but the Sheriff still wanted answers he would never get. After he died, Mom had closed their Café but was going to reopen soon.

"I'm sorry we won't be back for the reopening of the Café, but we'll see you at Thanksgiving."

"That's okay honey. It'll do you all good to start fresh somewhere. How is Stan?" My mom was the only person allowed to call Baron Tristan Mordecai Stan.

"Tristan is okay, he's not happy about the divorce, but he can visit the kids whenever he wants."

"Have you heard anything from Batu?"

"He's staying in Mongolia, and I don't expect to hear from him anytime soon. I promised the kids we would do some tourist stuff today, so I should get going. I'll call you once we're settled in the new house. Love you!"

"Love you too! Hug the kids for me."

I hung up and shook my head. My mom was unflappable. She is a descendent of a Knight Templar, and her mother had told her about the vampires looking out for us. She had kept that family secret from me and the identity of my biological father. She was now the matriarch of a family of vampires and mortals, who looked after her and helped with the café. People in Rossville just thought she had gone off the deep end after my dad had been killed and tried to act as if everything was fine. Sheriff Fleming was looking for answers about my dad's death. Hopefully, he would get back to the normal crimes of busting meth labs, spousal abuse, and underage kids drinking by the river.

I turned to the kids. "Grandma loves you. Now, where do you want to go?"

Des responded first, "The Gumball Wall! It's really gross."

Tomas added, "Yeah, and the Underground Tour, beneath the city."

Jacques said, "I want to take Lug to a park."

Marie petitioned, "The Aquarium! I want to see the octopi."

Teri was looking at a map and routing the tour. "Underground Tour first, then Gumball Wall and lunch at Pike's market, then the Aquarium." She turned to Jacques. "And we'll take Lugosi for a walk when we get back, I promise."

The Underground Tour was in Pioneer Square, where settlers began building the city. They didn't have much regard for the indigenous people, who preferred to live on higher ground that the periodic high tides would not easily flood. The tour guide took us down old stairs to damp passageways under the sidewalks where we had just walked. It was a dark labyrinth of passageways hidden below the city. My heightened sense of smell caught the faint scent of the undead a few times. The underground would have been a perfect place to hide from daylight. The kids were intrigued by the stories of greed, stupidity, and the early settlers' audacity that led to Seattle's founding. I was amazed that around the turn of the twentieth century, a Madame of a brothel, who was one of the wealthiest people in town, gave a large sum of money to the city for public education. She never even got a statue.

I was caught up in the tour guide's stories and hadn't been paying enough attention to the kids. Des took advantage of the opportunity to hide in a dark alcove and jumped out, scaring Marie, who fell backward in a puddle. Then Tomas scared Jacques by touching his shoulder and yelling rats. The guide was already losing his patience when a huge rat scurried across the passageway, and Teri skewered it with a knife. When we got to the end of the tour, a supervisor told us to leave and never come back.

Des complained, "I wanted a t-shirt!"

"Then you should have behaved yourself," I responded.

Jacques, enjoying his brothers being reprimanded. "I like Seattle!"

We left the Underground and headed to the Gumball Wall, which is the weirdest tourist attraction. It is just outside of a theater where years ago, people began sticking their gum on the wall before they went in, I mean thousands of people. A section of this old brick wall next to Pikes Market is covered in gooey globs. It was cleaned off once, but soon people covered it again with nasty chewed-up gum. I had to tell the kids a dozen times, "Don't touch it! Don't stick Jacques to the wall!" They took a lot of selfies, and then we found a restaurant for lunch with a view of the Sound and wonderful, rich dark coffee. I fell in love with Seattle that day.

After lunch, we stopped at a clothing store and got a few things since we only had the clothes we had packed for the week in Las Vegas. Teri picked out a plaid shirt and a quilted vest that could hide a few small weapons. The kids insisted on knit caps because "That's what everyone wears here."

When I asked the saleswoman for umbrellas, she smiled and said, "Just get a hoodie." Apparently, the only people you see with umbrellas are tourists. Walking around in the rain without an umbrella is a Seattle thing. I had a lot to learn about the Pacific Northwest.

Our next stop was the Aquarium which I located on a pier jutting into the Puget Sound. The first exhibit is a series of tide pools. It seemed like a good idea for the kids to explore the coastal sea life up close. Marie was pointing something out to Des. "Look, a tiny octopus in those rocks." He leaned forward as far as he could, then, with a shove from Marie, went headfirst into the exhibit. Des pulled himself out with a little help from Teri. He had a small cut on his cheek. I put myself between the siblings. Marie and the others were laughing. A young woman on staff came over with a towel. I guess this wasn't the first time.

Marie noticed a group of people watching scuba divers on the pier alongside the Aquarium. "What is happening out there?" she asked the young woman that was toweling off Des.

She responded enthusiastically. "Once a year, divers release a female octopus carrying fertilized eggs from the dock. Then she will find a place to attach the eggs until they hatch."

"That is so cool!" Marie said excitedly. "I love octopi. They are extremely smart."

"Octopus!" Des said in a disgusted tone.

"Don't be a hater," Marie replied with a self-satisfied grin.

I told the kids that we had to get going and pick out something from the gift shop. I got a hoodie with an orca with a friendly, toothy smile. Des and Tomas got shark t-shirts, and Jacques found one with a whale tail coming out of the water. And of course, Marie got an octopus t-shirt.

We left the Aquarium and headed to Cupcake Royale, a local spot the hotel concierge recommended. I bit into a tiramisu cupcake and felt like I had died and gone to sugar heaven. The coffee was great as well. We headed back to the hotel to take care of Lugosi as the sun was setting. For the Mordechai clan, this had been a peaceful day.

We found a little park by the hotel, and the kids played with our new pup. He was so cute, loving, and happy all the time. A couple of young women stopped to pet Lug. Des and Tomas trying to impress them, began boasting about how they had rescued him at a gas station. Their dad would have been proud. Marie came over and stood with Teri and me.

"Mom, I think I smell one, you know...."

I inhaled and looked around. Marie was right. I did not realize she had inherited my strong sense of smell. "I think it's male, Common Caste. We'll go back to the hotel." Teri got the boys. I put my arm around Marie and I scanned the people in the area but did not see anyone that caused my gut to twinge. The scent faded until we got into the lobby. A handsome Latino with an L.A. Angel's baseball cap leaned against the wall by the elevator.

"Nice hat!" I told him.

The kids yelled, "Angel!"

"Aw, my favorite semi-vampire family, how are you?" Teri came over and hugged him. The boys were excited to see someone who had valiantly fought with them in the "Battle of Vegas."

"We're fine. A few mishaps, but I think we'll like it here."

"Did the Baron send you to keep an eye on us? I've got it handled!" Teri declared.

"Really?" he smiled. "The Salinas police didn't think so."

"That was Lady Pauline," I responded.

"Some detective called the Baron, and he got pretty upset. You know your ex-husband's temper. Lady Pauline is laying low till this police inquiry blows over. Anyway, the cops don't have any evidence connecting you to any crimes. But to be on the safe side, I hope you'll just order in tonight and watch movies. The local nocturnal crew has been ordered to stay away from all of you."

"Where are you staying?" I asked.

"At your husband's place. I got here last night. He's got a plush condo nearby. It is sweet."

"Okay, Sir Angel, you want to join us for movie night?" I would not invite just any vampire, but Angel was a SoCal friend. He did not have HH blood, but like Batu, the Magus had recently promoted him to Haute Caste status.

"Sure," Angel suggested, "we can watch a Fast and Furious sequel."

We ordered pizza and watched horrible car chasing, beat the crap out of people, movies, until midnight. Angel went with me to walk Lugosi while Teri supervised the kids. I wanted to ask him some questions away from their curious, eager little ears.

It was cool outside, with a faint dampness from the Sound. The traffic noise of the city was a quiet hum at this hour. Lugosi stopped at every poor tree, trying to grow in a small square of exposed earth. "What's the news? Is Alexander behaving himself?"

"Yeah. Your blood has kept him humbled. He can't believe how it has diminished his powers. He is learning how to care for Hannibal's elephants. It's the perfect punishment. A nightly reminder of his defeat. The Magus wondered if I could get a donation to take back with me. I've got the equipment in my backpack."

My blood had a vampire antigen that weakens the undead. No one expected that when I was born. "Sure. I don't like getting stuck, but it's worth it to keep that pompous ass in his place. How is Tristan?"

"The Baron is not a fun person to be around since the divorce but give him time. I've heard several vampiresses talking about their desire to make him feel better. Honestly, though the Baron is an incredibly powerful vampire, I don't see how the two of you stayed together this long."

"We lived apart most of the time," I put my hand on Angel's arm. "There is another night 'person' nearby." My gut had that familiar feeling when something was not right. Lug began to growl.

"Baroness," a woman's voice called softly.

We turned to see a strikingly beautiful woman with long curly blonde hair, violet eyes in a black bustier and torn jeans. Hell was missing a seductive demon.

"Pomp!" Angel said. "C'mon, you know what the Magus said."

"But mon cher, it would be impolite not to welcome her to my city."

"Not now. Wait till you're invited," he responded. Angel moved between us. For an instant, I saw ugliness in her face that was shocking. Lug growled, and I grabbed him in my arms. Angel said, "The Magus will hear about this."

She spat on his shoes and said something in French I did not understand. I had enough and moved beside Angel. "I don't want to hurt your feelings, but I have no desire to meet and greet any vampires at the moment. If you ever want to be on my good side, leave us alone for now."

She glared, then disappeared down an alley, and Angel turned to me. "That burst into flames look was for me. She knew me when I was Common Caste. She doesn't like having me set limits with her."

"Pomp? Let me guess. That's short for Pompadour?"

"Yeah, she loves to talk about her nights at the French court. I'm glad you cut her off. The Magus sure knows how to pick them."

I snickered as we walked back to the hotel. "Pomp should hook up with Alexander."

"You won't tell the Magus what I Just said, right?"

"Nope. We're cool. I'm only going to tell him how well you protected us."

Back in the room, Angel went into the bathroom with me to draw some blood. He was very good with the needle. It barely hurt at all. He filled three tubes, then placed them in a container with some ice. He explained I would not see him again for a few months. I gave Teri a break from her official duties to spend time with Angel, and Lug slept by the door while she was gone. I opened one eye when Teri made it back at the crack of dawn and collapsed on a couch. Once you've been with a vampire, I guess it's hard to be satisfied with a mortal. Maybe one night I would find out if that was true.

34

Pompadour was not happy, which made her hungry. She drove her Jaguar home for a quick change. Getting into a little black dress and putting a comb in her hair was nothing compared to the layers of finery and wigs she had once squeezed into at Versailles. Dangling sapphire earrings and a large diamond ring were the final touches. She pulled up the Worthy Targets file in her area and smiled. It was the drug company CEO's night to play cards at the Rainier Club.

She drove to the exclusive club and parked nearby. The doorman welcomed her into the lobby and checked her membership card. She took the elevator up to the bar knowing that Heinrich Bledsoe would be finished with his game soon, then stop by for a nightcap before leaving. She liked stalking a victim who was obsessive-compulsive about his schedule.

The thin, tall man in his fifties looked distinguished in his blue Armani suit and a pale pink shirt. He sat in the same place at the bar every Thursday night. He had noticed the young blonde before, but she had never been so close to him. She was ravishing. Heinrich reminded himself that though he might be thirty years older, some young women liked more mature men.

"Good evening, I'm Heinrich. May I order something for you?" he inquired.

"Bien sur, mon cher, a glass of cabernet," she smiled sweetly.

"What brings you to Seattle?"

Her faint perfume was intoxicating, jasmine and roses with a hint of spice. He leaned closer. She took a sip of wine and answered, "Hematology research. The study of the human body is compelling, no?"

He looked into her violet eyes and felt as if he had been mesmerized. Some of his competitors were at the club that night, and he did not want them to see him leaving the club with her. Gossip about his behavior would not sit well with the board.

"I would like to get to know you better, but this bar is a bit crowded, don't you think?"

"Let us have a rendezvous, but you must promise not to bore me with talk of corporate details." She took a slow sip of wine. Other than blood, vampires only drank wine and other clear liquids and occasionally small amounts of raw beef.

"I have a private room on the next floor. Would you like to meet me up there?"

Lady Pompadour merely smiled. He was glad she did not want to discuss his career. He whispered the room number, then went to the elevator after stopping by a table to chat with some business acquaintances.

He had not won at cards that night, but he thought his luck was about to change. He had an hour before he generally left the club. "Plenty of time," he thought. He knew that the Rainier Club staff would never discuss anything that happened there. It was a safe place for the elites of Seattle to discretely let their hair down. He made himself a scotch, neat, and sat on the bed. After several minutes Pomp entered.

"Don't you want to know who I am?" She slowly walked over to the bed.

"I'd rather you show me who you are," he replied.

She took his drink, placed it on the dresser, pushed him down on the bed, and straddled him. He was very excited by her aggressive moves. He started to pull the straps down on her dress. She pinned his arms, head-butted him so hard he fell back, unconscious, then placed her hands tightly about his neck. As he started to come to, she pushed her hair comb deep into his mouth to silence him. He began flailing, but he was no match for her strength.

"Heinrich, your company flooded the market with addicting pain pills, ruining the lives of countless human beings. I will show you the same consideration you showed them."

His eyes pleaded for help as she bit deeply into his carotid artery. "Merde!" she spat out his life fluid. "Blood thinner!" He stared at the angry vampiress in shock. She carefully disengaged from him as he bled onto the sheets. His head was resting in a pool of blood. The pain faded as his life quickly slipped away. She took a razor blade from a pocket in her bra and slashed his neck and the wrist on his left hand. Then she put the blade in his right hand. She had noticed that he was right-handed earlier in the evening. She had heard about the mistakes Pauline had made. She did not want this death to look suspicious. Perhaps it was better that she had not feasted on him.

Vampires do not reflect light the same as mortals, and this anomaly has aided them from being tracked by modern technology. Security cameras would only show a blur rather than her image when she left the room. Vampires also did not leave fingerprints. The whorls and ridges fade away after they are transformed, and lab equipment show inconclusive results when their DNA is tested. All the same, she was very careful to remove any trace of her visit. Her faint perfume would not linger. There would be no evidence that anyone had been in the room with poor suicidal Heinrich. A vampire computer geek who adored Pomp had forged a membership card and would now make all traces of it disappear. She was still hungry but would have to make do with bagged blood. She had not seen that medication in his medical records. At least she could tell the Magus she had taken out a Worthy Target and about the omission in the file.

She hoped that would help in case he was upset about her attempt to meet the Baroness. She had done it on the spur of the moment even though she knew that she was violating "protocol." She should have waited to be invited. She left the club and drove her Jaguar through the streets of Seattle with Edith Piaf singing her lungs out on the stereo. The thought of the Baron spending more time in Seattle improved her mood. She was overdue for his royal touch.

Chapter 4

The House on the River

In Mongolia, Batu was getting emotionally and physically prepared for his transformation. Being estranged from his family made his decision to transform easier. Batu walked outside to feel the rays of the sun warm his skin for the last time. The old Mongolian woman, who looked after the Princess, regarded Batu with curiosity as she worked in the garden. He smiled back to put her at ease, but she turned away. Two of the mortal royal guards nodded to him. Batu had served with them when he was first allowed to work for the Princess. He would be viewed differently after tonight. The vampire world and their servants would no longer see him as a mortal to command. He was still trying to take in what it meant to now have Haute Caste status. Batu did not have rare HH blood, but his service to the royal family and the Magus had gotten him this coveted title. He wished he could explain what he had achieved to his family, but they would just think he had joined a cult. He would miss daylight, but it was a small price to pay. To his surprise, a tear ran down his cheek. Batu quickly went back inside to prepare. He had to drink the herbal tea the Princess had ordered for him and get more rest before the ceremony.

At the hotel in Seattle, we slept in until eleven. Trying not to wake Teri, I quietly got the kids up, packed, and ready for the ride to their new home. I woke up my sleeping ninja at the last minute.

Not used to seeing her sleep so late, Tomas asked, "What's up Teri?"

Jacques inquired, "Are you okay?"

Des rolled his eyes. "She was talking to Angel for hours last night."

Marie looked at Teri and said, "Just ignore them."

We left the hotel and had salmon tacos at a Pike's Market café. They were amazing. Then we wandered around getting bread, fruit, cheese, and chocolate croissants so we could survive in the wilderness. I should have asked Angel about the caretaker of the property. All that he had told me was that he lived in a small cottage behind the main house.

We had started for Snohomish County a little too late to miss the commuter traffic. The Seattle traffic reminded me of Los Angeles. Once we got off the highway, everything changed. We drove by beautiful, placid Lake Stevens, and the GPS took us close to the foot of the Cascade Mountains.

"Wow!" Tomas said.

Des complained, "My phone signal is weak."

"Look! An eagle!" Jacques exclaimed.

Ahead of us, circling far above the tall trees, the majestic creature seemed to welcome us. We drove into Granite Falls, which was just like Rossville, small-town U.S.A. We drove past the high school. There were a lot of trucks with mud tires and Jeeps in the parking lot.

Marie said, "I bet Grandma would like it here." She did not sound enthusiastic.

A few miles outside of town, we saw a cardboard sign hung on a mailbox. "Bienvenue Miranda!". I was just glad it did not say, Baroness. We drove down the gravel drive until we came to a large modern two-story home on the Stillaguamish River. It stood in a clearing surrounded by incredibly tall pine trees. A smaller house stood nearby with closed shutters. We piled out of the car and stared at the primal beauty all around us.

"Look," Marie said, pointing. "a waterfall!"

On the far side of the river, a small waterfall trickled down the granite cliffs. We had moved to paradise. As Lug and Jacques ran down the slope to the water, I looked over at Teri.

"I'm on it!" she said and followed close behind.

The triplets and I entered the house. It was spacious, with large windows offering spectacular views. The furnishings reminded me of a hunting lodge. Above the stone fireplace, there was a bouquet of fresh lavender and roses. I found a note on the coffee table.

Bienvenue Madame,
I will greet you and the children at sunset. I prepared a meal for you. It's in the refrigerator. I hope you will be comfortable here.

Guillaume

What was it with all the French vampires? We explored the house. After surprisingly little arguing, the kids claimed their rooms. There was comfy bedding, beautiful furnishings, and some beautiful tribal tapestries on the walls. The small bookcase in the master bedroom was empty except for copies of my books. Every room had a view of the mountains, and some had views of the river and the waterfall. This was a perfect retreat from the crazy vampire world and from my past. It had not even been a year since my father had been killed. I sat on the bed and took a deep breath. This was our haven. When Tristan visited, he would stay at a condo he owned in Seattle. I would have no flashbacks of making love with him in this bed. It was a new start for my head and my heart.

Teri and Jacques came running up the stairs, following Lugosi. He ran to greet me and jumped on the bed.

"Lug, No!" Teri yelled too late.

He shook and covered me in river water. "It's okay," I laughed. Teri grabbed one of the plush towels from my bathroom, and Jacques helped dry him off.

"Mom, can we stay here?"

"As long as you want, this is home now." I smiled.

I yelled to the kids to put their stuff away. When I opened the bathroom drawer, there was a small bottle of perfume and a card. It was Midnight Fleur, a lovely blend of exotic flowers. I opened the card,

Miranda,

This scent reminded me of you. It is parfum, its beauty is lasting, and it has many complex layers to explore. We both have a year to adjust and heal so that our reunion will be sweeter. Please allow your love for me to conquer your anger towards me.

Batu.

Tears began to flow. "You bastard!" He must have arranged for Guillaume to put this in the drawer for me to find. I had stopped wearing perfume when I separated from Tristan. The scent he had given me was like a claim on me. I was not about to start wearing Batu's scent, no matter how good it smelled.

"Fuckin' men!" I exclaimed. I had tried using other cuss words in place of my old favorite because of the kids, but "Freakin!" just didn't do it for me.

I went to the kitchen in search of coffee and found a Keurig, a pound of Tony's coffee beans next to a grinder, and reusable pods for the Keurig. We were being watched over by an environmentally conscious vampire, which should be interesting. The fresh coffee was delicious. I walked out on the patio and sat in an Adirondack chair, and sipped the heavenly dark brew. It was about an hour before sunset. I sent some text messages letting everyone know we had arrived safely. The summer days were long, which was fine with me. I had heard the undead rarely visited the Seattle area until the long winter nights came. I would be settled in and prepared for them before the long nights began.

In L.A., the Magus awoke to find a text message from Miranda.

The house is great. We love it here.

He was relieved that her mood had improved. After the battle with Alexander in Las Vegas, she had been quite hostile and had berated the Magus for putting the children in danger. He had ignored her tirade because he knew how special she and the royal offspring were to the vampire world's development. The Magus thought she did not understand what a character-building event it was for the children. The research concerning her blood was fascinating. He had one of the tubes of Miranda's blood sent to Lily so she could continue her research. The other two tubes went to Hannibal so he could continue to vaccinate Alexander. Hann reported that Alex was moping around, depressed because his campaign to rule the vampire Houses failed, and he was banished to Hannibal's elephant refuge in the California desert. The Magus felt satisfaction when he thought of Alexander cleaning up after the elephants. He rose from the velvet chair in his study and went out on his patio overlooking Paradise Cove. His tall, slight frame was incredibly strong and agile. He pushed back his mane of straight black hair and stared out into the dark ocean. Thirty-eight years ago, he had arranged for Connie Ortega to have a sexual encounter with Sir Omar. He had no idea the extent to which their daughter would impact the nocturnal world. He believed their offspring would be gifted, but she was so much more. She and her children were a wonder to the world of the undead.

A servant announced that Baron Mordecai had arrived. He joined the Magus on the patio. They nodded to each other, though the Baron nodded a little more deeply. "Good evening dear Magus." They were the most powerful nocturnal beings in existence.

"I've just heard from the Baroness. She is happy with their new home," the Magus told Tristan.

"Miranda, happy? I hope for all of our sakes it lasts."

"To feel love is divine. To feel love is also hell," the Magus contended.

"She is my plague and my cure," Tristan sighed. "Any news from the House of Cups?"

"Kyoto is doing everything possible to make amends for his unfortunate behavior. The Princess is allowing him to continue his blood studies in a small lab in her monastery." The Magus waited for Tristan to get to his real concern.

"And Batu?"

"He has been found deserving of our gifts. The transformation will occur when darkness encompasses the Mongol plains. Do you have concerns about his character?"

Tristan looked out on the ocean. "He is difficult to read. I will reserve my criticism as it may be due to his attraction to the Baroness. He saved her from harm twice, and I hate being in his debt."

"Of course. I believe Batu will be helpful to the Princess as she consolidates her new House. I was pleased to hear that Kyoto has been giving the Princess sound counsel. I hope you will be able to forgive him. I believe that he only wanted to transform the Baroness to save her from mortality."

Anger flashed in his eyes. "When she transforms, I will be the one. It will be of her own accord and desire. He had no right to try and coerce her. I shall never trust him again. I understand your ancient friendship, and Miranda's hatred of bloodshed caused you both to be lenient."

A servant announced that Lady Sarah had arrived. The beautiful redhead wore tight jeans and a scoop neck t-shirt, emphasizing her tiny waist and ample cleavage. Turquoise bracelets adorned her arms. She joined Tristan and the Magus on the patio, bowed to the Magus and said, "Good evening. I hope I'm not intruding."

"Not at all Lady Sarah." The Magus gestured for them to follow him into the study. Two walls were lined with dark walnut bookcases filled with leather-bound books. A large fireplace with a carved malachite mantel took up much of a third wall. On the top of the mantel was a large ornate gold clock. In front of the fireplace was an antique dark blue sofa, flanked by side tables with exotic vases filled with peacock feathers. Facing the sofa on each side were matching gold velvet chairs. The fourth wall, made up of sliding glass doors to the patio, were hung with heavy dark drapes that would block out daylight.

The Baron and Lady Sarah sat on the sofa, the Magus across from them in an antique velvet chair. "I have news for you both," Sarah began. "Lady Lily wanted me to share some results from the latest blood sample. She is now on her way to Mongolia to confer with Kyoto."

"Continue," the Magus nodded.

"She finds that the Baroness's blood is evolving, showing ever more vampire qualities, yet the Baroness is still quite mortal. The aging process is slowing down. Normally we have to give mortals regular doses of our blood to add to their longevity. Miranda had been given some HH blood at times but not near the amounts it would take to affect her so dramatically. Lady Lily says this is happening on its own. There is no explanation for the properties her blood exhibits. The vampire antigen affects us but does not block her supernatural qualities."

The Baron smiled. "This is great news."

"No one can know of this besides us, Lady Lily and Kyoto," the Magus stated in a serious tone, "I will send them a message. If this is true, the Baroness must be allowed to discover what is happening to her over time. She will struggle with the emotional and physical impact on her changing nature. Our awareness will allow us to be supportive. We still do not know how this will play out. The anti-vampire toxic quality of her blood may diminish or get stronger. She may begin to age suddenly. We will verify the extent of her evolution by continuing to monitor her blood when more is drawn for suppressing Alexander's powers."

Tristan responded, "How will this affect the offspring? Their aging process and development are quite mortal so far. However, they are brighter and exhibit greater physical strength than other children."

"Of course. Like their mother, they are still a mystery of creation." The Magus was quite concerned with their development. It is why he had chosen a very special Common Caste vampire to look after them. "I hope you will be able to visit them frequently, perhaps spend the winter at your place in Seattle."

"I have already made arrangements to visit twice a month, but I can visit more often. Much depends on the Baroness."

The Magus added, "Lady Pompadour tried to meet her before being given permission. The Baroness chastised her and refused to meet with her."

"I'm sure she did," the Baron wished he could have seen that encounter. "I'll discuss strategy with Pomp when I visit next week. In time I hope she will be able to influence my family to respect our ways."

"There is another matter I must inform you about," Lady Sarah said. "Lady Pauline was a bit careless dispatching of a Worthy Target while looking after the Baroness and the children. This has caused a detective to look into the death of this drug dealer. As she is of my House, I take full responsibility."

To Sarah's relief, the Magus smiled. "Rookie mistake. I'm certain Lady Pauline will learn from this."

"I assure you she has," Sarah replied.

"A detective from Salinas called and left a message with my butler. I ignored it. Perhaps I should contact them personally to stop this investigation now," Tristan suggested.

Sarah responded, "He is Detective Takeda, from the Salinas police department. Teri informed me that he briefly questioned the Baroness a few days ago and had not contacted her since."

The Baron responded indignantly, "I will not allow Miranda to be the subject of an investigation. It will be my pleasure to stop this detective."

The Magus turned to Tristan. "Let's not be too heavy-handed. This mortal is just doing his duty. He must be fairly bright to have found some connection between their visit and the crime and then follow the lead to you. Perhaps we have been remiss to leave the bodies of our Worthy Targets behind. It might be useful for us to have assets in the criminal justice system. Let's just try to convince him that your ex-wife had nothing to do with this crime."

In preparation for Batu's transformation ceremony, Chang brought a small, sturdy Mongol horse with great strength to the main building's front steps at sunset. The breed was largely unchanged since the time of Genghis Khan. A special saddle had been created for Princess Khunbish. She wore a jeweled headdress with long strands of jade beads hanging down the sides. Her red silk tunic had gold buttons and dragons embroidered on the sleeves. Chang helped her onto the steed. Sir Steve and Batu followed behind as their procession walked to the monastery. Batu wore a plain black tunic that wrapped loosely about his chest. He thought to himself what a suitable match he would be for Miranda once he transformed and developed his vampire abilities.

There were few electric lights in the ancient building. Lanterns and candles illuminated the entrance and stairs to the room for the ceremony. A monk lit some incense as they entered, then hurried away. Kyoto welcomed them. There were several carved chairs inlaid with turquoise and malachite. The monks never used these, only the Princess and her guests. An IV pole with a bag of blood and some medical supplies looked very out of place.

"Please excuse the bright light, but it will be helpful," Kyoto turned on a light that gave the room a harsh glare. The Princess seated herself on one side of the medical equipment. "Sir Batu, if you will, please kneel here," Kyoto pointed to a large cushion on the ground in front of the Princess. Batu kneeled, facing his royal sovereign. Steve handed the Princess a tiny dagger with a razor-sharp blade.

She fixed her gaze on Batu, and in Mongolian, asked him, "Are you certain?"

Batu responded in Mongolian, "Tiimee," with a small nod, though his voice was a bit shaky. The vampire wannabe had to be committed to the ceremony to avoid deadly injuries.

Kyoto took one of Batu's arms, inserted a needle into a vein, attached the tube connected to the blood bag then started the flow of the HH blood. It was a mixture of his blood and the Princess'. It was a rare and special honor to receive the blood of the ancient Haute Caste. The Princess expected much of the young Mongol she would make her knight. Batu prepared himself for the pain which would come next. She leaned forward, and he stared into her intense dark eyes. Batu saw her sharp fangs, followed by searing pain as she bit deeply into his chest. The Princess felt a sense of elation as she drank his mortal blood. Steve stood behind Batu to keep him from collapsing. "Miranda!" Batu cried before falling back. The Princess released her fangs from his chest, made a small cut to her wrist with the dagger, then held it up to Batu's parted lips. He swallowed the salty warm, bitter elixir. Her blood and the IV revived him. He began to feel the power of the undead surge through him. The exchange of bodily fluids temporarily weakened both transformer and the transformed. They would recover by the next night, and Batu would have a new appetite.

"Thank you," he uttered. "I shall try to merit your generosity."

The Princess smiled. "You are now a Knight of the House of Cups." She wiped her blood-red lips with a silk handkerchief. "Sir Batu, you will serve this House alongside Sir Steve. You are guardians of the House of Cups. May your speech and behavior uphold our code and your proud Mongol heritage."

"Of course," Batu responded. Chang helped him to his feet and took him out of the monastery to a horse that would carry him back to his new home. Chang would watch over him for the rest of the night.

The Princess turned to Kyoto. "You believe his seed will produce a child by the Baroness?"

"Yes, he seems very healthy, your Highness. I believe he will become a magnificent example of our kind. He is already quite strong, clever, ambitious, and ethical. He will honor your House."

Then she turned to Steve. "You'll encourage their relationship?"

"Princess, no one can say what the Baroness will decide or do, but she does have strong feelings for him. When he is ready, he will return to her, with or without my meddling."

She appeared amused. "You're lucky. I have strong feelings for you, insolent prig."

"Yes, I am," he responded.

Steve helped her down the stairs and onto her horse. They rode double, with him behind, supporting her gently. She could not use her amazing will to bring her strength back instantly. It was the first time he felt so protective of his assassin Princess. "You may ride me tomorrow," she muttered and fell asleep in his arms in the moonlight.

Chapter 5

Des Takes a Swim

I walked down to the Stillaguamish River, called the Stilly by locals. We were close enough to let us hear the lullaby of the dark, blue-green water rushing against the rocky banks. I could easily imagine a bear and her cubs strolling along the river's edge, searching for a salmon or trout for dinner. We would have to be careful Lug did not become a snack for some predator. Most of all, I imagined my dad, Pete, telling me how great the fishing would be if I only had the patience for it. When the world stood still for a moment, the grief monster would creep out of some dark corner of my brain. I would never get the picture of my dad's battered body in the emergency room out of my head. He never regained consciousness after the attack by the crazed monks who were simply going to abduct him. Kyoto and Alexander had chosen the wrong mortals to carry out their plan.

I thought about the unlikely heroine who came to our defense. The vamp-wolf that my mom named Sally had taken revenge on my father's attackers. Afterward, we ensured Sally was safely tucked away with a dear friend, James, at his ranch in Montana. We hid her from the suspicious sheriff who had investigated the bizarre deaths of Pete's killers. Sally was the only vamp-wolf in existence. I had wanted her destroyed when she first showed up near our farm in Rossville. Bart had told me everything, and everyone has a purpose, so we waited for Sally to reveal her reason for being. It turned out that she was a wild avenger who would not wait for a trial to dispense justice. I only wish that she had killed the monks before they had mortally wounded my dad.

I sent a text to my biological father, Omar Sadeghi, who tried very hard to fill the void my late father had left.

We are safe. The kids are being rotten to each other as usual.
All is good. Love this place.
Hugs Miranda.

He was a dashing vampire whose home was in Qatar. He typically wore traditional Arabian garb, except when involved in an assassination. It's hard to be inconspicuous in white flowing robes. Dark hair managed to peek out from his headdress. It was where I got my unruly curly hair. He was usually very somber, but the kids could always make him smile. He, like Tristan, was particularly incensed when they found out that Alexander had fathered Jacques. He was very protective of his family. Since Pete's death, Sir Omar and I had grown very close. His significant other, the vampiress Anastasia, was also very fond of us. The vampire side of the family has smothered us with concern since Pete's death. Now that the rebellion has been quashed, we have a chance to establish a more normal life.

"Madame, Bonsoir!"

I turned to see a young man with wavy brown hair to his shoulders, wearing a fitted denim shirt and tight jeans. "Guillaume?"

"But of course, who else would be here?" He stood with arms crossed, waiting for me to come up to the house.

"The hunchback of Notre Dame?"

"Alors, you're joking, no?"

"Yes," I responded. This was going to be fun.

The kids piled out of the house and sprawled on the patio furniture.

"Who is he?" Des asked, nodding his head at Guillaume.

Guillaume whipped around to face them. "It is rude to speak about a person as though they are not present."

"Sorry," Des responded.

Jacques took the opportunity to score points. He jumped up from his chair and extended his hand. "I'm Jacques."

Guillaume smiled. "Yes, you have a resemblance to him, to your very great grandfather." Jacques shook his hand. "I am Guillaume, a distant relative."

"Seriously?" Tomas stood up and stared at him. "You're one of our ancestors?"

"Our bloodline was protected. I discovered who the guardian demons were, and I was allowed to join. I was an exception to the rule. Are you Tomas, the firstborn?"

Tomas seemed to stand a little straighter. "Yes." He extended his hand as well.

Marie approached him next. She put out her hand, and he started to kiss the back of it. She abruptly pulled it away from him. "Knock it off. Just shake my hand."

Guillaume displayed a sly smile. "Of course, mademoiselle Marie. It is an old custom in France. I meant no offense. You are truly a modern fille." He shook her hand.

Des finally walked over to him. "I'm Des. I just didn't know who you were. We've been through a lot lately." They shook hands.

"No problem, I have heard about your adventures. Now you are home. Let me show you a gift from the Magus." We followed him to the back of a small barn behind his cottage. Under the eaves were boxes without bottoms.

Marie's eyes lit up. "Bat houses!" She had never met a creature she did not adore. "Will they start to look for food soon?"

"Yes, Marie, they will hunt for their dinner. Which will keep us free of flying insects."

I had no doubt this was a gift meant for my daughter. Teri joined us with Lug.

"This is our bodyguard, Teri Park. This is Guillaume."

"Mademoiselle," he purred.

"Hi!"

"I presume you are proficient with a sword?" Guillaume asked.

That got the kids' interest.

"Not my preferred weapon," she replied

"Would you be interested in fencing lessons?"

Almost in unison, all four kids said, "I would!"

Guillaume pointed to an outbuilding that looked like a small barn. "Come, that is where we shall practice." He walked over and slid one of the large doors to the side.

I stood in the doorway as Teri and the kids rushed in to examine the swords hanging on one of the walls and the protective equipment laid out on a long table. Masks were hanging on another wall. The kids, of course, began trying them on.

"We should make a horror movie," Marie proposed.

"Yeah, the Cult of the Masks!" Des responded.

Tomas ran with it. "A group of teenagers finds some masks put them on, and become possessed!"

Jacques added, "Their faithful dog pulls off one of the masks and saves them from something horrible."

"Sure, okay," Des said, "And Uncle Guillaume could be the creepy neighbor who gives the kids an old trunk with the masks in it."

"Enough! Let's go get dinner," I suggested.

Guillaume looked at me. "Creepy? Moi?"

"You have to be thick-skinned if you're going to hang out with them." As we were walking back to the house, I asked him, "Did Tristan ask you to watch over us?"

"Yes, but I had wanted to meet you for some time, so I was delighted when he honored me with this privilege."

"He thinks you're safe and that I won't have an affair with a relative. That's why he asked you. He is picky about the vampires he allows to get close to me. Jorge is gay, Bart is a Heirophant who only shares his bed with Jeanne. He doesn't see you as competition."

Guillaume smiled. "That is not why he chose me. I'm Common Caste, a very, very distant relative, and obviously French. I will explain why he trusts me some night. Madame, try not to jump to conclusions."

I decided to let it go for the moment, and we followed him into the kitchen. Guillaume pulled a large pot of Beef Bourguignon out of the fridge and put it on the stove to heat. Then he put some baguettes in the oven to warm. I told the kids to go wash their hands. There was also a large round of Camembert cheese, which he put on the counter. As I started to take some, he frowned, shook his head, and told me, "Let it warm to room temperature."

Teri looked mystified. "How long since you've had a regular meal?"

"You mean a mortal supper? Several hundred years, though, I never lost the love of preparing fine food. Sometimes I still taste the sauce."

"We met Madame Pompadour. Does she ever taste your sauce?" I asked.

He smirked, and Teri tried not to laugh. "Yes, she visits from time to time, or I go to the city. She chose the tapestries that hang on the walls. I admire her exquisite taste. She will not intrude on you and the children without an invitation."

"Why do you like her?" I asked bluntly.

"She is complicated, has a great intellect, and many talents."

"Whatever," I just spooned some stew into a bowl. After meeting Hannibal the Barbarian and Jeanne D'Arc, it was hard to impress me.

The kids came over and filled their bowls. Des pulled out a chair for Marie. "Mademoiselle." Just as she started to sit down, he pulled the chair back, sending Marie and the beef stew onto the hardwood floor.

"Desmon!" I yelled and helped Marie back up.

Guillaume picked up Des, who was just an inch shorter, and carried him outside. He tossed him to the ground and began scolding him in French. After a moment, he switched to English. "You must respect women! You would not be here if not for women!"

"My dad had something to do with it too," Des responded, then quickly regretted it.

Guillaume threw him over his shoulder and carried him, struggling, down to the river. Tomas and Jacques started to go after their brother, but Teri and I held them back. Guillaume tossed Des in the icy cold river. I never saw Des move more quickly than when he scrambled back onto the shore.

"Are we clear?" Guillaume demanded.

"Yes," Des said, shivering.

Guillaume put his arm around his student's shoulders and helped him up. "You will be an extraordinary young man."

"If I don't die of pneumonia," Des sniffled.

When they came back into the house, my chastised son went to put some dry clothes on. Marie approached her champion. "Thanks, but I can take care of myself."

Guillaume looked surprised. "Eh Bien, mademoiselle, I will take my leave for this evening."

I followed him outside. "Guillaume, thanks for everything. I have a feeling you may want to throw us all in the river at some point. Next time let's confer on a different way to modify their behavior."

"As you wish, though I would never do that to you. Until tomorrow night." He smiled and walked back to the fencing barn.

I had no doubt we were related. I would have prohibited the fencing lessons if anyone, but Guillaume was the teacher. I now knew he could handle them. When I sat back down at the table, supper was quiet, the siblings looking at Des and trying not to laugh.

Tomas put some salad on his plate. "The lettuce is kind of wet."

Marie added, "It is kind of damp here."

"Shut up!" Des shouted, which caused more snickers.

"I want the four of you to promise me there will be a truce. Help each other, as you did in battle in Las Vegas." I got some eye-rolling. "I mean it! At least act like you love each other, damn it!"

"Dear Desmon, will you pass the ranch dressing?" Tomas asked.

"It would be my pleasure," he responded, throwing the bottle at him.

"No computer games for 24 hours. Give me your phones and tablets. Now!" They reluctantly gave me their phones. Teri went off to find their tablets.

"I didn't do anything," Jacques whined.

"You're related. That's enough."

"Only fifty percent," he muttered and looked down at his plate.

"The rest of you take care of the dishes. Jacques, come with me." Tomas leaned over and whispered something to Jacques, then Jacques followed me out to the back deck. This would become the place where I would have important talks in the time to come. We were far enough from the kitchen that the kids would not overhear us. I turned my Adirondack chair to face him.

"Jacques, with everything that has been going on, I haven't had a chance to talk with you. I'm sorry. I know how difficult it is. I remember the shock when I found out Sir Omar was my biological father. It does not change how much we love you. Tristan will always be your dad in every way except you don't have his DNA." I looked at the sadness in his eyes and felt helpless.

"I don't want to be related to Alexander. He sucks!" Jacques sniffled.

"Sweetheart, there are worse things in the world than being Alexander the Great's kid. He's very bright, cunning, handsome, and resourceful. Jacques, you are your own man, not a clone."

He stared at me. "Do I look like him?"

"A little. I think you look more like my side of the family, like a de Molay."

"I hope Dad visits soon, or maybe I could call. I want to tell him that I don't care what Alexander says. I'll always be his son."

"He knows that, Jacques. You can call him when you get your phone back tomorrow night. Nice try."

I hugged him and asked him to feed Lug, and he headed back into the house. I stayed outside to look at the moonlight on the river. It was so peaceful here, at least for now.

In Vegas, an hour after sundown, Pauline was pacing in Anastasia's living room. She was in a denim shirt and jeans. Her long blonde hair fell loosely about her face.

A butler came in with a silver tray and three small crystal glasses with a dark red beverage. He left the tray on a small table and vanished.

Anastasia and Omar entered as though on cue. Anastasia wore a black silk blouse with matching slacks, high heels, and black diamond jewelry. Her platinum hair was in ringlets. This was a casual look for her highness. Omar, as usual, wore his traditional garb. He adjusted his robes as he sat down.

"Lady Anastasia and Sir Sadeghi, thank you for meeting with me."

Anastasia sat beside Omar and gestured for Pauline to sit on the sofa across from them. Omar began, "The Magus has asked us to deepen your understanding of our code. It seems that because of the recent events involving the rebels and the royal family, the Haute Caste did not properly educate you after your transformation. Sir Ruben was remiss in that."

Pauline was relieved by Omar's tone. She had fully expected to be punished and perhaps downgraded to Common Caste. "I'm so sorry to have caused any problems for the Baroness. I was careless. I assure you it won't happen again."

"No, it won't! "Anastasia replied in a soft and chilling voice. "Like other predators, we are careful not to overhunt, so we do not deplete our food supply. You must seek permission before an assassination. It is not enough that someone appears on the Worthy Target list."

Omar continued, "The number of targets removed is limited and set by our Parliament. We often do not meet that quota to avoid bringing attention to our kind. During wartime, we sometimes exceed that number. If one of our kind is attacked, an assassination is permitted. The Head of each House keeps track and grants permission."

"Please have some refreshment," Anastasia handed one of the crystal glasses of O-positive to Pauline and took one for herself. She took a sip and continued, "Lady Sarah stated you reported the assassination to her afterward. In the future, please contact her first."

Pauline emptied her glass. "May I ask a question?" Omar nodded. "Do these rules apply to everyone?"

Anastasia smiled. "No. Not to the most powerful or most ancient. But, interestingly, they seem to take fewer lives than anyone else."

"Lady Pauline," Omar began, "the repercussions from taking a life affects many. We cannot truly gauge how lives may be impacted. We carefully choose Worthy Targets because of their acts against humanity. However, each assassination affects mortal society and may have repercussions on us as well. In this case, the unintended consequences could have caused problems for the Baroness and her family."

Anastasia continued, "We ask that every assassin study his or her prey before carrying out the punishment. Do not just pull up a name on a list. We insist that you study their life, their family, and those who they have hurt. We must be sure their removal would benefit society more than harm it. Then inform the head of your House as they may have additional information of which you are unaware. Sometimes it may be more complicated than it appears. If one of our kind violates the code, the head of their House, or the Magus himself, will deal with the offender. Often harshly."

"I had no idea. Forgive me for being so stupid and rash. I acted like a gangster, not a sophisticated assassin," Pauline replied.

Omar added, "The Magus developed the code which governs the purpose for our unique talents, so we would not utilize them in a reprehensible fashion."

Anastasia continued, "The Head of your House will answer any other questions you have."

"I will honor the code," Pauline said abashedly. She had considered visiting that detective in Salinas but changed her mind. She would run everything by the Head of her House from now on. "Thank you." She bowed and grabbed her backpack. "I'll let Lady Sarah know you have enlightened me."

Chapter 6

Manny's Unplanned Vacation

"**A**re you serious?" Manny asked his captain.

"Some lawyer in Beverly Hills contacted the Senator's office about you harassing some rich asshole's ex-wife about the Pill King's murder." Captain Jenkins was losing his patience with Detective Takeda. "I told you to wrap up that investigation. I don't care what you call it. Say it was gang-related or some other bullshit. You need to focus on those damn home invasions and get the mayor's office off our asses!"

"I'd like to find out who murdered Phil Emerson. I thought that was my job," Manny said and closed the file on his computer. He didn't want the captain to see the info he was pulling together on Baroness Mordecai.

"You watchin' that detective show, Bosch again instead of working?"

"Fuck-off!" Manny barked back and immediately regretted it.

"Fuck-off? How about you enjoy five days on the beach. I think you need a little time to reflect on your career. Come back and talk to me when you want to act like a member of the team."

"I'm sorry, I...."

"Starting now!"

Manny was pissed at himself. He couldn't believe he had gotten himself five days off without pay. He shut down his computer, grabbed a couple of files, and headed to the parking lot. Everyone in the office got busy so as not to make eye contact as Manny left the building. He burned rubber as his old Mustang peeled out of the city parking lot. Then he slowed down and told himself he had to let this shit go. He came from a family of farmers who did not want him to become a cop. His great grandparents had struggled to get their farmland back after being incarcerated during World War II. His grandparents had raised their kids to be perfect Americans, active in their church, playing local sports, and serving in the military. Manny's parents were more laid back. His dad met his mom at a rock concert. Still, in the end, conformity ruled. Unless you were going to be a doctor, you were supposed to work in their agricultural business. He was so proud when he told his parents he had become a detective. If he got fired, it would be back to the farm, and worse, every day, he would be reminded that they told him he shouldn't have become a cop.

Maybe Jenkins was right. Maybe Phil got what was coming to him. Perhaps he was just another drug dealer taken off the street. Maybe. Manny went to his apartment and started packing for a road trip. He had to assure himself that there was no connection between the Pill King's death and a string of cold cases. If that were true, he would put this obsession with Baroness Mordecai to bed and return to Salinas to kiss his captain's ass.

A few hours later, Manny looked out his apartment window waiting for Molly, his neighbor and best friend, to come home. His twenty-pound black cat Trouble purred in his arms. He greeted Molly as she came up the stairs. "Hey, what's up?"

"I heard you were suspended. What did you do Manny?"

Molly was a clerk at City Hall and worked with the captain's wife. Rather than try and explain, he asked, "Could you watch Trouble for a few days?"

Her apartment door faced his. She opened it then turned around. The scowl on her face was worse than the captain's reprimand. "What's going on with you Manny?"

He followed her into her apartment, where he spent more time than in his own place. He plopped down on the sofa and let Trouble make herself at home. She had her own water bowl and dry food bowl there. Molly sat beside him. He looked into her hazel eyes and knew he had to be honest. "I think I've stumbled onto a serial killer. Jenkins thinks I'm being over-zealous. He wants me to shitcan the investigation into this drug dealer's death."

She pushed back her thick curly brown hair. She loved the earnest, needy look on Manny's face. She wanted to mess up the straight black coif that he put too much product on. Molly checked her desire to kiss him. They had decided to be friends three months ago because of personality issues. She sighed, "Seriously? And you won't let this go."

"I have a few things to check out. If the captain is right, I'll apologize."

"Yeah, and I'll win the lottery." She frowned. "You gotta promise me you won't go solo against some drug lord." Molly stared into his brown eyes, hoping for reassurance he wouldn't do anything crazy.

He smiled. "Never. Hey, you got any of that Jamaican chicken left?"

"Sure," she got up and leaned down to pet Trouble. She knew Manny was staring at her cleavage.

Manny blinked a couple of times, took a deep breath, and stood up. "I'll just finish packing and be right back."

"Get some cans of cat food and the cat box!" She called after him as he went back to his apartment. She picked up Trouble and whispered, "Why do I still love him?"

Chapter 7

The Stare Down

Tristan's private jet arrived in Seattle a few hours before sunset. He would be making his first visit to Granite Falls a few weeks after we had settled in. His butler, Clive, did not knock on the door of his darkened sleeping compartment until the sun's rays no longer posed a threat. Jasper, the chauffer, took care of the luggage when they arrived at the Baron's magnificent condo at the top of a building near Pike's Market. Clive walked out on the large balcony and gazed at the Sound. "Breathtaking!" he commented to himself. He went back inside to join Jasper, his brother, and the Baron.

"Sir, shall we leave for Granite Falls soon?" Jasper asked the Baron.

Tristan stood at the glass doors to the balcony considering his priorities. "Yes." He paused to send a text message,

Dear Pomp, I look forward to your company tomorrow night.

He smiled when he got her response.

You should.

Tristan had Jasper drive the Lamborghini so that he could focus on his talk with Jacques. Alexander's deception had wounded Tristan's pride. He could forgive that, but he could not excuse emotional harm to his youngest son. Alexander cared only for himself, and announcing that he was the child's father in front of the vampire world was heartless. Tristan's self-centered existence had been rocked by fatherhood. He could not imagine Alexander ever experiencing such a meaningful change of consciousness. His thoughts strayed to Miranda, her quiet beauty and passionate response to him in the past. He was not handling the divorce well. He longed to have her soft brown eyes look at him with desire again.

The Lamborghini glided to a stop in front of Miranda's house. Tristan climbed out and paused for a moment to prepare for his meeting with Jacques. Before he reached the front door, he heard Jacques yell, "He's here!" The door flew open, and Jacques ran outside to his father. When the other siblings joined them, they almost took Tristan down. I would have liked to take a picture, but the kids would be tackling a blur.

From the porch, I watched Guillaume help pull the children off their father, then he kissed Tristan on each cheek. That took the kids by surprise. Tomas looked at Des. "Don't even think about it!"

"Idiots! It's what they do in France," Marie said scornfully. She used her newly acquired knowledge of French customs to appear more sophisticated than her siblings.

Guillaume ignored them. "Good to see you my dear friend. With Lady Pomp's help, we made their home as comfortable as possible despite the lack of amenities. The baguettes they sell here are deplorable."

"Merci Guillaume."

Tomas piped up, "Dad, Guillaume is giving us fencing lessons."

"You're lucky. He is a fencing master. Why don't you get ready to show me what you've learned while I talk with Jacques?"

I walked inside and waited for Tristan to decide if he wanted to speak with me. Our last interaction had been rather contentious.

Tristan and my youngest child came into the kitchen.

"How are you?" he inquired, barely looking at me.

"Fine. Thanks. You might want to go into the living room to talk."

"Of course," Tristan replied.

I could see the backs of their heads as they sat on the couch.

"Please tell me what troubles you, Jacques," Tristan asked in a soft voice.

He looked up at the only father he had ever known. "I'm afraid I'll be like Alexander. He's a greedy asshole."

"What else?"

Jacques' eyes began to fill with tears. "That you won't love me like you love the others. I couldn't blame you. I'm not your son anymore...." The floodgates opened, and his body trembled.

Tristan put his arm around Jacque's shoulders. The emotional pain Tristan felt was unlike anything he had ever experienced before. Silent tears trickled down his perfect cheekbones. "Jacques, no one and nothing could ever change my feelings for you. You are and will always be my son." He paused to dry his face with a handkerchief, then handed it to Jacques. "Do you believe me?"

"I want to."

"Jacques, are you calling me a liar?" Tristan asked with a bit of a smile.

"No sir." He looked at his dad. "No, I mean, it's just...."

"Either I speak the truth, or I lie. Which is it?"

"The truth, you speak the truth." He dried his eyes.

"Remember that no matter what happens or what anyone may say, I will always be here for you."

Jacques finally smiled, nodded, and said, "Okay, Dad, I will!"

"Now why don't we go out to the fencing barn so you can show me how a Mordecai can handle a sword! You are a Mordecai, aren't you?"

"Damn straight I am!" Jacques called out as he ran out of the door.

I realized that I loved Tristan more at that moment than at any time in our relationship. I felt his presence behind me, and I needed a moment before facing him. I grabbed a mug and filled it with Ethiopian coffee that could keep a bear awake during hibernation. I slowly turned around. I could take his arrogance, his conceit, and his infidelity but not his pain. The look on his face almost made me drop my mug. I quickly put it on the counter. "Thank you!" I mumbled.

We wanted to hold each other. The desire, the need for comfort, was palpable. Suddenly Lug started barking loudly from the living room. Then we heard the kids outside scream, "Cougar!"

We ran out the door to see a large mountain lion facing Guillaume, who was brandishing a sword. Teri stood beside him with a Japanese throwing knife in each hand.

I yelled, "Jasper get the kids in the house! Now!" He wanted to stay outside and protect us, but he knew his first priority was to the offspring, so he rounded them up.

Tristan and I slowly walked up behind Teri and Guillaume.

"Allez!" Guillaume said. The cougar began to snarl.

Teri whispered, "It is such a beautiful animal. I don't want to harm it."

Tristan took a step forward and raised a hand. "I want all of you to walk backward towards the house slowly." The cougar seemed to fixate on him.

He lived with a panther, so I decided to follow his advice. Teri and Guillaume began to move back as well. We slowly backed up to the deck. The impressive, scary cat continued to stare at Tristan. I could feel my heart beating wildly. I imagined trying to stitch Tristan up after a cougar attack. Tristan and the cougar continued their stare-down for what seemed like an hour but was actually less than a minute. Suddenly the sleek beast turned and disappeared into the woods.

When Tristan joined us on the deck, I asked, "What just happened?"

"I told him he was not welcome here."

"Seriously? You can communicate with wild creatures?"

"Just like I do with you." He smiled.

"Damn, nice burn," Teri muttered and walked back to the barn with Guillaume.

Marie looked at her father and said, "I thought that cougars were afraid of people or at least tried to avoid them."

Tristan replied, "That is generally true, but they sense vampires as competing predators and want to protect their territory. Since you are part vampire, they will probably consider you the same way."

When we got into the house, the kids could not stop talking about how their dad had scared off a cougar. He counseled them, "No quick movements and never turn and run away. They like to chase their prey, and you aren't fast enough to outrun them. Stand tall and back away slowly. I don't ever want you to go after them. Understood?"

They became quiet and nodded, except for Marie. She asked, "But can't we have an understanding with them like you do with Delilah?"

"I raised her. That is different. I saved her from a smuggler. She was half-starved. It took time to establish a relationship of trust with her. The wild creatures here will come and go as nature intended. If you try to tame them, you will put yourself and the beasts in danger."

Marie accepted his response but was not happy with it. I just hoped she would never come across some abandoned, starved baby cougar. In Rossville, Marie had made friends with a vampire-wolf when she was five, and the belief that she could befriend all creatures had stayed with her. That incident scared the crap out of me, but she just thought it was a big dog. The wolf had been given the blood of a member of the Haute Caste years before, and unbeknownst to me, kept watch over us. The vamp-wolf, named Sally by my mother, now resided on my old friend James' ranch in Montana. Not long after James had taken Sally in, his long-time companion, a dalmatian, Gracie, had passed away, and I was glad he still had Sally for company.

"Now, show me what you've learned from Guillaume," Tristan said to the kids.

They ran ahead of us to get ready. As we walked across the grass, I said, "You're a surprisingly good dad."

"And a terrible husband?"

"Just take the compliment."

A flicker of a smile appeared. "You seem to like me better now that we're divorced. Does that extend to more intimate appreciation?"

"When hell freezes over!" I took off running into the barn.

I found a chair against a back wall. Tristan was aware that it was best not to push his luck, and so he did not join me when he entered. The emotional wear and tear we inflicted on each other needed a rest. I would never describe our relationship as toxic, more like combustible.

The kids lined up in their protective gear, looking like Stay-Puft Marshmallow ninjas. Guillaume looked quite serious as he inspected them. "Eh Bien, one at a time, starting with Marie, as she is a lady."

"She always goes first," Tomas complained. He was eager to impress his father.

"Let Tomas go first." Tristan grabbed a fencing foil from the rack on the wall.

"As you wish," Guillaume responded.

"Your funeral," Des muttered to his brother.

Without any safety gear, he began to fence with his oldest son. Every time Tomas made a move, Tristan would dance out of his reach with amazing speed and dexterity. When Tomas tripped over himself and fell, Guillaume stopped the match.

Des was next with a similar performance, though he lasted a little longer. Jacques said he could not even try to stick his father, so instead, he practiced with Guillaume. He had a natural gift for the blade. His balance and quick reactions were impressive. It was one of the few times in his life he manifested a talent that surpassed his older siblings. I loved seeing his look of self-satisfaction. Marie went last. She had requested to go against her dad, like Tomas and Des. Just as the lesson was about to start, Marie whipped her blade across Tristan's arm, cutting through his sleeve and drawing a little blood.

"What the hell?" Des cried out.

"Damn!" Tomas exclaimed. "You can go first next time."

Guillaume said, "Marie, the match had not begun."

Tristan responded, "She knew that. She used the element of surprise. Well done daughter!" He smiled at her as he wiped the scratch on his arm that had already begun to heal.

"Grandpa Omar told me once that he never waited for others to strike first. I didn't mean to hurt you. I thought it would only rip your shirt."

Tristan hugged Marie. "It is nothing."

When your grandpa and Dad are vampires, you get a pass for being a little overzealous when it comes to learning self-protection. I suppose in our weird world, that was a family bonding moment. I was just glad that Mom did not see it.

When the lesson was over, and the kids had put all the fencing equipment in its proper place, Guillaume announced that he had something to say. He looked at Teri, who had been quietly watching the fencing lessons. "Teri, you have proved yourself quite courageous. You are a mortal, yet you risked your life tonight to fight the cougar beside me. You have my admiration and my gratitude." He bowed to her.

Teri turned red, not used to such lavish praise. "It's my job."

Tristan replied, "You do your job very well."

I walked over and put my arm around her shoulders. "I agree."

Des yelled, "Ice cream!' and the siblings all ran back to the house.

Guillaume and Tristan followed behind them. I stayed with Teri. She looked at me. "I was scared to death."

"Yeah, but you didn't run. So welcome to our tribe. When a vampire says they owe you, it means they will always have your back. It's not said lightly. You impressed him, and mortals rarely achieve that. I consider you part of our weird family, and I'm glad you put up with us."

She smiled. "Maybe I should ask the Baron for a Lamborghini."

"Nice!"

In the kitchen, I watched the kids interacting with Tristan, and I realized how much they had grown. When they stood next to him in the kitchen, I saw teenagers, not children. They each tried to get his attention during the ice cream sundae building fiasco. The kitchen counter was covered with melting ice cream, nuts, cherries, and chocolate sauce. After watching them, I lost my appetite, so I began cleaning up the mess as they all went into the living room. Guillaume and Tristan sipped small glasses of blood as the kids demolished their sundaes. Teri had retired to her room, a bit overwhelmed by our lot. Vampires have a way of doing that to mortals, even ninjas.

The kids finished their sundaes and went off to play video games with Guillaume, who had become quite adept at the games. Even Des had warmed up to their guardian. Tristan used this moment to call me into the living room.

"What's up?" I inquired and remained standing.

He gestured for me to sit on the couch beside him. I was wary of being so close, knowing the effect his scent had on me. Too many memories of bodily contact to risk such proximity. I sat in a chair across from him.

"This dance again? You distanced yourself like this when we first met. Surely you're not afraid of your reaction to me now." The intense passion of his gaze was disconcerting.

I sat up straight. "Don't underestimate yourself. New subject. How long will you be staying?"

"You ask me to come here and now wish to know when I will depart? The Magus said you have borderline tendencies."

"The Magus is a sociopathic organized crime boss and serial killer. My mental health issues have developed since you entered my life."

He laughed, "Only you would dare to talk about the Magus like that." He paused and looked out at the river. "I don't know how long I'll stay, but I'll visit more frequently. I will meet with some of our kind in Seattle soon. Why don't you and the children come to my home tomorrow night."

"Pomp is one of your friends?"

He smiled. "Old friend. You could learn a lot from her. I'm sorry your first meeting did not go well. She is one of my favorite chess opponents, and her brilliance and beauty are remarkable."

"You are such a piece of work. I'd like a little alone time, but the kids can visit you with Teri and Guillaume."

"You can't be left unprotected at this time. We are not certain that we have identified and dealt with all the rogue vampires. You must come with the children tomorrow night. You need not interact with me."

I stood. "Whatever. I won't argue with you now, but there will come a time when you trying to control my life will end. Sometimes it feels like a stranglehold on me, and I wish I could just disappear, but I would never do that because of the kids."

"I gave you the divorce, but I cannot stop caring about you," he said softly.

"Try harder!" I walked to the doorway of the kitchen. "Tell the kids they have to be in bed by 3 a.m." I had this strange desire to kill something or someone. This was not good. I cleaned the kitchen and washed all the dishes by hand. I found that mundane tasks were soothing and calming. I decided to sweep and mop too.

Tristan pulled out his phone and sent a text,

Pomp, you were right, as usual.

The response came quickly,

How could you doubt me?

Chapter 8

Funeral Pyre

Lily was shown to Kyoto's sparse room by a silent monk and was surprised by the truly austere, spartan building. A stone stairway took her up a dark passage. The wooden door creaked open as the monk let her in, then disappeared down the stairs. The room had one of the few electric lights in the monastery. As her eyes became accustomed to the dim light, she noticed her former lord sitting on a tatami mat, sipping a cup of tea.

"Lady Lily, please join me," he gestured to her to sit with him.

She kneeled across from him. "How are you?" She was shocked by his plain robes and peasant demeanor. His hair, which normally was in a samurai topknot, was now pulled back in a single braid. He handed her a small cup of green tea.

"Well enough. I'm sorry, but I can't offer you proper refreshments. I have had to sup on cow's blood as our preferred nourishment is banned at the monastery. Though when I visit the Princess, she is kind enough to give me O-positive."

Lily could not hide her sadness. They had been lovers for two hundred years. It was difficult to see the once-proud Head of the House of Cups so humiliated. She uttered, "I am sorry."

"Lady Lily, I have been given a chance to redeem myself. I welcome the challenge that Miranda, I mean the Baroness, has given me. I will find a way to repay her kindness. Did you bring it?"

She nodded and pulled a small plastic box from her backpack. She popped it open to reveal a vial of dark red blood laying in ice chips. "It has been several days since it was collected."

"No matter, the properties I am studying will not be affected." He held it up to the light. "Excellent!"

She followed him into the adjoining windowless room that held his makeshift lab and noticed a bed in the corner. A generator, a gift from the Princess, powered the equipment needed for his research. It also allowed him to charge a cell phone which, was his only contact with the outside world, when the signal did not fail.

She said, "My findings concur with what you reported. Her vampire nature seems to become stronger but remains balanced by the antigens with no harmful effect as yet."

He looked at her. "Tell me, do you see any changes, anything that concerns you?'

Lily looked at the floor. She tried to form an impression of Miranda that would make sense. "Kyoto, she is starting to scare me. I have told no one else about this."

He placed the vial of blood in a small refrigerator. Then he turned back to her. "Lady Lily, you have reason to trust your reaction to her. Her blood is unique. There is a battle going on inside the Baroness. It is as though her two natures have called a truce while each side builds up an arsenal."

"Yes! That is what I sense and what the lab work leads me to believe."

"What have you told the Baron and the Magus?" He knew she was putting herself in danger by not being frank with them.

"Only that her aging process has slowed. They already see the vampire qualities becoming more apparent."

He touched her cheek. "My dear flower, you are right to wait before revealing more of the results. Let them think she is becoming more like us, for now. It is important they do not interfere with her evolution. I owe that to her."

"You tried to stop her development, but now you understand that was a mistake. Since I first examined a sample of her blood when she was a child, I realized we had a new creation. The Baron is delighted with the information I gave them. It was the truth, just not the whole truth." She trembled as he pulled her to him.

"I have missed you," he kissed her gently. She melted into his embrace. The old passion between them reawakened.

He carefully pulled away from her. "I'm not worthy of your beauty and grace. One day I hope to reclaim my place in your affection. "You are a Lady of the House of Cups. I am lower than the Common Caste. I once took you for granted. I was a fool."

She smiled. "Would you be disrespectful to my station by denying my desire?"

He was amazed by her response. "You would still want me? Even now?"

She began to unbutton her blouse. He folded her in his robes, and they fell to the floor, tangled in passion. Centuries of sensual memories triggered their pleasure centers. He whispered lines from a Japanese love poem. She applied delicious pressure that caused him to roll on his back. Their roles had reversed, but Kyoto did not complain. Lily inhaled the rare wine scent of his skin. "I've missed you!" As he entered her, she arched backward, reacting to the ecstasy of their bodies joining. He pulled her down against him increasing their sensual friction. She welcomed the strength of his arms. She kissed his neck, and the scent of his blood unleashed inhibitions. "Bite," she cried out as she held her wrist to his mouth.

"Not yet, my love," he smiled as their passion continued to build. Just when the sexual tension became excruciating, he said, "Now!"

Kyoto bit her wrist, tasting her precious HH blood, and felt infinite pleasure. She lifted his wrist and bit him tasting the blood that had delighted her since she had been transformed. There is a deep, sensual bond between a vampire and the person they have transformed. It does not fade with time. The sharing of blood during sex is a rare and significant act. She would not go back to Ruben. The sensitive Haute Caste would note the change in her scent and know that she was with Kyoto again. It was not an act of impulsive passion; she had received permission from the Magus. When Lily left Kyoto for Ruben, it had caused the ancient vampire to lose his way. The Magus thought that bringing them back together would help restore harmony and loyalty. He believed Lily and Princess Khunbish would prevent Kyoto from ever going against him again.

When the Magus got a text from Lily stating that Kyoto was cooperative, he thought. "Sex. Not fighting against me, progress! No executions for now."

I sat on the back deck, watching the kids playing with Lug. He loved to retrieve balls or sticks, anything he could fit in his mouth. It was such a pleasant moment until I felt someone was watching us. I had been wondering how Tristan could let us live here without more daytime security than Teri. He had impressed upon me that the danger from rogue vampires and their flunkies may not have entirely passed. I sent a text message to Teri, who was eating lunch. She walked out on the deck with half a sandwich. "What's up?" She was watching the kids and Lug.

"I don't know, but I could swear someone was nearby."

We both scanned the river and the dense tree line around the property. "Look!" I pointed to someone coming out from behind a tree. Lug started running towards them, barking frantically, with the kids following him.

A man appeared and picked up a small goat just as Lug reached them. "It's okay pup. Calm down."

Jacques caught up to Lug and grabbed his collar. Teri and I ran down to get between the intruder and the children. Teri pushed the kids back, and I faced the goat man.

"Sorry, my goat got loose. I'm Leif. I live just the other side of those trees," he said, pointing behind him.

He certainly looked like a Viking that washed up on the Sound. Tall, muscular, strawberry blonde, but not pale like Tristan, there was color in his cheeks, and he definitely had more brawn. His plaid shirt could not hide his broad shoulders. He looked like he needed a shave. I inhaled in his direction, he was mortal, but something was off.

He smiled at me. "You must be Ms. Mordecai."

"How do you know who I am?"

"Guillaume asked me to keep an eye on you guys," he replied.

"I will have to talk to Guillaume about that. We do like our privacy."

"I understand. I didn't mean to startle you. I just had to round up this little guy."

Marie came over to me and asked Leif if he had more goats, breaking the tension

"A dozen. I make cheese. I'll bring you some," he replied with a smile, then turned and disappeared into the trees.

Well, that answered my question about daytime security. As we were walking back, Teri said. "He's good. We didn't detect him till now. I think he wanted to meet us."

"I was thinking the same thing."

"Maybe he wanted us to know he's not nocturnal."

Taking the kids to visit Tristan at his condo, I rode with Guillaume in his Mini Cooper and Teri followed with the kids in my Jeep. Once we hit the road, I asked. "Who is Leif?"

"You met him?" he looked surprised.

"Yeah, he stopped by with a goat."

Guillaume chuckled. "It probably got away when he was trying to milk it."

"I don't like anyone keeping secrets that affect my family."

"I exist to serve Madame. You can trust Leif. He wants to make a good impression on our kind. Protecting you and the kids is his current mission."

"What did he do before goat herding?"

"He's still at it. He works at the Funeral Pyre."

"Seriously, the Funeral Pyre?" I said in a snarky tone.

"It's a club, and hard to get into. The elite Goth freaks of Seattle love it."

"You realize elite, and Goth should not be in the same sentence."

Guillaume shrugged. "Pomp has said that you and Teri are welcome any night. We could go while the children visit with their father."

"Let me think about it," I replied. Pomp wanted to cultivate a friendship with me. Maybe she'd change her mind once she got to know me. I'd bet my life she cultivated my husband, the Magus, and any number of Haute Caste vampires. In any case, my curiosity was piqued. I knew Teri would love to go to a club. "Okay, we'll go."

The kids were happy to hang with their dad while Terri and I went out for the evening. We went up to Tristan's condo with the kids. Clive had ordered pizza, and Jasper had brought ice cream cake for later. Four chess boards had been set up in the living room. The kids would be challenging Tristan, Clive, and Jasper. Tristan would show off, taking on two of them at once. The adults had been playing chess for ages, so you would think the siblings Mordecai might have been intimidated by their opponents.

"Cool!" Des sat down in front of the malachite and obsidian set. "I want to play Dad first!"

Once the kids were settled in, Guillaume, Teri, and I headed out. Teri was excited about the last-minute plan of going to the club. Like me, she had not dressed for it. "Can we stop at a store? There has to be someplace still open that sells more appropriate attire," she asked Guillaume.

"Right around the corner. I had an idea you might want to do that, so I called ahead so they would stay open." He grinned.

The End of the World Boutique and used book shop had everything an anarchist might want to wear. I found a pair of purple Doc Martens that someone had carefully painted skulls on. They were my size. Then I found a partially ripped fishnet shirt to go over a black sleeveless t-shirt. I tried on my new look in a tiny changing room that smelled faintly like a cat box.

When I came out, Teri said, "Now you look like you write vampire books."

"So do you!" I responded. She wore skin-tight black leather pants and a Sex

Pistols T-Shirt with "Bollocks" printed across the bottom.

Guillaume left the house wearing a tailored white shirt left open at the chest and dark purple pants. He was not about to touch that look. I gave the clerk my credit card and wandered over to the used book section. In the Paranormal Romance section, there was a copy of my first book about sociopathic ghosts. I picked up the copy and signed the title page. I looked around a little more, but my vampire book was not there.

"Hey, you going to buy that?" a clerk about half my age asked.

"You can double the price now," I responded and went over to sign for the clothes.

"She's Miranda Ortega. The author!" Teri sanpped indignantly, "You might thank her."

We left the store, and I felt jazzed about my new look. I would not wear it every day, but I would definitely buy more interesting clothes from now on.

Teri said, "We should get tattoos!"

"Only if it's Dracula. Tristan would love that!"

Every place was within walking distance from the condo. We put our old clothes in the Range Rover then went to the club. We came to an old brick building next to an expensive lingerie boutique. "Sir Henry is the landlord. You'll meet him tonight. He is one of the ancients and not a huge fan of the Magus. He was Cleopatra's lover, and Lena transformed him after the Queen's death. He is Haute Caste and has managed to distance himself from our society. He lets Pomp live on the top floor. The club is in the basement," Guillaume informed us.

We saw a few people at the back of the building, dressed like rock stars, go down the stairs. We followed them. A tall, muscular woman wearing a black bustier with a leather mini skirt was the bouncer at the door. Every visible part of her body was pierced in some fashion. I marveled that anyone could have so many holes in an earlobe.

A man in front of us, dressed in a suit, was being turned away by the bouncer. He tried to hand her a hundred-dollar bill, but she just snarled, "Get lost!"

He looked mortified. The woman with him tried to give her more money.

"There's a karaoke two blocks down where you can pretend to be Ozzy. Go before I give your companion a reason to wear all black," she spat on the ground.

"Doris, Bonsoir," Guillaume said. He walked up to her and kissed her on each cheek.

The tourists walked away, shaking their heads and complaining.

Doris looked Teri and me over. I inhaled in her direction. She was mortal. "Gilley is she Mordecai's...."

"Not anymore," I cut her off. "I'm Miranda Ortega, though I'm partly responsible for the Mordecai kids. This is Teri; she keeps us in line."

"Her?" Doris scowled. She was easily a foot taller.

Teri merely pulled a pant leg up enough to show a longer than legal knife strapped to her leg and smiled. "Yes, me."

"Welcome to the Funeral Pyre!"

We followed Guillaume down a hallway with paintings of French royalty on the walls. Marie Antoinette was right by the door to the main room. "Wow," I exclaimed. Dozens of small tables surrounded a stage. Tiny chandeliers with fake candle lights added an unreal quality to the dimly lit room. Versailles would have had mirrors, but here, there was only a tiled reflecting pool of water in front of the stage. Although vampires have no reflection in mirrors, some quirk allowed them to see themselves reflected in still water. Being extremely vain, they often would have small pools added as a "decorative" feature. I was not picking up the scent of the undead. The patrons were mortals who looked like they could be extras for a vampire movie. The women had powdered their faces to look pale, and the men seemed to be competing with the women for the best exotic eyeliner designs. There were a few rebels who wore a bit of dark red. If you ever wanted to know how many ways a person could wear black leather, velvet, and ripped jeans, just visit the club. I could see couples slipping off into curtained areas.

"Where are the night people?" I asked, trying to be tactful.

We sat at a table in front of the stage that had a "PRIVATE" card in the center. Guillaume smiled. "A few will turn up when the word gets around that you're here. This is Pomp's salon, where she reigns over mortals. She has always resented not being Haute Caste due to her blood type. This is where she holds court now."

"Do you think the Magus will grant her Haute status now that he has changed the rules?" I wondered if that was why she was so eager to meet me and get on my good side.

"That is something that must be earned," Guillaume replied.

A handsome waiter in a frilly shirt open to his navel came to the table. "Monsieur Guillaume, what do you and your guests desire?"

"I'll take him," Teri whispered to me.

"My usual," Guillaume turned to us. "Baroness, Teri?"

"Sake," Teri blurted out. I had to laugh.

"Coffee, strong black coffee for me," I said.

The waiter smiled at Teri and disappeared.

Suddenly a vision in black lace appeared on the stage. She had black weaves braided into her blond hair, pulled back with delicate chains. The same chains ran down her shoulders and over her perfect size D breasts, held up admirably by a leather bra. She did not need the white powder. Her eye makeup reminded me of the Kabuki mask Kyoto had worn when he abducted me. I shuddered for a moment.

"Are you okay?" Teri asked.

The woman on the stage raised her hands, and the room went silent. She glanced at her reflection in the water and looked satisfied. "Bienvenue to the Funeral Pyre. May you unleash your innermost secret passion here. Now the band Carnage!"

She was gone in an instant, and I knew the speed of her disappearance was not a light trick. Pomp was showing off for us. The band came on the stage, and many in the crowd gasped. The shirtless, muscular bass player had his hair pulled back by a black bandana. Despite the heavy makeup, I recognized him. "Leif!"

Teri said, "Wow. "He can herd my goats anytime."

They were all mortal, then the lead singer appeared. I could smell his Haute Caste blood despite the pot fumes. His long hair hung in braids, and he wore an open leather vest that emphasized his brawn, and leather pants laced up the sides. He snapped his fingers, and small flames around the stage ignited. I was not impressed. After all, I had been married to the second most powerful vampire, but the audience was awed. His eyes were golden brown and reminded me of a cat. The drums were hard, the guitar riffs were harsh, and his voice was full of raw rage. The sound felt like it was pushing us backward. The waiter arrived with the drinks. He managed to spill my coffee on the table and appeared mortified. "No problem," I yelled above the music and handed him a hundred-dollar bill. He looked relieved.

Teri loved her sake. She sipped it like it was an elixir from the gods. I was looking around and noticed Leif make a bowing gesture towards us. Teri smiled back, but I ignored him. I was not sure I wanted him around the kids or Teri. He looked like a wild man from Game of Thrones.

Guillaume downed his small silver cup of blood. His reddened lips were off-putting. When the first song ended, he said, "That's Henry."

I expected a more exotic name. "He's Haute, right?"

"He's an anarchist, won't use any titles, so just Henry."

"Does he get along with the Magus?"

"Barely, but he's close with Pomp."

They played two more songs I did not recognize, but I could understand Henry as he bellowed sentiments like, "Break their backs before they break mine," and "Sexual oblivion!" He had the crowd responding to his every word and gesture. He let them scream out their anger and lust. Freud would have loved it.

I noticed Henry staring at me as he came to the edge of the stage. His vampire presence exuded primal energy. I saw women and men at the nearby tables leaning forward. I pushed my chair back and crossed my arms. He had a barely perceptible smile on his handsome face. "For our dishonorable guests," he announced and began singing "Live and Let Die" to a hard metal beat. It was amazing. That old song had never seemed more relevant. Patrons stood and rushed to the foot of the stage like lemmings called to the cliff. Guillaume helped us grab our drinks and head to the back of the club.

A young woman jumped on stage, and Henry smiled wide enough to show his fangs. The crowd screamed. He pulled the eager young woman towards him. I yelled, "No!" and charged up to the stage like a bat out of hell. I threw people out of the way as I jumped on Henry, knocking him to the floor. The crowd cheered loudly. The young woman started to hit me, but Leif held her back. I looked at Henry and yelled, "She's not a Worthy Target."

He lifted me off of him like an unruly puppy. His fangs were once more concealed. He stared at me, taking inventory. His scent reminded me of Tristan. "It was just for show. They don't think it's real. I can see there is a vampiress beneath that boring mortal exterior. Show me more."

He began to kiss my neck. It was an exquisitely pleasurable experience. I felt my body flush with heat, and then I slapped him so hard my hand stung. The crowd shouted obscenities. I bowed and started to exit the stage. Henry just rubbed his cheek and smiled. To dissuade his fans from trying to harm me, he shouted, "Let my jealous lover leave!" The crowd laughed and parted as Guillaume and Teri stepped forward to help me get out. The adrenaline rush left me feeling shaky, and my pulse was racing. I took a deep breath. So much for Seattle nightlife. I could not get out of that hell hole soon enough.

Guillaume tried to reassure me. "Don't worry. He won't waste anyone here. He has better manners than that."

Teri asked, "Why are we leaving?"

"How much sake did you drink?" I asked.

"The Baroness is right to leave now," Guillaume interceded. "At the end of the show, the audience charges the stage, and some get invited backstage. Carnage fans are rather passionate."

"We're outta here!" I yelled.

I wondered why Pomp did not show up during the scuffle. I soon found out. We walked toward the Sound to admire the view in the moonlight to calm down. Guillaume broke the silence. "That was quite a performance. You left an impression on Henry."

Teri laughed, "Seriously, that was the most fun I've ever had at a club. I think you should be my bodyguard. I didn't know you had it in you! Guillaume held me back, said you'd be fine. He was right."

I shook my head. "I made a fool out of myself."

"Damn, Henry is hot!" Teri sighed.

"Teri, never, ever, ever get involved with a vampire like Henry. He's one of the powerful ancient ones. His touch, his scent and his voice are fucking intoxicating. He just plays with mortals and probably younger vamps too. He was so arrogant, showing his fangs. Pomp kept hers hidden."

Guillaume smiled. "Be careful about judging the ancient Haute Caste so harshly."

"You forget I married one," I responded.

Chapter 9

An Ace Up His Sleeve

When we got back to the condo, I found my kids and Tristan playing cards with Pomp! She had changed into a tight-fitting blue jean ensemble trimmed in pearls. Her makeup and hair were more natural. Tristan displayed a look of satisfaction when he saw my surprise.

"Back so soon?" he inquired.

I kept quiet. Teri responded to fill the awkward silence. "The club was great."

Pomp smiled. "Henry loves to perform."

Des yelled, "Royal Flush!"

Tomas threw down his cards. The other siblings looked equally disgruntled.

"He is quite good," Pomp said to Tristan, "he has a gift for counting cards and reading people like you," she almost purred.

I had the urge to slap her. She was not even trying to get on my good side. What was she up to? I was not about to stay longer and find out. I wanted my kids away from her. "Time to go! Get your stuff. We're going home."

The whining began, but Tristan shot them a look, and they quickly got their things and headed out with Guillaume and Teri. Tristan came over to me as I started out the door.

"May I visit tomorrow night?"

"Sure, but only with Clive and Jasper. You've never been lucky with trashy blondes. I thought you might have learned that by now." I looked into his eyes. "My gut tells me that Pomp and Henry are dangerous. I don't trust them."

He stepped closer and, in his most seductive voice, said, "Invite me into your bed, and I will never speak to them again. Until then, I shall socialize with whomever I please."

I stepped out the door and turned back to say, "You always underestimate women. You have no idea what Pomp is planning. Keep her away from my kids!" I got on the elevator with my unhappy brood.

Jacques asked, "Where did you guys go?"

Guillaume replied, "Henry's nightclub. It was entertaining."

"Yeah," Teri added, "Leif plays in the house band."

"Seriously?" Marie responded.

Something fell on the floor of the elevator as we got out. It was an ace of hearts, right by Des's feet.

"Cheater!" Tomas exclaimed and shoved Des.

Guillaume got between them, and they both calmed down. They did not want to piss him off. "Gentlemen, we are going home. Des will ride with me so that I can explain the importance of honesty and integrity. Oui?"

"Oui," Des responded, looking down at his feet. French never sounded so sweet.

The ride home was quiet. I was not sure what happened in the Mini-Cooper, but Guillaume appeared to be dedicated to teaching Templar ethics to the kids. I was glad they would hear about a moral code from someone other than me that they respected.

When we got back home, Des just said politely, "Good night Mom," and went off to bed without resistance. Tomas, Marie, and Jacques watched Lug run around for a little while outside, then turned in as well.

Teri and I sat in the kitchen. We were starving. I made peanut butter and banana sandwiches. Then I pulled out a box of Godiva chocolates. It was great. Wrestling with Henry had totally depleted me. I knew a couple of vampires I wanted to talk to about Henry. I was sure they had spent some nights at the Funeral Pyre.

We sat quietly, enjoying the chocolates. After a couple of minutes, Teri broke the silence and asked, "What are you thinking?"

"I'm going to invite Robert and Billy to visit."

"That sounds like a good idea. You can use all the allies you can get. Besides, they never stay anywhere very long."

Pomp stood beside Tristan, staring out at the water, listening to the sounds of the coastal city as it began to quiet down. She reached a hand up to his cheek and gently touched him. "Cher Tristan, let us not waste this night."

He bent down and kissed her. It was almost perfunctory, without passion. "You are lovely, but I am bewitched." He looked at her with sadness in his eyes. "I cannot feel whole without her. The Magus thinks that I am suffering from an acute case of love. I fear that it will be chronic. I appreciated your efforts to rattle her composure this evening at the club and here."

"Henry texted that he was impressed by her aggressive behavior to save an innocent from his bite. Leif was also helpful."

"Every violent surge brings her vampire qualities closer to the surface. I could smell the difference in her tonight when she returned. I will let the Magus know." He walked back into the condo. "Thank you. Now I must confer with the Magus."

"Au revoir," she said and showed herself out. She was used to the behavior of royals. One night she would be granted the same aristocratic status that she had at Versailles. She would find a way. For centuries she had paid her dues as a member of the Common Caste.

She headed to the club where Henry was entertaining a few female Goth fans after the show. The young women were a bit light-headed, intoxicated by Henry's scent. He would taste their blood and other pleasures. He did not take their lives or offer to transform them. He just preferred warm, fresh blood to bagged, sipped from a goblet. He paid his devotees well. He was careful to only take a little blood from each. They marveled at his "dental implants" and asked where they could get them. He just said, "It would diminish your lovely smiles."

When Pomp appeared, they quickly took the hint and faded into the Seattle night. She seated herself on a small love seat beside him. He stretched out, letting one hand rest on her thigh.

"It went well with the Baron," she told him.

He displayed a Cheshire cat grin. "The Baroness was an unexpected delight. The barely controlled rage. I wish she would attend every performance."

Pomp was aroused by everything about Henry but was careful not to let him know that. She would not allow anyone that much power over her. Pomp had never been a slave to passion. She stood and replied, "Perhaps it can be arranged for you to spend more time with her. Would you care if contact with her goes so far as to upset Tristan or the Magus?"

There was a sudden coldness in the room. "I lost all respect for them when they destroyed Lady Lena. I would enjoy causing them some discomfort. Come here. I seek more intimate conversation."

"It is too close to the dawn, mon cher," she said with a smile that promised another night.

"Pomp, you must have vexed the king," he responded.

"Louis was a lovestruck mortal. Sometimes, I miss my less complicated lover. Till tomorrow night." She went to her luxurious suite above the club.

Manny was frustrated. When he arrived at the Baron's mansion in Bel Air, he found out that Tristan was out of town for at least a week. It was apparent that Manny would get no useful information, so he left a card and asked if Mordecai would call him when he returned. He decided not to waste time and began looking into every aspect of the elusive couple's lives. His research included any legal issues involving Miranda Ortega-Mordecai and her ex-husband. He also was able to get information on the Baron's real estate holdings in SoCal. What bugged him was the lack of any pictures of Tristan Mordecai. How could such a wealthy publisher and international businessman have managed to evade photography or be filmed even once in the age of viral social media?

His savings were taking a hit being on unpaid leave, but he couldn't give up his investigation yet even though his faith that the Pill King's death was somehow connected to Miranda was beginning to fade.

He found a cheap hotel in Santa Monica that had all the charm of a homeless shelter. It was either this or sleeping in his car and showering at a gym.

He opened his laptop and began pouring over some of the files a friend at the L.A.P.D. had sent him. They were unsolved cases involving slashed throats. There was a Brit who had worked for a billionaire, Desmon Dontinae. A drug dealer, a child-porn producer, a pimp, a plumbing supplies salesman, and a Senator. A Senator! No one had been able to solve it, and it was ruled a probable suicide. A couple of crazy Italian monks had been picked up related to the drug dealer's death, but they were later released. He saw a note that one of the monks had been killed during an attempted abduction of a Peter Ortega in Illinois. WTF! Checking further, he found that Ortega was Miranda's father.

With all these connections, he felt better about his hunch. He took his portable printer out of his suitcase. He began putting up pictures of the unsolved murder victims, the monks, and Miranda on the wall with tape. The details surrounding Miranda's father's botched abduction and murder were beyond bizarre. He had contacted the sheriff in Rossville, who sent him some very disturbing pics of the monk's bodies after an attack. It appeared to have been a wolf or large dog. Sheriff Fleming requested he keep him updated on any breaks in the case, as he had reached a dead-end in Rossville. Manny now had an ally.

He researched Desmon Dontinae, thinking there might be some billionaire connection to the Baron. He spent an hour online and found nothing. How was that possible. He imagined a billionaire could afford the kind of security that could remove his presence on the internet to a great extent. But he didn't think it was possible to do it so completely. Just like the Baron. Strange!

At about ten p.m., he finished the last slice of pizza and shut down his computer. He was about to let ESPN lull his brain into the realm of sleep when someone knocked on his door. The cheap hotel did not have peepholes, so he pulled the window curtain back a couple of inches and saw a lone tall Latino. He picked up his gun and cracked open the door.

"What do you want?"

"I'm Angel. Baron Mordecai sent me to find out what it was you wanted. I'm a friend of the family," the stranger told him with a smile

"It's late.' Manny told him. "Why don't you meet me at the Starbucks down the street in the morning, about eight o'clock."

"I'm available now, but if you don't want to talk, I'll let him know." He began to walk away.

"Wait!" Manny did not want to be alone with this emissary from the Baron. "Let's talk at the bar on the corner."

"Whatever." Angel shrugged.

Manny closed the door, put on his shoulder holster, and pulled on a jean jacket. He peeked out the window again, saw Angel had started walking toward the bar and headed out, stayed behind his visitor, and followed him into the dingy crowded bar. Manny pointed to a booth in the back, against the wall, where he could watch not only Angel but the comings and goings in the bar. The waitress came over, Manny ordered a beer, but Angel declined.

"The Baron is quite the elusive mystery man. Let's start with who exactly he is," Manny said.

Angel smiled. "None of your business."

He needed a different tact. "Where was he the night that his ex-wife and kids were staying at a hotel in Salinas?"

"Las Vegas."

"Does he own a black Range Rover?"

"That might be the only luxury vehicle he doesn't own."

"I find it strange that there aren't any pictures of him anywhere online."

This question seemed to irritate Angel. "He likes his privacy."

Manny paused to sip his beer. "Does he know Desmon Dontinae?"

"You're in over your head. Be smart. Go back to Salinas, live a long life catching speeders." Manny started to get up, but Angel put a cold hand on his shoulder. He looked down to where Manny's gun was peeking out of his jacket. "Guns are pretty worthless. They just piss us off. Do yourself a favor, go home amigo." Then he turned and walked out of the bar.

"Us?" Manny thought as he finished his beer. "What the fuck did that mean?" Who are these people? He knew he would never get to sleep now.

I sat out on the deck, listening to the light Pacific Northwest rain long after everyone had gone to bed, except, of course, Guillaume. At four in the morning, he wandered out of the fencing barn and came over to sit with me.

"How are you?"

"Unsettled," I replied.

"Why?"

"I grew a half an inch in the last year. How is that possible?"

His eyes got big. "You're sure?"

"I measured myself tonight. I suspected it because my jeans seemed to be getting shorter. Do you know what is happening to me? And tonight, I felt something new. It was stronger than when I fought Alexander. Like an animal released from a cage." I was trembling a little as I spoke.

Guillaume gently placed a hand over mine. His touch was soft, cool, and calming. "Your hidden nature is beginning to reveal itself. We can't predict how it will be expressed. Haven't you noticed the height of most vampires? We always grow at least an inch, some more, after transformation. You are an unfolding mystery ma chère."

"I was afraid of that. I don't want to lose control and hurt someone." Tears were forming in my eyes.

"Tomorrow night I will begin your fencing lessons. It will help you learn self-discipline and control." He smiled.

"So, tell me, why did Tristan and the Magus want you to be around the kids and me?"

"Another time. Sleep well." He stood and retired to his cottage.

I stayed outside for another half-hour. I got a text from Billy,

**Your newly promoted Haute Caste friends would be
delighted to get the hell out of Rossville and visit you.**

I responded,

Hot damn!

70

Then I went to bed.

Chapter 10

Oh Henry!

A few nights later, a Triumph motorcycle, followed by a Cadillac, pulled up in front of the house. Billy and Robert had arrived. The kids were delighted to see their vampire guardians. They greeted them with lots of hugs. Then the complaints began.

"Mom wants to send us to school here, but I think it is a waste of time," Tomas whined.

Des added, "I think you should tutor us. I mean, think about the wisdom you could share with us."

Marie chimed in, "It's more important to know about vampires and the modern world than the Civil War."

I stopped the discussion. "You'll learn about both!"

Robert smiled. "Your mama is right. Y'all are smart enough to take it all in."

Jacques looked at Billy, his outlaw hero. "What do you think?"

"Knowledge is power Jackie," Billy replied and winked at me.

Guillaume came over to greet his old friends. "Sir Robert, Sir Billy, what a pleasure," he bowed.

"D'Artagnan!" Billy laughed. "Are you still playing with swords? Where are the other Musketeers?"

"Swords are so much more elegant than the crude weapon you carry," he nodded at the gun peeking out of Billy's vest.

Robert and Billy would "bunk" with Guillaume. His little house had three small bedrooms without any windows. Des looked at Robert and asked, did you bring your guitar?

"I never go anywhere without it!" he answered with a smile. We had all been charmed by his musical talent.

Robert took a basket from the Caddy's back seat and presented it to me. "From Danuta. She and Connie said ya'll better stay at least a week at Thanksgiving." looked in the basket, and there were several dozen chocolate chip cookies. My favorite! I could smell the cinnamon and knew she had used my dad's recipe. I jammed a whole cookie in my mouth. "She knew they would be safe with Billy and me. We'll see you in a little while." The kids followed them into Guillaume's house, with Des carrying Robert's guitar and Jacques lugging Billy's saddlebag.

I was still curious about his décor, but right now, I just wanted to devour a few more cookies in peace. I went into the kitchen and made a cup of Ethiopian heaven to go with the cookies. It brought back delightful, sweet memories of my old kitchen in Illinois. I sighed, and Batu's image filled my brain. Had he already been transformed? After the ancient ritual, each vampire developed a unique power. Had he found his special gift? I wondered what it might be. I closed my eyes as I stood at the counter, clutching the hot mug. I could almost feel him holding me like he did before he left for Mongolia. His scent, his dark eyes, our one kiss! Then the front door opened, and it all went away, like waking from a dream.

"Miranda, you should lock your door," Henry scolded me from the doorway in full seductive leather attire. He would have been hot in sweats!

"What are you doing here?"

Teri came into the kitchen from the back deck, "I heard there were cookies."

"Good evening Teri."

Teri's eyes got wide, and she stammered, "Uh...Hi! Great show the other night. It was great!" She was star-struck.

He smiled. "You're always welcome at the club."

"Why are you here?" I tried to sound calmer than I felt.

"Teri, why don't you run along and tell Leif I'll be over soon to work on a new song," Henry told her.

To my amazement, she almost ran out of the door. "What the fuck?" I blurted out.

"I am an old friend of Sir Bart, and he suggested I look in on you. He said you had the gift to read minds. Try mine."

"I trust Bart, but I can't say the same for you."

"I have managed to live outside the Haute Caste circus for a very long time. Bartholomew and I are kindred spirits. I might be able to help you."

He sat at the kitchen table and gestured for me to sit across from him. I liked the idea of having a large wooden object between us. Maybe I could break off a chair leg and use it as a stake. "You're nothing like Bart. He's the Heirophant. Who are you?" I sat directly across from him.

"Guess." He stared at me.

I sat down and focused my mental faculties on him, then closed my eyes. He came in loud and clear. I saw an image of him sitting on a throne, holding a scale in one hand and a sword in the other. "Justice!" I muttered and opened my eyes. Henry stared at me like a predator stalking prey. I started to perspire. "It's more than that. You want revenge." Suddenly I recognized his underlying scent. "It's because of Lena!" I stood and shut him out of my mind. I felt goosebumps, and my heart raced. I did not tell him everything I saw. "She wanted to destroy my children and me. What are your intentions?"

He stared back at me, but his eyes were less intense. "I mean you and your children no harm. I wanted to gauge your strength. You know that the Magus, and others, have used you and the children as pawns."

I moved across to the far side of the kitchen. I wanted even more distance between us. "I saw what your special power is."

He looked surprised. It was an uncommon sensation for Henry. "Really? Which one?" he asked with a smirk.

Just then, Guillaume, followed by Billy and Robert, rushed in, and they all stared at Henry. Guillaume, noticing my flushed cheeks and distress, came over and stood beside me. "Teri told us you were here."

Billy and Robert began joking with Henry. "We're Haute now, so you might not want us to play in your club patronized by the struggling masses," Robert said.

Henry smiled. "I would share your blues any night, but not your title, Brother Robert."

Billy asked, "How is Pomp? Still refusing your advances, I imagine."

Henry smiled. "But the Goth ladies love me."

The kids entered with Lug. He came over to me, looked up at Henry, and began to growl.

I said, "Good boy," patted his head, and he quieted down.

"Who are you?" Des asked. The kids stared at the rock star.

"Such an inquisitive family, so many questions. You should begin with, 'Good evening.' I'm an old acquaintance of your fathers, both of them."

I glanced at Jacques, who looked at the floor. "Henry was just leaving."

Henry looked at Billy and Robert. "Yes, I should be going. Leif is expecting me. If you'd like to join us, he's got a place up the hill."

Robert glanced at me, then said, "Sure, I would love to." He turned to me as he headed toward the door. "We'll see you later Baroness."

I was relieved when they left the house.

Marie asked, "Why did Lug growl at him?"

"Henry is good at making people uncomfortable, and I guess pups too."

"He's a jerk!" Jacques remarked.

"A Lithuanian jerk," Marie added.

I showed the kids the cookies. "Danuta sent these." They grabbed handfuls.

Tomas said sadly, "I miss her."

"We'll see her at Thanksgiving. Now go get your clothes out of the dryer and put your laundry away before your dad gets here."

Jacques walked away quietly and said, "I'm glad Henry's not my dad." I had nothing.

Batu woke up in the middle of the day, covered in sweat. "Miranda!" he cried out. In the darkness of his room, he sensed she was being tested. The undead constantly tested Miranda. Batu was not there to protect her. He lit a small candle and recited a Buddhist prayer to bring her serenity. Batu was not sure he had the right to pray anymore. He was just beginning to understand his powers. It would be dangerous to leave the protection and supervision of Princess Khunbish and Sir Steve so soon. "Less than a year to go my love," he whispered.

Tristan arrived at eleven o'clock. We were all out in the fencing barn. I watched the children's lessons, and it took trust in Guillaume to let them practice with real weapons, but he had warned them, in no uncertain terms, not to screw around. Tristan sat beside me and inquired about my well-being. His primal forest scent made me flash on an intimate moment.

"Unnerved," I responded. I was still a bit revved up from my contact with Henry and becoming irritated with Tristan.

"What happened?"

"There's no way Henry would show up here without your blessing. I don't know what game you're playing. He was unkind to Jacques."

Tristan looked satisfied until I mentioned our youngest, then his veneer cracked. "What do you mean?"

"He mentioned knowing Jacque's father."

"I'm sorry. Henry probably thought Jacques was proud of being related to Alexander. I'll explain the situation to him. Was he rude to you?"

"You knew how he would treat me." I glared at Tristan. "You think you can control people like pieces on a chessboard. My gut tells me Henry is a loose cannon. He let me look inside his head. He is very powerful and angry." I was getting a little too loud, and the kids looked in our direction. "You think your power will keep the Haute Caste in line. You should remember what happened to the Magus." I got up and moved to the other side of the barn.

Marie looked at Tomas. "Mom and Dad are at it again." They were waiting for Des and Jacques to finish practicing with Guillaume.

He raised his sword. "Let's distract them."

"Say that again ass-hat. I dare you!" Marie shouted.

"You suck at everything!"

They began lashing out at each other with their swords. I yelled, "Stop that!"

Marie's sword got stuck in Tomas' padding.

"Seriously!" he exclaimed and stomped on her foot.

"That hurt!" She ripped his padding as she dislodged her sword.

"You could've killed me!" Tomas bellowed.

Guillaume and Tristan pulled them apart before medical care would be needed. Guillaume shaking his head, said, "You both need to cool off!"

"No, please. We didn't mean it," they pleaded as Guillaume and Tristan carried them to the river. "We just wanted you and Mom to stop arguing."

My kids were working together. It was like a velociraptor moment from Jurassic Park, and I felt proud and scared at the same time.

Guillaume replied, "That does not matter!"

"Stop it!" Marie hit her father's shoulder as he carried her towards the river. That was something a lot of vampires wanted to do but would never dare.

They were tossed in like toys for Lug to retrieve. Des and Jacques were laughing their asses off. Lug jumped in the river, thinking it was a game, knocking them over as they tried to stand up. We all started cracking up. Even Guillaume smiled! They were cold and wet as they walked back up to the house. I noticed them share a high five as they went in. My kids deserved better parents.

While Tomas and Marie were changing into dry clothes, Tristan spoke with Jacques for a few minutes alone, and then they joined the rest of the offspring in the den to play computer games. When Tristan realized just how violent the computer games were, he got interested and started playing with them. However, Tristan would not play any game that had a vampire character. The kids later told me that he would make an excellent assassin. He had swift reflexes. Imagine that.

Guillaume joined me in the living room. "Are you all right?"

"My head is fried. I got a glimpse into Henry's mind." I looked to see his reaction.

"That was a mistake. Henry is ancient, like Alexander and Hannibal. I heard that he was Cleopatra's lover." He shrugged. "Henry does not feel any allegiance to the Magus, yet he follows the code well enough to avoid being censured."

"He was loyal to Lena," I almost whispered.

"She transformed him. We feel a special bond with the vampire who shares their gift with us."

"Who transformed you?"

He smiled. "A renowned swordsman."

"My father, Omar?" I had to think for a moment. "That means Templar blood and the blood of the House of Swords connects us."

"I have sworn to keep you and the children safe." He patted my hand. "Henry, for all his peculiar ideas, remains protective of mortals."

"We aren't just mortal. We're hybrids. I'm a fucking human Prius."

"You're still a mortal female, and they are still children, and Henry still respects the code."

"I keep hearing about this 'code,' can I get a copy of it?"

"I am sure that at the appropriate time, it shall be revealed to you." He stood. "I must put the equipment away. Good night cousin."

"See ya' tomorrow cuz." WTF! I appreciated the familial reassurance from him, but I was not buying that Henry was just shy of a vampire merit badge for good conduct. I stuck my head into the den and said, "In bed by two a.m. No arguments." I didn't even look at Tristan as I turned to go to my room. He followed me into the hall.

"Miranda, Jacques is fine. May I please talk to you for a few minutes?"

It was unusual for Tristan to say please to anyone. "Okay, in my room away from inquiring minds." I could see Des and Marie peeking into the hall. I had the spacious master suite. My windows looked out on the river, though at night, the view was limited. The sound of the river was always soothing. He stood several feet from me. I felt like we were tigers circling each other. I indicated he should sit in the chair by the window, and I sat on my bed. I had no intention of sharing it with him. "What is it?"

"I want you to understand my intention tonight. The Magus's allowed me to let you gain a sense of your powers." He gave me a second to respond.

"Nice that no one asked me," I responded coldly. If I didn't know better, I would say my ex was feeling sorry for me.

"When you looked into Henry's mind, whatever you saw is partially a reflection of your true nature. We can only see connections, similarities that exist in the other."

"You're wrong. You have no idea what Henry shared with me, and I will not reveal it to you." I stood with my arms crossed.

"I believe you protest too much," he replied with a smile.

I hated it when I amused him. My jeans suddenly unzipped and started falling down. "Stop that!" I almost lost my balance, pulling them up. "New trick?"

"I have revealed little of my powers to you. You have not been ready."

The lights in the room went out. I felt his arms about me. I pushed at the darkness. "No!" The lights came back on, and it appeared that he had not moved from the chair. "Thanks for thinking of me, but I knew enough about you to divorce your ass." I struggled to get my composure back.

"Henry has graciously consented to protect my family. Remember, I told you I would let you live here on the condition that you accept protection." He looked stern. The expression of lust had vanished.

"You should have asked me who I wanted to protect us. Why don't you go play with Pomp? I'm exhausted." I started to take off my shoes.

"Enjoy sleeping alone," he responded and left without another word.

Now his scent was in my room. I opened a window and took a deep breath. I was just starting to get a grasp of the extent of the many abilities of the undead. I was somewhat immune to their charisma and mind tricks because of my vampire DNA. I knew Tristan could lift people and objects into the air with his mind but turning out the lights and touching me from across the room was new. He needed to move on. I hoped Tristan would cut his stay in Seattle short.

In Rossville, Scheherazade was having difficulty staying within the parameters of her kitchen job. She began to take out the trash fairly frequently, especially when Sheriff Fleming was around. She was one of the few women who could look alluring in an apron while standing by a dumpster. Scheherazade removed the clips that held her hair back and let her hair cascade down her back. She undid a couple of buttons on her blouse to show a bit of cleavage escaping from a black lace bra. As Sheriff Fleming walked out to his car, she called out, "Do you have a smoke?"

The fact of the matter is that vampires do not smoke. She would pretend to be enjoying her smoke break, but tobacco did nothing for the undead except smell terrible. Of course, young Fleming had no idea with whom he was dealing. He just thought the poor young immigrant was impressed by his status as a law enforcement officer and his all-around good looks.

"Hi Sheri, sure." He handed her a cigarette. "Too bad you're not serving tables anymore." He thought she was one of the most beautiful women he had ever seen.

"I miss taking care of you every night," she purred.

"When do you have a night off? An Applebee just opened in Danville. I would like to buy you dinner."

"I don't know if they'll let me," she whispered and looked back at the café.

"What do you mean?" He started wondering if she was illegal.

"I owe Mrs. Ortega for taking me in. I don't get a night off."

He looked surprised. "Sheri, this is America. Everyone gets a night off. I'll just go in and talk to Connie."

"I don't want to bother you," she said with a sly smile.

"C'mon." She followed him into the restaurant up to the counter, where Connie was cutting a piece of apple pie.

"Hi! Sheriff, do you want a piece to go?" She glanced at Sheri. "Greg needs some help with the dishes." Scheherazade did not budge.

With all his courage, he said, "I think Sheri here deserves a night off. I'd like to take her to dinner tomorrow."

Connie looked at him with eyes that could fry an egg. "Her husband back home might not be so keen on that."

Scheherazade was amazed a mortal could be so clever. She feigned embarrassment and ran into the kitchen. Sheriff Fleming turned several shades of red, mumbled an apology, and did not return to the café for several nights.

Chapter 11

Manny Meets Delilah

"You can't be serious!" Kananga exclaimed. She stared at the Magus as though he had lost his mind. They stood facing each other in the living room of her mansion on the edge of Kinshasa, the sprawling capital of the Congo.

"Lady Mbuyi Kananga, I trust your judgment in all the affairs of our world as I trust Sir Sadeghi and Baron Mordecai. However, you have the distinction of being female and not related by marriage or blood to the Baroness. I am confident that you will be able to govern our society impartially while I am gone."

"How long? What if some of the Haute Caste refuse to accept my new authority?" She shook her head slowly, and her long braids cascaded across her shoulders.

The Magus took off his silk jacket and laid it across the back of the leather sofa. He put out a hand, and she allowed him to pull her close. She started to melt against him. The Magus slid a hand slowly up the side of her thigh. "You are magnificent," he whispered. He adored the sweetness of her scent, the softness of her skin. She leaned into him and bit his lip. "I have missed you," They kissed more deeply, gracefully falling on the sofa. Two perfect bodies, responding to ageless passion, and they quickly cast their clothes aside. His lips caressed her earlobes then traveled down to her breasts. She cried out as he entered her. She pulled his head back by his hair and flipped over so she could be on top.

"Much better my love," she whispered. She controlled the rhythm of the thrusts allowing the sexual tension to build up to an excruciating level before they climaxed. For a moment, they shared pleasure as one. She collapsed on top of him. Kananga was immersed in her sensory overload. She remembered when they first met at a village celebration centuries ago. She thought he was an Arab trader and just ignored him. The Magus had caught her scent as the beautiful young woman passed by him. She had rare HH blood, and she carried herself proudly. Somehow, he knew she would desire and welcome transformation.

In the distance, over the evening traffic noise, they could hear the faint sound of drums. He would go downriver away from modern cities to challenge his gifts and intellect and refresh the skills that allowed him to survive for centuries. The fight with Alexander had left him feeling vulnerable and out of touch. His existence had become too easy, and he had missed the plot to overthrow him. He knew that Kananga would never be surprised by her enemies. He wanted to sharpen his skills again, so he had come to her before he began his journey of rejuvenation. They had become lovers, centuries ago, after he had transformed her. They were bonded but not besotted despite their passion. He knew Lady Kananga was objective and logical. She would protect the vampire world while he was away.

I got a text message from Tristan saying he had to return to LA. The kids were bummed, but I was glad that his royal ass would be out of here for a while. I took the kids to get them registered for school in Granite Falls. I had Rossville send their school records. Their GPAs were great. Behavior, not so much. If someone picked on one of the kids, the siblings Mordecai would never forget or forgive that transgression. One kid who made fun of Jacques found "Judd Cooper has a tiny dick" burnt into the school's lawn with herbicide. It wouldn't regrow. They had to dig up the grass and the dirt under it and replant the entire lawn. No one could prove who did it. My kids were strongly suspected but would never confess.

I lined them up before I took them to school on the first day. They were fifteen and sixteen, and I would probably never get a chance to address them like this again. "No weird stuff. Your dad is a Lithuanian international businessman. Don't let them know how fast, strong, or smart you are. I know you'll get A's without trying, you'll get bored, but you'll have a social life with regular, normal people. You need more of that in your life."

"What if we hate it?" Marie asked.

"Why don't you just give me a lobotomy," Des quipped.

"Take band, or get in the school play, or the school newspaper. Try to find something you are interested in."

Tomas said, "We want a field trip to Henry's nightclub."

"Ask the principal," I responded. Most parents would say make good choices, but they expected honesty. "Don't fuck up. You don't want to make me angry. Now go!"

While Teri drove them to school, I paid a visit to the goat farm. Leif's house was a short walk from ours. He had a very modern log cabin. The front porch faced the road. I looked back towards our place, but it was obscured by spruce and cottonwood trees, even though it was close. I saw a Silverado pickup parked beside a small barn. In the fenced pasture, goats were grazing, running, and making weird noises. The slight breeze wafted their funky scent my way.

The wooden door had a bronze gnome doorknocker but no doorbell. I lifted the gnome's head and let it fall hard against the door. A voice coming from a hidden speaker said, "Just a minute."

The door opened, and a young woman in Goth clothes and last night's makeup moved past me, went behind the house, and then sped away in a corvette. "Good morning Baroness," Leif stared at me, shirtless with a seductive grin.

I frowned at Leif. "Get dressed. We need to talk."

"Sure. Make yourself at home. Be right with you." He gestured towards the living room and disappeared. I moved a guitar out of the way and sat on the couch.

A keyboard, guitars, speakers, and drums littered the room. I was glad we did not live closer. The heavy drapes covering a small window were slightly parted to allow in a bit of golden sunshine. My host returned wearing a Slayer T-shirt and a mug of black coffee. "Costa Rican," he said and set it on the coffee table in front of me.

"Thanks!" I took a sip. It was delicious.

He sat down on the other end of the couch and turned to face me. "What's up?"

"What exactly is your job?"

"Bass player, goat farmer, and your chief of security."

"You're barely an adult. You are going to protect us? How?"

He picked up a remote, and a large TV screen on the wall lit up with a dozen windows showing every inch of my property from every possible angle. There was even one from a camera near the top of one of the giant cedars. "I monitor you and the kids. In return, I get this house, a truck, goats, and I get to play in Henry's band. I was on the street when I met him. He helped me turn my life around. And by the way, I'm twenty-one."

I looked at his sweet face. "Leif, do you know who Henry, Pomp, and my ex-husband really are?"

"Yeah, you can say the V-word. I'm sworn to secrecy. Who would believe me anyway? But I can't figure you out. They never let regular people get close to them. I gotta know, are they really the Baron's kids?"

I wasn't going to explain about Jacques' father, so I said, "Yeah, daddy is a vampire."

"Wow. So, what's the deal with you?"

I thought it might be a good idea to leave him a little afraid of me. "I'm half-vampire and descended from the Knights Templar."

"What the fuck! I knew you weren't normal." He leaned back a little on the couch. "You don't....uh...."

"Drink blood? No. I'm pretty much a vegetarian. The kids are omnivores." He relaxed a little. I finished my coffee. "I could try and ban the kids from coming over here, but they have issues with authority. Just keep the Goth groupies away from them."

"The ladies always leave in the morning. I think they're afraid I'll ask them to clean up goat shit."

"No alcohol or drugs around my kids. None!"

"Not a problem. Henry won't let anyone in the band if they drink or use."

"I guess you don't consider blood as a drug." He stared at me, clearly at a loss. "What instruments do you play?"

He looked around the living room and smiled. "All of them."

I sat for a minute thinking, then asked, "Would you give the kids music lessons? I think it might help them make friends at school. Also, they get bored easily. Maybe music will keep them out of trouble."

"Yeah, sure. I suppose."

"All right, great! We'll work out details later." I got up and left him looking a bit confused and unsettled. I walked back to the house, a little more comfortable with my neighbor. It was still weird that he was okay with vampires, but my gut told me he meant no harm and was grateful to them. I was not buying the Saint Henry propaganda. I was glad he was good to Leif, but I had to wonder about his motives. Henry had a lot of anger that he kept well hidden. I felt it in his music and saw it in his mind. He was a complicated vampire, not someone I needed in my life at the moment.

At nine in the evening, in Bel Air, Tristan was just starting an online meeting of the Heads of the Houses. Vampires' images could not be seen using webcams, so they used avatars, graphic representations of themselves. The display had several rows of boxes. The top row had a single dark box where the Magus' avatar would usually appear.

Below that were two more. Tristan's Tarot identity/avatar was on the right. It was the emperor sitting on a throne adorned with golden ram's heads wearing a red silk shirt.

Anastasia, the High Priestess' avatar, to the left, appeared in light blue robes, and a diamond crescent pendant adorned her neck.

The next two rows were for the Heads of the Houses. So as not to offend anyone, they would appear in the order they logged on.

Sir Omar represented the House of Swords based in Qatar. He was at Lady Anastasia's home in Las Vegas. His avatar was dressed in traditional Arab robes, wearing a plain white kufiyah. Behind him, on the wall, hung an ornate sword.

Sir Jorge represented the House of Arrows from Caracas. His avatar wore a purple shirt and held a golden bow in its hands.

Lady Sarah of the House of Plows, Toronto, was a vision in black leather and turquoise jewelry.

Sir Cesare Borgia representing the House of Pentacles, London, was in New York on his way to Seattle. From his penthouse suite, his avatar was a portrait of him in fifteenth-century Italian finery.

Princess Khunbish of Mongolia joined for the first time representing the House of Cups. Batu had helped design her avatar. Her image wore an elaborate beaded headdress and a voluminous silk robe embroidered with gold thread.

Lady Kananga of the House of Wands was at home in the Democratic Republic of the Congo. Her avatar had intricate braids and a gold lion's head pendant.

Tristan sat at the desk in his library, wondering if he should start the meeting, but before he could decide, Kananga took the lead. Her avatar had long jeweled braids and exuded an aura of authority.

"Dearest members of the Haute Caste. You have all received a communication from the Magus notifying you of the temporary transfer of power. He is taking time to recover from his recent ordeal in Las Vegas." There was some faint whispering from the other Houses. "I have accepted his request to watch over our affairs until his much-desired return."

Tristan and the others were impressed by the tactful way Kananga announced her takeover. She knew that their egos were easily bruised. The Haute Caste were obsessed with their place in the vampire hierarchy. Being Haute Caste was not enough for them. Lady Sarah always felt slighted, by the others, as she and the House of Plows were only two hundred years old. Tristan, the rightful heir in terms of, seniority, power and gifts, had difficulty understanding why he had been passed over. Cesare Borgia knew that as the head of the House of Pentacles, he had the most experience dealing with political intrigue. He had helped infiltrate Alexander's rebellion and save the Magus.

"How was the Magus at your last encounter, Lady Kananga?" Tristan inquired.

"He reminded me of the Magus from long ago, seeking adventure and new challenges."

They all knew that meant they had made love. Kananga was not known for being sentimental. She would not like to think she had displayed her feelings for the Magus.

Omar, always the good soldier, responded, "We will, of course, respect his wishes. Your willingness to lead our society in his absence is appreciated by everyone, I am sure," he added pointedly

"Do you know when he will return?" Princess Khunbish did not beat around the bush. She was also a bit cranky, being awake at noon for this meeting.

"The Magus said he will return when he understands his purpose more fully," Kananga responded.

"Will we act on the plan to allow the Common Caste to be members of our governing body?" Lady Sarah asked. Her avatar had long auburn curls, like her own, which spilled over a black vest.

"Perhaps," Jorge paused, "it would be wise to give the Common Caste time to organize themselves and choose a representative from each House." The House of Arrows representative wore a turquoise shirt and held a feather in one hand.

Anastasia was not happy with that proposal. "Giving them time is fine, but so many of them? I thought there would only be one or two permitted to participate in our Parliament." Of all the undead, she was the least comfortable with those in the lower spectrum of their society. The other Haute Caste understood that having seen her family killed by rebellious commoners made social equality distasteful to her. Her avatar displayed royal finery and platinum curls.

Kananga knew she had to make a decision in the absence of the Magus. If she did not appear strong and decisive, they would not support her for long. "One member of the Common Caste from each House shall be chosen to participate as equal members of our Parliament. In the interim, I may have a couple of them join us."

It was quiet for a minute, which meant they had accepted her decree. She felt relieved.

Sarah spoke, "Baron, are the offspring well in their new home? Is there anything required of our Houses to promote their well-being?"

"Guillaume is tutoring them, and we have sufficient mortal help during the daylight hours. Sir Henry has agreed to impart some of his knowledge to the Baroness to help her understand her growing powers."

Kananga added, "With her consent, of course."

Jorge responded, "Sir Henry may be due for a special commendation."

Omar replied, "I am grateful he has accepted this challenge."

Kananga asked, "Princess Khunbish, what of Sir Batu and Kyoto?"

The royal avatar responded, "All is well in my house. Sir Batu has transformed and gained powers very quickly. His strength, speed, and intellect are remarkable for such a newly transformed and young vampire. We shall choose his first Worthy Target soon."

It was good that no one could see Tristan's face at that moment. Jealousy cast an evil pall on his handsome features. He picked up a marble chess piece and crushed it in his bare hand.

"Kyoto continues to show remorse and has been working on his blood research while staying in the monastery," Lady Khunbish said.

Kananga added, "Thank you, Princess Khunbish, for allowing him to serve his exile in your House."

"Lady Kananga," Sir Borgia decided to make his presence known by ending the session. "is our all business complete?"

Kananga felt the slight. "One more item, Sir Borgia, how is Lady Antoinella? Since she has elevated to Haute Caste status, has her past treachery been erased?" Rogue members of his House had been responsible for the first attempt to harm the Baroness when she married Tristan and other deceitful incidents. Kananga was letting him know she had not forgiven his House their transgressions.

His avatar did not reveal his emotions, but everyone could hear the anger in his voice. "Her attempt to protect the Baroness during Alexander's revolt resulted in her being awarded Haute Caste status by the Magus. Yes, she is your equal now." That was clearly a snub.

Anastasia responded quickly, "The Haute Caste title, dear Cesare, has never given anyone the powers that centuries of nocturnal survival have finely honed."

Kananga refused to engage further with Borgia. "Our session is over. Good night." The screen went dark.

After coming back from his meeting at the bar with Angel, Manny had barely fallen asleep when a loud pounding on his hotel room door woke him. He grabbed his gun, looked at the clock, and yelled, "Just a minute." He pulled on his jeans, went to the door, and looked through the curtains. It was that guy who worked for the Baron. He opened the door a crack. "What do you want from me? It's 3 a.m.?"

Angel smiled. "Nothing. You're not my type." Manny didn't know he meant blood type. "The Baron is back. Now is your one chance to talk with him. Take it or leave it." He started to walk away.

"Wait!" Manny grabbed a shirt and slipped on his beach shoes. He hurried out the door and followed Angel to the parking lot where a chauffeur was waiting in a Bentley. It felt sinister, creepy. "I'll follow you." If something happened, he hoped someone would find his car.

"You better. I wasn't going to let you put your cheap ass in this fine ride." Angel sneered and got in the back of the Bentley.

Manny was insulted and relieved at the same time. He already knew where the Baron lived. He loaded the address in his Waze app, but he followed the Bentley as requested. The chauffeur was careful to stay just below the speed limit. At the Baron's mansion, the electric gate rolled back, and he pulled up behind the Bentley. The front door opened. A butler with a British accent barely looked at him. "Good evening Angel. Detective, the Baron will see you in the library. Follow me."

Manny had never been in a house with a library, or a butler, or electric gates, for that matter. The elegant foyer with a curving staircase reminded him of the stately homes in old movies. The house was quiet except for their footsteps. Suddenly a cockatoo went flying past them, and a plump woman wearing an apron chased after it. "Ruben, come back here!"

"In there," the butler pointed to a double door. Then he hurried off in the direction of the fleeing bird.

Angel opened one of the doors. "Good evening, Baron. Detective Takeda is here."

Manny looked past Angel and saw a tall, platinum-blond man, dressed all in black, standing behind a huge mahogany desk. "Yes. Thank you, Angel, you may leave us."

Angel whispered to Manny, "It's been nice knowing you." Then he walked away.

Manny's first thought was, "I could take him." However, he did not want to try out that theory. He walked over and extended a hand.

Tristan ignored the outstretched hand and merely said, "Sit down." Manny awkwardly pulled his hand back and sat on the sofa. Tristan faced him in a leather chair.

He stared at the earnest detective. Manny began feeling a sense of dread creep over him. He decided the deep blue color of the Baron's eyes had to be contacts. He had never seen anyone so pale.

"Leave my family alone," the Baron stated with a coldness that rattled Manny. He had interviewed murderers, rapists, and career criminals who would kill their own mothers and had not felt so intimidated. He couldn't understand why.

Manny tried to calm himself by responding with the facts. "I have just been investigating leads in a murder case. Your ex-wife was driving a car the night of the murder, which matched a suspect's vehicle."

"Cossacks," Tristan muttered.

"Excuse me?"

Tristan ignored the question. "Tell me about the character of the victim."

Typically, Manny would not have said much. For some inexplicable reason, he felt compelled to answer, "A lowlife and a known drug dealer, but we had never been able to make any charges stick."

Tristan replied with a small smile. "So, the world is better off without him."

Resentment started to build in Manny, countering some of Tristan's power. "I never said the victim was male."

"I had the incident looked into. Did he have any redeeming qualities?"

Manny replied, "That is irrelevant. Saint or sinner, he was murdered. It's my job to find the killer, and I intend to do just that."

"Do you? Would you be prepared to protect yourself from someone who could kill another so easily, so cleanly?"

His intense stare was making Manny increasingly uncomfortable. The detective suddenly wanted to flee, but he was not about to show fear. He looked the Baron right in the eye. "I can take care of myself."

"Delilah," Tristan called. A sleek black panther came out from behind the desk and settled near Manny's feet.

"What the hell!" Manny exclaimed, jumping up.

"My cat scares you? Imagine if you came face to face with a bloodthirsty, deadly assassin? Go back to Salinas, detective." He waved his hand in dismissal.

Manny was happy to take the hint. No one appeared to show him out. They must have figured he would not dare look around, and they were right. He got in his old Mustang and burned rubber in the drive heading out. He wondered if James Bond felt like this when confronted by the head of Spectre. He used to think Vegas was the capital of strange rangers, but not anymore. "What was that all about?" Manny muttered as he turned onto Sunset Boulevard. He headed west toward the ocean to find an all-night café and clear his head.

Chapter 12

The Great Pretenders

On Saturday, the kids got up around eleven, which was fine with Teri and me. I wandered into the kitchen seeking coffee as they headed out the back door.

"Leif is going to show us how to milk goats!" Marie exclaimed excitedly.

"And play guitar," Des added.

"And drums," Jacques said.

I looked at Tomas. "I'm lead singer material."

"Have fun! Be back for dinner. Your dad is coming over tonight."

"All right! Dad is back in town!" Jacques exclaimed as they left.

It was good they wanted to see him. Honestly, I still liked looking at Tristan, and the sex was always great, but living with him? No thanks. Perfect vampires are incredibly annoying. I took a sip of the dark brew that soothed my soul.

In Rossville, Grigoryi noticed Connie at the far end of the property, standing under a tree by Pete's grave. He stepped off the back deck and walked towards her. The former vampire-hunter, monk, was happy to bake bread for the café. He had not been involved with Pete's murder, but he felt a duty to help the woman who had been made a widow by another monk, with whom he had once known and worked. He had made peace with his past and accepted vampires as part of the unnatural order of things. He was small in stature and big in heart.

"Connie, are you okay?"

She stood up a little straighter and wiped her eyes before turning towards Grigoryi. "Fine. Just visiting with Pete."

"I'll leave you alone. I'm sorry if...."

"Greg, if you don't stop apologizing for being a kind person, I'll let Camo bake the bread."

"No, please," he started to laugh. "I'll try not to apologize so much."

She looked out at the corn and soybean fields surrounding their property. It was all starting to turn brown. The fading summer colors matched her mood. Connie was glad that Miranda and her grandkids would visit for Thanksgiving and reassure her they were doing well. She was happy they were in a new place, away from the sadness they had experienced here, but she could not bring herself to move away.

They walked back to the house in silence. Danuta and Camo were at the café, supervising the local help getting ready for the dinner crowd. Jeanne and Bart would be up soon. Connie would have to break it to them that Scheherazade had taken off last night. She had found the door to Scheherazade's room open in the morning, and all her belongings gone. Only the scent of jasmine remained. Pity, she used to like that scent. Connie would not miss the drama that had swirled around the femme fatale, although she was concerned about where Sheri would go next.

Jeanne sat up in the darkened bedroom and gently touched Bart. "My love, I fear that Scheherazade has gone. I had a vision that woke me." She quickly got out of bed and dressed.

Bart rolled on his side. "I know. She ran off with the sheriff."

"You saw it too?" She combed her long dark hair.

"I saw her secretly meet with him next to the dumpster behind the Café last night."

"How appropriate," Jeanne mused.

"Should we go after her?" Bart asked.

"No, I think it is important to remain here with Connie."

Bart rose from the bed and approached her in all his naked splendor. She reached up and brushed his brown curls off his face. Their spirits had become intertwined over the centuries. He lifted her up and carried her back to bed.

"Allow me to mess up your lovely hair."

"Lord Bart, duty calls. We must inform Connie," she said but did not resist him.

"You are French. Your first duty is love." He countered.

"Bien sur." She kissed him passionately as he laid her on the bed.

His hands elicited pleasure with every caress. She felt his hardness and yearned for the joining of their bodies. He held off entering her until their exquisite sensual play had created almost unbearable tension. Their rhythmic dance finally began, and the wood-frame bed creaked. Jeanne pushed him over and climbed on top, crying out as they drowned in their perfect climax.

After several minutes she sat up and rested a hand on his muscular chest.

He smiled. "If the nuns only knew how passionate you are."

"Or Grigoryi the ex-monk, he still has trouble looking at me directly."

"Try cussing around him." He stood and got dressed. "Time to talk with Connie and then call the Baron."

"And Lady Kananga." She buttoned her denim shirt. "You know where Scheherazade has gone don't you."

"She was not hard to read. Her thoughts were always focused on Alexander. She is obsessed with adding the once-great ruler to her list of admirers. She is even more vain than Anastasia."

"Is that possible?"

The kids returned from Leif's place, ready to rock the world.

Tomas announced, "Lead guitar and back-up vocals."

Des acted cool. "Bass guitar. Felt like I've played for years." He grinned at Tomas. "And lead vocals."

Jacques showed me his hands. "I've got the perfect fingers for the keyboard."

Marie was quiet. "Hey hon, how did it go?" I asked.

"Okay. Can we get a goat?"

"What if you just help Leif out. He's got quite few. You don't have to be in the band."

"What do you mean? I'm the drummer. We need a name for the band."

Des smiled. "The Vamps!"

Jacques responded, "Dad will hate it."

"Yeah, the Vamps!" Tomas said.

Marie added, "Tell Dad we're just going through a phase."

During dinner, Teri and I listened as they discussed the broad spectrum of music they wanted to draw upon. Marie liked German techno, Tomas was underground trash rock, Des was all about female indie bands, and Jacques was a huge fan of my parent's classic rock.

"Work with Leif. I'm sure you'll come up with a unique sound."

"Teri, who is your fav singer?" Jacques asked.

"Henry," she said without having to think about it.

From the doorway to the dining room we heard, "Good evening."

We looked over and saw Henry wearing a torn t-shirt and tight blue jeans that showed his great build. His braids hung loose to his shoulders. He looked like he just stepped off the cover of a romance novel. Damn! Lug walked over to him and sniffed his hand, then laid down. I wondered if Henry was using his gift on him.

"Henry, I didn't hear you knock. Come in." The kids looked puzzled as he pulled up a chair and joined us. "Coffee or tea?" I asked.

"Or blood?" Marie quipped.

He smiled at Marie, and she felt like climbing under the table. "Nothing thanks."

Teri came to the rescue. "Tomas plays lead guitar like you."

Henry regarded Tomas respectfully and said, "Study the masters, Hendrix, Santana, Knopfler, Van Halen, Freddie King. I'm sure Robert will be glad to help you when he visits again."

The charm was working. I could sense the kids were open to him, accepting him.

Des added, "We're all in the band. It's called The Vamps."

"Seriously? You are your mother's children. Let me know when you're ready to play in a club, and you've changed the name."

Jacques looked down at his plate. "He's making fun of us."

"No, I'm not. I know your heritage. It will take time, perhaps a year or two, but you'll become a band worth listening to."

He boosted their confidence. I wasn't sure they needed any confidence-boosting. "All right, but for now, help Teri with the dishes while I talk with Henry. Your dad will be here soon."

I headed out to the deck, and Henry followed me outside. We sat facing each other in Adirondack chairs. "Thanks for encouraging them."

He smiled. "What did you want to talk to me about?"

"I don't trust you, but I have a proposition for you. I want Tristan to think we are having an affair."

"Why would you want him to think that?" His eyes lit up. "Not that I am opposed to it."

"I only want him to think that we are. It's to protect someone else."

He smirked. "Is it someone I know?"

"Who it is doesn't matter right now," I replied flatly.

"We shall have to touch to be convincing to your ex."

I looked into the eyes that had charmed Cleopatra and felt a tug. "Stop it!" I demanded.

"It's coming from you, Miranda. You have a great capacity for sensual passion. It's a gift you have yet to learn to control."

I stood and walked to the edge of the deck, leaned against a post, and focused on the sound of the river to calm my brain. I turned to Henry. "I have controlled it. I was a virgin when I married Tristan."

His eyes widened. "So, the rumor was true. Who else have you been with?"

"Did you place bets on my sex life?"

"No, Ruben did. Sometimes I can't abide his attitude towards the fairer sex or his appetite for gossip. You still did not answer me."

"Snacking from adoring fans isn't exactly supporting women's rights," I replied. He just shrugged his shoulders and waited for me to respond. We stared at each other, and finally, the silence got to me. "The answer is no one."

"Not even Batu, and yet you will do anything to protect him."

"I never said it was Batu."

"You are an enigma, but I enjoy puzzles and have been solving them for a long time. I can help you learn to apply your sensual abilities to your advantage," he said with enthusiasm and approached me.

"I have no doubt. I don't want to be Mata Hari."

"I heard Tristan is a gifted lover, but it was your chemistry with him that made it sublime. He understands that. He can't find that same satisfaction with anyone else."

"All this time, I thought Tristan was responsible for all those rockets exploding in the moonlight. So, I might have a sex life after Tristan?"

Henry looked serious. "He does not wish you to. His ego expects you to pine for him. After the Magus destroyed Lena, Lady Kananga advised me not to let what happened to Lena control my life. I saw the wisdom in that and decided not to seek revenge on him or the Magus. But if I ruffle the Baron's feathers, I'll sleep better."

I felt uneasy. "You must know I was partly responsible for Lena's demise." I searched his face, but there was no hostility towards me.

"She was wrong to go after you and the children. She brought it on herself. I would have preferred a less final punishment." He looked towards the house. "Tristan has arrived. What is your choice? Shall the show begin?" Henry put his arm around my shoulder and played with my hair with the other hand. "Just a kiss, a natural kiss."

Henry slowly, softly kissed me. The tenderness of his touch was overwhelming. I responded to the healing balm of his affection. Wow! I did not need to act. He pulled away.

"I allowed myself to feel what you felt. Thank you. It has been centuries since I experienced such pure passion."

My eyes got big. "You can take in and mimic my responses?"

"It has allowed me to please my lovers more fully."

"That's not natural, Henry."

"It was for me," he grinned.

Tristan opened the sliding glass door. He was not amused. "Henry, shouldn't you be entertaining the masses at the Pyre?"

"We start at one a. m." Henry pulled me close to his side. "You should come by."

Tristan said coldly, "I return to L.A. tomorrow night. I thought you should know Scheherazade has left Rossville. I believe she'll try to contact Alexander."

"Thanks for the tip," I replied. Scheherazade could stir up the Common Caste against the Haute Caste and my family.

"You always surprise me." Tristan looked at me as though I had delivered a hit to his gut. Then he went back into the house to see the children.

Let's walk by the river," Henry said and led me by the hand. "I'm sure Tristan will keep an eye on us." The pebbles crunched under our shoes. It was peaceful and beautiful at the river's edge. He halted and faced the rolling water. "I will protect you from Scheherazade. I heard about the snake attacks on you and Antoinella. Treacherous bitch!" The serious tone of his voice made me a believer. I suppose Cleopatra's death might have had something to do with his resentment of snakes.

"Why do you take such pleasure in pissing off my ex?"

"There is a rivalry," the charm returned to his voice. "He is more powerful because of his natural ability enhanced by the blood of the Magus, Lena, and Kyoto. I have emotional intelligence, which comes from being almost as old as the Magus. You are his emotional Achille's heel. He had never been involved with such an unpredictable woman. At this moment, I have no doubt he is trying to fathom how you could be infatuated with me."

"I don't want to hurt him. I just want to distract Tristan and protect Batu."

"Enjoy your good deed," he purred and pulled me close for another tender kiss.

Sometimes you have to sacrifice. I came up for air. "Henry, who do you want? I can feel it despite your skill."

"You should always listen to that inner voice."

"Teri?"

He responded, "Our secret."

Henry left after our walk by the river. He refused to discuss his attraction to my friend and bodyguard. I was good at keeping secrets but not at hiding my concern for others. This would be tough. Though I was relieved, Henry and I were both faking it. I was in the kitchen getting a snack when I heard Tristan slam the front door as he left. Des wandered in. "What's up with Dad?"

Before I could respond, Tomas entered and said, "He was just letting us win the video game all this time. He kicked ass tonight."

"What did he say?" I asked.

Des grabbed some chocolate fudge ice cream out of the freezer. Tomas handed him a bowl. I could tell they were trying to come up with a tactful response. Des spoke, "He yelled something about Henry when his dragon melted my army."

Tomas added, "There aren't any Henrys in the game."

Marie wandered in at that point. "Why was that vamp here? I didn't think you liked him."

"That was before I saw him and Leif at the club. He's amazing on stage."

"Is that why you kissed him?" Jacques asked. I hadn't seen him come into the kitchen.

"That is none of your business." It was the best response I could come up with at the moment.

Chapter 13

The Magus Brings Down the House

The Magus woke as the moon was rising over the plain that sloped down to the river near the city of Mbuji Mayi in the Congo. He came out of the house at the center of a fortified camp, which provided secure daytime sleeping quarters. Lady Kabedi and Sam, one of her aides, were conferring with members of the Baluba tribe about poachers. The Magus was becoming increasingly hungry as the blood from rodents and small game were not enough to sustain him, and blood banks were non-existent in the bush. That hunger renewed his instincts, and the hunt sharpened his skills. It was why he had returned to the Congo.

Their guards were paid well, provided with new uniforms, weapons, and phones. They traveled in Jeeps with 'Moonlight Safaris,' painted on the sides to add the look of a legitimate business. The end of the rainy season brought lush vegetation. The primal jungle scent, mixed with the smell of mortals, further whetted the Magus' appetite.

Lady Kabedi and Sam, one of Lady Kananga's aides, approached the Magus. "We have located a Worthy Target. He has killed three elephants over the last month. The local chief has asked for help protecting the remainder of the herd, and we can trust him." Sam explained in earnest. He had known the great grandfather of this chief in the days when he was still mortal.

"Lady Kabedi, if you will accompany me, I shall be of need of your linguistic abilities. Sir Sam, I would appreciate it if you handled any of the other poachers who come your way. I'll leave it up to your discretion if any are to be pardoned," the Magus told them.

"Of course." Sam nodded, then returned to speak with the chief.

The Magus followed Kabedi, trekking a mile upriver, then another mile into the bush where the elephants often stayed. With their enhanced vision, they were able to see well in the darkness and they sidestepped an eight-foot-long slithering black mamba. The Magus marveled at Lady Kabedi's tracking skills and her agility in the bush. They passed several of the trees in the area, stripped almost clean of leaves by the great beasts. In places, the brush was nearly impassable, and Kabedi used a machete to clear the way. They picked up the scent of mortals and knew they were getting close. The lethal duo moved silently towards a clearing. The sound of an elephant crying out broke the quiet. Then a man's harsh voice yelled commands. Kabedi and the Magus stood in the cover of some bushes. Anger rose in them both as they saw nets and sharp weapons used to subdue the elephant. One of the men aimed a rifle at the elephant's head.

The leader, in his native language, called out, "Don't harm the tusks!"

In Tshiluba, Kabedi shouted, "Stop! Or be killed!"

The leader, Kalonji, gestured to the ragtag group of poachers to halt. Their boss looked surprised and pissed off. He stared at Kabedi and said, "I hate to destroy such beauty, but you get in the way of my profits." He turned back to his men. "Get rid of them. Quickly!"

A dozen armed men started towards them, and a few circled behind. The Magus turned to Kabedi. "Tell them if they run to the village now, I will spare their lives."

Kabedi translated what he had said. Something about her words, her tone, and the fearless stance of Kabedi and the Magus made the poachers stop in their tracks.

Kalonji yelled, "Cowards!" and broke through his men and stood before the Magus with his rifle pointed at his head. "To hell with you!"

The Magus raised his hand and held it inches from Kalonji's chest. Kalonji's face twisted in pain. He dropped the rifle, grabbed his chest, and fell to the ground. His screams of pain made his men step back. Blood spread over his embroidered shirt as his chest ripped open. Kalonji's men started to come to his aid. Kabedi, with lightning speed, turned, raised her arm, and dropped the closest attacker, his head split cleanly open with her machete.

The poachers looked at their leader on the ground, turned as one, and fled into the jungle. Kabedi began to free the elephant from the nets and examine its wounds. The Magus knelt beside the poacher and lifted his throat to his lips. He drank deeply of Kalonji's blood. The ecstasy of fresh blood combined with the adrenaline rush of the fresh kill caused a sense of unworldly pleasure.

He dropped the body and cleaned himself off with water from a canteen. He felt a sense of purpose, unique to his kind, renewed in him. The Magus walked over to the elephant. The wounds were deep, but he could stand. The Magus helped Kabedi apply the salve that Hann had sent them. The great beast realized they were trying to help him and stood quietly.

Kabedi said, "It is fitting that the elephant survives, and those poor excuses for human beings should perish." She walked over to the man she had killed, slit his wrist, and trickled blood into a cup. She quickly emptied the cup then steadied herself as the blood rush filled her being.

The Magus looked over the injured elephant and said, "Let's walk him to the river. He will need water. We will make arrangements to send him to Hann's refuge. I don't think he will survive in the wild with these injuries. I will ask Marie to name this new resident of the sanctuary."

Kabedi smiled. "I'm sure she will be pleased, Magus."

"What did they yell as they ran away?"

Kabedi replied, "They said that you were the devil."

"Indeed."

94

The Magus stared at the repugnant display of elephant ivory in the small warehouse in Kinshasa. Pure anger welled up within him. Not sadness, or hopelessness just rage. It began to seep out of every pore. He let out a blood-curdling scream that caused even Kabedi and Sam to move away from him. "Get out!" he yelled, and they quickly exited the building.

Standing alone in the center of the Bilombo Export Company building, he raised his arms, and the beams that held up the metal roof began to crack. As debris fell around him, the wooden crates stacked from floor to ceiling began to ignite as though small bombs were going off. In minutes, the flames enveloped the building. Black plumes of smoke escaped as the heat blew out the windows.

Alerted by one of the guards, Charles Mercator, the company Vice President rushed to the docks. The thin, balding Belgian jumped out of his Mercedes and started screaming at his warehouse guards. Suddenly a figure emerged untouched from the flames and smoke. The workers cried out and fled into the night. "You are worthless!" Mercator screamed after them.

"You are the scum of the earth, monsieur!" the Magus declared with cold fury.

Fear seized Charles as he backed up against his Mercedes and tried to open the door. The Magus leaped on him and threw him to the ground. He looked up with terror in his eyes and asked, "Who is your boss? I'll pay you double!"

"The elephants," the Magus answered and spat on Mercator's face. "Now, I shall collect your ivory." He put his hand under the struggling man's jaw and tightened his grip till the jaw began to splinter and crack. A garbled scream erupted from the Belgian as blood flowed down his chin onto his shirt. The Magus reached into Mercator's mouth, ripped out a handful of his bloody teeth, and threw them on the ground. Then he dropped the shocked Belgian.

Kabedi drove up with Sam in a Range Rover, ready to take the Magus to the airport. The Magus looked down at Mercator and said, "I will let you live so that you will see my face in your nightmares and forever hear the lamentations of the elephants you ordered slaughtered." The man lay on the ground shrieking as the Magus got in the car. "Such a waste of human flesh. And humanity considers us monstrous."

Kabedi drove, and Sam sat with the Magus in the back. He handed the Magus a small cup of O-positive. "I thank you on behalf of the magnificent creatures you have saved. If you had taken his life, no one would have cared, but I appreciate your self-control."

The Magus knew that the Belgian was the actual owner of the company. Since the government required every corporation have 51%, African ownership. Mercator pretended his butler Bilombo, was the company president, but everyone knew the truth. The Magus felt satisfaction thinking about the pain he would endure and how difficult it would be to eat with a crushed jaw.

They arrived at the airfield and pulled up next to the Magus' plane. Before boarding, he said to them, "I'm ready to return to my station and my home. I'm grateful to both of you and Lady Kananga for assisting me. Africa has made me remember everything that truly matters to me."

Kabedi responded, "It has been an honor dear Magus. May Africa continue to be in your heart and mind."

"My plan for the future of our kind is now crystal clear."

As his private jet took off, Sam turned to Kabedi, "What is his plan?"

"I would bet that it involves Miranda and the offspring."

He smiled, "Only an idiot would bet against you."

Outside of St. Louis, Scheherazade emptied Sheriff Fleming's cash wallet of cash, then tossed it in a trash can. She had lifted it and ditched him before she slipped away with a trucker at a diner. She knew Fleming would be too embarrassed to report her crime. She still had access to a bank account that had ten thousand dollars left in it.

She had received a text from a contact in the House of Pentacles. The Magus being in Africa, recovering from his abduction, distracted the Haute Caste and made it easier for her to take off. She would find Alexander and sympathize with his terrible punishment. The Magus was mean and petty, making him clean up after elephants when he had once ruled most of the known world. Scheherazade was sure he would reward her for her loyalty.

The fifty-something skinny trucker reached across the seat and rested a boney hand on her knee. He badly needed a shower. She whispered, "Why don't you pull over into that shopping center."

"No problem, honey." He pulled the semi into a deserted back corner of the parking lot. As he leaned over toward her, she put her arm around his neck, surprising him with her strength, and put him in a sleeper hold until he passed out. She took a sip of blood from his wrist—just a sip. The last thing she needed was getting sanctioned for an illegal kill. The vampiress was in enough trouble. She checked for witnesses, but he had parked in a poorly lit area. "Thanks honey," she said as she emptied his wallet. Scheherazade found a hotel and paid for two nights. It was good to be free.

It didn't take long for Mom to call with the news about Scheherazade. She told me about the rumors that Sheri and the Sheriff went off to St. Louis, where she gave him the slip and took his wallet. News and gossip travel fast in a small town.

Mom laughed and said, "The Sheriff hasn't shown his face since he got back."

"You tried to warn him."

"Yeah, well, he's a little dense. So, how are the kids?"

"Fine! They are starting a band." I had to chuckle. She used to ask about me.

"Lord! Pete would have loved that. Anyway, since Sheri is gone, I'm thinking of visiting Sally and James in Montana after you come here for Thanksgiving. Camo says he would go with me. Do you think that would be okay?"

"Sure. James would love to see you. Maybe you could cook up a cheeseburger for the wolf. Then you can come to Seattle."

"Oh, Hon, I don't want to leave the café that long. How is Stan?"

I was waiting for that question. "He's okay. He is here visiting the kids. We're all adjusting."

"Well, give him a hug for me. I have to supervise the new help making chicken and noodles. Everyone says hi. Love you all!"

"Love you Mom!"

My mom would never mention vampires on the phone. As Tristan's housekeeper, Tillie, said, "It takes some getting used to." My mom had been aware of our family connection to vamps for years and never told me. Those pesky family secrets. She wanted to visit the wolf that had been enhanced with vampire blood because the poor creature almost died trying to save my dad. Sheriff Fleming had become pretty frustrated trying to track down the wolf that had left bloody footprints. I bet that he was even more frustrated by Scheherazade using him to escape from Rossville. It rarely goes well when mortals get involved with the undead. Being part vampire, I was hoping that, in the end, it would be different for the kids and me.

What was I going to do about Henry's desire for my bodyguard? Rules, I needed some rules for our fake relationship. Number one would be Henry could only visit Granite Falls when Tristan was in town. Number two would be that he could not be alone with Teri. That was a start. Staying rational around Henry was difficult for me. I had no idea what it would be like for Teri if the passion were real and mutual. I had some immunity because of my genes and experiences with the vampire world. Even though Teri had been part of our household for a while, she was an innocent mortal. She could not work for us forever. I knew Henry would patiently wait for his chance while slowly drawing her into his web. If I told Tristan what actually was going on, then Batu would be endangered again. Could I trust the Magus with my fears? No, but I did trust Kananga as much as you can have confidence in your relationship with any nocturnal bloodsucker creature of the night.

I sent her a text message knowing it would probably be a day before I heard back. I now paid attention to what time of night it was in other parts of the world. Vampires could be quite irritated if their daytime rest were disturbed. Sleeping all day was one of the things that made me wonder if I would ever go there. Another was my tendency to throw up when I had seen people killed. On my second date with Tristan, he "assassinated" a pedophile/drug dealer. I ran from the scene and lost my dinner. He told me, "You should work on that." I was tempted to keep Dramamine in my purse in case we went on another fun date night.

They were able to operate in plain sight at night because no one believed in them. Tristan, as my publisher, even had me write a book that flattered vampires. Vampires do not like the creepy depiction of Nosferatu, and Dracula was also offensive to their vanity. My book was sort of autobiographical, but no one ever suspected that. It sold pretty well, and the vampires in my book were okay with how I portrayed them. I've never met an ugly vampire. Some are mean, jealous, greedy, and despicable but always as attractive as hell. I wondered what Batu would be like now.

Batu woke up at sunset and got on his horse for a wild ride across a Mongolian valley. His long thick hair flowed in the wind as he rode. He loved the scent of the brush. His arrows seemed to find their targets more easily. He jumped off the horse and landed on his feet. He had adjusted quickly to sleeping during the day and was losing his taste for food. After an intense ride, he now craved a cup of blood. His body temperature had become cooler, and he felt his senses becoming more acute. Now transformed, a new strength flowed through him, and like all vampires, his image was no longer was reflected in mirrors, and strength pulsed through him. The night before, he had lifted a small Mongol horse to the delight of the Princess. He would make her House proud.

When he returned from the ride, Lily was waiting in his suite. He was surprised to see her wearing a kimono instead of her usual western clothing.

"Lady Lily." he bowed to her. "I am honored by your presence." He was getting the hang of the whole Haute Caste royal speak.

"The Princess has asked me to examine you to be sure you are well."

"What kind of wellness check did she have in mind?" He slipped off his shirt and headed for the shower. Modesty was never a concern for Batu.

"She has been keeping close watch over you and knows that you haven't had sex recently. She believes that may cause melancholy, which could impact your development." Her slight smile was discernable.

Batu stood under the spray of water without a word. It seemed like years since he had been with a coed at the University of Illinois, but it was only several months. He could not refuse a check-up ordered by the Princess. Besides Miranda, the Princess was the last person on the planet he wanted to anger. He hoped his medical "check-up" would not be publicized in Seattle.

Lily let her kimono slip to the floor. She entered the shower and began to soap his back with hands that were very adept at soothing muscles. When he turned to face her, she observed. "You appear to be in good health."

Chapter 14

Refuge

Hannibal heard that Scheherazade was heading in his direction about the same time he received a message about the new elephant the Magus had shipped to the refuge. He would much rather deal with a wounded bull elephant than that conniving femme fatale. Alexander was depressed but made an effort to fulfill his part of the bargain, helping care for the elephants. Hannibal knew the ancient warrior was an honorable egomaniac and would have been arrogant but merciful had he won. That caused Hannibal to give Alexander the task of checking on the health of the members of the herd with Dr. Mayi rather than cleaning up elephant waste.

Miranda's blood had been administered to Alexander only once since his arrival. It seemed to diminish his Haute Caste vampire power. Hannibal kept the tubes of her blood in a small, locked refrigerator in his master suite. He did not want anyone to dose him with her blood.

Cassie was enjoying Alexander's company. She had a tryst with him back in the day when he was conquering the world, and he had sought the advice of the oracle. Now she flirted with him but had yet to bed him. Hann wondered if the loss of Alexander's powers made him less attractive. Cassie was complicated. She would only have sex with a vampire after performing a ritual that involved a hot bath, sensual oil, and sandalwood incense. Hannibal was much more impulsive and direct when the mood struck him. He had little patience for her painstaking approach. Their partnership revolved around a deep respect for each other, a dislike of the modern world, and a love for the elephants they protected. The Magus had transformed them both, which added to their powers and affinity for each other.

Cassie stood by the tiled fire pit in a long purple cotton dress. Her brown hair fell in shiny waves down her back. Dangling gold earrings sounded like tiny wind chimes when she moved. Having finished his nightly check of the elephants, Hann joined her in his work boots, jeans, and leather vest. Alexander emerged from the ranch house in an impractical white shirt and tight jeans.

"We need to talk," Hann said bluntly to Alexander.

"Good evening Lady Cassandra, Sir Hannibal. What is the matter?"

Hann watched his reaction closely. "Scheherazade is probably going to pay us a visit."

"I'm surprised she stayed away this long. She thinks she wants me," Alexander remarked wistfully, "but I'm no longer the powerful Haute Caste vampire she desires."

"Yes, you are," Cassie responded. "Miranda's blood produces a temporary condition. In time, the Magus will allow you to reclaim your ancient powers."

Hann added, "When you accepted the judgment of the vampire realm, you were lucky to have been granted mercy."

"I will see my son, Jacques," Alexander stated with conviction. "That is my right." He realized the demand sounded foolish considering his situation.

Cassie touched his arm and looked into his handsome face. "Xander, that will be up to the child. You cannot force a relationship on him."

Her touch was very calming. He did not mind that she was using her abilities to influence him. "Jacques will desire to know me once I am restored to my former state."

"If she contacts you, you must let me know," Hann told him.

"Of course."

Cassie searched Alexander's mind. "You are hiding something."

"Only my desire for you," he replied with a seductive smile.

"That's not a secret. What is it?" Hann asked.

Alexander knew smoke screens were useless around Cassie. She could always see into his soul. "I did get a text from Scheherazade, but I did not think much of it until you just told me she was no longer captive."

"Show us!" Hann demanded.

Alexander produced his phone and pulled up his messages with Scheherazade. "She whines about Rossville and uses rather rude language to describe my son's grandmother. I have not been responding. Truth be told, I have little interest in her. The last message...."

Hann grabbed the phone. He read the text out loud, "My Lord, I will come to your aid. Allow me to serve you again and help you attain your rightful place in our empire."

"You didn't think to share that information with us before now?"

Alexander appeared amused by the text. "Our empire? What did she conquer?"

Cassie said, "More like who did she conquer. I recall a Maharajah, Sir Omar, Sir Borgia, and a few others." She looked at Hann, who shifted uncomfortably.

Alexander added, "She is irrational. I did not take it seriously."

Cassie said flatly, "You should always take women seriously." She left to visit with the herd.

"I will pass this on to the Baron. He may decide to pay us a visit," Hann said.

"Too bad he will not bring the Baroness," Alexander replied. "Having her blood mix with mine gives me a sense of her. She is nothing like she seems." He stopped before revealing more about how her blood was affecting him.

"I would not speak of her when he visits," Hann told him and went into the house.

Alexander stared into the fire. Where the tips of the flames turned to smoke, he saw Miranda standing by the river's edge. After a moment the vision vanished. He smiled. "My new love."

I stood on the bank of the tree-lined Stillaguamish River as it tirelessly made its way to the Sound. The fresh scent of the pine trees and the gentle sound of the water splashing over the rocks invigorated and calmed me at the same time. Then it happened, that same sense I had a year ago, during my abduction, and the Magus used his ESP to help find me. Just for a second, I felt someone lightly touch my cheek. Then it was gone. Maybe he was checking on me from his retreat in the Congo. Who knows, maybe Tristan was fucking with me. The sensation was too short-lived for me to identify who was thinking of me. Batu could not have developed that ability so soon. I was beginning to think that relationship was doomed from the start. For years, we had secretly adored each other. But we never so much as shared a kiss until the day I got divorced. Then he took off to become an elite nocturnal being. I sighed, then walked back up to the house.

Teri returned from school with the kids. Tomas shoved Des as they got out of the car. Within seconds they were rolling around on the ground with fists flying. Teri jumped out of the car and tried to break them up. Marie got out her phone and started taking a video. Jacques stood to the side laughing. I yelled, "Stop it!" to no effect, then added, "Or no fencing!" It worked like magic.

Teri helped them to their feet. Des had a bloody nose, and Tomas had blood dripping from his mouth. Des looked at his bro and said, "Dracula."

"Go get cleaned up. Then we'll talk in the living room. Now! Marie stop filming!"

She grinned. "I just sent it to Dad."

"I'm sure he'll be proud."

Jacques shook his head. "Tomas is in love again."

Teri and I went to the living room to get ready for the meeting. "What happened?" I asked.

"Just as we got to the driveway, I heard Des say something like, 'Ashley? Are you serious?' Then they just started hitting each other, and it spilled out onto the driveway."

The kids wandered in one by one. Des finally appeared with a large bandage across his nose. "Is it broken?" I asked.

"No." he looked sheepish.

"Then lose the bandage!" He winced as he removed it, but it looked straight. I hoped he was just trying to get sympathy. "Can you breathe?"

He snorted.

Teri said, "He's fine."

"When two people fight...," I started to say.

The kids chimed in, "...they are both to blame!"

"That's right, so I don't want to hear about whose fault it is. I just want to know what you were arguing about."

Tomas spoke up, "It's nothing."

"Des?" I asked.

"He farted in my face."

They all started cracking up, even Teri. "Don't let anyone come between you.

You've got to have each other's backs."

Des replied, "Whatever."

Jacques grinned. "Tomas has Ashley's front."

"You little asshole," Tomas reached for his brother, but Teri got between them.

I blurted out, "I don't care who she is. Love is always a mistake." The kids looked at me wide-eyed. "When you're so young," I quickly added.

Teri said, "Go do your homework so you'll have time for Guillaume's lesson." After they left, she turned to me. "That was harsh."

"I'm just making it up as I go. You will make a great mother one day."

I was a little tearful. She gave me a hug. "You're just telling them the truth."

Several hours later, I got a text message from Tristan,

Who won?

Leif came by that night and watched Guillaume do his thing with Teri and the kids in the barn. He had changed from his goat herder garb to a Lucifer T-shirt and had even combed his red hair. He paid close attention to Teri. After she put her equipment away, he approached her. I watched his body language as he leaned towards Teri, smiled, and made eye contact. It was obvious that he was interested in her, and she clearly enjoyed the attention. My gut told me something was not right.

"So, is it okay if I go to the club with Leif Saturday night?" she asked me later.

"Only if I go with you."

I did not tell Teri I was going so I could guard her. I knew Henry was finding ways to get closer to her. He was clever, powerful, and had remarkable powers. I would go to the club to keep up the appearance of a growing relationship with him and watch out for Teri. I wondered if Pomp was involved in a plot to corrupt Teri. How could anything happen at the club without the former French aristocrat's knowledge?

At midnight Tristan's Bentley pulled up to the main house at the elephant sanctuary. Cassie was there to greet him. "Tristan, always a pleasure. How is your family?"

"The children are doing well," he said nothing about his ex.

Cassie smiled. "Xander and Hann are in the war collection barn. Not my favorite place. I will talk with you later." She kissed him.

Tristan pulled her into his embrace and kissed her passionately, then gently released her. It had been centuries since he had shared her bed. "Of course," he replied.

It was a bizarre moment, even for Tristan, to see Hannibal the Barbarian and Alexander the Great pouring over old maps discussing ancient battles. "Good evening," he said, "no new campaigns, I hope."

"Tristan, welcome!" Hann said.

Alexander merely nodded. "Excuse me. I'll make my final rounds of the

102

elephants."

Tristan watched him leave. "He appears to be keeping his word."

"Yes. He has complied with receiving the Baroness's blood and performs any task required of him." Hann looked at Tristan. "He is taking this fall from grace better than I ever imagined."

"What of his powers?"

Hann rolled up a map. "Cassie says his powers are just below the surface, but I don't sense the powerful personality that commanded armies. Still, he is quite clever. Warriors always dream of their next battle. He said I should have never used elephants in battle. They make too much noise." He smiled. "That was the point, to scare the enemy before we even engaged them."

"You're enjoying his company," Tristan remarked. He did not add that Alexander was using his ability to charm the old warrior.

"We are two of a kind. We remember the strategy, the calculations, the blood and guts which won our wars. Now battles can be launched by a computer, a thousand miles away. One bomb can destroy a city. I know there are still troops on the ground that pay the price, but for the leaders, it has become far too impersonal."

"I can still make it very personal with Alexander," Tristan responded coldly.

While they talked, Alexander made the rounds in a jeep, checking the electrified security fence that encircled the refuge. At the far end of the sanctuary, he got out and appeared to be checking a gate.

A figure called out from the shadow of an old, abandoned shed outside the property. "Lord Alexander, what do you wish me to do?"

He responded without looking up, "Scheherazade, I will meet you here tomorrow night at this time. I shall need a very fast car."

"Of course."

He got back in the jeep and continued his normal nightly inspection. Cassie had watched the surveillance camera that showed a tiny heat signature get back in the vehicle. Still, he appeared to be carrying out his normal duties. The muse could sense a vampiress' presence but was unsure if it was a premonition or real-time. She had never been close to Scheherazade. That vampiress was not one to be friends with other females. It was too bad the femme fatale was her own worst enemy. The powerful vampires that Scheherazade obsessed over seemed to become bored with her. Cassie did not like to see someone allow themselves used and then cast aside. She had read enough of Alexander's future in the Tarot cards to know he had no plans that included Scheherazade, yet there was a powerful female in his future.

Tristan was waiting in the living room of the ranch house when Alexander returned. He stood and faced him. "I would like to talk with you alone."

Alexander merely nodded and sat on a leather sofa across from him. Tristan remained standing. Alexander looked at the Baron as though sizing up his greatest foe. "Out with it," Alexander demanded.

"Jacques is as much my offspring as the others. I will do whatever is necessary to protect him." Tristan sat down in a high-back velvet chair.

"He is also my son," Alexander responded without a trace of remorse or fear.

"I comfort him. I provide for him. I teach him our ways. What have you done for him?"

"Provided half of his DNA." A slight smile appeared on Alexander's face. "You must see the resemblance when you look at him?" Alexander expected a flash of hot anger, but there was none. An uncomfortable sensation began to creep over him. Tristan projected cold rage on him, and a sense of impending doom filled his head.

The Baron jumped to his feet. "Enough! I will allow you to continue to exist, but only if you never cause any harm to my son Jacques."

Alexander regained his composure. Charm would not help him, but emotional intelligence could. "You are gravely mistaken to think I might wish anything but the best for Jacques. He is more precious to me than my own existence. Consider how difficult it has been for me to watch him grow up from another corner of the world. I had to be sure you would not reject him."

Tristan started to respond, then stopped himself. Cassie entered and brought them each a cup of blood in goblets. They drank up. "It is getting late. Good night Cassandra, Alexander."

To Alexander's surprise, the Baron went to his suite alone. Cassie did not pursue him. "The Baroness is affecting us all," he thought.

Chapter 15

Manny Does Seattle

After his encounter with the Baron, Manny sat in the café, thinking about his next move. He pulled out his computer and started going through his notes to figure out where to start. While looking through his emails, he smiled and quietly said, "Ha! Gotcha!" He had sent an email that looked official to Teri Park's parents stating she had a parking ticket in Salinas and requested her current address. They replied with an address in Granite Falls, Washington. Satisfied with his plan to continue his investigation, he closed his laptop and went back to the motel for a couple of hours of sleep. When he woke up, Manny drove north to Salinas to visit his cat, Trouble, and Molly before continuing on to Granite Falls.

The big cat purred loudly as he rubbed against Manny's shoulders from the back of the couch. Manny was checking his computer for any new information. "Missed you too."

"Me?" Molly responded from her kitchen. She was filling bowls with veggie chili.

"Yeah, you too."

Molly walked over and pushed his laptop screen down. "Eat!"

He put his computer to the side and took a big spoonful of her chili. "Habanero, nice!" She always managed to put just the right amount of heat in her cooking. He grabbed a chip and dug into a bowl of guacamole. "Remind me why I don't marry you?"

"Because we would kill each other if we lived together."

"Yeah, there's that." He smiled.

"So why aren't you ready to return to work?" She gave him the "I'm really worried about you" look.

"I met the Baron. This billionaire tried to shake me down, intimidate me so that I would stop my investigation. He had a fucking black panther as a pet, staring at me. It will take more than that to scare me off."

"Wow!" she said shaking her head.

He was glad she did not dismiss his explanation. "They are all hiding something. The Baron, his wife, and her friend. I've got to figure out what is going on, who killed the Pill King, and how they all are connected." He took another mouthful of chili. Trouble rubbed against his arm.

"James Bond, you might be out of your league. If it's organized crime, shouldn't you turn this over to someone else, like the FBI? You're scaring me." She picked up Trouble and held him in her lap. "Maybe you should take a real vacation."

"One of the Baron's staff has been following me. I noticed his car last night parked down the block. If they wanted to kill me, they've had lots of chances."

She got up and went to the apartment window. She looked down the street at the parked cars, but they all looked empty. Was Manny starting to lose it? "I don't see anyone."

"His name is Angel. He's been keeping tabs on me but not interfering." He did not mention the comment about, "It's your funeral."

"You do need a guardian angel." She picked up the dishes and took them into the kitchen.

"Do you mind taking care of Trouble for another week?"

"Where are you going now?" She was done trying to argue with him.

"Granite Falls, Washington."

On Saturday, after a fifteen-hour drive, Manny arrived in Granite Falls. Nestled in the Cascade Mountains, the town was once a major hub for mining and the lumber industry. Only fifty-five minutes north of Seattle, yet it seemed like he was in another state. There was a four-way stop at the center of town. It did not seem like a place that would meet the Baron Mordecai's standards. On the corner Omega Pizza beckoned to him. He decided to grab a bite before going to their residence.

While waiting for his food, Manny asked the young waitress about the Mordecai family. She was friendly but did not know anything helpful. Manny got the "everything" pizza and a coke. Normally he would have gone veggie and drank water, but it might be his last meal. His phone signaled an incoming text and he pulled out his phone. Molly sent a photo of Trouble carrying her cheeseburger off the kitchen counter with the caption, "She misses you."

He looked down and realized he had finished the whole pizza. He was surprised that a local restaurant in an out-of-the-way town had such great food. He paid his bill and a teenager, maybe a freshman in high school, came out from the kitchen as he was about to leave. She was a cute girl with long red hair and bright blue eyes. "Did you ask about the Mordecai family?"

"Yes, I'm visiting them for the first time and worried my GPS might cut out on me up here."

"Just go down to Jordan Road, follow it through the traffic circle. You'll pass over the bridge, then turn right. There's a big house, with a little one next to it at the end of the road."

He looked at her name badge. "Thanks Ashley."

"Alright! They were here," he thought to himself and took off in his Mustang.

He followed Ashley's directions, and a little way out of town turned down a road lined with overgrown blackberry bushes and towering spruce trees running along the bank of a river. Now and then, a glimpse of a mountain capped with snow would appear and made him want to stop to look at the view. If he survived this case, he would have to come back and go hiking. Manny pulled into a gravel drive and parked in front of the house. He climbed out of the car and went up to the porch. Before he got to the door, it opened.

Teri looked out at him. "What the fuck are you doing here?"

"Hi Ms. Park, I'd like to ask Ms. Mordecai some questions. Is she home?"

"Let me check." She closed the door in his face.

She returned a few minutes later and simply said, "Go away!" Then closed the door again.

Manny felt frustrated but not defeated. He got back in his car and drove a short way down the road, and parked behind an abandoned shed, overgrown with vines, where he could watch the entrance to Miranda's property.

I watched his car drive away from my upstairs bedroom window. "Damn! Sheriff Fleming back in Rossville was easy to work around but not this stubborn detective. I never thought he would show up here after Tristan had scared the crap out of him. Until he had a search warrant or charged me, I could avoid him. Was he brave or stupid? I told Teri to keep this from Tristan and Guillaume for now. I did not want them to hurt him unnecessarily.

I hoped he was gone and got back to the important question of the day. What would I wear to the club? I rummaged through my dresser and pulled out a Black Sabbath T-shirt. Vintage! Then I found some skinny black jeans and my lime-green Converse All-Stars. I was set. I hoped Teri would tone down the sex appeal tonight. She had no idea how turned-on Henry was. I was not sure if his attraction was based only on her HH blood. Teri was darling, amazing with weapons, and very bright. Still, the icing on the cake for vampires had to be her Haute Caste potential.

I stood on the back deck and watched the sunlight fade, the trees casting their long shadows on the ground. Lug joined me and leaned against my leg. I patted his head, and he rubbed his muzzle against me. I wished I could find a man as easy to love as Lug. My old friend James was that kind of man. It was as if Tristan had written his name across my heart in permanent, maroon-colored ink ending any chance of a relationship with James. What was it about these nocturnal demons that made them almost irresistible? I would have to keep my wits about me tonight to keep Teri and me safe. Vampires did not play fair.

The kids inspected our outfits before we headed out the door. Teri got a thumbs-up from the fashion police for her purple mini skirt, tiny black t-shirt, and black chains. Marie said my lime-green shoes were, "Cute if you were eight." I did not change them. Leif arrived ready for the show. This was the first time the kids saw the goat herder in his full leather regalia with heavy black eyeliner and his hair held back by a bandana.

"Cool!" Des exclaimed.

Marie said, "I want those boots!" He was wearing snake print Doc Martens. He high fived his fans.

Tomas said, "Take us to the club."

Jacques added, "C'mon we're the Baron's kids. You can sneak us in."

I responded, "You're my kids and you're not going near that place till you turn thirty."

Guillaume trying to distract them said, "The street hockey equipment you wanted came. You can teach me how to play tonight. Not as scandalous as the Funeral Pyre, but much better for your health."

"Have you met the Mordecai offspring? Be sure and have the first aid kit nearby. We're outta here."

The club was already crowded with night people when we arrived at ten p.m. Strange rangers with money to burn packed the place. When Teri and I were seated at the reserved table in front, people craned their necks to try to figure out who we were. I heard someone say, "They belong to Henry." They? What rumors had he started? Maybe it was to protect us. I wanted to give him the benefit of the doubt, but it wasn't easy.

At eleven p.m., Pomp took the stage. She radiated beauty and desire. She was wearing white lace that left little to the imagination. Small pink ribbons adorned her long blonde curls. The jeweled handle of a small dagger was peeking out of her garter. People were pushing close to the stage. "Carpe Noctem! Welcome my lovers of the night." A sly smile came to her lips. Pomp did not flash her fangs like Henry. She bent down and raked a nail across the cheek of a young man leaving a bloody cut. He tried to get on stage, but bouncers held him back. She licked her finger. "Take pleasure wherever you can find it."

Pomp disappeared, and a spotlight fell on a far corner of the dark stage. A veiled woman in black and glistening gold fabric stepped forward. She began to swirl to the center of the stage. Faster and faster, she moved as though her feet did not touch the ground. Then most of the material fell to the floor. Her see-through skirt shimmered, and a large snake covered her breasts! It was Scheherazade!

"Come on Teri. We're outta here!" She did not argue as we headed for the exit. As soon as we were outside, a figure stepped out of the shadows to block our path.

"Baroness, I am delighted to see you again." He started to reach for me. I stepped back.

"Alexander! You escaped Hann?" I expected to hear an elephant trumpet in downtown Seattle. I could smell the scent of my blood mixed with his.

Henry burst out of a side door of the club. "Leave them alone! They do not desire your company." He looked pissed.

"That is not what I sense." Alexander's intense gaze caused the same sensation I had felt on the deck earlier but couldn't identify.

"Stop it! Both of you!" I yelled.

Henry had enough. He smiled like a Cheshire cat. He picked up Alexander like he was a child's toy and threw him over several parked cars. Impressive. Teri's eyes got big, she grabbed my arm, but we did not move. Scheherazade came out of the club and lunged at Henry. She screamed as he snapped her neck and dropped her on the ground.

Manny had followed us from Granite and witnessed everything. He came out from behind a van and pointed a gun at Henry. "Stop right there and get down on the ground!"

I screamed, "No!" as Henry headed for the detective. Teri jumped in front of Henry. He put his arms around her and gently moved her aside.

"Detective, get out of here! You have no idea what you're dealing with," I told him.

"I just witnessed two murders."

"No, you didn't. Look!" I pointed behind him. Alexander was walking back towards me. "He's fine. They are just stunt people practicing their skills." It was the only explanation I could think of on the spot. Manny did not look convinced until Scheherazade sat up, rolled her neck, and smiled at him. "Just leave now. I promise I'll talk with you tomorrow at my house, around noon," I told him.

I was hoping that things would finally start to calm down. A light rain began to fall but no one seemed to even notice. Alexander took advantage of the situation to put an arm around my shoulder and kiss my cheek. I could feel his seductive power again. I turned and pushed his arm away. "Knock it off!"

"Who is this stupid man who dares point a weapon at my Baroness?" There was a threatening icy tone in Alexander's voice.

Manny holstered his weapon. "Who are you?"

"You don't want to know," Alexander replied with a hint of a threat.

Manny did not back down. It just was not in his DNA. He looked at me. "Are you okay with them? Do you want me to take you and Ms. Park home?"

I finally breathed. "I'm fine. They are all old friends. Please leave. I'll see you tomorrow."

"How gallant of you. For the sake of the Baroness, I'll spare you." Alexander said.

I glared at Alexander. "What is wrong with you people, 'I'll spare you?', You're not hurting anyone. Just shut up." I looked back at the detective. "Forget I said that."

Luckily, Manny was paying more attention to Teri, who seemed to be enjoying the company of the other "stunt" man. "Okay, tomorrow at noon in Granite Falls." He was trying to look as though he was not alarmed by the insane scene he had witnessed. Something caught Manny's attention. A huge snake started crawling down the leg of the "stunt" woman.

"Snake!" he yelled and pulled out his gun again though he didn't think he could shoot the snake without hurting the woman. His hand holding the gun was shaky, and he began to sweat.

Henry pushed Teri out of the way and leaped on Scheherazade. He tore the snake off of her, and it began to wrap itself around his neck. Henry gripped its head in one hand as it tried to bite him, then grabbed the body with the other. With a quick motion he ripped the head clear off! He threw the head on the ground, and it landed beside Manny's feet. Scheherazade cried out, "My baby!" Manny, startled, jumped back and shot at the snake head.

Alexander stepped in front of Manny, used his psychic charm on him, and quietly said, "Trust me. Everything will be fine." He slowly reached out and took the gun away from the shaken detective. I could see how shocked he was. I remembered feeling that way the first few times I encountered Tristan. I felt so sorry for him. Manny stood there looking stunned, as if he had just been run over by the "what the fuck truck". He was going to have a lot of questions. I wondered how I would be able to explain to him what he had just witnessed.

I walked over to him. "Welcome to my world Detective Takeda. Please, just go now. We'll talk tomorrow. You can have your gun back if you promise to leave now."

"Fine. Just give me my gun." He clearly could not believe he had let someone take it from him. Alexander handed it back. The eye contact between them was hostile and challenging. Manny did not want to be taken advantage of again. I was surprised by how quickly he was recovering. Vampire influence can leave you with a bad hangover. As he got in his car, I heard him mutter, "God, I hate snakes!"

When I turned around, Teri was closely checking Henry for any snake bites. I was not in the mood to deal with her vampire crush. Scheherazade had gathered up the remains of her serpent, and I gave her my best, "Eat shit and die!" look.

Alexander stepped in front of me. "I know that you can feel our connection. I want to talk with my son, but that is not the only reason I risked the wrath of the Baron and the Magus." His eyes now looked at me with warmth and desire. Henry made me feel hot and bothered. With Alexander, it felt as if he had put a warm, soft blanket around my shoulders and pulled me closer with his presence.

"Did you think I would be taken in by your tricks? Damn vampires! You are all such arrogant assholes!" Honestly, I wanted that warm, soft blanket, and he knew it. "Teri, we're out of here. Fantastic performance Henry!" I glanced up at Pomp's windows above the club. I saw her for a second watching us. "Tell Pomp to leave Teri and me alone!" I knew she was behind this insane circus. Someone had to have allowed Alex and Sheri into the club with that snake. Henry would never have allowed that.

"You weren't so bad either, Baroness." Henry bowed to me and headed back into the club.

Teri got in the driver's seat, and we took off in silence. As we headed north out of Seattle on Interstate 5, she finally spoke. "I was just making sure Henry was okay."

"No, you weren't. You're in love and lust with him, and he's fixated on you. I'm not jealous. Henry and I were faking it to upset Tristan. I know you won't take my advice, but you should run away from him like your hair is on fire."

Henry's performance lit up the stage with lust, anger, and dark desire. Later the young women that thought he was really into them were all over him in his undressing room. He was hungry after killing the snake and being so close to Teri.

The female groupies loved the way he savored their offers of blood. The euphoria they experienced when he accepted their offers would bring them back again.

Pomp sent a text message to the Baron,

You were right. He wants Teri.
What shall I do with Scheherazade and Alex?

Tristan replied,

Send the snake charmer to India.
Alex may stay at my condo in Seattle.
I will deal with him later. You have done well.

Chapter 16

Scheherazade Loses Her Head

Before Manny arrived, I sent the kids and Lug to Leif's place to learn about goats. I figured that he had enough sleep by noon to handle them. I wore a Chicago Bear's T-shirt and tried to look as normal as possible.

Manny was right on time. I asked Teri to stay with me for the question session in case I needed her to back up my story. It wasn't that I didn't trust Teri to control herself, but I asked her to leave her weapons in her room. Poor guy, I was a little surprised he actually showed up. I decided he deserved a better explanation than stunt performers. I hoped he could handle it.

He walked into the house and looked a little wary as if he was expecting us to attack him. "Detective Takeda, you're safe here. It's just Teri and me." We settled in the living room. He picked a chair in the corner with a view of the front door. "Do you want coffee or tea?"

"Coffee, black, please."

Teri went into the kitchen to get us coffee.

"I'm sorry about discharging my weapon last night," he said.

"You don't need to apologize. Who knows, that snakehead might have bitten you."

Teri brought coffee and put a plate of cookies on the table.

"Thanks," he took the mug and started to relax a little.

"What do you want to know?" I asked.

"What the hell is going on? To start, what happened last night?" He stared at me and then Teri. "I almost went home last night, thinking I was losing it, but I know what I saw."

"We were guests at a private nightclub and ran into some people we did not expect to see. The woman with the snake was one of them. We started to argue over a private matter when you got there."

"That does not explain how that one guy could get thrown over several cars then get up as if nothing happened. And what was going on with the woman? I could have sworn her neck was broken. It was like watching the X-Men."

"Movie stuntmen. They're amazing," Teri said.

"I didn't see any cameras," Manny replied. "I'm not a fool."

"No, you're not." I decided to tell him the truth. "You better put the coffee down."

He stared at me for a minute, then put his mug on the table. "Okay. Talk to me."

"What I'm going to tell you will change your life forever, and you won't be able to tell anyone about it because they will question your sanity."

Teri leaned over towards me and whispered, "Are you sure about this?" I just nodded. Teri looked back at Manny. "If I were you, I would just take the hint, forget all about it, and get out of here. Ignorance is not always a bad thing. Trust me!"

"That's what the guy said last night, then he did some mind trick and took my gun. Just tell me the truth. I can't promise I won't have to arrest you, but I'll only do what I am required to do under the law."

I laughed, which surprised Manny. "You won't arrest anyone. It isn't illegal to be a vampire."

Silence. Manny looked at me and then at Teri thinking it was a joke. "You want me to believe you're a vampire?"

"I'm not, but the X-Men and the snake lady in Seattle last night are. Teri and I run around in sunlight. We're just regular flesh and blood like you."

"Is it a drug ring? Some PEDs or super steroids that jack them up and increase their pain tolerance. Are they part of a cartel? Is that why they went after Emerson?"

I tried not to laugh again, "Emerson?"

"The man you and your friends killed in Salinas."

"No, it's not about drugs," Teri answered.

I added, "Teri and I did not kill Emerson."

Teri continued, "We advised you to leave, but you demanded the truth, and now you have it. I know it's hard to accept. It took me a while."

He looked suspiciously at the mug of coffee. "Did you drug me?"

"Nope! We just answered your question." I went over to the bookshelf, grabbed a copy of my vampire book, and handed it to him. "Read my book, then maybe we can talk again. Till then, I've got nothing more to say to you. You should leave now." I opened the door and went out on the deck.

Teri felt sorry for him. "Look, I searched for every possible explanation on the planet before I accepted their weird truth. These freaks are legit."

"Just tell me what is really going on. I'll protect you," he said in earnest.

Teri looked in his deep brown eyes and shook her head. "Dude, you pissed off the Baron. The only reason you're not a meal is because the head of the vampire world thinks you might be useful. You are the one that needs protection." She picked up the cookies and went back into the kitchen, afraid she might have said too much.

Manny sat alone for a minute before leaving. He just wanted a break in the case and find the murderer. Instead, he had stumbled into the middle of a bunch of nocturnal beings whose existence he couldn't accept. Manny looked down at the book Miranda had given him, and went back to his car, trying to figure out his next move.

Early that evening, before opening Henry waited for Pomp in the empty club. He sat in the center of the stage, playing a melancholy tune on his guitar. She walked onto the stage in a short black dress, fishnet stockings, and high heel boots. She sensed that he did not have his normal pleasurable response to her presence.

Cold anger showed in his eyes. "Your ambition has made you sloppy and dangerous to all of us. You are no longer welcome here." He put his guitar in its case. "I understand your fixation with powerful vampires. I can excuse allowing Alexander to be here, but not Scheherazade and her snake. You put the Baroness and Teri at risk, not to mention that detective. I have no doubt the Baron gave permission, but you neglected to ask for my consent. This is still my club. Do you imagine the Baron will be your next king? You delude yourself. You are Common Caste trash."

"Bastard! How dare you insult me! At least I was given a title by the King of France. Cleopatra chose suicide over you. You'll spend years craving the love of that protected mortal, Teri. You don't deserve to be one of us!"

"Fortunately, I was born with HH blood." He raised one hand, and she started to choke. She fell to her knees. Her face showed panic as she clutched her throat. Henry slowly made a fist then lowered his hand as she fell on her side. He picked up his guitar and stood over her. "Pity, your lovely voice will never be the same. You are banned from the Funeral Pyre. I don't care where you go. Have all your possessions gone by the end of the night. You will never understand what it means to be Haute Caste." He walked away into the shadows.

At dinner on Sunday, the kids discussed goat herding, ignorant of the crazy weekend Teri and I had experienced.

Des said, "I don't think I'm cut out to work on a farm."

Tomas shook his head. "You didn't work. You just watched us."

Marie added, "And ate goat cheese."

"How is Leif?" I asked.

"Fine," Jacques responded between bites of pizza. "He said Pomp isn't at the club now. She might be hanging out with Dad more."

I shot a look at Teri; she just shook her head.

Tomas asked, "Will you let us go hear Leif's band rehearse?"

"No, not at the club. Maybe if they're at Leif's place."

Even Teri agreed with me. "Your mom is right. You're just too young for the club scene. But I'm sure Leif will help you form your band."

Billy and Robert wandered into the kitchen. They found their beverage of choice and filled a couple of small glasses and Robert quipped "Good evening Mordecai mortals."

Tomas asked him, "Will you give us guitar lessons tonight? Leif let us borrow a guitar."

"Sure," he mussed Tomas's wavy hair.

Billy smiled. "And I've got an extra harmonica."

114

"Put your dishes in the sink, and get your stuff ready for school tomorrow, then meet our house musicians in the living room."

The kids did not argue because they desperately wanted to be in a band. Teri and I told Billy and Robert what had happened at the club.

Robert responded first. "You know there has to be a Haute Caste vamp protecting Pomp. She would never have allowed Alexander or Scheherazade near her without permission."

Billy added, "It wasn't the Magus, and I don't see Lady Kananga having anything to do with those dishonored fools."

Teri asked, "Was it the Baron? I don't understand. I thought he hated Alexander."

"Tristan is a jealous asshole." I wondered what other stunts he might pull.

Billy laughed, "How the mighty fall." Robert finished his glass of blood.

I admitted to him, "You were right about Henry. He tried to protect us." Teri looked like she was about to sigh.

Robert went on, "Pomp is going to be sorry. Henry owns the club and the building. She was just his guest. Though I've heard she's squirreled away a fortune."

"Maybe I should console her," Billy said.

Robert laughed, "Yeah, you could try, but then I'd have to play at your funeral."

Out-of-tune guitar picking called our heroes to the living room. Billy and Robert patiently began teaching them about music. "Your instrument is your best friend. Your music will always be with you," Robert told them.

We listened to Billy play a melancholy tune on his harmonica while Teri and I finished cleaning up the kitchen. I would never have believed that housework was becoming my moment of Zen. A bit of normalcy in a bizarre life. It's not that I liked doing the dishes, but it was a predictable act with an expected outcome that solved a problem. I wished I could fit Tristan in the dishwasher.

Lady Kananga was irritated with the Haute Caste on the West Coast of North America. When she got word about the debacle in the parking lot in Seattle, she ordered a flight to London and arranged a meeting with the Heads of the House of Plows and the House of Pentacles for the next night. The vampire world was not going to fall apart on her watch. How dare the Baron make decisions to allow Alexander to stay in Seattle and send Scheherazade to India without consulting her. Because of his inability to be impartial in affairs that involved the Baroness, the Magus had put Kananga in charge.

When her plane touched down in London, she called him, even though it meant waking him up. "Tristan, we have to talk."

"Lady Kananga, is this about the Magus?"

"No, it's about you. How could you allow Alexander to go free and offer him sanctuary in Seattle?"

Tristan yawned then answered, "He has lost much of his power, and Hann agreed not to pursue him. I regard this as a family matter. Jacques has requested to meet with him."

"You were never a good liar. You want your son to see his biological father in a weakened state." Her tone was becoming angrier. "Haute Caste will be arriving in Seattle in a few nights to assess the situation." She abruptly hung up.

Tristan smiled. He rarely lied, but Kananga was right. He had stretched the truth. Jacques had said that one day he knew he would have to speak to Alexander. He just was not sure when he would be ready. Tristan was amazed that she had seen through his plan to expose Jacques to a Common Caste version of Alexander the Not-So-Great. She did not know about Henry and Teri. He laid back down but had difficulty falling asleep. Delilah stood next to the bed. He reached over and rubbed her head. "You're the most reasonable female I have ever known." He would have to return to Granite Falls sooner than expected.

Scheherazade was infuriated at being banished to India in the Magus' absence. Though Scheherazade's ancestors had come from Persia, she adopted wearing saris to look more exotic. Not much about her rang true. She had convinced Pomp to allow a stopover in London to pick up some of her possessions. She planned on disappearing in Europe long enough that the Magus might grant her forgiveness. A young vampire who was a Common Caste member of the House of Pentacles greeted her jet. He had served her when she had been a favorite of Cesare Borgia. She had taken him under her wing and into her bed, and he was still under her influence. He handed her a Chanel purse with cash and a fake passport. She told him she would contact him if she needed anything else and quickly left the terminal.

Scheherazade was famished and headed to Pop Brixton, a courtyard that had been fashioned out of shipping containers and strung with festive lights. There was a variety of cheap and sometimes exotic food that brought lots of people to the market. The scent of spices, smoke, and grease filled the air. Scheherazade only paid attention to the scent of O-positive blood as she walked through the market. She found a balding middle-aged man drinking a pint of a dark brew at a bar near the edge of the courtyard. Behind him, unused shipping containers formed dark alcoves. She stood beside him and smiled.

He looked up at her. "Harry's my name. What will you be drinking?"

"Sheri," she smiled. "My name is Sheri. Red wine."

"I'm afraid this is a whiskey and beer bar."

"Let me have a sip of yours. Maybe I'll like it." She brushed up against him.

He almost spilled the beer handing her the mug. She pretended to take a long slow drink of the nasty brew. "Lovely."

"That's what I was thinking," he said with a grin. He looked her up and down, noting her attire. "I've been to India on holiday. It was a bit too hot and steamy for my taste."

"Why don't you tell me more over there, where we can find a more private place to sit and finish your beer." She pointed to a barely lit area behind the bar.

"After you m'lady," he chortled.

They sat on a cement block and leaned against a shipping container. They could still see some of the twinkling lights from the market. Away from the crowd, it was easier for Scheherazade to focus on her prey. She slid over against him and took the drink, setting it on the ground. "Later Harry," she purred.

His eyes got big. She started to lean into him and brushed her lips against his neck. "I didn't know Indian women were so affectionate." He started to perspire. Harry had never imagined having sex here, at Pop Brixton, though he had imagined quite a few exotic locations. "Steady Harry, don't get ahead of yourself," he muttered to himself and awkwardly put his arms about her.

Sheri smiled at him as she was about to take a bite. He stared at her wide-eyed, totally mesmerized.

Movement behind Scheherazade broke his concentration. "What's this?" Harry blinked, looking beyond Sheri. "We're having a private moment here!"

"Leave or it will be your last moment," a handsome man with wavy hair in an expensive suit stared at them.

"Cesare!" Scheherazade exclaimed.

A gorgeous woman with long black hair appeared next to him and added, "That's his wife you are manhandling," Antoinella told him, nodding in Cesare's direction.

Harry looked horrified. "She was trying to seduce me!" He pushed Scheherazade away and scrambled to his feet.

"Leave us!" Cesare commanded.

Harry ran away and did not look back, vowing that he would never go to Pop Brixton again.

"I didn't even know we were engaged," Scheherazade responded, getting to her feet.

"You have compromised and insulted my House for the last time," Cesare stated.

Antoinella swiftly and silently moved behind her, grabbing her wrists. "Allow me," she said.

Fear seized Scheherazade as she picked up the scent of HH blood that had been recently given to Antoinella. She tried to break free, but the other vampiress' strength had been enhanced by Cesare's blood. "Let me serve you. Let me fill your nights with pleasure," Scheherazade pleaded.

Cesare nodded and Antoinella let go of one wrist. As Scheherazade swung around, Antoinella produced a large razor-sharp knife and slashed her throat. With lightning speed, Antoinella moved out of the way of the blood spray, which decorated the shipping container shielding them from view. Scheherazade fell to the ground.

Cesare approached the dying vampiress and pulled her head up by her hair. "Such a waste of talent!" Her eyes pleaded with him to relent and give her another chance. "You should never have unleashed your snakes on our kind." He glanced at Antoinella, who touched the scar on her neck from a cobra Scheherazade had attacked her with during Alexander's attempted coup in Las Vegas. She handed Cesare the knife. With powerful cuts, he completely severed her head.

Antoinella smiled. "Well done my love." She produced a small cup and held it below the head. When it was full, they each took a drink. They paused to feel the rush and to experience their reward for removing the traitor. She held up a sack, and he dropped the head into it. Under cover of darkness, they left her body in a market dumpster and covered it over with garbage. They carried her head back to their Rolls Royce.

"Where to Sir Borgia?" the Common Caste chauffeur asked.

"I hear the Thames just south of the Ferris Wheel is lovely this time of night," Antoinella said.

"Yes. That will be a perfect spot." Cesare was looking forward to ending the night with Antoinella after disposing of the head. A kill always enhanced their sexual encounters, and this kill was particularly satisfying. He sent a text message to Kananga.

We have cut off the head of the snake.

Chapter 17

Forbidden Fruit

The kids were jubilant as they piled into the kitchen after school. "Well done, my man," Des grinned and gave Tomas a high-five.

Even Marie complimented her brother, "Fucking hilarious!"

"What happened?" I asked.

Teri rolled her eyes. Jacques just smiled and said, "Respect!"

They grabbed snacks and settled around the kitchen table.

"I was walking across the basketball court during gym, and this senior yelled out, 'Hey Tomasina, I'm calling ICE on your Mexican ass,'" Tomas told me.

Des added, "Then Tomas walks to center court picks up a ball, and makes a perfect 3-point basket."

Marie added, "Then he bows to the racist asshole."

"The coach came over and made the kid apologize. I guess I'll be on the team now."

"Thanks for not beating him to a pulp. I'm sorry you had to deal with that." It was probably better that I wasn't there when it happened. "Just be careful showing off." I took a sip of coffee. Racism was making its ugly presence known in our protected world. "Your Grandpa Pete would be proud, but please don't tell your dad. I'm not sure what might happen to that kid."

Marie grinned, "I heard Ashley call him an ass-wipe when he walked by our lockers."

Tomas just smiled then checked his phone.

"All right, Leif is expecting you for band practice, but do your homework first."

Des said, "That won't take long."

Jacques jumped up. "Cool!"

After they had gone, I told Teri I wanted to talk to her on the deck. We settled into chairs looking out on the river. "I want you to know that I am not jealous. Henry and I both told you we were just trying to get Tristan to stop focusing on Batu. I'm warning you to stay away from Henry because no one did that for me when Tristan started pursuing me."

Teri looked at me like I didn't understand. "Henry isn't like your ex."

"He is more like Tristan than you realize. Egotistical seductive vigilante serial killers."

"He saved us from that snake!"

I flashed a knowing smile. "Henry hates snakes but loves forbidden fruit. There's this whole biblical vibe here. He wants a taste of your apple."

"Actually." She moved her hair away from her neck. Just behind her ear were two tiny puncture wounds.

"No! When did...?"

"The night at the club. It was so quick that I didn't realize it had happened till I touched my neck and then noticed his lips were slightly red. I got this euphoric sensation, but it didn't last. Maybe it was the sight of him ripping the snake's head off that killed the mood."

"That's not good. Henry will literally hunger for you now. I mean full-on obsession. He follows his own ethics, not the rules. I think he intends to do everything but transform you." She heard me, but I could tell it was not quite registering. She was lost in Henry-land. "Teri, you have to get away from him."

"I don't want to leave."

"Said the fly to the person trying to free her from the spider's web."

"Henry is not forcing me." She was starting to get angry.

"Listen to me. You were with Angel, right? I mean, you've made love to a vampire." She nodded. I continued, "Did he bite you?"

"No," she smiled. "The sex was great. He's in shape and unselfish. His endurance was amazing. It was exhausting."

"Angel is a normal vampire." That sounded weird, even to me. "Think about it. Henry has not kissed you; he just took some of your blood without permission, and he has you believing it's love. He's one of the ancients." I tried to keep my voice level. "I'm not sure you know what that means. They affect us like a drug. They are unbelievably powerful. He started out screwing Cleopatra, and that was when he was still mortal. You thought Angel was overwhelming, Henry is off the fucking Richter scale, and you're saying, 'Bring it on!' Really?"

Teri was pissed. "Henry warned me that you would try to get between us. I liked it better when you didn't care about my personal life." She got up and slammed the door as she went into the house.

Wow! I needed reinforcements. I sent out a couple of text messages. Henry was starting to get under my skin. I had to find a way to shield her from his powers. I needed to ask for Tristan's help. I was not looking forward to our next conversation.

Sir Steve entered the bedroom of the Head of the House of Cups and bowed. Princess Khunbish lay on her side, supported by decorative pillows. She gestured for him to join her. "What news?"

He lay beside her and ran his hand gently over the length of her body. "Scheherazade is no more."

"Sir Borgia?" she inquired while unbuttoning his shirt.

"And Lady Antoinella. I hear they share everything these nights. Sir Borgia had ignored her for many years, and now he is mesmerized by her."

Khunbish played with his curly blond hair. "I owe them for dispatching the vampiress that was involved in the attempt to kill Batu in London. Perhaps I should offer his service to them."

He loosened her tunic and began to kiss her shoulder. Soon he was on top of her as they quickly shed their clothes. He pulled the jeweled combs from her hair and let her long dark hair fall about her face.

She put a hand against his chest. "You didn't answer me."

"My lady, I cannot possibly consider your request and ravish you at the same time. Only a woman is capable of that."

She smiled. "Then continue."

He loved the softness of her skin and the strength of her response to his touch. He kissed her breasts. Then she flipped him over with one of her famed wrestling moves. Steve did not mind her dominance at all.

"I'm at your mercy," he said.

She rode him like one of her prized horses. Pleasure consumed them until they could not hold back the release of sensual tension any longer. Khunbish collapsed on his chest, and he held her in his arms. They fell into the deep sleep of their kind as the sun began to rise. It was the first time Steve had been allowed to stay in her bedchamber. It had been a century since either of them had allowed another to become a significant intimate.

In another part of the palace, Batu turned off the light and lay alone in his bed. His one night with Lily had proven that he was a fully functional vampire. Lily had suggested another tryst for his health, but he declined. She was a skilled lover, but not his love. He did not want any rumor of them having an affair to get back to Miranda. Batu was not sure he would be able to wait a year before he could be with her again.

He was becoming aware of his powers and how to control them. One night he and Chang were crossing the street in town when the brakes on a bus failed and was about to run down a couple crossing the street. Batu raised his hands and sent out an energy wave that pushed them back onto the sidewalk. Chang and Batu disappeared before anyone had noticed them. The couple was confused but grateful to be alive. He stared at his hands and thought. "Oh shit!" There was also a new connection to Miranda. He had a feeling it was probably due to her psychic ability, not his, since he was not sensitive to anyone else. He lay in bed and tried to sense what was going on with her but felt nothing. He turned the light back on and started to read Shakespeare's sonnets. It was going to be a long day.

The next night in London, Kananga greeted Cesare and Antoinella in her Knightsbridge home. Her butler asked if they wanted refreshments, but they politely declined. He left and closed the door to her study. They were seated in modern oak chairs with bright fabric cushions around an oak and glass coffee table. A collection of small carved African animals made from semi-precious stones were on the table. Kananga wore western clothing on this night. A black silk jacket and black jeans with high heels. Cesare unbuttoned his Armani suit jacket as he sat down. Antoinella also dressed to show respect for their interim ruler. She straightened her little Chanel black dress and pearls. She was uncomfortable but chic. It was worth it.

As they settled in, the butler showed Sarah, the Head of the House of Plows, into the room. She wore a burgundy satin blouse and leather jeans. Lady Kananga welcomed her. "Thank you for coming on such short notice.

"Lady Kananga, it is always an honor to meet with you," Sarah said.

"The House of Pentacles always appreciates a visit from you," Cesare added.

"Sir Borgia, Lady Antoinella, I give you my thanks. The Magus also conveys his appreciation for your swift action dealing with the traitor to our kind." She handed Antoinella a small emerald-green box. "From the Magus."

Antoinella opened the box to see a beautiful four-carat canary yellow diamond pendant. Her eyes lit up. "It is beautiful. I am very grateful."

Cesare rose and put the precious jewel around Antoinella's neck. "My House appreciates this recognition. You must know we had wanted to finish her in Las Vegas. Justice has finally been served."

"We will keep her demise secret for now. We have only informed Princess Khunbish and Sir Steve." Lady Kananga informed them.

"Surely the Baron will know," Cesare said.

"The Baron had knowledge of Alexander and Scheherazade's visit to Seattle and did not discuss it with anyone," Kananga replied. The implication was that the Baron did not clear it with Kananga.

Cesare was surprised. "His relationship with the Baroness clouds his judgment."

"Yes, Sir Borgia. He allowed Alexander and Scheherazade to be there after Scheherazade aided Alexander's escape from Sir Hannibal's sanctuary. Pomp was also involved. Sir Henry has banned her from his club and no longer speaks to her."

"That must have been some quarrel," Sarah remarked.

Kananga replied, "Sir Henry crushed her voice box, and now she speaks to no one. She may never regain her voice."

"What happened?" Antoinella asked.

Kananga smiled. "Have you met Teri Park, the bodyguard for the Royal offspring?"

Antoinella understood immediately. "She has HH blood."

"Yes," Kananga replied.

Sir Borgia looked surprised. "I never paid any attention to her. I was never close enough to catch her scent."

"Sir Henry has, and he has a wicked temper. Scheherazade must have threatened Teri somehow. Knowing Scheherazade, she probably attacked her with a snake," Antoinella remarked.

"Yes. There was an altercation in the Funeral Pyre parking lot, witnessed by the detective from Salinas. The Baroness is handling it, but I believe cooler heads are needed."

Cesare spoke in a cold tone, "Sir Henry greatly diminished Pomp's powers. Her lovely voice was seductive and compelling. He had no right. She was foolish, but his response was cruel and excessive. She must have been following the Baron's orders. I can't see the Magus being involved."

"The Magus has been made aware and is returning to Los Angeles. Sources tell me that the Baroness requested Lady Pauline and Sir Angel assist her as she fears for Teri's safety," Lady Kananga said.

"It's ironic that a bodyguard would need protection," Antoinella quipped.

Lady Sarah said, "I'll leave for the U.S. as soon as possible." She was embarrassed that Kananga would know what was happening in her House before she did.

Cesare observed. "The Baron and Sir Henry can be quite treacherous. At the moment they are acting in unpredictable ways. I must insist on going as well. If Sir Omar were not the Baroness' father, I would suggest his involvement as well."

"Sir Borgia, I am glad you have offered to go. The Magus thought you might wish to intervene. Lady Antoinella, I believe the Baroness would be glad to see you again," Lady Kananga noted.

Antoinella smiled. "Of course, she will." She played with the diamond. "There was a time that jealousy kept us at each other's throats but taking down Alexander together changed that. By the way, what will happen to his greatness?"

"The Baron is toying with him. He is allowing Alexander to stay in Seattle. Alexander waits for permission to visit with his son," Kananga responded.

Cesare spoke, "More cruelty. I much preferred the Baron when he was married to the Baroness. He was much more, shall we say, pleasant. Can we not get them back together again?"

Sarah laughed, "Have you met the Baroness?"

"And then there's the Mongol," Antoinella said. "What's the news of the newest Haute Caste member?"

Kananga displayed a knowing smile. "He is progressing nicely. The Princess believes he will be quite formidable in time. Lady Lily has the same opinion of his rapid development since his transformation."

"Really, despite his common blood," Sarah tried not to laugh. "She is fortunate to be 'assessing' him."

"Please keep me posted on the situation in Seattle. It will be a few nights before the Magus is presiding over our world again. I shall stay in London until he returns to the West Coast. Sir Borgia, if you would like, I could discipline the Common Caste involved in Scheherazade's escape from the airport."

"I would appreciate that. We shall make arrangements to leave tonight," Sir Borgia replied.

"May I fly out with you?" Sarah inquired.

"Of course, Lady Sarah, there are four sleeping compartments on my jet." He was always happy to show off the wealth of the House of Pentacles.

The next night Kananga felt energized by the proposition of teaching the vampire rabble of London the importance of loyalty. She had her chauffeur drive her to the Underground Club in Camden. She knew that the Pentacles had a private room off the main area in the basement. Her braids hung down over a black leather jacket, and she wore a miniskirt with tiny spikes around the hem. It helped her move through crowds. She only had to say, "Piss-off!" a few times to interested men and women before getting to the private room. An aide accompanying her headed to the DJ booth.

The loud metal music made the place vibrate. In the dimly lit private room, Kananga could see several vampires taking "sips" from vampire groupies. The West Coast trend had made its way to London. As she entered the room, the aide cut off the music. In the sudden silence, heads popped up. The vampires pushed the mortals to the ground as they realized who had just entered. "Get out!" A blond vampire with a purple satin shirt said to a young man lying at his feet. The mortals got the message. They quickly pulled on their clothes and scrambled from the room.

"Lady Kananga." The blond vampire bowed, and the others followed suit. A vampiress with long blue hair pulled out a wooden chair and placed it beside Kananga.

She did not sit. She coldly surveyed the vampires, assessing who might be the most influential. It wouldn't be the one who told the human snacks to leave. That would be too obvious. She stared at the young woman with blue hair. The leader would be a quiet vampire with manners. "Who helped Scheherazade last night?"

"I'm Sophie, Lady Kananga. I would gladly be of any assistance, but I was not involved in that unfortunate event."

She met Sophie's eyes. The Common Caste vampiress felt a sudden throbbing headache and sudden nausea. She clutched her stomach and broke away from Lady Kananga's gaze as the dry heaves started. "Sophie, who was involved?" Kananga demanded.

The vampiress held up a hand, and Kananga stopped the pain. Sophie slowly straightened up. She took a deep breath and steadied herself with the chair. "Bryce and Collin were with Scheherazade last night. They left with her and haven't come back. None of us were involved. We wouldn't go against the Haute Caste."

The vampire in the purple shirt asked, "May I speak?" Kananga nodded.

"I'm Paul. Bryce and Collin tried to talk us into helping Scheherazade, but we would never go against you. We told them to go to bloody hell, your ladyship."

"They will end up there," Kananga responded. "Find out where they have gone. I will reward whoever locates them, and I will mention you to the Magus."

Murmurs went through the room. Sophie asked, "Has the great Magus returned?"

"He is on his way back to Bel Air. I am here because Sir Borgia, Lady Antoinella, and Lady Sarah are on their way to meet with the Haute Caste in the West. Do you want me to report that members of his House were at this club when they should have been hunting down two dishonorable Pentacles?"

She had never seen vampires vacate a building so quickly.

An hour later, in Liverpool, a ship was just pulling away from the docks as Paul and Sophie's Mini Cooper came to a screeching halt. "Bollocks!" Paul spat out.

"You're sure that's the ship?" Sophie stared past the glare of industrial lights and tried to make out the small freighter's stern.

"Yes, damn it!" Paul kicked a trash can and sent it off the end of the dock.

"Well, at least we can report they are on their way to India. We won't look like complete fools." She pushed her long blue hair out of her face. "I thought Lady Kananga was going to destroy me. That was the first time I felt an Ancient's power." Sophie shuddered for an instant.

"It's a fuckin' miracle she didn't. I don't think Bryce and Collin will be so lucky. Thanks mate, for keeping me from getting involved with those idiots. C'mon, it's an hour before dawn."

Chapter 18

Scheherazade: The Sequel

Marie and I stood near the barn and looked up at the bat houses, watching the bats take off to hunt for food. They looked like they were being shot out of cannons as they quickly disappeared into the evening sky.

"It's strange that they're a symbol for vampires," Marie observed. "They just seem like large flying mice to me. They aren't mean at all. They take care of each other and never fight."

"I don't know why Bram Stoker came up with that," I wondered out loud.

"The Magus sent the bat houses to get on my good side. After all his scheming and trying to manipulate all of us, that's something I'll never show him. He can't win me over that easily. Anyway, I have to go. We have band practice." She went to work on her drum skills. Even though they had all made incredibly fast progress learning to play their instruments, I was still glad they practiced at Leif's.

I stood looking at the river, thinking about how the Magus and all his minions constantly try to control us. I was glad she wanted to stay away from that nocturnal maniac. I remembered Bram Stoker on his death bed in Tristan's mansion. He had been kept alive with doses of HH blood for many decades to atone for his depiction of vampires, which they considered a grievous insult. Tristan finally "pardoned' him when Stoker agreed to pose as my college Professor and convince me to write a vampire book that showed them in a more accurate light. Such a tortured soul. I wanted my kids to find ways to avoid the vampire world insanity. Not that I was a great example.

"Bon Soir Miranda," Guillaume greeted me. I was startled, still unused to how the undead could move so quietly.

"Hi Cuz! Did you know Bram Stoker?" I asked.

He looked surprised. "Of course, such a scandal. The poor Irishman fell in love with the Baron's mistress Simone and was so jealous he wrote a book that described us as ugly blood-sucking monsters. Your husband never forgave him."

"My ex let me bury him."

"No! He finally let him die? I did not know he could be so merciful."

"It was a wedding present."

"Ma chère, you have had a positive effect on him." Guillaume smiled like he was proud of me. "Do you have time for a fencing lesson?"

I did feel like killing something, even if it was only pretend. "Sure."

I followed him into the barn and strapped my protective gear on over my jeans and sweatshirt. It annoyed me that Guillaume did not wear any protection. Teri came in. When she saw me, she started to leave.

Guillaume called out, "Mademoiselle, you need practice as well." Teri hesitated and Guillaume told her to get ready. A few minutes later, Teri and I were facing each other with pointy weapons in hand. "Remember, it is about discipline, timing, balance, and precise strikes," Guillaume reminded us.

With the friction over Henry still an issue, we regarded each other as opponents. The hostility in the air was palpable. We danced about till Teri lost her patience and lunged, but I managed to slip out of the way. Her frustration heightened. I felt a sense of calmness come over me. I was not the one struggling with the mixed emotions of a budding affair with a vampire. She tried to stick me again, but a quick movement left me unscathed. Then I struck so fast it even surprised me. The point of my blade rested just above her heart! She dropped her weapon with a look of shock.

"You moved like a vampiress! Bravo!" Guillaume exclaimed.

I dropped my weapon and started tearing off my gear. "Teri, I'm sorry. I didn't mean to..."

From the doorway of the barn, I heard someone slowly clapping. "It's your true nature," Tristan said.

Teri rushed past my ex and went into the house. I felt my brain chemistry getting back to normal, at least normal for me. "Can we talk?" I asked Tristan.

Guillaume politely excused himself, left the barn, and closed the door. I went over to a corner where there were a couple of chairs. "Come sit." I invited him.

Tristan looked at me with a bemused expression. He was so fucking handsome and self-assured. Damn him! I sat down as he strode across the room.

I nodded at the other chair. "Please."

"I'll stand, thanks." He wore a white shirt open to mid-chest with his gold Templar pendant drawing attention to his muscular chest. He had given me the pendant once, but I returned it. It looked better on him. His blue eyes pulled me in, but not like I was drowning. I had learned to tread water over our years together. His scent was still like a walk in a forest, but there was something else.

"Pomp! You've been with Pomp!"

He smiled. "You wish to discuss my sexual partners?"

I quickly recovered. "No. I wanted to talk with you about something that happened at the Funeral Pyre."

"Pomp wrote out an account of what happened for me,"

"Wrote?" I said confused.

"Sir Henry crushed her voice box."

He was waiting for my reaction. "That Bastard! I'm not on Team Pomp, but she didn't deserve that. Will she recover?"

"I'm relieved you do not approve. Pomp will heal in time, but her voice, likely will never be the same. The Magus will return in a few nights, and there will be a meeting of the Parliament to discuss this affair. Is that all?"

I was not sure I was looking forward to the Magus back in charge again. "Not even close. You must have known Alexander and Scheherazade were visiting Seattle. Why did you let that happen?"

He sat in the chair across from me. This was starting to feel like a chess match. "To see if you were really involved with Sir Henry."

"So, the parking lot fiasco was to find out who Henry wanted to fuck?" I had underestimated how obsessed Tristan was with me.

"Crudely put, but yes."

"You've got to move on. Seriously." I paused, trying not to enrage him. I shifted the discussion. "Now Henry is using his considerable charm and chemistry on Teri. She is so taken in by him right now she even got in an argument with me. I told her she should get away for a while, but she refused."

"Like me," he responded. I felt him starting to touch my neck with his shadow self. It was slight but enough to make me move my chair back a little. I could tell he was amused, but I had more pressing issues to discuss.

"Will you help me keep her away from Henry? I'm afraid he'll do everything but transform her as long as she is watching over the kids and me."

"She's an adult. Teri has HH blood, and she is fully aware of who Sir Henry is."

"Yeah, well, I thought I knew who you were too." His shadow touch was starting to move down my shoulders. "Stop it!" I got up and stood behind the chair. The sensation ceased.

"I'll speak with Sir Henry because the children like Teri, and it might be difficult to replace her."

I was on a roll. "What about Alexander?"

"I will ask Jacques if he wishes to see him. If not, I'll continue to ban him from contacting our son. I accept that they will meet sooner or later, and I would like to be available to Jacques when it happens. Alexander is also interested in you. He is due for another dose of your blood. Do you wish us to continue the treatment? The Magus is leaving the decision up to you. In any case, his powers will probably take months to return."

"Funny thing, you know that phantom touchy thing you just did to me? Well, 'his greatness' has been doing it too. I think my blood is connecting us in some way. Has Lily said anything about this?"

He looked surprised. "He is contacting you? That means your blood is not inhibiting all his abilities. It seems to be increasing some. He is becoming more telepathic, like you. I must speak with Lily and the Magus." He looked at me. "What will this mean for the children?"

"I don't know, but no one is sampling their blood, and I won't give anymore to Alexander. I don't believe concern for our well-being is the reason for the Magus' research."

"As you wish. You'll have to fend off Alexander's advances. He will try every way possible to get close to you. I said this would happen when we divorced. My fertile Baroness, you are quite intriguing to the Haute Caste. I won't use my power to touch you again. I don't want you to confuse my affection with Alexander's flirtation."

"You mean sexual harassment. I'll demand that he stop as well. For what it's worth, I knew it wasn't you."

A slight smile came to his face. "You are indeed a vampiress. You have the power to block any attempt to be influenced by others. It is time you accept your true self and use it. I just witnessed you move with the speed and grace of Lady Kananga. One request?"

"What is it?"

"One last kiss?"

I looked into his beautiful, seductive, deep blue eyes, inhaled his scent, and responded, "Hell no!"

He laughed and walked out of the barn.

"What the fuck!" I exclaimed. I sat down and took a deep breath. I wondered what was happening to me.

Tristan entered Jacques' room and found him reading a book about the Knights Templar. "Jacques, we must talk."

"Sure," he closed the book and stood almost at attention.

Tristan sat in the chair by the desk, but Jacques remained standing. "Alexander has been punished for attempting to overthrow the Magus, as well as conspiring with Kyoto to orchestrate your conception. He has been caring for Hann's elephants as ordered and has complied with having his powers diminished. He risked the wrath of the Magus and me to speak with you and is now in Seattle. I told him it is your decision whether you care to grant an audience."

The triplets were just outside Jacque's door listening to every word. Tristan sensed their presence but ignored them. They would find out anyway. Jacques sat down and said, "I knew he was here." His eyes got big. "I had a dream he had escaped, but I didn't tell anyone. I guess it was a vision."

Tristan appeared concerned. "Do you have them often?"

"No. That was only the second one. The first one was the night before we rode Hann's elephants. I saw that we would win."

"Jacques, you must tell your mother or me whenever this happens. Do not be afraid or ashamed of such a gift."

"Okay." Jacques was quiet for a minute, then said, "I've had time to think about what he did, and I think I should see him. I don't want to hang out with him, just not be strangers. Like Mom, she had two fathers. At least I found out earlier than she did. I was angry at first, but not so much now." He looked at Tristan for reassurance that he was making the right decision.

"Embrace your heritage to help you explore your destiny."

Jacques got up and hugged his father. Tristan felt that rare experience of his eyes watering.

The triplets ran in. "We should be there too!" Tomas said.

"I still haven't forgiven Alexander," Marie added.

Tristan nodded. "I'll set it up soon. Jacques, I'll ask Guillaume to bring you." He looked at the siblings. "Alone!"

Des hopped on the bed. "That's okay. I didn't want to see Alexander the Not-So-Great anyway."

Bryce paced the deck of the freighter in the hazy moonlight. He ran a hand through his short brown curls and straightened his dark suit. "What if it doesn't work?"

Collin leaned against the metal door to the galley. He had battled for Scotland against the Crown during his mortal life. He swept his long dark hair away from his face. "Don't worry, I'll sew her up, just like I did on the battlefield. C'mon, you dobber. We best get to it!"

They went below deck into a small compartment off the galley. At Scheherazade's direction, they had kept watch on her from a distance in London. After her beheading, they followed Cesare and Antoinella and retrieved her remains which they laid out in a large wooden crate with ice. The smell of death permeated the room. They carefully lifted her body out of the crate and laid it on the long food prep table, then Collin retrieved her head from the crate. Bryce took a perfumed handkerchief from his suit pocket and held it over his nose. Collin scoffed, "Why did they ever transform your worthless arse?"

"May I remind you my breeding allowed me to be acceptable as Sir Borgia's chauffeur. Without me, you would never have found her head."

"Well, you'll have to dirty your royal fingers. Hold her precious head in place!" Bryce managed to find plastic gloves. Collin did not bother. Hoping contact with the ancient vampiress' blood would benefit him, he had taken a sip when Bryce was not watching. Sensations were heightened, including the putrid smell. He readied the needle and thread. "Bryce, Hold her steady!"

The gray skin was tough, but Collin managed to force the needle through. Bryce stared at her glassy dark eyes, hoping for some spark. She had been so beautiful, talented, and commanding. They would have done anything for her. Collin slowly, painstakingly, sewed her neck in perfect alignment with her head. He made dozens of small stitches to reduce scarring.

"Slowly rotate her head as I move her body on its side," Collin demanded. "Now, move her hair out of the way."

Bryce arranged the blood-caked hair so that her neck was bare. He would shampoo her once beautiful thick mane when they finished sewing her up. He was disgusted with the leadership of the House of Pentacles. "The Italian assassin and his whore will pay!" he proclaimed. "A worthless Prussian ruled our House, and now it is ruled by the Pope's bastard. It should be one of us!"

"Hey mate, put me in charge. Hand me the jar with the salve."

Bryce opened the small black bag that Scheherazade had given them when she got off the plane. Inside was a note with the instructions,

Use these items if I'm discovered.

He pulled a glass jar out and carefully handed it to Collin.

130

The Scot opened it and inhaled deeply. The scent of frankincense, myrrh, turmeric and other ingredients started to waft over the room, covering the stench of death. He applied the balm completely around her neck. "Now, the tea!"

Bryce opened a thermos filled with tea that smelled like Vicks VapoRub. Earlier, he had tasted it and almost vomited. Bryce wondered whether he was about to poison or revive her. He handed Collin a cup of the brew. "Bottoms up!"

"Hold her!" Collin demanded. Bryce positioned the still lifeless body so that Collin could pour some of the bitter tea into her gaping mouth. The liquid began to bubble as it trickled down her throat. Then Collin opened a small bottle of aged blood and slowly poured it into her mouth. Bryce brought over a bowl and pitcher of water and gently washed her hair with a shampoo that smelled of coconut. Collin cracked open a small porthole window that had been blacked out and breathed in the night ocean air. They cleaned up all traces of her blood. Bryce tossed the bloody towels out of the porthole. Collin helped Bryce dress her in a long pale blue robe. "I hate seeing her this way."

Bryce responded, "Scheherazade prepared for any possibility. She amazes me." He glanced out the porthole. "Sunrise soon."

Collin closed the porthole and locked the compartment. Bryce handed him a sleeping bag. They laid down on either side of her on the floor. It would be a long day. Sleep did not come easily as they waited to see if she would revive. They would be the scourge of most of the Haute Caste whether she survived or not.

"This is a fine mess," Collin muttered.

Bryce's phone vibrated to wake him up just before sunset. He wanted to be the first to greet the vampiress. He stood over her and gazed at the seemingly lifeless form. They were all promised immortality when they transformed. She should not have been executed. The well-mannered vampire socialite felt anger and grief rise to the surface. As he touched her cold gray cheek, searing pain rocked him as her fangs tore into his wrist! "No!" he cried out and ripped his arm away from her grasp. Luckily, she was still weak. He wrapped a towel around his hand.

"Thanks for waking her up Bryce," Collin said sarcastically. He threw a bag of blood at Scheherazade, careful to stay out of her grasp.

She chugged it and demanded, "More!"

He handed her the second bag. "That's all there is my lady, unless you want to be dining off the crew. Though that might make it a wee bit difficult to get to India." Collin sucked out the little bit of blood remaining in the first bag.

She sat up slowly, still dizzy and confused, as the blood began to nourish her body and allow it to replenish her supply of vampire blood. "I remember Cesare ...."

"Sir Borgia and Lady Antoinella." Bryce replied, "They tried to destroy you. I watched them throw your head in the Thames, and I retrieved it."

Her hands went up to her neck and felt the stitches that preserved her existence. She felt an odd sensation, gratitude. "You have risked much to save me." She did not actually say thanks, but it was close.

"We're headed for the Port of Kandla," Collin told her. "We thought the Haute Caste might be more charitable towards you if you stay in India for a bit."

Scheherazade slowly swung her legs around off the table. Collin decided it might be a good time to get some fresh air. "I'll take a stroll...."

She grabbed him and threw him to the floor, then leaped on top of him. Scheherazade's ravenous hunger drove her to act like a wild animal. She bit his neck deeply and held down his arms as he tried to fight her off. She needed more blood than they had given her. Collin cried out, "Bitch!" He almost pushed her back, but blood loss made him weak, and he fell unconscious. Bryce shuddered as he shrank back against the cabin wall. He made his way to the door and escaped to the deck. "What had we done?" he asked himself.

A half-hour later, Scheherazade emerged, looking replenished. She approached Bryce as if nothing had happened. She had covered the stitches in her neck with a silk scarf. With a charming smile, she said, "I decapitated him. You may dump the pieces overboard." He just stared speechlessly. "I need you to be my chauffeur."

"Of course," he responded and went back into their compartment to take care of Collin's remains.

Chapter 19

The Parliament Meets

Manny had returned to Salinas and was in a bad mood. Molly had stopped by after work to check on him. She knocked, and he yelled, "Come in." He came out of the kitchen. "Hi Molly, thanks for watching Trouble."

"You're welcome. So, what's up? You ready to go back to work?" She plopped down on the couch, and Trouble jumped in her lap. The pudgy cat began purring. "Hey Trouble."

"I don't want to talk about it." He was clearly irritated.

"Aren't you expected back?"

"Why don't you become a cop? Then you could get paid for interrogating people."

"Manny!"

"Not now!'

"Okay," she got up in a huff. "Something is burning." Molly slammed the door as she left.

"Damn it!" He ran into the kitchen. His veggie burgers were smoking. He threw the pan in the sink. "Fuck!" His smoke alarm went off. He opened all the windows and tore the smoke detector off the ceiling. Trouble just stared at him from under a living room chair.

He almost started to cry, out of frustration and guilt, but crying was a cardinal sin in his family. Manny took a deep breath and sat on the floor near his cat. Trouble came out and curled up in his lap. He pulled out his phone and sent a text to Molly,

I get the asshole of the week award. Sorry!

A little while later, she texted back,

Come over for Mac-n-Cheese.

He went over to her place with a sheepish expression. She just shook her head and handed him a plate, and they sat at her kitchen table and ate in silence.

"If I tell you what is bothering me, do you promise not to say I've lost my mind?"

She could see how serious he was. "Manny, just tell me."

He related the strange scene in the parking lot of the Funeral Pyre. He stopped, wondering if it would be wise to go on.

"Are you bullshitting me? Were you drunk?" She pushed her plate away.

He shook his head. "I wish I was. I was stone-cold sober."

"He tore the head off of a snake?" she asked wide-eyed.

"Yeah! I have never seen so many freaks. One guy gets tossed over cars like he's a football and then just gets up and walks away. I could swear that snake-woman's neck was broken, but she acted like it was nothing."

"Then what happened? What did they tell you?"

"Miranda Ortega, the writer, told me to come to her house the next day, and she'd answer my questions." He omitted the part about handing his gun over.

"Did she?"

"Yeah, well, sort of. This is the part where you promise not to tell anyone what I'm going to tell you. Unless something happens to me."

Molly looked worried. "What've you got yourself involved in?"

"I'm not sure. I drove up to Granite Falls and met with her and Teri Park. Ms. Ortega started out telling me to forget all about it and go back to Salinas. When she realized that wasn't going to happen, things got even weirder. They tried to convince me that I was dealing with vampires." He waited for her response.

"Jerk! You had me scared for a minute. I was thinking organized crime or some kind of cult." She got up, picked up her plate, and put it on the counter. She turned back to Manny. "Vampires? Why not werewolves or zombies?"

"I'm not making this up. That's what she said. I told her that I thought they were involved in drug dealing, and she got extremely pissed."

"Baroness?" Molly turned and stared at him.

"Her ex is a Baron. Have you ever read any of her books?"

She leaned back against the counter, looked up at the ceiling, thinking for a minute. "Yeah! Years ago, I read a book about some hot, psychotic ghosts. That's her?" She sat back down at the table.

"Yeah. That's the woman who told me the people in front of the club were vampires."

Molly got her laptop out and googled the writer. The short bio on Wikipedia said she was married to Baron Tristan Mordecai, a publishing mogul. "Okay, she is a Baroness who also had a vampire romance bestseller. Maybe you should read it. What have you gotten yourself involved in?"

"I'm not buying the vampire crap she was trying to sell me. Maybe they are involved with some kind of new designer drug. That would explain the strength and recovery of those freaks. Maybe it isn't even illegal yet."

"I can't find even one picture online of the Baron and almost no info about him. How is that possible?" Molly exclaimed.

"I met him. In the middle of the night, one of his goons came to my hotel and said I had to see him right then or forget it." Molly's eyes got big. "I went to his mansion in Bel Air. It was unbelievable, servants, everything. He made some vague threats, and while we're talking, a black panther strolls into the room and

134

sits next to him. It's his fuckin' pet."

"Who is this guy? Who have you pissed off? Maybe you should let this go." She closed her laptop. "I'm serious. With that much money, he could make you disappear."

He bit his lip, sat quietly thinking, then responded, "I must have some kind of protection. Maybe 'cause I'm a cop. He could easily have made me disappear in L.A."

"Take the hint Manny. How many days leave do you have left?"

"Four."

"Let it go Manny. Go someplace where you can chill. I'll take care of Trouble." Molly did not like the smirk on his face.

"I think you're right. I'll go to Vegas."

"You're up to something. Maybe I should go with you."

He was not about to drag her into this. "I'll just see a show, do a little gambling, maybe go to Hoover Dam."

"Just don't gamble with your life," she said and hit him in the shoulder.

I got up early and sat out on the back deck to greet the sunrise. I rolled up the sleeves of my robe and held out my arms to the sunlight. An hour later, I was a little chilled but content. Nothing had changed. Sunlight still did not harm me. Good to know. Whatever happened during the fencing lesson did not seem to have made me less mortal. I went back inside and got breakfast ready for the kids. They ran through the kitchen, grabbing breakfast burritos and yelling something about a delivery. I followed them to find out what was going on.

Tomas stood in front of the garage, inspecting a dozen large boxes with fragile and flammable warning labels. "Tomas, what did you order?"

My son was stoked. "Wow, that was quick." He looked at his siblings. "Help me move this stuff into my lab."

"You have a lab?" I asked incredulously.

Des smiled. "He does now." He pointed to the garage. "Today, my brother, the mad scientist, begins his quest to invent the perfect sunscreen."

Teri came up and stood next to me. "Seriously?"

I had to ask, "For Lithuanians?"

Tomas laughed, "Yeah, so Dad can go outside during the day."

Marie added, "Our chemistry teacher, Mr. Cramer, used to work for a pharmaceutical company. He told Tomas what to order."

"It's my science fair project."

"How did you explain that to your teacher?" I asked.

"I told Mr. Cramer that my dad has solar urticaria, and I wanted to develop a sunscreen so people with that condition can go out in the sun," Tomas explained.

I felt in awe of the kids at that moment.

Teri picked up one of the boxes marked 'Flammable. "Don't blow anything up or burn the place down."

I looked at Teri. "I'm going to order a few fire extinguishers. Maybe I should talk with Mr. Cramer."

Teri said, "That is an excellent idea." I didn't know what was going on with the Henry mess, but she was in a better mood. Nothing like vampire love to make you psychotic.

Teri called out, "Okay guys, time for school. You can do your mad scientist thing later. In the car now."

That evening Sir Henry was waiting at the Baron's Seattle condo. He stood on the balcony, enjoying the view, and considering how much he loved being in Seattle, especially with Teri Park's arrival. Suddenly he was lifted several feet in the air. He tried to grab the balcony railing, but a force moved him out over the street so quickly he was left floating in the air. He looked around and saw the Baron standing in the patio doorway. Tristan's stare was pure malevolence. "Shall I crush you like you crushed Pomp's voice box? I'm sure you would heal, in time."

Pure defiance seized Henry. "You wish you could," he grinned. Then he put his hands together, and a small electrical charge broke the Baron's hold on him. As he started to fall, he spun himself towards the balcony below and surprised the downstairs neighbor's cat. Then he climbed back up to the Baron's condo and jumped down on the patio facing him. "Shall we talk? Or do you prefer more Haute Caste games?"

They settled in the living room, sitting across from each other. The Baron began, "The children are very fond of Teri. She is an important caretaker. The Baroness does not want you to seduce their bodyguard."

"And does the Baron also have an opinion on my sex life?" he asked, thoroughly amused.

"None. I have no problem with you having an affair with a mortal." Tristan signaled to Clive, who entered with two small plates of cubed raw steak and cups of blood.

"You had a relationship with a mortal. You must understand my attraction," Henry said.

They held up their glasses almost in a salute, then downed them.

Tristan continued, "The Baroness is hardly your average mortal. Her father is the Head of the House of Swords, and she has Templar blood. Teri is a very adept martial artist and remarkable with our children, but she is not part vampire." They began to eat the cubes of raw meat.

"You neglected to mention that she has HH blood. She could become a magnificent Haute Caste vampiress." Henry paused and looked at Tristan with a menacing gaze. "Stay out of the way of my relationship with Teri. If not, I will tell the Parliament about you plotting with Pomp, which resulted in the public display of our powers in front of the mortal detective."

"I will not bargain with you! I am not hiding my actions. You engaged in a false affair with my ex-wife to upset me. I allowed the truth to be known. Pomp helped expose your deceitful behavior and your affection for the mortal."

"At the risk of exposing our kind to police scrutiny. Don't you ever admit to making a mistake?"

Tristan bristled and pushed his plate away. "In fact, I do. I trusted Lena."

Henry raised his voice, "Lady Lena was magnificent! The jealous Haute Caste elite destroyed her because the great Magus felt threatened." He crushed the crystal glass in his hand and let the glass shards fall to the table.

Tristan stared at Henry. "Believe the fantasy. She tried to murder the Baroness and my daughter Marie." Henry looked unsure for a moment. "Lena saw them as a threat to our kind. She wanted to eliminate hybrid mortals and the Magus. Lena would have taken control of our world through treachery. She did not want children to be born to vampires. I respected her once. She used my blind devotion to deceive me."

Henry felt the sadness in Tristan's response, which he had not expected. Henry stood and said, "I have business with the Magus. I leave tonight. As to Teri Park, she will be the one to decide how our relationship progresses. I will abide by whatever she decides, and I expect the same of you and the Baroness."

"And with the blessing of the Magus, of course."

They merely nodded to one another, two ancient beings paying each other respect, then Henry departed. Tristan wanted to hate his age-old counterpart, but he could not. Their shared knowledge, abilities, and history made them vampire brothers. When he first heard that Miranda appeared to favor Henry, he was not happy, but at least she had chosen one of the ancient undead. Lena's ability to sew discord and upset the progress of the vampire world was still apparent given Henry's response. He wondered if there were still other vampires hoping for revenge on her behalf. He sent a text to the Magus,

Henry will visit soon. He seeks the truth about Lena. Welcome back.

Alexander had been listening from an adjoining room. He entered the living room and sat in a leather chair near the Baron. "Well, well, you upset the anarchist."

"Yes, honesty will do that," Tristan replied.

An ornate water-filled gold bowl sat in the middle of the coffee table. Alexander leaned forward to admire his reflection. His wavy shoulder-length brown hair nicely framed his cheekbones and expressive eyes, one blue and one green. People always stared the first time they met him, but he did not mind. He tore his gaze away and looked back at the Baron. "I cannot properly express my gratitude to you for allowing a meeting with Jacques."

"It's my son that you should thank."

Alexander did not mention that he was also Jacques' father. "You could have sent me away until he was an adult. I would have abided by your wishes as you have been honorable and merciful since my defeat."

Tristan regarded the ancient vampire with suspicion. Being flattered by Alexander made him want to take a shower and kill someone at the same time. "What are your intentions towards the Baroness?"

Alexander thought for a moment, searching for a truthful yet nonprovocative response. "I don't know. I hope she will allow me to become better acquainted with her."

Tristan smiled. "I will not interfere, but if you cause her a moment of displeasure, your punishment at the elephant refuge will seem like a holiday. Good night Alexander. I'll be with Pomp at the Four Seasons."

"Give her my regards."

Tristan stood. "It was at her behest that I'm allowing you to stay in my home. I'll give her your thanks as well."

"Of course," Alexander responded. Once Tristan left, Alexander pulled out his laptop and hacked into the security system at Miranda's property. He was able to see the kids taking Lug out for his last walk before bedtime. Alexander focused on the smallest figure. It was grainy, but he could make out Jacques. "My dynasty," he muttered.

The Haute Caste members of the vampire Parliament met online the next night. The Magus was back at his home on the cliff overlooking Paradise Cove near Malibu. He had slept well during his day flight and felt refreshed when his private Jet landed in Los Angeles that evening. Tristan went online from his mansion in Bel Air. After clearing several security barriers, his screen came up. The top row had a single dark box where the Magus' avatar would appear once everyone else was present. Below that, Tristan's Tarot identity/avatar was on the right. Anastasia, the High Priestess' avatar, was to his left.

The avatars of Lady Sarah (House of Plows, Toronto), Sir Omar (House of Swords, Qatar), Sir Cesare (House of Pentacles, London), Princess Khunbish (House of Cups, Mongolia), Sir Jorge (House of Arrows, Caracas) and Lady Kananga (House of Wands, Kinshasa) came on the screen.

At the bottom, two vampires shared the final square. They did not have HH blood and were the first members of the Parliament, other than Tristan and Anastasia, that were not Heads of Houses. They were the first members representing the Common Caste. The Magus had recently promoted them to Haute Caste status as a reward for their roles in the defeat of Alexander's coup attempt. Angel and Robert were sharing a computer in my office.

Angel's avatar wore a backward baseball cap and an Anaheim Ducks hockey team T-shirt.

Robert's avatar wore a frilly white shirt, black vest, and multiple gold rings on his fingers.

I was allowed to sit in the room with Robert and Angel to observe, a first for me. I was also told not to say anything during the meeting. That would also be a first for me.

Once everyone was online, the Magus' avatar lit up. He wore a red robe and had an eternity symbol pendant. All of the images were amazingly lifelike. It was as close as they could come to having their actual faces displayed. Ironically, the vainest creatures on the planet had no use for mirrors. I wondered if that would stop my kids from transforming. During Parliament meetings, the Magus insisted on following formal protocol, and all would be addressed by their titles, although

I rarely did. "Good evening to all of you. The Parliament is now open. I wish to extend my gratitude to Lady Kananga for taking care of my responsibilities while I was away. The beauty of the Congo has replenished me," the Magus informed them.

Lady Kananga nodded graciously.

Tristan asked, "Shall we discuss the incident in Seattle?" He wanted to put out his version first.

"You may begin," the Magus said. He was curious to hear how the Baron would spin the tale.

"I allowed Alexander and Scheherazade to be in Seattle after his premature departure from the elephant sanctuary and hers from Rossville. They were present at the Funeral Pyre when the Baroness and her bodyguard made an appearance. Sir Henry became upset when Scheherazade produced one of her pet snakes. Their struggle resulted in Alexander being tossed in the air over several cars and the snake being beheaded. A detective who has been following the Baroness witnessed the altercation. He fired his weapon at the snake's head, and fortunately, no Seattle police were involved. I take responsibility for Alexander and Scheherazade being present."

The Magus asked, "Is this the detective from Salinas who is investigating Lady Pauline's dispatch of the Worthy Target?"

"Yes."

Lady Sarah added, "Lady Pauline regrets not being more careful during that assassination and for not seeking approval ahead of time."

Sir Jorge spoke, "It is imperative to protect the Baroness and the children from undue police attention. Didn't Pompadour and Sir Henry know the detective was watching the club? How could they have allowed this public spectacle?"

"Sir Henry has asked me to speak on his behalf," Lady Kananga said and paused. The Baron was surprised that the rogue vampire had confided in her. The Magus nodded. "Sir Henry told me that Pomp allowed the scene at the club per the direction of the Baron, so he could see who Sir Henry would try and protect."

The Parliament was quiet for a very long minute. Finally, Omar broke the awkward silence. "For whom did he show the most concern?"

"Teri, the bodyguard," the Baron responded.

Angel found the nerve to speak, "She has HH blood. I understand that she is protected from transformation."

"All true Sir Angel," the Magus agreed.

Anastasia was more concerned with me. "I do not believe it is appropriate to set up a trap to discover if someone is attracted to another. I think the violation of the privacy of the Baroness is at the root of this embarrassing situation. It has exposed our kind to further scrutiny by this detective."

"Bingo!" I blurted out. Unfortunately, everyone heard me though they could not see me. The Magus decided to ignore my comment. Robert turned towards me and put a finger to his lips. Angel was trying not to laugh.

Sir Borgia added, "One positive outcome is that Scheherazade met a timely end in London."

"I wish that were true. She is now aboard a ship on her way to India." The

Magus informed them.

"That's not possible!" Sir Borgia exclaimed.

I was sitting on the edge of my seat. "What the fuck?" I muttered.

"I have contacts in London who have reported that two members of the House of Pentacles recovered her remains. I assume that they were successful in reviving her."

There was a moment of stunned silence. Sophie and Paul had reported their findings to Lady Kananga, who had spoken directly to the Magus. Lady Kananga did not want to embarrass Sir Borgia. She had hoped the Magus would have handled this situation more discretely. She also did not trust Borgia.

"I should have been informed!" Sir Borgia complained.

The Magus nodded. "I just learned of this traitorous act. My concern is where she will go. I fear she will head to the House of Cups because of her resentment of the Baroness and Sir Batu."

All waited to hear how Princess Khunbish would deal with the unwanted visitor. "My House will not allow her to cause any harm to Sir Batu to get to the Baroness. She will not escape justice."

"I do not doubt your ability to make her regret her behavior. For now, I will spare her life. We shall discuss this further at a later date." The Magus clearly wanted to end the discussion.

"Of course." Her avatar nodded consent.

"I should punish her! She is of my House! I must know more about who was involved." Sir Borgia was pissed and embarrassed.

The Magus stated calmly, "She is no longer your concern. Now, what about Sir Alexander?"

Wow! Smackdown by the Magus. "That must have pissed off Borgia." I thought.

Tristan spoke up, "Sir Alexander remains here as my guest. My son Jacques has granted him an audience."

"Princess Khunbish, what news of Sir Batu and Kyoto?"

"Magus, Sir Batu is showing intellectual and physical prowess beyond my expectations. Kyoto is humbly continuing his research while staying with the monks. Lady Lily has graciously been assisting him. We have found the first Worthy Target for Sir Batu. I feel he will be ready in the next few weeks."

I felt relief mixed with sadness. The tiny optimist inside me had hoped Batu would never actually bite anyone. I wondered how the Baron reacted to her report. Avatars did not show emotion. You had to pay close attention to their voices.

"Excellent!" the Magus said nodding.

"I have a request from Kyoto," Lady Khunbish went on, "he requires more blood for his studies. He is constructing a genetic family tree that requires blood from the Baron, the Baroness, Sir Omar, Sir Alexander, and all the offspring."

The Magus responded first, "I will leave the decision to cooperate to those involved. Please tell him that we will discuss his request."

The Baron answered, "I shall cooperate, and I have no doubt Sir Alexander will too, but I cannot speak for the others. I do not think the Baroness will agree."

Angel shot me a "don't do it look." I bit my tongue and shook my head. Kyoto did not request a sample from my mother. He may have rightly assumed I would never get her involved in his research, or maybe this was just an attempt to get blood from the kids and me.

"Is there any other business?" the Magus asked.

"I have a question from the Common Caste," Sir Angel said.

"Of course," The Magus responded.

"Will they be allowed Worthy Targets instead of always drinking from a bag?"

I never realized they were not allowed to assassinate criminals like the Haute Caste. It took guts to ask this in front of all the heads of the Houses.

"I will seriously consider your request Sir Angel."

Angel sat up a little taller in his chair.

"Good night to you all. May moonlight greet your waking."

The screen went blank.

Robert had a smug look on his face. "Billy owes me $50!"

"Billy bet Miranda would stay quiet?" Angel said in surprise.

"He understands the fairer sex less than I do." He went off in search of Billy.

Angel got up. "Lady Pauline and I are going to talk to Teri about Henry. Wish us luck."

After they both left, I sat and tried to collect my thoughts. I was sure Khunbish could handle Scheherazade, but still, she had been resurrected after a beheading. She was a tough and ruthless vampiress. At least she was not near my family. What was the Magus up to? He must know I would not allow him to get any samples of my children's blood. Lug wandered in and leaned against my leg. "Good boy," I patted his head. "You're the sanest member of this household." He looked up at me with soulful eyes like he agreed.

Henry was waiting in the Magus' living room for the Parliament meeting to end. Like many of the Haute Caste, he had a private jet, which allowed him to travel at his convenience. His phone chirped. Henry was surprised to see a message from one of the Mordecai children.

Leif gave me your #.
Call it off with Teri if you ever want a chance with me when I'm older.
Marie

"Indeed, a true Ortega-Mordecai." Henry had no idea that the little Baroness knew how the vampire world gossiped about who might stand a chance with her when she came of age. When he heard the story of Marie's kidnapping as a baby per Lena's orders, he immediately understood why. She was the key for a vampire to be part of the Mordecai royal dynasty. The clever young female now leveraged her availability in the future to save Teri.

Clever and somewhat ruthless. Adorable. Henry wondered if Marie's siblings knew. He guessed not. Teri had quite a fan club. "Amazing!" he said out loud.

"What is amazing?" the Magus asked.

Henry had been so wrapped up in his thoughts that he did not realize the ruler of their kind had entered. The Magus sat across from him, waiting for an answer. Henry knew the Magus too well not to be honest. "I just got this text." He held up his phone for the Magus to see.

He read it and looked surprised. It took a lot to surprise him. "So young and so aware. What will she be like when she matures fully? Now, what brings you here?"

"I came to discuss my relationship with Teri. I had thought that nothing was going to dissuade me from pursuing her, but now I don't know." Henry stood and walked to the large windows overlooking the garden that led to the cliffs over the ocean.

"If Teri desires to be in a relationship with you, and it does not interfere with her duties to the children, it will be allowed," the Magus pronounced solemnly.

Henry turned suddenly. "I am surprised that you have become so lenient about relationships with mortals."

The Magus glared at Henry then broke off eye contact. "You have my answer. You may leave now!"

Without another word, Henry left the Magus' mansion.

Chapter 20

Manny Goes to Vegas

Pauline was pissed. She paced the deck at Miranda's house. This was the first time Pauline had seen either Teri or Miranda since checking on them at the hotel in Salinas. "You have no idea who you're infatuated with," she told Teri emphatically. "One of his gifts is charm. He could make the Queen of England want to fuck him in front of an audience. Teri, you have got to believe me. This is a terrible idea."

"What if I want to become like you?" Teri looked at Pauline, hoping to stop the tirade.

"You can't transform because you're hot for someone! There's no going back. You must be sure you want nothing more than to be one of us for eternity."

Angel came out on the deck. He could see that Teri was close to tears. He went over to Pauline and said quietly, "I'll fill you in about the meeting later. Let me talk with her alone."

"Good luck!" Pauline said to Teri, walked over to her Triumph, and sped off.

Angel sat down next to Teri. She looked at him and asked, "Am I crazy?"

"No," he managed a smile. "Just under the spell of one of the most experienced lovers in history. Don Juan was an amateur compared to Sir Henry. He messes with your brain chemistry. Don't you feel a little hungover after having contact with him?" He looked at the sweet young woman and felt her struggling with the dark side of their reality.

"Yeah, but it made me want to spend more time with him. I don't think he is like this with everyone, I...."

Angel put one finger gently on her lips. "You didn't have that experience with me. He is a legend among the undead. Pomp is one of the few who can block his abilities. It's why she was his partner for so long. Did you hear what he did to her?" She shook her head. "He crushed her voice box and threw her out of the club because of the snake."

Teri looked shocked. "No, he wouldn't...."

"He is an ancient Haute Caste vampire, almost as powerful as the Baron. When he's pissed off, it's terrifying. You must have had a glimpse of that when he attacked Scheherazade." Angel had never seen Henry enraged, but he could imagine what it might be like.

"Will she be okay? I think he was just protecting me."

"She will be, in time, but her voice may never be the same again. You will too, but it's gonna feel like you're withdrawing from a drug. You gotta stay away from him." He felt her emotions close down as a wall of denial went up.

"Maybe we were meant to be together, like Miranda and Tristan."

"Yeah, that worked out great."

Her phone beeped, she looked at the message. "Angel, I've got to answer this."

Teri ran into the house, and Angel just shook his head. He had no doubt she would continue her relationship with Henry. Out of concern for her, Angel had secretly installed an app on her phone that enabled him to monitor her calls and texts. He opened the app on his phone and heard Teri talking to Henry.

"I have spoken with the Magus, and he understands my feelings for you. Please do not leave the children. They still need you. In time we will be together. I promise," Henry explained.

"They were wrong to try and get between us. When will I see you again?"

"Soon my love," Henry told her softly.

"Not soon enough," Teri declared.

Outside, Angel snarled, "Fuck Henry!" and threw his phone down. Luckily it landed on the grass. No one lied about the Magus, so it had to be true! He didn't get why.

Manny drove his beat-up old Mustang down a street of mansions in Las Vegas. The car Ms. Ortega had been driving in Salinas was registered to Omar Sadeghi, who lived on Winter Palace Drive. Manny knew he would probably annoy some rich asshole, but he had to check out any possible leads. Manny was running out of ideas and time. Someone knew who killed the Pill King, and he was sure it was not a vampire. Manny arrived at a modern white palace with columns and a fountain in front, topped with a bronze eagle wearing a small crown. He got out of his car and went up to the heavy double doors. Before he could even knock, a butler opened the door and motioned him inside. He guessed they had high-tech security. He started to say, 'I'm....'"

The butler interrupted, "Detective Takeda, follow me."

He was shown to a library; as an avid reader, he was amazed by the number of books lining the walls, including Arabic titles and a few other languages. He was so absorbed in the collection that he didn't realize a man dressed in flowing white robes, trimmed with gold embroidery, had entered and had been watching him for several minutes.

"Please be seated," Sir Omar gestured toward a grouping of a burgundy velvet sofa and chairs.

"Thanks," Manny replied and sat. He was a little embarrassed that he had not seen or heard anyone enter the room. He noticed a sword almost out of sight, hanging at the man's side. He wondered if that was a normal custom. The man said nothing more and stared at Manny. "I was hoping to speak with Mr. Sadeghi,"

Manny finally said.

"I'm Omar Sadeghi."

"I'm with the Salinas Police Department," he said, although he was sure Sadeghi already knew all about him. "Do you own a black Range Rover?"

"Actually, five."

"Excuse me?"

"I own five, though a relative has taken one to Granite Falls."

"Did you drive..."

"I never drive."

"We have an uninvited visitor?" Manny turned and saw Anastasia, coldly staring at him from the door to the library. The exquisite platinum blonde woman wore a black lace blouse and mini skirt. He thought she must be in films.

"Yes, but he was not unexpected. Detective Takeda, this is Ms. Romanov."

Manny stood and felt like he should bow. "Hello. I'm sorry if I have inconvenienced you." He felt the need to be highly polite.

"Be seated," she commanded, and he did. Anastasia sat on the sofa next to Sadeghi. Manny guessed they were a couple.

The butler entered and asked, "Tea or coffee sir?"

"Coffee, please." Neither Sir Omar nor Lady Anastasia responded. "I'm sorry to bother you both, but a black Range Rover was seen leaving the scene of a murder in downtown Salinas. The same night a woman by the name of Miranda Ortega-Mordecai was in Salinas. She had a black Range Rover that is registered to you."

"Do you have a question?" Anastasia asked.

The butler returned with a silver coffee set. He poured coffee into a delicate porcelain cup. Manny took the cup and said, "Thanks." The butler left. Manny's hand had a tiny tremor as he took a sip. What was it about these people that made him anxious? The coffee gave him a moment to calm down. He took a sip of coffee then asked, "Did anyone else drive one of your Range Rovers to Salinas that night?"

Omar smiled. The detective was brighter than he expected. "Yes. One of my friends had checked on my family members that night to make sure they had traveled safely to Salinas. She did not stay long and drove back here." Vampires disliked dishonesty even when dealing with mortals. He was concerned a traffic camera might have picked up Pauline's car, and he did not want to appear to be hiding anything. Omar knew Tristan had tried to warn the detective off and was surprised by Manny's tenacity. "You have spoken to Ms. Ortega and the Baron. Still, you pursue my family. May I ask why?"

"Because he is an idiot!" Anastasia abruptly stood up and walked out.

Manny stared at Sadeghi. "Because you all act as if you want me just to walk away from a murder investigation as if nothing happened."

"Our family values its privacy. You have nothing but a vehicle seen in the vicinity. Are there no other black Range Rovers in California?"

"A gas station attendant saw a woman in a similar vehicle with Nevada plates that night. What is the name of the friend who was in Salinas?"

"Her name is Pauline. I'll ask her to contact you."

He decided not to ask for a last name. Something else was bothering Manny.

"Mr. Sadeghi, how are you related to Ms. Ortega?"

With a flat affect, he responded, "She is my daughter."

Manny stared at a man who looked about thirty years old. "Seriously?" he blurted out. He could not help himself.

"I think I have answered enough of your questions."

The room suddenly felt colder. Manny held out his card. "Here is my...."

"No need," Sadeghi replied. "We know where to find you. I advise you to go home now. Good night, Detective." He rose and left Manny alone.

The detective scanned the glass coffee table. Neither of them had touched anything. There was no chance of lifting a fingerprint. It probably wouldn't be a good idea anyway.

The butler appeared in the doorway and said, "I'll show you out, sir."

Manny slowly got up and followed the butler out. The luxurious home did not provide any clues as to the source of their wealth. He thought maybe Sadeghi was from an OPEC country. Anastasia was gorgeous. She was probably Miranda's stepmother, so there was no point in trying to question her. Manny decided that Omar Sadeghi must have spent a fortune on plastic surgery to look so young. He would check into a hotel for the night. Manny was not about to abandon his investigation.

Teri and the kids were in the barn putting their gear away after a fencing lesson. I was in my room writing when the offspring had surrounded Guillaume and demanded to talk. He told me about the incident with them later that night.

He gestured for them to pull up chairs. Teri stayed to listen out of curiosity. Tomas began, "Guillaume, we have some questions about the family. The vampire side."

"Go on," Guillaume said.

Marie continued, "We want to know everything. We want to know what's true. There are so many myths that we aren't sure what to believe. The only thing that seems true is staying out of sunlight. Is silver actually toxic to you?"

Des added, "And the whole having to be invited in, or can't be around crosses, or being repelled by garlic, shape-shifting into bats, and not crossing running water. What's that all about?"

Guillaume smiled. "I think you've been watching too many old movies. You saw the film *Nosferatu*?" They all nodded except Teri. "The Magus advised one of the writers. He was not happy when the vampire was depicted as a bloodthirsty hideous gnome."

"I thought it was funny," Marie remarked.

"Sunlight is dangerous to us. Our skin cells have lost the ability to tolerate exposure to the sun, and we are hypersensitive to ultraviolet rays. We don't get a sunburn; we fry."

"I'm going to find a way to prevent that," Tomas declared in a serious tone.

"I wish you success." Guillaume smiled. "The idea that we have to be invited in is Victorian rubbish. We are not prone to asking mortals permission for anything except permission to transform them. Shorts invented the idea that they could ward us off by using a cross. It made them feel like they had some kind of supernatural protection. Some of us had to escape from a grave after our families had buried us. There were a lot of crosses surrounding me when I woke up."

Des asked, "You had to dig yourself out of your own grave?"

"That's messed up," Jacques remarked.

Guillaume explained, "Your father was one of the Haute Caste who helped me escape from my coffin. It was important for my family to believe I was dead." He looked grim. "To answer your other question, we are quite sensitive to scent, and the smell of garlic is just annoying. The shape-shifting myth arose from our speed of movement."

Guillaume suddenly disappeared and Tomas exclaimed, "Where did he go?"

"Over here!" the vampire called from across the room. In a flash, he was back in his chair.

You're even faster than Dad!" Jacques observed.

"Stoker decided to write that we had turned into bats to explain our sudden escapes. Personally, I don't mind being compared to such noble creatures."

Marie smiled.

"It used to be more difficult to cross water. We have to travel at night. In ancient times, bridges were few and far between. Crossing a river at night by torchlight is difficult and often resulted in slips and falls. You can see how that might be bothersome."

"Do you really like the taste of blood?" Jacques asked quietly.

They all stared at Guillaume. "Yes. It is a salty delight that revitalizes us. Though I threw up the first time I drank a cup. It is, as they say, an acquired taste."

Teri touched the tiny marks on her throat, quickly removed her hand, and left the barn. Guillaume noticed but said nothing.

"Any more questions?"

"What about silver?" Des asked. "Sarah wears silver rings."

"Lady Sarah," Guillaume replied, "prefers jewelry designs significant to her house in this new world. However, although it looks like silver, her settings are platinum. Though it will not kill us, silver can cause a severe allergic reaction to a member of the Haute Caste. If wounded with a silver weapon, it takes longer to heal if you have HH blood. The Common Caste can wear silver but prefer gold to be like the Haute Caste."

Marie looked at the bracelet on her wrist that had been her grandmother's. "It's not affecting me."

Guillaume smiled. "One only becomes sensitive after transformation."

Marie asked their ancient tutor, "Do you ever want to die?"

He stared at her with a satisfied grin. "Marie, you are a most philosophical young person. That is the point of all this, isn't it? Did I make a mistake? Do I regret transforming?" He leaned forward and touched her cheek. "Being French, I only regret having to give up cheese."

Marie looked displeased. She was not satisfied with his answer.

Des remarked, "So would Mom and Leif."

Tomas asked, "What do you fear?"

Guillaume responded with a sad smile, "We fear two things, sunlight and permanent beheadings. I believe I have given you much to think about. That is all for tonight, mes enfants!"

I was surprised by how subdued the kids were that night when they came into the house after their fencing lesson. Tomas told me that Guillaume wanted to talk to me. I walked across the yard and stopped for a few minutes to watch the moonlight shimmer on the water. I inhaled the wonderful calming scent of the towering fir trees and listened to the river splashing over the rocks. These moments always comforted me and brought me peace. I walked over to Guillaume's house and knocked on the door.

He called out, "Entrée!"

Guillaume had decorated the living room with French Provincial furnishings. He chose colors in shades of light blue. A big difference from the dark heavy furniture and red and black drapes that the Magus and Tristan fancied. Guillaume gestured for me to be seated, then went into his kitchen. After a few minutes, he returned with a perfect Cappuccino in a beautiful bone china cup for me and a small cup of espresso for him.

Madame," he bowed, then placed the glorious brew before me. "Let us enjoy our coffee before we talk."

He appeared amused as I inhaled the wonderful aroma. "This is amazing? Where do you get the beans?"

"Bellingham, it's Tony's coffee. I have it delivered the day after the beans are roasted."

"Will you double your order?" I put down my mug.

"Bien sur."

"What's on your mind?" I sat back and looked at his kind face. Guillaume did not have the aura of darkness I usually detected with the other undead. He told me about his conversation with the kids. "I thought they were getting close to asking about how we choose Worthy Targets. I stopped the discussion before they got up the nerve."

"Thank you. I know they are mature for their ages, but I don't want them to dwell on that aspect of your reality."

"Miranda, I have something else to tell you. Jacques is very curious about the Templar side of the family. I was relieved he did not ask me about that tonight. His research will not find a Guillaume de Molay." His expression was earnest.

"Are you saying we aren't related?"

"I did not lie about our familial ties, but I was not born Guillaume."

I was not connecting the dots. "What's your real name?"

"Giselle," he answered and waited for my reaction.

"But that's a woman's...." I stared at him.

"Yes. I arrived in a female body, but it was not a good fit." Guillaume paused, giving me time to process this information. "More coffee?" he finally asked.

"No. No, thank you." I looked at his handsome features and saw a man. "You're transgender?"

"I'm a man who was once mistaken as a woman. When I was fifteen, I often dressed in men's clothing. My excuse was that I worked in a stable, and it was easier. Over time I wore male attire more than skirts. I was just considered odd and left alone by people who knew my family. Being connected to the Knights Templar was secretly respected. When I was eighteen, some soldiers tried to rape me to make me act like a woman. They came out of the local inn, drunk, and attacked me when they came to the stable for their horses. I tried to fight them, but they acted out their rage against life on me. Just when I thought I was about to die, the violence suddenly ceased."

I stared at Guillaume wide-eyed.

"Shall I continue?"

"Yes! What happened?"

"A vision in white robes began slashing the rapists with a long sword. At first, I thought he was an angel sent to take me to heaven. He moved so quickly I barely saw him cut them. Then blood started spraying from their throats on the walls and straw-covered floor. The horses bolted from their stalls. I looked up, and there was Sir Omar. The Magus stepped out from behind him. He extended a hand and helped me get to my feet. I was shaking and started to throw up. The Magus supported me, so I would not fall over. The world went black. I woke up in a fine carriage and was taken to a chateau that belonged to the Baron."

"My father and the Magus saved you?"

"I'm descendent of Jacques de Molay. We are blessed and cursed by our bloodline."

"You can say that again. I also tend to throw up at the sight of blood."

Guillaume displayed a tiny smile. "I got over that. The Baron was the same then as he is now. He had difficulty understanding my nature. The Magus showed remarkable insight and insisted I start a new life among them as Guillaume. In time I requested to be made a vampire by Sir Omar. As the centuries passed, the nocturnal world only knew me as a man. As medical interventions became available, I was able to change my body to fit my true identity."

"Wow," was all I could say.

"Do you wish the children to know? If not, I could tell Jacques my birth records were destroyed." There was a palpable sadness in his voice. My eyes were tearing up.

I gently touched his hands. "Guillaume, think about it. They've accepted that their dad and grandpa are vampires. You being transgender may surprise them, but it is something they can handle. You can tell them whenever you are ready."

He gently took my hands and said, "Merci beaucoup Baroness."

"So why did my ex want you to watch over us? I mean, besides being family."

"I love Jeanne. I met her shortly after I was transformed. She is with Sir Bartholomew now, but she may come back to me some night. I have never been with another."

"After all these centuries, that's devotion." Guillaume and Bartholomew were similar in their simple monk-like lifestyles, very unusual for the undead. They were both lost in love with a saint. Unlike Bart, Guillaume was very attentive to his appearance. "Tristan knew you would never mess around with me. I bet he was shocked when he could not seduce you."

Guillaume grinned. "It was a very long time ago, but I do recall he attributed my refusal to a rare medical condition."

"Ha! I'm surprised he didn't say that when we got divorced."

That night I lay on my bed and thought about Guillaume's courage, that he had no one to turn to for support and acceptance until the vampires intervened. The Magus had rescued him, understanding what it was like to live as an outcast, being harassed and threatened. I would never have known Guillaume was born Giselle and had been through two transformations. The many worlds within him explained his compassion and why he was never quick to judge others. I was grateful for his positive influence on the children and wondered what their reaction to Guillaume's secret might be. Des would probably say, "That's cool!" and the others would feel the same way. The undead world was full of the weird and unusual. Ironically, this was one of the more ordinary things that our family had encountered.

Chapter 21

Alexander Makes Amends

"I require more blood," Kyoto said humbly to Princess Khunbish and Steve.

They sat on cushions around a low table in her palace, two hours after sunset. She stared at the once-proud samurai. His show of humility barely concealed his nobility.

Steve spoke up, "The Magus agreed to help with your research."

"I would like to discuss this with him directly," Kyoto replied. He looked at the Princess, then lowered his gaze.

"I might arrange that if you give me a good enough reason. How will your research benefit my House?" Khunbish said.

Kyoto smiled. "I notice you did not invite Batu. Do you not wish him to know of my hematology studies?"

The Princess shifted on her cushion and adjusted her jeweled headdress. Steve waited for her to answer. She looked at Kyoto. "My knight, Sir Batu, might be swayed by his attachment to the Baroness. Sir Steve can be more objective about your work. Tell us why we should continue to support your research."

"Her blood has many interesting properties. Lady Lily and I have studied the Baroness' blood since her birth. Think about how her blood diminished the powers of Alexander. There is a biological civil war within her body. Her vampire nature tries to assert itself, but it is held in check by her mortal nature. Every blood sample shows her to be an evolving species. I'm certain it is the same for the offspring, but without samples of their blood, I can only hypothesize."

Steve could see that the Princess was becoming frustrated. He pressed Kyoto, "Fascinating, but how could this research help our House?"

Kyoto cleared his throat, then went on. "I believe the royal blood would have an interesting effect on the Common Caste who dare act against the Haute Caste."

She leaned forward. "Continue."

"The Haute Caste powers are diminished by Miranda's blood. I believe the Common Caste would have their vampire natures destroyed, reducing them to mortals if they did not perish. Without research, I can only guess how they might react. There are many variables, and of course, how the aspect of age might play a factor. Think of it as a merciful alternative to beheading them. I suspect that the this evolution is more pronounced in the children."

The Princess smiled. "Though I prefer the rebellious and ungrateful among the Common Caste to be totally eliminated, I do appreciate the cruelty of your mercy." She gestured to Steve. "Allow him to call the Magus."

Sophie and Paul anxiously waited for an audience with Lady Kananga. Before leaving London for the Congo, she was questioning the Common Caste one by one. They were doing their best to act as if they had never associated with Scheherazade. Every member of the House swore their loyalty to the Magus. Sophie and Paul were the last to be seen. They noticed that all who left her presence seemed beaten down and relieved to be leaving in one piece.

"You two are next. She'll see you both together. Good luck," Lady Kananga's aide told them.

Kananga sat in a high-back velvet chair wearing an orange caftan embroidered with gold thread. She was regal without trying. "Sit!'" she pointed to a pair of wooden chairs.

Paul said, "Good evening." He wore all black for this solemn occasion.

Sophie forced a smile. "Lady Kananga, we are honored." Centuries ago, Sophie had been a lady in waiting at the court of King Henry the Eighth. She knew all too well that displeasing people in power could have terrible consequences.

"What have you found out?" Kananga demanded.

Paul started to talk, but Kananga raised a hand to stop him.

Sophie took the hint. "Scheherazade is in India. Her ship landed in an industrial port. I do not know her current whereabouts. Only one of the Pentacles survived. She attacked Collin and threw his body overboard. Bryce escaped from her when the ship made port. He sent us this message before disappearing. Here is his last text." She handed her phone to Kananga.

> *Terrible mistake!*
> *Perhaps I will ask for forgiveness in 100 years.*
> *She is mad and treacherous.*
> *I do not know her plan. I shall disappear now.*
> *Your Pentacle brother, Bryce.*

Kananga handed back the phone. "You have confirmed what I had already heard. You will tell me if he contacts you again."

"Of course."

"Our world is changing due to the mortals who we have accepted into our world. The repercussions are only starting to be known. I share this with you because I want you to understand how the royal family's welfare impacts the Common Caste. It was the Baroness who spared Scheherazade. How that act of mercy will play out, only time will tell.

I had long desired to see some of you granted Haute Caste status. A few of the Common Caste have protected the Royals and fought for the Magus. That caused him to see the Common Caste in a different light. Your loyalty is paramount to the

152

survival of our society and the continued promotion of the Common Caste. The unique powers of the Haute Caste offer vital protection to all of our kind from ambitious mortals who hunt us."

Paul observed, "We need each other."

Kananga nodded. "Precisely."

They had no idea that the cold Lady Kananga and other nobles had their backs or appreciated them. They had always felt like beggars at the undead table.

Sophie bowed, then raised her head. "We are honored to be of service to you and the Magus. We shall let the others know how the Royals and Haute Caste value our role in society."

Kananga was pleased. "Did you know that Sir Robert and Sir Angel participated in the Parliament meeting, representing the Common Caste?"

"We had heard rumors, but no one believed it," Paul told her.

"I will be returning to the Congo tomorrow night. Sophie, I leave you in charge until Sir Borgia returns." Sophie's eyes got big. "If anyone should question your authority, show them this." She handed Sophie a gold lion's head pendant with diamond eyes. "Sir Borgia looks forward to working more closely with the Common Caste of his House."

"I am honored!" Sophie said in a hushed voice.

"Sophie, you are quite capable and intelligent." She turned to Paul. "I have heard that you are a skilled masseuse. I would like a back rub."

"Of course." he looked a little anxious.

"Relax, I chose you because all I desire is a back rub."

She picked up a small bottle of spice-scented oil and handed it to him. Then she let her caftan fall off her shoulders to her waist. She was exquisite. As regal when she was half-naked as when she wore fine robes. She moved to a backless chair. "Begin."

Sophie tried not to laugh as Paul almost dropped the oil. He took a deep breath to calm himself.

"Sophie, you would do well to become better acquainted with Lady Antoinella. The Baroness fought Scheherazade to protect her. Despite some earlier doubts, it is clear she is loyal now."

Sophie commented, "It is amazing that the Baroness would protect the Common Caste."

"She is American. She struggles with her royal status, and she is raising the offspring with the same egalitarian views. Of course, she has no idea of the impact she and the children have on our world. Paul that feels fantastic."

"Thank you for telling us about the Baroness," Sophie responded. "Until tonight, we only heard rumors of her attacking vampires she did not like. A mythical mortal who fought the undead."

"And won the heart of Baron Mordecai," Paul added.

"All that is true, but she only attacked those who tried to harm her or her children." Kananga decided to let them be in awe, though the relationship with the royals was hardly that simple. "Thank you, Paul. Your skill is extraordinary. Good night." She pulled up her caftan. Paul blushed a tiny bit, which is very uncommon for a vampire. The Common Caste vampires bowed and left without another word. Once outside on the street in Knightsbridge, Paul held out his hands and said, "These hands massaged Lady Kananga. Her skin was so soft and beautiful. Her muscles so perfectly defined...."

"Are you still gay?" Sophie asked with mock concern.

"Of Course! Don't be ridiculous," He scoffed.

"Hey, speak to me with the proper respect." As she fingered the gold pendant.

"Don't be getting too full of yourself. I was the one who got to touch her," he said smugly.

They walked down the boulevard lined with beautiful old homes. Sophie declared, "One day I'll own one of these mansions. I will!"

"Loyalty has its rewards," Paul replied. "Poor Bryce! I imagine he's living in some hovel where he has to scrounge for a decent bloody meal. What a fool!"

They hurried off to the club to share all they had been told with the others of the House of Pentacles.

I drove into Seattle with Jacques to prepare for his meeting with Alexander. I vetoed Tristan's plan to have Guillaume bring him because I wanted to monitor their interaction. I had to be sure that my son would have a natural response to his biological father without Alexander using any vampire telepathic charisma shit. We went to Pike Place Market for dinner before heading over to Tristan's condo.

With four kids, it was rare to have any one-on-one time with any of them. We sat at a table looking out on the beautiful Sound as the sunlight faded. I munched on a plate of hummus while Jacques devoured fish tacos. "Are you okay? We can cancel this and just go home. Whatever you want."

He took a bite, chewed it slowly, then swallowed. He carefully wiped his mouth with a napkin, then folded it and placed it back in his lap.

"Mom, I want to talk to him." Then he proceeded to finish the rest of his dinner.

"I never told you this before, but you do bear a resemblance to him. Except both of your eyes are the same color."

Jacques was quiet during the rest of the meal. I looked out on the darkening sky and prepared to be a lioness if needed tonight. I did not trust Tristan's judgment. I was sure his motive was to strengthen his relationship with Jacques and show Alexander as a lesser vampire. Alexander got the name "The Great' while still mortal. We finished our meal and walked to Tristan's condo.

Clive greeted us at the door. I was always happy to see the enhanced mortal who had known me since I first entered the world of vampires. Before the kids were born, the Common Cast vampiress, Simone, attacked Tristan out of jealousy at Point Mugu, and Clive had protected me. Since then, he and his brother Jasper, Tristan's chauffeur, had been injured a few times protecting me and the offspring. I owed them a debt that I could never repay. Clive remained a stoic, very polite Brit. He was always meticulously groomed from his thin mustache to his crisply pressed suit.

"Good evening Baroness Mordecai, and young Baron Jacques."

"Hi Clive, good to see you," Jacques said and started to shake his hand, but Clive indicated that would not be proper.

We went into the living room. Alexander rose from the couch, and Tristan made his entrance as we walked in. My keen sense of smell was almost overwhelmed as male hormones filled the room. It felt like two bucks about to fight for dominance. Some things didn't change when males were transformed. Alexander's wavy shoulder-length hair looked vintage rock star. He wore black leather pants and a tight T-shirt ripped down the front showing his muscular body. Tristan wore a navy silk suit and a barely buttoned white shirt. His long pale mane framed his aristocratic face perfectly. It was like a contest of who could out macho the other.

Jacques stopped in his tracks. He could feel the friction between the two males. I coaxed him, "It's okay, just sit down."

"Hello Jacques, it is so good to finally have a chance to speak with you."

"Yeah, sure. Hi." He sat across from Alexander.

Tristan walked up behind Jacques and patted his shoulders. "Your mother and I will be in the next room."

We walked into the dining room. I sat in a chair that allowed me to see Jacques through the doorway, but I could not hear what they were saying. Tristan sat beside me and touched my hand lightly. It was enough to send a little electric shock through my system. "Stop it!" Then more softly, "You're such a fucker."

"It would be my pleasure."

I moved to another chair to put some space between us. "What kind of agreement have you made with Alex?"

"We will abide by Jacque's wishes. I am confident that my relationship with him will be stronger than anything he establishes with that sperm donor."

I was uncomfortable with that last comment. "Your description might be apt, but please don't use that expression around Jacques or me."

"Sensitive, are we? That surprises me. Though Alexander does tend to get under people's skin."

"What is wrong with you?" I stood and went into the kitchen.

Clive asked, "Coffee Baroness?"

"Yes, please, and some silver bullets."

His eyes got wide. "Madame?"

"Just coffee." I went back into the dining room. "For Jacques' sake, Tristan, try not to be an asshole."

We sat in silence, though Tristan barely concealed a smirk. Clive brought me the coffee and freshly baked chocolate croissants. Heaven!

Tristan finally said, "I miss you. I did not mean to be offensive, though what the Magus has decided will be worthy of your scorn."

"Cut the 'I miss you' crap. What did the Magus decide now?" I took a big swig of coffee. I know I sounded harsh, but I could not leave him any doubt about my conviction to stay apart.

He looked at me with those amazing river blue eyes, and I had to swallow quickly to avoid coughing. He was still the most strikingly handsome man I had ever known. And the most aggravating. "The Magus will allow Henry to pursue a relationship with Teri, providing it doesn't get in the way of her care for the children."

"And you agree with that?"

"Teri is an adult and capable of making her own decisions about her intimate life."

"Henry is not the guy next door. He's an emotional predator who has found a victim with HH blood," I responded.

"Perhaps he truly cares for her. It would not be the first time a vampire has fallen for a mortal."

"Yeah, and they'll ride off on unicorns to their castle in the sky. You and the Magus make it hard for me to like vampires."

"The Magus wishes to meet with you."

"What about?" I knew this had to be important.

"I'll let him tell you."

"Then his lowness will have to come to Seattle. Excuse me. I'll be on the balcony so I can be alone." I grabbed a chocolate croissant. Tristan sat there with a self-satisfied grin. He was glad to still get a reaction out of me. Outside I took a deep breath. "What the fuck!" I hoped Jacques was having better luck.

Alexander waited for Jacques to speak. His father, King Phillip II, had been distant, and fear of him had caused his mother to flee the royal court with a young Alexander. His father was assassinated when Alexander was twenty, which put him on the throne. He wished to have a better relationship with his son. Jacques stared at the ancient vampire. "What should I call you?"

He smiled. "I was called Alexander III of Macedon of the Argead dynasty, Hegemon, Shahan Shah, Alexander the Great, and other titles."

"You had a lot of names."

"I ruled over most of the known world. A son was born after the world believed I had perished. I never knew him. The title of father pleases me more than my other names. You may call me that or whatever name you feel comfortable with."

Jacques was aware the conqueror had difficulty with rejection. It was strange to think he was Alexander the Great's Achille's heel. "I'll call you Alex."

"Very well. I did not get along with my father. I hope that you and I shall be closer. What do you want to know?"

"I read about you. I was surprised you were married three times. I just thought you liked, you know, Uncle Franco and that Hephaestion guy."

Alexander expected questions about his military conquests, not his sex life. "Your curiosity is interesting. Hephaestion was my closest life-long friend and advisor. He was like my twin. We were one soul in two bodies. The historians have misconstrued our close friendship. I trusted him with my life." He paused and then continued, "I have always chosen my partners based on intellectual and sensual affinity with me. For the most part, I have been with women because their emotional insight intrigues me, and of course, I wanted an heir. However, a few men have been important to me. Sir Franco was useful for my plans. Sometimes relationships also serve political purposes."

"Like wanting an heir? I'm not Alexander the fourth."

"No. You are Jacques Omar." He smiled. "You and Hann's damned elephants

156

defeated me." His voice got a little loud. "Do you realize that is my only defeat?"

Jacques sat back. "Yes." He smiled. "That was awesome."

"I have no kingdom to share with you," Alexander said.

"But you know a lot. Hann said I should listen to you." Jacques did not like to see him downcast. "I called him about meeting you tonight. He thought it was a good idea."

Alexander's eyes lit up. He offered his hand across the table. "You'll allow me to teach you?"

Jacques shook his hand rather formally. "Yes. As long as you don't try to overthrow the Magus again."

"Even a brilliant military commander can learn from a mistake, though if not for those great beasts, my plan may have succeeded. I want you to know that I would not have assassinated the Magus. I would have made him an honored advisor. I just built the guillotine to impress others of my capability." He watched Jacques' response to his confession carefully.

"I believe you. It would've been stupid to destroy the one guy who knows the most about vampires. And you're not dumb. But you didn't promise not to go after him again."

Alexander smiled. "I will not act against the Magus unless it is to protect you."

Jacques was surprised by the response, but he liked it. "The Magus protects us."

"Just know you have another protector. Jacques, you are the only family I have in this world," Alexander confessed with a sad smile.

Jacques had not thought of that. He was glad he had a lot of relatives. "It sucks that you're so alone."

"Not anymore."

"Do you still want your Pug back?" Jacques asked.

Alexander considered how Connie had claimed his beloved Pug, when Jorge had abducted her, to punish him for having an affair with Franco. "I miss Lady Penelope, but I will not take her from your grandmother. I know she takes good care of her."

"Yeah, you're smart not to mess with Grandma. She calls her Piglet, after Winnie the Pooh's friend."

"I'm not acquainted with Winnie. I still prefer Penelope, but I'm sure she does not care by which name she is called." Alexander looked at his son. He was mystified by the things Jacques was curious about. "You want to know about my intimate relationships and whether I love my dog? Have you no questions about my military conquests?"

Jacques shrugged. "Oh, I read about those. Conquering Persia was lit! You were a badass!"

"Thank you," Alexander accepted the compliment with a satisfied smile.

Jacques wanted to end the first visit before it got uncomfortable. "It's about time to go. I'll see you again soon." Jacques went to say goodnight to Tristan. Alexander looked over and saw Miranda on the balcony.

I heard the sliding glass door open, and without turning around, I said, "Tristan, not now."

"Might I have a few words with you?" Alexander asked.

I turned to see the handsome, powerful vampire humbly asking to speak with me.

"Why not."

He approached me slowly as though trying to see how close I would allow him to stand. When he was a foot away, he stopped. I could smell his light, almost floral scent. He smiled, aware that I was taking stock of him. "May I call you Miranda?"

"I don't care what you call me. How did it go with my son?"

"Excellent! He is remarkable, intelligent, and kind." The mighty conqueror looked pleased. "He would like to continue our talks. I feel it is important to have your permission."

This was different. It is rare for vampires to ask for permission of a mortal. I remembered Alexander was a brilliant tactician. This was the perfect approach to use with me. "You never cared about my permission before." I glared at him. "You don't have to try and win me over. This is about you and Jacques. It's up to him."

His gaze was intense and compelling. "What I did to you was wrong. I do not deserve your forgiveness. I am forever in your debt."

"You and Kyoto used my body for an experiment!"

"I will do anything; take any punishment you deem necessary for my transgression." The sadness in his eyes was getting to me.

"I just want you to be decent to my son." I felt drawn to him. He was not using any undead power of attraction like Henry. This was pure natural charisma.

"I will do everything to protect him and all of your children." Alexander gently touched my cheek, and I let him. "It's not just about Jacques. I want to please you in any way I can. I will do anything to earn the privilege of spending time with you."

He leaned forward and gently kissed me. I allowed the intimate moment, but I'm not sure why. The tenderness, the restrained passion, was exciting. I felt a sensual volcano stirring below his façade of polite control. He started to pull me closer, but I broke away. He did not try to stop me.

Jacques came out on the balcony with Tristan. By the looks on their faces, they had seen us. "Let's go Mom."

158

Chapter 22

Batu's Initiation

Teri stared at me in the kitchen with her eyes big as saucers. "Alexander the Great came onto you?"

"Yeah, well, I had his kid," I tried to sound calm. Seriously, I was a mess. I picked up a mug of coffee and sat down at the table across from her. "He just started talking to me on the balcony, and one thing led to another. He is a clever fucker."

"I guess. What's he like?"

"Like riding in a Rolls Royce naked. That's how he made me feel with one kiss. It felt like his natural self, not a vampire on steroids." I stopped, not wanting to get into a comparison with Henry.

"And?"

"That's all. It was glorious for a few seconds, but I'm not in the market for another egomaniac vampire. Been there, done that."

Teri grinned. "That's why we're talking about him at two in the morning. Got it. Tristan must have been pissed."

"That was a bonus, but I hated to see the confused look on Jacques' face. I heard the Magus approved of you seeing Henry, so there's not much else anyone can say." Teri grinned. "I'll see him Saturday at the club. Guillaume said he'll look out for me while Henry is on stage."

"Just be careful," I said even though I knew she was deaf to my advice. "News flash, the Magus will probably make an appearance soon. He wants something from me."

Her blissful countenance changed to concern. "Seriously? What does he want?"

"Tristan wouldn't tell me."

"I'll see if Henry knows anything. I gotta get some sleep. I'm exhausted! Teenagers wear me out."

I was left alone to ponder my weird life, but not for long. The good thing about vampires is that you can always find someone to talk to in the middle of the night if you have insomnia. Billy and Robert wandered in and pulled a bag of blood from the fridge, which they shared.

"Baroness, to what do we owe the pleasure of your company this fine night?" Robert asked with his lovely soft Southern accent.

"The Magus sent word he wants to meet with me, and Alexander kissed me.

I'm a bit rattled. I'm telling you so that you can correct any rumors. He kissed me. Then I broke it off. That's all that happened."

Billy grinned. "Methinks, you liked it."

"Why?"

"You didn't call him an asshole," Billy with a smile.

"Shut the fuck up Billy! Goodnight, Robert." I hated it when vampires were right. I was not going to lie, so I went to bed.

Kyoto sat in front of a computer, patiently waiting for the Magus' avatar to appear on the screen. He was pleased that his old Samurai image still represented him. His confidence had returned, despite his continued role as a servant to the House of Cups. Finally, the image of the Magus appeared in all his mysterious glory for their online meeting.

"Kyoto, what do you wish to discuss," the Magus asked in a stern tone that held none of the warmth of their previous relationship.

"Thank you for agreeing to speak with me, I have continued to research the Baroness' blood, and I find she continues to evolve. She remains mortal, but her blood is showing immune system changes that resemble Sir Omar's biology."

"This evolution has been expected. What is your point?" the Magus asked impatiently.

"We know her blood can diminish the powers of the Haute Caste, but we do not know how it will affect the Common Caste. As one who was convinced to act against my better judgment, I believe we should be prepared to deal with more folly as the Common Caste feel a sense of power. I would like to develop an agent, like the blood given to Alexander, that will have a similar effect on the Common Caste, should the need arise."

"How do you believe such an agent will impact the Common Caste?"

Kyoto was encouraged by this question. "It diminished the powers of Alexander, so I believe it may destroy the Common Caste's vampire nature."

"Rendering them mortal?" the Magus asked, clearly intrigued.

"Or dead."

"Is it not the same thing. This is splendid! You must continue your research."

"To do so, I will need more royal blood from the Baroness. I would also like to continue to study the offspring's blood. They might offer an even more powerful serum."

"You will have samples to study. Good night." Without waiting for a response, the Magus' avatar disappeared.

Kyoto shut down the computer, content that his research would proceed. It would be a few hours yet until sunset. As he drifted off to sleep, he hoped to move his laboratory from the stark, unadorned monastery to Khunbish's palace soon.

Batu had been unable to sleep. His first kill was scheduled for this evening. The

Worthy Target, Hulagu a wealthy, local leader, who regularly physically abused his wife and children. One night in a drunken rage, he severely beat his wife then went on to beat his horse to death. His repeated acts of cruelty fueled resentment in the townspeople. The official story was that his wife had some unspecified accident, and that the horse was put down due to a grave injury. No one believed that. The Target's wife had become so afraid that she took her children and fled to a relative in a neighboring town. Her leaving sealed his fate. Batu's stealth would be tested as the official had guards outside his residence.

Batu sent a message to Teri,

Tell Miranda I dedicate my first kill to her.

He did push-ups and lifted weights to help pass the time. He lit incense and watched the smoke trail while he tried to calm his nerves with meditation. Batu still felt his decision to become a vampire was the right thing for him. He hoped tonight would not make him regret his decision. Batu looked into the small reflecting vessel built into his table. His muscles had become more defined, and he was much stronger and more agile than he had been as a mortal. He fervently hoped Miranda would appreciate what he had become.

On the outskirts of the city, Hulagu walked out of his spacious modern home towards the yurt a few hundred feet behind the main structure. His secretary was waiting for him there. She hoped the powerful man would leave his wife for her. She was a good employee, but he wondered how long he could continue the affair before having to replace her because of rumors. He enjoyed the way his secretary flattered him. His wife no longer praised his virility.

He was close to the yurt when all the lights in his compound went out. In the darkness, he heard footsteps coming up behind him. Batu would need to work on his ability to stalk silently. Hulagu turned, ready to call a guard. Chang had gone along with Batu and rendered the security guards unconscious. Batu stopped a few feet from his target.

"Good evening Hulagu."

The stranger, clothed in black, made Hulagu very uneasy. "What are you doing on my property? How did you get in here?" He cried out for the guards.

"They are not available right now," Batu informed him with an icy stare.

The young woman, hearing loud voices, peeked through the window and became alarmed seeing Hulagu confronted by the two strangers. She turned to the small kitchen area, grabbed a knife, and pressed herself against the wall next to the doorway.

"You have no business with me, be gone!" Hulagu was trying to sound bold and defiant, but he was starting to tremble without his guards.

"You have abused your wife and children, exploited the townspeople, and killed a beautiful steed. You are a disgrace to all Mongols!"

"It was my horse. Leave immediately, or I'll have you thrown in prison!"

Batu leaped on Hulagu, knocking him back through the doorway of the yurt to the ground inside. He bit deeply into Halagu's neck and silenced his garbled cries. His hunger made him oblivious to the young woman hiding inside. The rush from his first kill was euphoria on steroids. The woman jumped from her hiding place onto Batu and stabbed him in the back. He swung about so quickly and with such force that she flew back against a heavy wooden pole and fell to the ground unconscious. As Chang entered the yurt, Batu steadied himself as the rush of fresh blood invigorated him. He looked down at his bloody shirt. The Haute Caste were usually much neater.

Chang looked at the body of Hulagu, shook his head, and said, "He was a disgrace to the name of the great Hulagu Khan!" Then he asked politely, "May I?"

Batu nodded, and Chang drained Hulagu of most of his remaining vital fluid. Then he looked at the crumpled body of the witness. "What would you like to do with her, Sir Batu?"

"She had been used by Hulagu and should not be harmed further. We shall leave her at the doorstep of the monastery. They will see to her and explain that demons attacked her." Batu took a handkerchief from his pocket and wiped his face and hands. He had removed a menace to humanity. He would focus on that rather than think of it as murder. He had never felt so alive. Then he felt the pain in his back. He turned his back towards Chang. "Would you mind?"

Chang pulled the kitchen knife out. "The monks will see to you as well. I think it would be better if we did not let the Princess know a mortal wounded you."

Chang lifted the young woman and carried her to their car. "I admire her bravery."

"And her aim," Batu responded. "She almost got my spinal column. Mongol women are formidable foes. One should not piss them off."

Chang laid her on the back seat. "She is quite pretty."

"You drank too much blood," Batu responded.

"Look how she attacked a much taller, stronger stranger. Can you imagine if she were angry with her lover?" Chang insisted.

"Don't be a fool!" Batu admonished him. "Don't get involved with locals."

When they got to the monastery, Chang said, "You did well. A quick, clean assassination."

Batu was surprised by the praise from the Common Caste vampire. Chang had been one of Alexander the Great's rebel commanders during the attempted coup in Las Vegas. "Thank you."

They delivered the young woman to the care of the monks. Dr. Kyoto joined them. The ancient vampire was stoic about Batu's kill. He told Batu, "You always remember your first."

Batu asked, "What will become of his wife and children."

"The Princess will see that they are taken care of," Kyoto told him.

Chang turned to the monks. "When she regains consciousness, please tell her that demons attacked her lover. They spared her because she fought bravely."

Kyoto looked at Chang. "Mongol women are more feared than the men. It is why the Magus chose Princess Khunbish to be the head of the House."

Chang said nothing more until they were in the car headed back to the mansion. "Batu, I did not understand why you were given Haute Caste status until tonight. It was an honor to assist with your first assassination."

"I was enhanced by the blood of two ancient vampires when I was transformed. Their gifts have changed me in ways I am just starting to understand. It was exhilarating when I felt the life force of my first Target seep into my body. What must it be like after hundreds of assassinations? How do you control your thirst?"

Chang shook his head. "Though Common Caste I have had the honor of assisting in the elimination of three of the scum of the earth. Each time I felt reborn by their vital fluid. Since Scheherazade, a Common Caste vampiress, transformed me, and I don't have HH blood, my powers have not evolved like yours have. I will never be your match."

Sapna was bored by most of the women in his hi-tech business circle. The few he was interested in were respectful of their marital vows. He stopped at the Taj Rambagh Palace bar in Jaipur to look for international women seeking a taste of local culture. The 19th-century palace reminded him of the glorious days when the caste system worshipped his Brahmin family. He wished he had lived in that era. An elephant adorned in finery stood in the courtyard to welcome visitors with its caretaker. At the entrance, a brass platter held a pile of fresh rose petals.

Despite the humidity, Sapna wore a suit. He was tall and moved like an athlete due to his years of playing soccer. In the bar, he noticed a strikingly beautiful woman in an expensive sari. He was drawn to her, ignoring the tourist in the black Chanel dress who tried to flirt with him.

"Good evening. May I buy you a drink?"

Scheherazade smiled. "I can buy my own. Perhaps you can entertain me with a story of intrigue and passion."

Sapna felt an overwhelming attraction to the mysterious woman. "Anything! Anything you would require, daughter of Kali."

She then took a sip of wine and said, "A more private place to talk would be appreciated."

"Of course!" He left to pay for a suite. She was fluent in several languages though she was raised speaking Farsi and English. She enjoyed pretending to be a member of India's highest caste. He returned, and they followed hotel staff to a luxurious room that overlooked magnificent gardens and water fountains bathed in moonlight. The scent of roses and jasmine filled the room, and soft lighting gave the room a romantic glow. Delicacies and a tea set were on a balcony table.

She looked about as though considering whether the accommodations suited her. "This will do."

As soon as they were alone, she sat on the plush bed and indicated he should sit in the nearby chair. He realized he had not introduced himself. "I am Sapna. What shall I call you?"

"Scheherazade," she paused as his eyes lit up.

He was mesmerized by her voice, her eyes, her scent. He felt utterly captivated by a woman for the first time in his life. "I don't understand, but I am at your mercy."

"Come here," she laid back against the large, embroidered silk pillows.

He took off his jacket and joined her.

Scheherazade unbuttoned his shirt and ran her hand lightly over his chest. He moved closer. Her hand went up to his throat and stopped over his pulsing carotid artery. She allowed him to kiss her, gently at first, then more demanding. She whispered, "You have HH blood."

He pushed away as though cold water had been thrown on him. "What?"

She smiled. ". "You have HH blood."

He had been approached before by medical researchers who wanted him to participate in hematology studies. He always refused. "How do you know that? You waited in my favorite bar to seduce me because you are interested in my blood?" He tried to control his arousal by this beautiful and dangerous woman. He started to get up. "I'm not a lab rat."

She leaped on him and threw him back on the bed. He was so excited by her strength that he did not resist. "You are amazing. Who are you? What do you want?"

Scheherazade straddled him. "Everything! And you will help me get it!" She began to kiss his neck. With every ounce of her self-control, she moved down his chest as he unzipped his pants.

"I'll give you anything you want!" Sapna cried out. He was totally in the beautiful stranger's control. Her sari fell away, and his senses were rocked by the strength and scent of her body. He kissed her breasts, teasing her nipples with his tongue. She bent down and kissed him deeply. He entered her again and again as he sought more intense levels of pleasure. She pinned his wrists above his head and cried out in pleasure." Excitement overwhelmed his brain chemistry. He shook as he climaxed. Scheherazade's fangs pierced the soft skin of his neck, and she drank deeply. Sexual release and pain rendered him almost unconscious. He could feel himself become weaker but had no desire to pull away.

She withdrew her fangs before it was too late.

He closed his eyes as he whispered, "I am yours."

The kids stood in front of the high school and waited for Teri to pick them up. Jacques said, "Mom is a wreck."

Des responded, "C'mon, our family is a total freak show. She's doing her best."

"Alexander," Marie added, "might be a disaster, but he's hot."

"Seriously?" Tomas asked. "C'mon chicks can't keep away from Dad. There's no way Alexander is better looking than him."

"Mom said I kind of look like Alex," Jacques said with a grin.

Des turned to Jacques as she pulled up. "Hey, ask Teri."

They piled into the car but were unusually quiet, which bothered their bodyguard. "What's up?" she asked.

Jacques got up the nerve. "Teri, who would you want to be on an island with,

Alexander or Dad?"

"Henry!" she sighed, and they all started laughing.

"So, what about you guys? Is there some vampire you like? C'mon, you can tell me." She glanced at their faces in the rearview mirror.

"Shut up! Don't tell her anything. She'll go straight to Mom," Tomas said.

Des teased. "Tomas is in love with Lady Kabedi."

Shoving and elbowing ended with the straps of Tomas's backpack around Des's neck.

"She's beautiful!" Teri responded, hoping to calm Tomas down.

"Too beautiful for his ugly ass!" Marie said as she ducked down in the front seat.

Jacques added, "Des thinks Pomp wants him."

"Stop it, and I won't say a word to your mom. Just take the straps off Des's neck. He looks a little blue." Tomas pulled the backpack off of his brother's neck.

"Thanks," Des started rubbing his neck, then he shoved Jacques.

When they got home, none of the kids said a word about the discussion in the car. Teri wanted to win their trust, so she did not tell Miranda about their discussion. Whether she ever did become a vampire or not, she wanted to be on the good side of the Mordecai offspring.

I found Tomas in the garage setting up his laboratory. He had received shipments of all the chemicals and oils recommended by his chemistry teacher. "I've got parent-teacher conferences tonight. Anything I should know before I go?" I asked him.

"Not really. Will Alexander show up?" he said with a shit-eating grin.

"Keep it up, and you'll never get to drive the Lamborghini."

"C'mon, Mom, I just wondered who will be there. Is Dad back in Seattle?"

I looked at the Bunsen burner, beakers, and other glass items strewn about the wooden table. "I don't know if he'll make it, but we're going to need some fire extinguishers."

"I've got this handled," he asserted with the perfect confidence of a teenager.

After dinner, I drove the winding road to Granite Falls High School. The actual falls were on the edge of town, a great place to admire the power of mother nature as the Stillaguamish River crashed against slabs of granite on its way to the Sound. I parked the car and walked down to the bottom of the falls to admire the power of nature. The natural beauty calmed me down as I prepared to act as if our family was normal.

The teachers were favorably impressed by the kids. The math teacher said she had asked Marie to help tutor some of her peers in algebra. Jacque surprised his history teacher when he complained that they did not study the battles of Alexander the Great. Des was enthusiastic about being in the school band and suggested they play Purple Haze, since Jimi Hendrix was from Seattle. Surprisingly, none of the teachers reported any behavior problems. Just as I sat down with the English teacher who had Tomas and Des in her class, Tristan showed up. Ms. Grisham, a cute petite brunette, was practically salivating as my husband introduced himself. It was her first year teaching, and Ms. Grisham said she took an interest in all her students. She was certainly taking an interest in my ex.

"A divorce can be hard on children. Do you get to spend much time with them since they moved here?" she asked, looking directly at Tristan.

Tristan managed a concerned expression. "I am able to flex my schedule."

"Is there some problem with their behavior or grades?" I asked.

"They are very bright," she smiled at Tristan then glanced at me. "It's just that they've requested to study some dark literature by authors like Neil Gaiman, Stephen King, and Bram Stoker. It's not the type of literature I use in my classes."

"Maybe you should think about it. I'm a writer, and my genre is paranormal. I think that's why they like those authors. You might want to add books by L.K. Hamilton and Christopher Golden to your list of great reads too. Your students will never be bored."

She snidely replied, "Yes, I've heard your books sell, but I teach the classics. Like the works of Shakespeare, Dickens, and Hugo." She looked to Tristan, hoping for his approval.

"My ex-wife's novels are well-written. I'm her publisher," he stated flatly. "They have been translated into French, Spanish, and German."

"I had no idea," she replied sheepishly.

"You realize Dickens wrote about ghosts. Unless there is something else, I think we're done here." I stood and walked out of the room.

Tristan joined me in the hallway. "Were the other teachers so plebian? How could our children ever be challenged here?"

"I liked the others. The chemistry teacher is all that's left. He has encouraged Tomas's experiments."

Someone had taped a note to the door of the classroom that read, "Mr. Cramer is ill this evening. He apologizes for not being available to the parents. He may be contacted by phone next week if anyone wants to speak with him."

"That's weird. Tomas said he was teaching this today." I looked at Tristan, and my gut said something was not right.

"Perhaps he caught something from one of his students. I'm glad to be out of here. I'll meet you back at the house."

As we walked out, Ms. Grisham found us and asked to speak with "Mr. Mordecai." Of course, she did. I left them in the hallway without another word. He hated to be called "Mr."

Chapter 23

Movie Night

When I got back from school, Teri was in the kitchen with Leif. They were discussing the show on Saturday. "I'll go in early with you. Maybe I could help at the door. Henry won't have time for me till later."

Leif looked up. "Hey Baroness, how did it go? Did anyone get suspended? That was my major."

"I almost decked the English teacher. I left her trying to reassure the Baron she was qualified to teach our offspring." I shook my head. "And the chemistry teacher was a no-show. Other than that, it was fine."

I went and checked on the kids. They were hanging out in the den watching a movie. They paused it to see if they were in trouble. Des asked, "We're good, right? The teachers love us."

"Yeah, thanks for trying to be normal." I smiled. "Your dad will be here soon."

"Cool!" Tomas replied and got back to the movie.

I saw what they were watching and had to laugh. Then I went to my room to write. I wanted to focus on the plot for my next book while the ideas were fresh in my mind. The English teacher's comments made me want to get back to my craft.

I heard Tristan's Lamborghini pull up. I figured it would take about ten minutes before he came into my room fuming. I could hear him talking with Leif and Teri, and then he went down to the den. Suddenly his voice got loud. "Turn that abomination off! How dare you! A vampire that turns against his own kind!"

"Dad, it's just a movie," Des replied.

Tomas added, "*Blade* is cool. He's part vampire, kind of like us."

Marie turned it off. "Don't take it personally. Those vampires are only kind of like you."

Jacques wisely said nothing.

"I think you should be going to a better school," their father exclaimed.

"We can start our own private school. We'll call it Nosferatu High," Des remarked.

Tristan's stormed down the hall to my room. When he collapsed on the bed, my laptop bounced up. "Your mortal influence has made them insufferable and disrespectful."

"I thought you said you liked them better once they started talking," I said smugly.

He sat up. "You're not helping. I want to kill something, but there are no Worthy Targets nearby."

"I don't know. Grisham is kind of a waste of blood."

He grinned. "Jealousy becomes you!"

"It's her pretentious attitude towards literature that offends me. You can fuck her anytime."

"That's what she said."

I hit him with my pillow, which was not a great idea. He mistook the gesture for foreplay and was soon on top of me. "Get off!" I yelled.

He complied by rolling onto his side. The door to the bedroom had been left open, and we became aware of four sets of eyes watching us.

Marie asked, "Are you back together?"

"No!" I jumped up off the bed. Tristan smirked. The kids looked relieved, but not because of my response. It was because their dad no longer seemed murderously angry at them.

Jacques said, "We just wanted to apologize. We like vampire movies."

Des added, "I mean, if you were in the mafia, we'd probably watch all the Godfather films."

I had heard enough. "Before I make you an offer you can't refuse, go to bed! You still have school tomorrow."

They hugged us and wandered down the hall, discussing what might happen if Blade went after the mafia. I wondered if anyone or anything could phase them after all they had experienced.

I decided that I didn't want to give Tristan any wrong ideas and left the room. He reluctantly got up and followed me into the kitchen.

Teri and Leif were still in the there. After a moment of uncomfortable silence, Teri asked Leif, "So, how are the kids coming along with their band?"

"They're progressing amazingly fast. I've never seen anyone learn to play as quickly as they have. I've been teaching them some of the classics. Velvet Underground, the Sex Pistols, and The Clash. Des has a gift for screaming his heart out. Marie gets very intense when she drums. Tomas struggles with his riffs because he tries too hard and needs to let it rip more, but he'll get there. I tell him to stop thinking about the music and focus on feeling it. I told him that's what Henry told me."

It was apparent from his expression that Tristan wasn't completely following Leif.

"And Jacques, how is he doing?" Tristan asked

"He gets bored and tries to make playing the keyboard more complicated than it needs to be. It's hard for him to be a team player," Leif replied.

"Jacques' biological father struggles with that as well," Tristan mused.

"Thanks Leif, I have learned more from you about the kids than at the school tonight."

"We spend hours together working on their sound. For what it's worth, I enjoy it." Leif smiled. "They are interesting people."

168

Teri added, "Bring them to the club some night."

Tristan and I both said, "No!"

Tristan turned Teri. "Your relationship with Henry may continue. He has made his feelings for you clear to the Magus and me. Do not let it affect your job. The club is not appropriate for the offspring."

"Understood. Good night," Teri said and went to her room.

"I better check on the goats," Leif said and was gone before I could say anything.

"I hate to have to say this but thank you for sticking up for me at the parent-teacher conference and for setting limits with Teri. I like you so much more now that we're divorced."

"I haven't changed." He started to lean forward just as his phone chimed with a text.

I moved away from him. Saved by the bell. "What's up?"

He replied, "Ms. Grisham."

"You're right. You haven't changed." He glared at me and left. I heard him peel out of the driveway as I went to bed. "Asshole!"

The Lamborghini pulled into the dark, deserted parking area for the falls. Tristan got out and walked to Ms. Grisham, who was leaning against her Subaru. "You were perfect." He carried her to the Lamborghini and laid her on the still-warm hood.

"I would prefer the leather seats," she teased.

"Can't blame her," a man's voice came out of the dark.

The Baron turned to face the middle-aged mortal. "Give me your report, then leave us!"

"Yeah Cramer," Grisham said impatiently, "Make it quick."

Gladly. I'll continue to avoid your ex as long as possible, but sooner or later, she'll see me. If she recognizes me, what do you want me to say?"

"Just tell her you're added daytime security for the children. Is everything else set for next week?" Tristan did not have the same confidence in Cramer as the Magus.

"Yes. I don't like it, but I'll do it."

"I don't care about your preferences. Just be careful. You may leave now."

Cramer walked away as Tristan pulled Grisham into the Lamborghini. He did not want to see how they would manage in that tight space.

Tristan enjoyed the enthusiasm of the mortal. He pushed the button that lowered the back of the seat. She was overwhelmed by his physical prowess. In the tight confines of the car, she pulled off her top and pulled Tristan's head towards her. The ancient lover kissed her deeply, then teased her nipples with his tongue. She lightly bit his neck. Foreplay that vampires adore. Tristan whispered, "Pomp has taught you well." He did not enter her until she became aroused enough to feel nothing but pleasure. It did not take very long.

Back at work in Salinas, Manny sat at his desk and stared at his Starbucks coffee as though an answer might suddenly appear in the cappuccino foam. He still found it impossible to let go of his obsession with the Pill King murder, and its connection to the bizarre world of Miranda Ortega. Organized crime was the only logical explanation. He was sure the Baroness and Teri Park had a good laugh at his expense after telling him he was chasing vampires. To hell with them! He was going to find out the truth. Every computer search, internet, and criminal database all came up with dead ends. He knew what he had to do next.

"Dr. Barnes will see you now," the receptionist said.

Manny walked into the examination room of his high school buddy. "Manny, what brings you here?" He looked concerned. Manny had never come to see him at his office. He only saw him at the sports bar when the 49ers were playing.

"Hi Fred." They shook hands. "I have a favor to ask you. My job has been very stressful lately, and I need a month off, but it can't look like I'm...you know, having some kind of psych issue."

"Manny, if you're having trouble with stress, maybe I should refer you to...."

"No, that's the problem. If I go to a shrink, that will go into my file, and I'll always have that hanging over me. Can you just say I'm anemic, or I've got Hep C, or rabies, something that could get me some medical leave?"

"Rabies? Why not the plague?" Fred teased.

"I'm sorry. I used up all my vacation time, and I just don't know any other way besides quitting to get some time off." Manny started to leave.

"It's too bad you've got mono. You'll have to be off work at least a month, or maybe two."

Manny broke out in a huge grin. "Thanks Fred, I owe you!"

"Well, there is a parking ticket I got." He smiled. "Let me write this up for you." He handed Manny a face mask. "Wear it when you turn in the paperwork. Come see me when you're better and I'll clear you for work."

Manny headed back to police headquarters. Captain Jenkins seemed relieved when he turned in his medical leave documents. "You haven't been your old self. I guess this explains it."

Manny mumbled thanks through his mask and left, not knowing if he would ever be able to return to his old life. Despite his mixed feelings lying about being sick, he was focused on the mysterious Miranda Ortega, like a heat-seeking missile.

When he got back to his apartment, Molly gave him shit as usual but agreed to take Trouble. She promised to research any leads he fed her.

"I hereby deputize you as my resource person and confidante. If forty-eight hours go by and you haven't heard from me, go to the Chief." He was trying to joke, but he sounded serious.

"OK, Detective Whatever, just remember Trouble is counting on you to return.

She hates it when I shoo her off the table." Molly looked concerned. "If I don't hear from you, I'll call the FBI, forget the Chief."

"I believe you would." He looked at Molly like he was seeing her for the first time. "We'll have a long talk when I get back." Then he kissed her quickly and ran out the door.

"What the holy fuck," she muttered. "God bless Miranda Ortega." Molly scooped up Trouble, turned out the lights, and went back to her apartment. She looked at the cat. "That forty-eight hours starts right now."

Manny set his GPS for Rossville, Illinois. He was determined to find out everything about the writer from the cornfields. He did not notice the BMW, with dark tinted windows that was tailing him. A tracking device had been attached to Manny's car so that his shadow could stay quite a distance back. It was ten o'clock, and they could follow Manny most of the night, then catch up with him again after sundown. They hoped he would sleep part of the day.

Saturday night, the scene at the Funeral Pyre was crazy. Since Pomp left, word had gone through the music underground that the Pyre was now less like a nightclub and more of a hardcore music venue. Everyone who was trying to make a name in the underground music scene was there wearing their best Goth finery. Most sported multiple tattoos, pierced body parts, fully or half-shaved heads, and hair color of every imaginable hue. Teri knew she looked pretty boring in her tight black T-shirt and ripped jeans, but it made her stand out. She kept hearing, "Who's that bitch?" as Leif escorted her to the table closest to the stage.

A handsome man and an extremely sexy woman with dark hair came over and sat at her table. Teri looked surprised and told them, "This is a private table reserved for Henry's friends."

"Exactly. Good evening Teri," he replied with an Italian accent, "I'm Cesare, and this is Antoinella, from the House of Pentacles."

"Oh, I'm sorry, I didn't recognize you. You were in Las Vegas when...."

Antoinella interrupted her, "Apology accepted. How is the Baroness?"

"Fine" She felt at a loss for words. "Uh, do you come to Seattle often?"

Cesare responded, "No, the summer nights are short, and then it is so wet the rest of the year. We prefer more temperate climates with longer nights all year."

"We're here to be of service to the Baroness," Antoinella continued, "Tell her we'll call on her soon."

Teri looked up as the room darkened, and Henry's band came on the stage. She turned and asked, "Have you heard Henry...." Teri realized they had disappeared. "Okay...," she muttered, a little shaken. She would deliver the message.

Henry lit into a deafening, raucous set that got the crowd yelling and bumping into each other. Teri noticed several couples heading off to the dark corners of the club. A bartender brought her a glass of wine and screamed above the din, "From Henry!"

She sipped it while looking at the object of her lust and adoration. Henry's stage presence was electric. Everyone stared at him like they were trying to absorb his passion. Women would throw themselves on the stage, only to be thrown back into the crowd by security. Henry gave her a sly smile between songs. Her longing to be alone with him was almost unbearable. Then he called out, "This is for Teri." He pointed to her, and she wanted to crawl under the table. "It's something called Insatiable!"

Every word of the song was about sexual desire for her that could never be satisfied. The band and the crowd began chanting, "Never Enough!" As the song ended, Henry jumped off the stage, picked Teri up like she weighed ten pounds, and held her in a tight embrace. The crowd went crazy, screaming for him. As he carried her backstage, a man, dressed in black leather, tried to grab her. Henry shoved him and he sailed backward, knocking several people down.

Henry removed three very disappointed women from his dressing room with an embarrassed smile and closed the door. "I'm sorry, they sneak in here when I am on stage." Henry took off his leather vest and wiped the sweat from his face and muscular torso with a damp cloth that smelled of spice. "Did you enjoy the set?"

She jumped on him and kissed him passionately. He wanted to experience her purely, so he repressed his seductive power. They fell upon the couch and searched feverishly for ways to pleasure each other. Henry had sensed the depth of her passion, and now he fully experienced it. The softness of her skin soothed him. Her agility and strength amazed him. He kissed her neck, nearly overwhelmed by her HH scent. She deftly unfastened his leather pants as he pulled off her shirt and kissed her breasts. His lips teased her nipples. She lightly ran her fingers over his penis as he gasped in delight. "Now!" she demanded, and he entered her. The friction of their bodies allowed them to be lost in all-consuming pleasure until they collapsed together in a shuddering climax.

Lying under him, she whispered, "Insatiable?"

He pushed himself away. "Only with you, my love." His hand lightly moved over her neck, to her breast, down her body, and finally to her clitoris where it rested. He smiled. "The center of my universe."

She pushed his hand away. "Henry, I don't know if I should be flattered or offended."

He kissed her. "I never want to offend you." He got up and pulled a box out of his jacket pocket and handed it to her.

She stared at his magnificent nakedness before her eyes shifted to the box. It was black lacquer with an eternity symbol in red on top. She opened the box to find a gold medallion with an ornate eye design with a large emerald as the pupil. "It's exquisite!"

"It's the Eye of Ra. I have had it since the time of the pyramids before I was transformed. It is for protection and health. The vampire world will know what it means."

"That you're mine!" she responded. "Then get rid of those Goth groupies."

He was surprised by her self-assuredness. "I was concerned I would overwhelm your senses, your thoughts. Yet you dare order me to do something?"

"Right, I'm your girlfriend. It's my job, I'm supposed to., Miranda warned me, but it just feels like we're supposed to be here now. I feel your ability, but only in a really good way. Like my life's been some fucking hard jigsaw puzzle that I could never finish till I met you." She held up the necklace to him. He fastened the clasp around her neck, and it rested just above her breasts. "I'll never take it off."

He told her wistfully, "Cleopatra gave it to me."

"Shut up!" She pulled him down on top of her.

Chapter 24

Betrayal

I got a call from the school nurse Monday morning as I came into the house after playing with Lug. "Mrs. Mordecai, there was an accident at school, and Tomas cut his arm. It was a deep cut but not critical or life-threatening. As a precaution, we sent him by ambulance to the Cascade Valley Hospital E.R. We've been calling for half an hour, and when we couldn't reach you, we contacted Tomas' father, and he gave permission to have him treated."

"Okay, I'm on my way to the hospital!" I hung up and yelled for Teri. We jumped into the car and took off. She ignored speed limits and blew through red lights. All the trauma of my father's murder played in my brain. "Do you think it was just an accident?" I blurted out, but Teri did not answer.

We ran into the E.R., and they showed me to a small, curtained area. The doctor was stitching up a gash on Tomas' lower arm. He was pale from blood loss and pain, and his skin tone reminded me of Tristan. He was kind of woozy from the pain meds.

"Tomas," I touched his uninjured arm with tears in my eyes.

"I'll be okay," Tomas mumbled.

I looked at the young doctor. "I'm his mom. He has HH blood, so do I. He can only take blood from someone with HH."

Teri added, "I have HH too!"

"I'm Dr. Karen Hastings." She continued to work on closing up the wound as she talked. "Tomas already told me. I had never heard of it before, so I contacted a friend who is a hematologist about your blood type. He did lose quite a bit of blood, and a transfusion is indicated. I'll send you both over to the lab to have some blood drawn."

I touched Tomas's head, which felt cool. I looked at the monitor and saw that his body temp was 95°F. "He's cold."

"Nurse, blankets from the warmer," the doctor ordered. "His temp was 98°F when he came in." She seemed surprised by the sudden drop in his temperature. "Please go to the lab now."

I hated to leave his side, and I wished that it was night, so Guillaume could help heal him with some of his blood. Teri and I would have to do for now. The lab found our blood healthy and compatible with Tomas's. Once we had the all-clear, the doctor sent us to donate blood.

I was a little faint when we got back to Tomas, not from blood loss, but from the sight of my child in the E.R. A woman was leaning over him. Ms. Grisham! "Get away from him!" I yelled, which caused the staff to wonder what happened. I looked at the nurse. "I only want my family and Teri here." Being a small rural hospital, security tended to be a bit lax.

"Of course," she responded and escorted the teacher out. I looked through the curtain and noticed Ms. Grisham talking to a man. He looked familiar, but I could not place him. They disappeared as soon as he saw me. I had too much on my mind to worry about them.

I held Tomas' hand and willed myself not to cry anymore. I could not stand to see my son like this. Though I had regularly attended church as a child with my parents, I was not particularly religious. Even so, I prayed the healing properties he inherited from his father and grandfather would kick in. I was counting on God to work in mysterious ways.

Dr. Hastings had the staff set up the transfusion of the blood I had donated. I watched the precious life-sustaining fluid drip down from the bag through a tube into his arm. Within minutes his body temperature started to rise. He looked a little less pale. I turned to the doctor and said, "Thank you."

"You might thank his teacher, Mr. Cramer. He did a great first aid job, stopping the bleeding."

I got that feeling in my gut again. The queasy feeling that told me nothing was what it seemed. "Are you going to need the rest of the blood?"

"The rest of the blood?" she questioned.

"We both donated," Teri told her.

"Whose blood is that?" I demanded.

Dr. Hastings looked at the code on the bag and checked the computer. "It's Ms. Park's. The computer says it was all that had been collected."

I went immediately homicidal, but I was not sure who to kill. Almost anyone at the hospital could have been bribed. The doctor did not seem in on it, but someone surely was. I made myself focus on Tomas. I would stay by his side until he was discharged. I whispered to Teri, "Go talk to the lab technician who drew our blood. If I see her right now, I'll probably kill her."

Teri quietly slipped away and found the woman in the parking lot, who had feigned a sudden migraine and asked to leave, right after she had finished collecting their blood. Teri snatched the keys from her hand as she approached the woman's car. "Give me those back!" the lab tech yelled. She looked scared. "I'll scream if you don't!" She backed away from Teri.

"Do you really want to tell your boss you sold the blood?" Teri stepped forward.

The lab tech's eyes got big. "You have no proof! You didn't see anything!"

Teri smiled. "Not till now." She held up her phone and played their conversation.

"Shit! I knew I shouldn't have done it." She started to get tearful. "The science teacher from the high school said he wanted to keep it at school in case there was another accident. It didn't sound right, but I needed the money."

"When did he make this deal with you?"

"Right after you two finished donating and went back to the E.R."

"What a stupid, greedy bitch." Teri threw the keys into a dumpster. She wanted to do more, but any violence would have been caught on the security camera and attract too much attention. Teri walked away and headed back to the E.R.

When Teri told me what she found out, a wave of cold anger took hold of me. I guessed that some of the Haute Caste wanted our blood so badly they would go to any length to get it. This could not have happened without the consent of the Magus. Why did they want it so badly? Was Tristan in on this? My alliances in the vampire world were shifting quickly. I looked at Tomas and knew what I had to do. Calm settled over me. My attempts to distance us from the undead society had failed time and again. I would go after any vampire and mortal who harmed my children. I would make the Haute Caste involved in this attack afraid to go to sleep at dawn. I would no longer try to be merciful.

"Call Leif, tell him to pick up the kids and keep them at his place till we get back. Tell him not to trust anyone, especially not any of the teachers."

I called the high school and explained that Leif was coming to pick up the kids and that they were not to go with anyone else. Then I texted the same message to the kids and added,

Don't trust Cramer or Grisham!

Marie texted back,

We R OK. Will wait 4 Leif.

Jacques replied with a sad emoji. Des asked how Tomas was, and I texted him that he would be O.K. Then I texted Billy and Robert and asked them to track down Cramer and get the blood back before he could give it to the Magus

Tomas had fallen asleep, and I held his hand, trying to make some sense out of this craziness. I was now sure that Tomas' injury was not an accident. Who could I trust in the vampire world? If the Magus was behind this, most of the Haute Caste would take his side. Whoever planned this knew about our healing abilities. We didn't come back as quickly as the undead, just faster than normal mortals. The wound was scary and painful, but despite the blood loss not life-threatening. I guess when the Magus had protected us, he was just keeping his pets healthy for his experiments. He had a lot to learn about human nature. Now I was beginning to regret that the kids and I had helped rescue the Magus during the rebellion. I didn't believe that Alexander would have done this to his own son.

It was essential to know who I could count on. I could not believe my father, Omar, or Anastasia would be involved in this. I would definitely put them on Team Miranda. I was afraid the other royal Houses would side with the Magus, though Kananga was an independent thinker. Borgia and Antoinella sort of owed me, but who could trust a Borgia? Lily and Kyoto got off on researching us. They were probably in on this. I wondered what they would do with my blood. The Haute Caste were fearful of its properties. I hoped whoever stole my blood spilled some on themselves. I had to figure out who the hell Cramer was."

Teri had been quiet, allowing me to process the crisis. She was startled when I finally spoke. "The chemistry teacher! I will do everything I can to find out who he really is." I didn't realize I had said that out loud. I looked at my friend and bodyguard. "Thanks for donating blood. I owe you an apology. What I said about Henry and you, just forget it. He has rebelled against the Magus for years. It looks like I'm going to need him as an ally. I guess my first impression was wrong about him."

She smiled and hugged me. "I knew you would come around."

Just then, Tomas woke up a little groggy. "What's going on?" He looked at his bandaged arm and the almost empty bag of blood hanging on the stand. "I'm gonna kill Des! This is his fault!"

I looked at Teri with tears in my eyes. "He's going to be fine."

A short time later, Tomas' color had returned, and his temperature was back to normal. The doctor was amazed at his quick rebound. I thought it best not to have her do any more testing or asking too many questions. I convinced her that I could take care of him at home and would be sure to follow up with our doctor. She reluctantly agreed to discharge him. We could not get out of that hospital fast enough. I sat in the back seat with Tomas leaning against me. Teri took it slow so the curves would not jar him on Jordan Road. Darkness was starting to fall over the mountains.

"Tomas, why are you upset with Des?"

"He was trying to impress a girl, fell backward into me, and it caused me to slam my arm down on a beaker that broke and slashed my arm."

I did not want him making Des feel like crap when he did not deserve it. At least not this time. "I don't think it was your brother's fault. I'm not going to explain it now. Just trust me on this."

"You're the only person I totally trust. I think you're wrong, but I hurt too much to kick Des's ass," he said and closed his eyes.

As we walked into the house, the kids and Leif were all over Tomas. The concern they displayed for Tomas was touching. Marie told him, "Ashley called and asked you to call her tomorrow when you feel better." Tomas made his way to the couch and gingerly sat down. Jacques came over, put a pillow under his arm, and Des brought him a bowl of ice cream. Lug sat by his feet and stared up at him, sensing something was wrong.

"I think I need another pain pill," Tomas moaned, a bit more than necessary.

"The doc said you're not due for another three hours," Teri stated.

I tried not to smile. "Teri, would you text Henry to see if he can come over?"

"I already heard from him, and he said he'll be here soon," she replied.

"I imagine Tristan will be here soon too," I added.

The kids looked at me, trying to figure out what was going on. Guillaume rushed in before they could start asking questions.

"Tomas! Mon cher, what happened to you?" He gently touched my son's forehead and looked at the bandaged wound.

Tomas grimaced. "It was an accident at school."

Guillaume turned to me. "May I assist in his healing?"

"Of course. I had hoped you would."

I followed Guillaume into the kitchen. He poured some V-8 into a glass and then cut his finger to allow blood droplets to fall into the juice. I put my hand on his shoulder. "Thank you."

I handed the glass to Tomas. Everyone knew what was in it. "Do I have to?"

I started to tear up. "It will make you stronger."

Jacques frowned. "That's a lot of blood."

"No, it's not. It's mostly V-8. It will help you heal faster."

Des said, "Maybe you should put it in beer."

Marie had had enough. "Just drink it, you wuss!"

Tomas closed his eyes and emptied the glass. I was relieved that he kept it down. "I hate V-8!" he groaned.

Guillaume chuckled. I was glad he was not offended. The kids didn't realize that it was considered an honor to receive blood from an ancient vampire like Guillaume.

"I'll fix some stew," Guillaume said. We were all glad that he was going to cook.

We heard a car approaching the house. "Henry's here!" Teri's face lit up! She ran to the door to greet him.

A few minutes later, I heard Tristan's Lamborghini pull up to the house. "So is he," I muttered as a dark cloud descended on me.

The kids looked at each other, wondering what their father had done this time. I tried to be reassuring. "It's okay. I just need to talk with your dad." I kissed Tomas's forehead and went outside.

Teri and Henry found me first. "Miranda, how is Tomas?" Henry asked.

His concern was genuine. Henry had his arm around Teri's shoulders. His Levi jacket and jeans gave him a softer look than the chains and leather he usually wore. I wished I had someone to hug at that moment. "He'll be okay, but I need your help. I would like to see you both privately in the barn after I talk to Tristan."

"Of course," Henri replied, and they headed off to the barn.

I was sure they were glad to have some time alone in the barn as they waited for me. I went to the edge of the deck, stared out into the growing darkness, and heard a coyote wail in the distance. I could have made that sound at that moment. The evergreen scent from the old trees surrounding our property and the sound of the river rushing over the rocks comforted me. Tristan spent several minutes with our son before he came out and joined me.

"Miranda, he will be fine!"

"I know. Guillaume gave him some of his blood. I won't lie to the children. I am going to tell Tomas that you were involved." My emotions were locked up tight, as I spoke in a cold monotone that surprised him. He once said he would not lie to me. I was counting on that now. The evening light magnified the shadows in his face. There was no softness, no look of tenderness. "Are you going to tell me what

178

this was all about?" I demanded.

"It was not supposed to be so severe. Tomas or Des were to be injured just enough to require stitches. Damn Cramer! I knew he was not capable of following orders."

He confirmed my worst fears. "Orders from the Magus?"

"Yes, believe me, I would not have consented if I had known Tomas would have been hurt so badly. I'm not a monster!" He looked at me, seeking forgiveness.

"Monsters hurt children." I kept my voice down. "You knew I would never consent to their blood being used for experiments, so you agreed to this heinous scheme. How could you?" I stared at him with an expression of disgust. "Doesn't the code say that no children may be harmed?"

"It is important for the well-being of us all to know more about the properties of your blood. I know you are angry with me, but it is a small sacrifice for knowledge. Pain builds character. It will help Tomas in the long run. He is hardly a child anymore."

"He's my child. We're done." I said in a quiet voice that rattled him to his core. He was used to me yelling and throwing objects, not cold hatred. "I was a fool to think you were a caring father. You will have limited access to the children. My blood was weaponized. What will he do with the newest blood samples? The Magus has no intention of helping us. He only wants to use us. I once thought we were fated to be together, and now I know fate has a far different plan for me. Get out of my sight." I turned my back to him.

"I didn't want to see any of our children harmed but I can't risk alienating the Magus." He stormed off, muttering about me being unreasonable. I heard the screech of his tires as he spun out of the drive. I stood in the moonlight and stared down at the river. The dampness of the night suited my mood. A deep darkness that I had never known before crept into my heart. This was different than the sense of grief when my father was killed. This was a foreboding of the actions I would have to take to protect the children and myself.

As soon as the sound of his car faded, I headed to the barn, where I found Teri and Henry fencing. I could see he was holding back his speed and strength to allow her to feign competing with him. Most vampires would parade their superiority. "Thank you for coming so quickly."

Henry bowed to Teri and put his sword up. Teri playfully tapped his ass with her blade. He raised an eyebrow but let it go. Damn, they were sweet. I had never imagined Henry being so loving and playful.

"Is the Baron gone?" he asked.

"Yes. I told him to leave. I can't stand to look at him right now. Did Teri tell you everything?"

"Yes. Except why you wanted me here."

I pulled up a chair, and they did the same. I knew that any decisions we made tonight could put us at odds with the head of the vampire world.

"I misjudged you. I thought you would take advantage of Teri. I was wrong. You appear to truly care for her."

Teri touched his hand. "He does, and I have found my missing piece."

Henry smiled at her. "Baroness, I understand your sadness and anger. You are better than the Haute Caste, who have tried to manipulate and trick you. I realized I could not abide their society centuries ago. I had to create a separate existence, without antagonizing them to be able to survive."

His voice was calming, and I let him use his power on me to help me focus. "I don't require revenge." I paused to consider my need. "I want them to be so afraid of us that they will respect the children and me. I must stop the Magus from trying to control our lives. No one will be allowed to interact with us without my permission. I will do it with this!" I pointed to the site where I had given blood.

Henry leaned forward, sniffed the air, then sat back and stared at my arm. "I thought you were just HH, but your blood has an odd scent, not like any HH I have ever encountered. I realize you have received some Haute Caste blood over the years to help you survive, but your scent is not like any other Haute Caste."

"My blood diminished Alexander's powers temporarily."

"Yes. I heard about that. I don't believe anyone expected a mortal with vampire antibodies to threaten our kind. Still, here you are." He looked at me with a slightly amused expression. "If you don't mind the comparison, Dracula has created Frankenstein."

"Henry!" Teri glared at him.

"It's okay. He is right. There has been a lot of unexpected upheaval in the Haute Caste world because of my birth. The Common Caste rebellion was sparked when I was granted royal status and when my kids were also considered royal." A sad smile came to my face. "When I first met Tristan, he compared me to Mary Shelley, but you're right. I'm closer to the monster. At least that's how I want the vampire world to see me. How can I frighten the undead?"

"Weakness. Your blood makes us uneasy, but that's not the only threat you and the children pose to our kind. We suspect you have powers you are ignorant of, and most of us want to keep it that way."

"And you don't?" With Henry's unspoken permission, I searched him with my ability to read people. I had to know if I could trust him. My head started to ache. I closed my eyes and took a deep breath. "Enough."

He smiled. "What did you find?"

"What is going on?" Teri looked from Henry to me, very confused.

"You want me to bring it on." I studied his amused expression. Then I turned to Teri. "He wants to be the one to transform you."

Teri's eyes were as big as saucers. "If I transform. That's a big if."

Her words reminded me of when I met Tristan. For the first time, I felt like Teri would be okay whatever she decided to do.

"What do you mean, bring it on?" she asked.

Guillaume came to the door of the barn. "The kids are eating dinner. May I join you?" I nodded, and he pulled up a chair.

I touched his hand. "Cousin, I would like you to stay, but it might not be in your best interest. We're discussing how to get the Magus to fuck-off and leave the kids and me alone."

"How can I be of assistance?" He never even paused to think about the harm he could bring on himself.

Henry explained, "Help me teach her how to unleash her power."

180

"Bien sur!"

I didn't speak French, but it was clear he was willing to do anything to protect my kids.

Teri asked, "Do you remember when we were fencing, and you moved so fast that you were only a blur. Is that what you mean?"

Guillaume stifled a laugh and dismissed her comment with a wave of his hand. "Pfft, that is nothing. Henry, would you kindly start a fire."

"I don't think that's a good idea in the barn," I said.

Henry lifted his hand, and some papers on a table in the corner started to smolder. Guillaume looked at me. "Put out the fire."

I started to get up and go over to the table. Henry reached over and pulled me back into the chair.

Guillaume said, "Extinguish it with your mind Baroness!" I stared at him for a second like I thought he was crazy. "Focus Miranda!"

Adrenaline and something else in my DNA cause my brain to feel like it was turning up the juice. I stared at the table and raised my palms towards the papers burning on the desk. The flames and smoke began to get worse.

"Miranda! Don't let the Magus win!" Henry whispered in my ear.

Suddenly coldness seemed to emanate from me. The temperature was falling, and moisture made the air seem heavy. My head throbbed, frost formed on my hands, then I saw snowflakes! They swirled around the desk, cleaning the air of smoke and killing the flames. I was causing this freak storm! I shivered so hard my body shook. "I've had dreams like this," I muttered. "I would be somewhere, and suddenly snow would start falling...."

Guillaume put a blanket around my shoulders. Teri pulled it tight around me. She smiled. "That was amazing."

"That's nothing compared to what she is capable of," Henry said.

The air in the room cleared, leaving a dusting of snow that quickly dissipated as it began to warm up.

I looked at Henry. "I don't understand. Tristan never told me, not even a hint. How did you know?"

"About your power? I'm a student of the elements and the Zodiac. I'm Leo, a fire sign. You are Scorpio, a water sign. Our powers are related to the time of our births. The Baron is Aquarius, an air sign."

"He lifts people into the air!"

"Yes," Guillaume responded, "and he can manipulate the wind, among other abilities. Ma chère, there is much you have not been told despite your years with us."

"What is the Magus?" I looked at Henry.

"Capricorn. He is of the earth. Have you ever noticed how many quakes there are in Los Angeles?"

"But you're all undead. As far as I know, I'm still mortal."

Henry shook his head. "That is the mystery and the threat. You can walk in daylight and have Haute Caste powers. That makes you the vampire world's worst nightmare. You wanted to cause fear and trembling among us. When this becomes known, you will."

Guillaume touched my shoulder. "Be careful. You need to learn better control. Try a small rainstorm before you try a blizzard. You must appear ignorant for the time being."

"That won't be hard. I feel exhausted right now. I just want to take care of Tomas then go to bed. I'll think about conquering the world tomorrow."

Teri nodded in agreement. "Good plan! It has been quite a day for you."

Henry added, "I'll talk with Alexander. We have put our differences aside. His fondness for you and Jacques will assure his allegiance and secrecy."

"Maybe I should start a new vampire House," I said as I headed towards the door with the blanket around my shoulders like a child pretending to be a queen.

"The House of Templars," Guillaume suggested.

I looked at my cousin. "I don't think the Templars would appreciate the irony."

Chapter 25

Cramer Confesses

As darkness descended, Cramer took back roads between the hospital and Granite Falls. He nervously glanced in the rear-view mirror but did not see anyone following him. Because of the thick trees, the satellite radio connection faded to silence. He just wanted to deliver Miranda's stolen blood and find another employer. The Magus paid well, but his assignments were difficult to stomach. Would the Magus let him just walk away? The small ice chest containing Miranda's blood, that he had gotten from the lab tech, shifted in the back seat as he rounded a corner a little too fast. Jordan Road was hilly, full of twists and turns, and had a 35-mph speed limit. He was going over 50-mph and having trouble staying in his lane. He saw the timber truck come across the centerline too late. He jerked the steering wheel to avoid the truck but lost control of the car, went off the road and down the steep incline. His head banged against the side window, and everything went black. The car finally came to rest in the Stillaguamish River. The cold dark water rushed into the car and woke him. He was confused but able to undo his seatbelt as self-preservation kicked in. The door was jammed! The windows would not open. He wondered if he would drown or freeze first. He pounded against the window in a desperate, yet vain attempt to escape the rising water. He promised to turn his life around if only given a chance and hoped some guardian angel was having a slow night and would hear his prayer.

A voice outside the car shouted, "He's alive."

"Give me the hammer!" a second voice yelled.

Suddenly the glass shattered, and two hands reached through the window. Whoever it was, gripped his shoulders, pulled him out, and dragged him to the riverbank. He sputtered and tried to stand. It was too dark for Cramer to see who they were. He was picked up and carried up the bank by two men, wearing waders and rubber boots. When they got up to the road, they roughly dropped him to the ground, then turned and waved to the timber truck driver, who climbed back into his rig and drove off.

Cramer realized he had been rescued by darker angels than he had been hoping for. They got him into the Range Rover and covered him in warm blankets. His head had cleared enough to realize vampires don't usually run around in waterproof clothing.

"You set me up! You had him run me off the road!"

Robert replied, "Leif knew a guy. We had to make it look like an accident. In a few hours, you can call the cops, report the incident and tell them you're fine."

"You could've killed me."

"Naw," Billy responded, "We would've just brought you back one way or another."

Robert added, "You can thank the Baroness, she wants to talk with you. We wouldn't have been so merciful."

"How is Tomas?" Cramer asked.

"My, my, you gonna pretend to care about him now? Bless your heart," Robert said.

They rode in silence to Leif's place and parked beside the goat pen. Still a little shaky, the smell made Cramer start to gag. He covered his nose with the blanket as he followed them to the house. Leif poured a couple of mugs of coffee and indicated their reluctant guest should sit at the kitchen table. "You look like hell," Leif said and handed him a mug.

"I need a doctor!" Cramer protested.

They ignored him. Robert turned to Leif. "Now you get to babysit this waste of human flesh. It's almost dawn."

Billy looked at Cramer. "You've failed the Magus, which will not go well for you. I would advise you to accept any deal the Baroness offers you. We'll return this to the donor." He held up the cooler. "Adios."

Leif handed Cramer some dry clothes. "These will be a little big, but it will do for now. You can run. I won't stop you. I don't care what they do to you."

Cramer went into the bathroom to change. He was shivering as he changed into Leif's Seahawks sweats. Limited options ran through his mind. The Magus enjoyed torture, but the Baroness was an unknown. With a shaky hand, he combed his hair to look more presentable.

Cramer sat down at the table. "I'll cooperate." He grabbed the mug and took a swig. His head throbbed. "I probably have a concussion."

"Too bad," Leif remarked and started cooking breakfast. He handed him his phone. "Better call the cops."

Teri was already up, I had checked on Tomas, and she was getting breakfast for the kids. As I started for Leif's place, she said, "Give him hell!'

"Billy and Robert already took care of that."

The sky was becoming gray, and a fine mist added to the soft shadows of the trees. I carried a flashlight to keep me from tripping over fallen branches and roots. I took a deep breath of the damp morning air and prepared myself. It would take all my self-control not to throttle Cramer.

Cramer stood up as I entered the kitchen. I stared at him and finally remembered where I had seen him before. Fifteen years ago, he had flown us to Rossville when I moved the babies away from Los Angeles. "You were the Magus's pilot!"

He looked miserable, like a wet rat trying to dry out. "I'm truly sorry. It was not supposed to be so bad. Just enough to warrant a few stitches and some blood work. The Magus had me get a teaching degree so I could watch over them in high school. I was all set to move to Rossville, but when you moved to Granite Falls, the Magus arranged to have me hired at the high school here."

"You and that English teacher bitch!"

"Yes. We both work for the Magus. He wants samples of blood from your kids, but I'm not sure why. He would never confide in me."

I moved closer to him. "Look at me! Do you want to be one of them?"

"No!" he was repulsed by the idea. "I just did it for the money. Now I know it wasn't worth it."

I could read him well enough to know he was telling the truth. "You want a chance at redemption?"

He looked at me wide-eyed. "You mean going against the Magus?"

Leif injected, "There are a lot of us on Team Miranda, including very powerful vampires. You can help her, or we can turn you over to the Magus without the blood. Your choice."

Cramer searched my face for some sign of strength or power. I guess he found something. "I'll help you and the kids."

"What exactly did Magus ask you to do?" I sat across from him, and Leif put a mug of coffee in front of me.

He shrugged. "Besides getting blood, I kept him updated on how the kids were doing. He was irritated that I only had Des and Tomas in my class. He also wanted reports on Marie. Sandy, Ms. Grisham, reported to him on Marie and Jacques."

"What did you tell him?"

"I told him that Tomas has an amazing memory, and he never needs to take notes. Des reads people well, and he can work people to get what he wants. I don't know what Sandy has told him about the other two." He nervously took a sip of coffee.

"Where is Grisham now?"

"Since we have been outed and can't get the blood the Magus wanted, she took off. She had been in contact with Pomp, so she probably has gone there looking for protection from the Magus. Sandy had a tube of Tomas' blood to give to the Baron to pass on to the Magus."

"Fuck!" I hit the table with my fist so hard my coffee almost spilled.

"They especially wanted your blood. That's what I had in the cooler."

"If you hear anything, I mean anything from other vampires and their associates, you must tell me. If you do what I tell you, I can help you."

"I don't think anyone will confide in me now."

"I would like to cut you like you hurt my son, but I want someone looking out for them at the school. Can you do that Cramer?"

I stared at him and searched his thoughts, and I found remorse and guilt. "Yes. I'll look after them. I promise."

"I've got a car you can use. I'll let the Haute Caste know that you helped Tomas after he was hurt and that you're under my protection." I wasn't sure how much that was worth, but we would soon find out.

Leif added, "You can stay here for now when you're not teaching. Safer."

Manny was tired from his forty-hour, cross-country drive to Rossville. Still, he managed to get a glimpse of Miranda's place before heading to a hotel in Danville. The small city had big houses around Lake Vermilion, and tiny homes on the poor side of town near the V.A. Medical Center. Not a big tourist stop. Manny was ripe and sore from the long drive and sleeping in his car. He was looking forward to a long hot shower and a bed. As Manny got out of his car, he noticed the Harley in the hotel parking lot that he had seen on the road a couple of times. He leaned against his car, waited to see what the biker would do now. Knowing he had been spotted, the biker looked at him, made a quick phone call then left. Whoever was having Manny tailed wouldn't give up so easily. It was getting dark as he checked in and then walked over to the Big Boy's restaurant next door to get something to eat. He ignored the meth head, who was panhandling as he went back to the hotel.

Once in his room, he took a long hot shower. He loved feeling clean. Hand sanitizer and rest stop bathrooms could only help so much. To be on the safe side, he had put his gun on the vanity, close at hand. He got out of the shower, looked in the mirror, noticed the dark circles under his eyes, and shook his head. "What a dumbass!" He hoped his gut was right. He dried off, picked up his gun, and walked out of the bathroom.

"Good evening Detective," the panhandler that he had seen earlier was sitting on his bed, calmly watching him.

Manny stood in the bathroom doorway with a towel wrapped around his waist. "How did you get in here?" Manny pointed his gun at the intruder.

The bearded man did not flinch. "This hotel's security doesn't present much of a challenge. I mean you no harm and that pistol is useless." He smiled and added, "I am only armed with my wits."

"Who are you, and what do you want?"

"I am Bartholomew. I take care of the Baroness' mother, Mrs. Ortega, and look after the horses. Why did you come here?"

Manny kept his gun pointed at Bart. "I'm investigating a murder in Salinas, California. The Baroness was driving a vehicle spotted by a witness near the scene of a crime. I don't think she did it, but someone she knows might have. I'm here to follow up on leads. Any light you can shed on it?"

Bart could sense Manny's fear, which he was trying very hard to conceal. "I realize you think you are doing your job, but I would advise you to get a good night's sleep then go back home. No good will come of prying into the affairs of the Mordecai family. They had nothing to do with your murder case. If you try to make contact with Mrs. Ortega, you will forfeit any protection you are being afforded now." Bart stood and turned towards the door.

"Protection? From who? By who?"

"Trust me, you don't want to know," he said and walked to the door.

Manny was not backing down. "I want answers!"

186

Bart turned and looked at him with pity. He hated when mortals got involved in their affairs. He knew that the Baroness had already divulged their true identity, but it seemed Manny needed more proof. 'You're on what we call the "No Bite List', so unless you do something foolish, you have nothing to worry about from us." He smiled just enough to show his fangs. "Good night, and I hope for your sake goodbye." He quickly left.

Manny locked the door, still wondering how Bart had gotten in without him hearing. It was going to be a long night. He had an appointment with Sheriff Fleming in the morning that he would keep. "No Bite List," he muttered, "You've got to be kidding me!" Manny got dressed and laid down on the bed. He turned on the television, flipped through the channels looking for something to help him relax, and settled on *Blade*. Maybe he would learn more about the creatures these people pretended to be.

Manny managed to get about 6 hours of fitful sleep before his alarm went off at eight. He texted the sheriff, and they agreed to meet at the Mad Goat Cafe. Manny pulled into the strip mall and parked next to the sheriff's SUV. Fleming was already inside chatting with a cute barista at the counter.

Manny headed in and walked up to Fleming. They shook hands, and Fleming waited while Manny ordered.

"Cappuccino please. 12-ounce, triple shot, dry."

The barista smiled. "You know the difference between a latte and a cappuccino?"

"Yeah, I do," Manny wondered if he should have just ordered a regular cup of coffee.

"Okay. Sometimes new customers aren't sure. Any flavoring?"

"No, thanks."

They sat at a small table and waited for their coffee. Fleming started, "Thanks for coming all this way. It's great to work with you. What can I tell you about the Ortega murder?" He was anxious to discuss all the horrible details of the biggest crime in his short police career.

"Thanks. I think I've read enough about the details of the investigation. I just wanted your take on the Mordechai's. Miranda and her husband. Any suspicious behavior? Were they ever questioned about any other investigations?"

Just then, a small man in his forties entered the coffee shop. "That's weird," Fleming observed.

"What?"

"That's the little Italian guy who bakes bread for Connie Ortega at her cafe. I've never seen him in Danville before."

Grigoryi did not make eye contact with them. He just ordered and stared at some artwork on the wall. The barista signaled to Manny to come and get his beverage. When he walked up to the counter, Grigoryi glanced at him nervously. Manny thought he heard the man mumble, "Forgive me." He bumped into Manny, sending the cup of hot cappuccino crashing to the floor.

Fleming jumped to his feet, glaring.

Grigoryi feigned innocence. "Accident. So sorry!" He hurried out before getting his coffee.

Manny wiped the coffee off of his favorite Nikes. "Damn, at least it's only my shoes."

They sat back down as the barista cleaned up the mess. Fleming looked upset. "You think that was on purpose?"

"I do. It seems no one wants me asking questions about the Mordecai family."

The barista brought Manny a fresh cup.

"Thanks."

Fleming went on. "The Police Chief in Rossville is fond of Mrs. Ortega. I just thought you should know. They had a waitress that ripped me off and left town, but I was told to let that go. Something isn't right there, but I can't be of much help. The whole thing with Connie Ortega's husband was weird. We never were able to find out why anyone would want to kill him. It looked like some kind of wild dog or wolf killed his attackers, but we never were able to track it down. Another odd thing was that Pete was buried at night on their property with just a few of her husband's family from out of state there. I've already lost too much sleep trying to figure out what's going on. Sorry I couldn't be of much help. I better get going. Good luck."

Manny stared at his cappuccino. He wondered about the funeral in the dark. "It can't be," he thought and looked down at the coffee stains on his shoes. "Shit!" he muttered. He knew he wasn't going to get any cooperation here. He would have to pursue other leads.

He sent a text to Molly,

No luck. Coming home.

Teri and I gathered the kids together after breakfast. We sat around the living room. The only sound was Lug licking himself. I looked at Tomas and began. "It is not easy for me to tell you what has happened without becoming angry, but I will try. Tomas's injury was not an accident."

"I knew it." Tomas glared at Des.

"It wasn't Des. The Magus was behind it."

Des chimed in, "Bro, I tried to tell you."

I shot Des a look, and he fell silent. "The Magus told your father he needed blood samples from each of us for research. They knew I would not allow it, so they devised the plan to have you get hurt at school, but it went too far. Cramer was supposed to arrange for you to get a minor injury, but Des got in the way at the last second, and you were cut worse than planned."

Marie's eyes were big. "Mr. Cramer is working for the Magus?"

Teri said, "Grisham and Cramer."

Jacques surprised me by saying, "That's fucked up." He never cussed.

"Dad?" Tomas asked, looking down at his bandaged arm. "I thought he would never harm us. How could Dad be part of this?"

Marie said angrily, "Why did we help save the Magus' ungrateful ass? Dad won't go against him, even for us."

"But we will," I stated calmly. They all looked at me. "We are establishing a new House. I have been thinking about how we can protect ourselves, and now I am sure of it. I doubt the Magus will approve, but I know there are others that I can convince. I'll tell you more when I have worked out the details. No more running away from them. I'll demand representation and a voice in Parliament. You can't tell your dad yet."

"Who can we trust?" Jacques was tearful.

"For now, Henry, Guillaume, Alexander, and Leif. Cramer is willing to help us, but he'll have to earn our trust. I think others will help too, but it will take time to get their support. You have to keep this a secret."

"The Magus is a sorry asshole," Tomas looked down at his bandaged arm. "So is Dad."

"I won't stop you from seeing your dad, but be careful what you say around him. For what it's worth, he was upset that you were so badly injured."

Des shook his head. "I've lost all respect for him. The vampire code is a joke."

"Couldn't we just join the House of Swords?" Jacques asked, wiping his eyes.

Marie looked over at him. "Mom has to be in charge. It's about time."

Ben Lather had been a real estate agent for fifteen years and had experienced the wave of wealth that billion-dollar corporations had brought to Seattle. He had helped hundreds of people buy luxury properties. It was a little unusual to meet a client at midnight. Since they wanted to see a multi-million-dollar home he had listed, so he adjusted his schedule. He was used to eccentric clients and learned to cater to their requirements. Ben pulled up to the gate, keyed in the code, and drove up the drive to the front door. He got out of his Escalade and waited for the client to arrive. At age forty-five, he still had an athletic, sun-tanned appearance that helped him charm the clients.

A Jaguar pulled up to the house, and a ravishing young blonde woman stepped out of the car. He was surprised she was alone. At this price level, clients usually came with a spouse, partner, or a lawyer.

"Ms. Pompadour, good evening. I'm Ben Lather." He put out his hand, but she ignored it.

"Good evening," she whispered in a scratchy voice, "Laryngitis," she explained

The house was on the shore of Lake Washington and the lights of the city reflected on the calm surface of the water. It looked like a mansion from an old Hollywood movie. Pomp liked the classic luxury of the home and the dramatic view of the city. That made it a perfect place to entertain the Haute Caste. She had made a fortune in the stock market, and now it was time to show the vampire world how clever she was. She did not need Sir Henry or any other vampire, though she enjoyed the Baron's company. Because of Sir Henry's assault, she now had the attention and sympathy of many of the Haute Caste. At the French Court, she had become very good at using others misfortune to her advantage. She had grown tired of the Funeral Pyre and the Goth groupies. She no longer had to associate with Sir Henry to be with the Haute Caste. Miranda's move to Seattle had been the perfect opportunity for her.

She glanced around at the mansion and the surrounding property. "I'll buy it," she announced.

He was surprised. This had to be a prank. Ben looked around to see if someone was in the bushes, shooting a video. He would not put it past his jealous coworkers. "Don't you want to tour the residence?"

"I watched a video tour online. I'll pay cash. My personal banker will contact you tomorrow. Goodnight," she croaked out. Pomp caught the scent of his AB blood. She briefly considered how easy it would be to dispose of his body in the lake, but she did not want to find another real estate agent.

Speechless, he just watched the beautiful young woman climb back into her car and drive away. Her perfume lingered. He wished she had agreed to see the inside of the mansion. He had wanted to be alone with her there. Ben shrugged, then considered the vacation he would take with part of his commission. He had no idea how close he had come to never closing another sale.

Chapter 26

The House of Sun

I sat with Tomas on the back deck, and gazed at the river as the sunlight faded. The sky turned gray as the sun slipped into the Sound beyond our sight to the west.

"A bald eagle!" Tomas pointed to the large predator gracefully soaring above the tree line to its nest a few miles upriver.

"They make me nervous because of Leif's baby goats and Lug, but they are beautiful to watch. It's so amazing to have eagles in the neighborhood. I don't know if I'll ever get used to that."

"Kind of like vampires," he grinned.

"I think I prefer birds of prey."

"I'm glad Cramer is okay. Being pressured by the Magus has got to be fuckin' terrifying. Anyway, I could use his help with the ultimate sunscreen." His eyes had the look of an old soul. Hard to believe he was only sixteen.

"You can forgive him just like that? I can't," I said.

"C'mon, you know how manipulative the Magus is," he replied.

Teri came out on the deck with her cell phone in her hand. "Henry just left Seattle. He and Guillaume want to meet with you in about an hour." She looked at Tomas. "House business." He just shrugged.

"I'll be here." I was anxious about what their response to my plan might be.

She got back on the phone. "No problem Henry," then she walked back inside to finish her conversation.

Tomas just rolled his eyes. "Adults are crazy."

"Yeah, well, you're almost there. A car came up the drive from Omega Pizza. Looks like it's time for dinner."

Tomas ran his fingers thru his hair. The driver stayed in the car, but the cute redhead Tomas had a crush on, got out of the car carrying a couple of pizza boxes. "Hi, Mrs. Mordecai."

"Hi Ashley, come in," I took the pizzas from her, and she followed Tomas and me into the kitchen.

"Tommy are you okay?" she said and touched his good arm. They were darling.

"He's fine!" Des called across the kitchen.

Tomas was turning red. I paid Ashley for the pizzas, making sure to give her a nice tip.

Lug ran over and almost knocked her down. He brought comic relief to the teenage angst that hung over us. Tomas yelled, "Lug, stop it!'

Ashley looked down at Lug, "It's okay. I love Labs. Lug is a funny name."

Jacques pulled him off her. "It's short for Lugosi."

"Like the vampire? Cool!"

She had no idea how relieved we all were to hear her say that. The delivery driver honked the horn. Tomas said, "C'mon'" and walked her out to the car.

Marie punched Des in the shoulder. "Jerk!"

"What? He is fine. He just got sympathy from Ashley. Maybe I should get hurt."

Marie replied, "Just say the word."

"Enough guys!" I shook my head. "Des, grab the salad from the fridge, Marie, get plates, Jacques, grab some napkins."

Tomas came back in with a big grin. "She wants me to go with her to the b-ball game against Mirror Point."

"Sure, that sounds like fun. We can all go. I'll talk to Teri and Leif about it."

His grin faded. "Everyone?"

"We'll leave you and Ashley alone." I smiled. "A normal outing would be good for all of us."

Des smirked, "Tommy, pass me the salad."

Tomas shot back, "You are such an asshole."

Teri came into the kitchen as we were cleaning up. While we ate dinner, she had been primping.

"Wow!" Jacques said.

She wore tight black jeans, heels, and a low-cut red blouse. Gold bangles adorned her wrists, and she smelled of exotic flowers.

Teri smiled at us and went out the front door as Henry pulled up in a red Corvette. He came up to her and kissed her like he hadn't seen her in weeks.

They realized they were being watched and headed off to the barn for the meeting. I grabbed my Levi jacket, followed them and patted the Tarot card in my pocket. The cooler nights were starting to remind me of home. We would be going to visit Mom soon. I had to tell her about our adventures here, and I was not sure where to begin. Maybe I would skip the part about Tomas getting hurt.

Henry, Guillaume, and Teri were sitting and talking as I entered the barn. Teri got up, put her hand on Henry's shoulder, and said to him, "I'll see you later at Leif's," she gave a little wave to Guillaume and me. "I'll leave you guys to it."

Henry watched her until the door swung shut. "You've got it bad," I said to Henry and sat down with them.

Henry wore a tailored shirt and black slacks like he was attending a business meeting. He smiled. "I'm more content now than I've been in ages. Literally."

I just shrugged. I was not in the mood to hear about his happy love story.

"When Teri told me what you wanted to discuss, I was not surprised. Lady Cassandra contacted me months ago." Henry began, "She told me that she had a vision about you. She said you must create a House and that sunlight would be your symbol.

Guillaume added, "Like Louis the 14ᵗʰ, the Sun King."

Henry continued, "She saw Guillaume, Alexander, and me as your knights."

I was relieved they seemed to be on board before I even laid out my crazy idea. I owed Cassandra big time for that. "No mention of Tristan or the children?"

"When I asked about the offspring, she said their story has yet to be written." Henry leaned forward and touched my hand. "I have never known her prophecies to be in error."

"My story has been written? I don't think so."

"I think it is more shocking that Sir Henry would be a knight. It shows the magnificence of the new House and attests to your power."

"I haven't agreed to anything yet." He held out his hand, and a little flame appeared.

Without conscious thought, I reacted by holding my hand over his. Droplets of water fell from my palm. His flame quickly vanished. We stared at each other, then started laughing. "I didn't mean to...."

Guillaume raised his hand to stop me. "Never apologize for your power."

Henry added thoughtfully, "Guillaume is right. For the Haute Caste to take you seriously, we must be your knights, including Alexander. That will be a challenge. You might invite lady Cassandra to be your counselor. She understands you have misgivings about her but wishes only to protect you and the children. She may be helpful with Alexander."

"Let me guess. They were fuck buddies once."

"I would have said lovers, but though crude, your description is apt," Henry replied.

Guillaume cleared his throat, "Alexander has never been subservient, though he made the pretense with the Magus. You are the mother of his child. That changes everything. You must persuade Alexander."

I was not sure about what they were expecting of me. "You realize I don't have an undead wish, at least at this point. I will have to rule as a mortal or no new House."

"But of course!" Guillaume enthusiastically agreed.

Henry continued, "It is why Lady Cassandra insisted we be the House of Sun."

"Kananga! She knew!" I thought about the last time I had seen her before I left for Seattle. "She gave me this." I pulled out the Sun card. "She said it was my future."

Guillaume and Henry looked at me with solemn expressions. "That, my dear Baroness, was a sign. Lady Kananga also has visions," Guillaume said. She rarely tells anyone of her insights. It is one of the reasons she is so powerful."

Guillaume stood and bowed to me. "I will gladly be a knight to the Baroness Ortega-Mordecai of the House of Sun."

Henry nodded. "As will I."

I looked at these two powerful creatures and felt a little sick. Maybe it was the pizza. I've always had a weak stomach. I must have looked a little green because Guillaume handed me a wastebasket. I lost my dinner. Henry gave me a handkerchief.

Guillaume looked at Henry. "I think that means she accepts."

"Without a doubt. I'll tell Alexander you want to speak to him. Perhaps I should start addressing him as Sir again," Henry said. "You can give him back his title as a bargaining chip." He went to the door. "You must excuse me. Teri is waiting for me at Leif's."

I sat up and wiped my mouth. "Yeah, go! Go!" Head of the House of Puke was more like it.

"I have some ginger and chamomile tea that will help you. If you drink it once a day, it might help you handle this new responsibility better. I'll leave it in the kitchen. Don't worry; I'll clean this up," Guillaume said.

I wandered back to the house and laid down on the couch in the living room. That was a very weird and somewhat rocky start of the House of Sun. Take that Magus!

Pomp was disappointed that the Baron was not spending the night. Tristan got out of the elegant, canopied bed and began to look for his clothes in the candlelight. Still, she hoped he would continue to seek pleasure in her bed now that the Baroness had foolishly dismissed him. The nerve! That mortal bitch had no sense of how lucky she was to have mated with the Haute Caste's second most powerful member. She wished she was fertile and could provide the Baron with a child. It would give her such a hold on him.

"Dear Baron," she rose from the bed and let the sheets fall to expose her perfect breasts. "When shall I expect you again?"

He was annoyed when she feigned devotion. He knew she held no great affection for him. She adored his power. He got dressed quickly. "I have no idea." He walked out without another word. Pomp sorely missed Versailles. Even the king had never dismissed her so rudely.

She sent a text message to the Magus.

A tube was received and is on its way to you.
Your servant, Pomp.

Though she had little to do with the affair, she would take as much credit as possible. There was an immediate response,

One tube?

She texted back as her hopes of any reward faded.

Yes, that's all.

She put the phone on the bedside table and grumbled, "Merde!" Pomp had wanted to celebrate tonight. She expected the Baron to feel satisfaction in her bed and that the Magus would express gratitude for the samples of royal blood. Why

194

was she unable to win their respect? Pomp had to change her focus. More and more, Pomp felt betrayed by the powerful males she had relied on. Henry, the Baron, and the Magus were at times abusive, offensive, or unappreciative of her talents. Her speaking voice was better but would never have the same soft, seductive quality. She would need a new strategy to help her rise in the vampire court. She blew out the candle by her bedside table and lay in the dark room, considering her options.

Batu woke with a start from a bad dream. He had seen Miranda standing alone as snow piled up, almost burying her. She had tears in her eyes that became crystal drops as they fell down her cheeks. She called out his name, which caused him to wake. Groggy, he sat up and oriented himself. He reached for his phone and sent a text message to Miranda,

I know you suffer. Let me comfort you.

She had not directly communicated with him for months. He sent a message to Teri,

What the hell is going on?

Batu threw back the silk covers on his low bed and grabbed his clothes. He was leaner and more muscular than before, and the contours of his face were more pronounced. The transformation highlighted all his best features. He pulled his long straight black hair back with a leather tie then summoned a servant.

An old woman brought him a small glass of blood and a pot of tea. She made no attempt at conversation with one of the lords of the night. She bowed, then left. Batu sipped the blood slowly as though savoring a fine wine. He was aware that his breakfast was spiked with a little Haute Caste HH blood. He suspected it was from Kyoto. That dishonored vampire would do anything to stay in the good graces of Princess Khunbish. Batu appreciated the favors she bestowed on her Mongol knight. Still, he secretly hoped she would find someone to take his place so that he would feel free to leave if Miranda should need him.

His phone chimed, and he read the text message from Teri twice, slightly confused.

The Monarch butterfly is coming out of her cocoon.

A minute later, he got an unexpected text from Miranda,

Miss you.

He was still capable of human reaction. A single tear fell down his cheek. He was forgiven. Batu suspected his phone messages were being monitored, probably by Sir Steve. He decided not to press his luck by responding. He put on a dress tunic in preparation for his audience with the Princess. Then he lit a stick of incense and meditated on the challenges of his new existence.

There was a knock on his door. "Princess Khunbish will see you now."

Batu had a sense that something was wrong as he headed to the audience chamber. He picked up a familiar scent as he got close to the heavy wooden door and felt his fight or flight response start to build. Batu stood in the doorway and bowed. The Princess gestured for him to enter. As he walked into the room, he saw Scheherazade. "You!" he spat out and put his hand on the jeweled handle of a knife at his waist.

The vampiress looked at the Princess for protection. "Please, your highness."

"Sir Batu, let us hear what this renegade has to say."

Steve gestured for Batu to stand on the opposite side of the room from Scheherazade, next to Chang. A man who appeared thin and weak knelt on the ground beside their uninvited visitor. A small puncture wound was visible on his neck. When Batu stared at him, the man adjusted his collar to try and hide it. The vampires in the room could smell his HH blood.

"I brought you a present. My servant." Scheherazade nodded toward the kneeling man next to her.

The man appeared afraid to speak. He stared down at the floor. Scheherazade looked about the chamber. The Persian rugs were elegant, and Scheherazade knew the House of Cups had riches, but it was not as grand as she had expected. The only comfortable seats in the room were for the Princess and Sir Steve. She had spent a considerable amount of Sapna's money to get to Mongolia and look presentable. Gold bangles jingled on her wrists when she moved her arms. If she did not get help from this House, she would have to resort to larceny...again.

The Princess spoke, "Chang, take the poor mortal to the kitchen, tell the staff to feed him, and arrange for his lodging." He looked up at the Princess like a dog grateful for a bone. "You will be our guest. We will discuss possible employment with you tomorrow night."

"Thank you," he croaked as he followed Chang out of the room.

Sir Steve was irritated. "I dislike the way you've treated your servant. He might have died before you arrived."

"He is stronger than he looks." Her voice was harsh.

"Show us your neck!" The Princess demanded.

Scheherazade approached the couple and bowed. She unwrapped the silk scarf she had wound around her neck and revealed her scar. The femme fatale managed to let her tunic slip below one breast, then pulled it up quickly. Her pretense at modesty fooled no one. Though her neck was almost healed, a slight scar would remain, a constant reminder of her punishment. It was uncomfortable for the undead to face mortality. Batu wished to avert his eyes, but he kept his gaze on Scheherazade because of his distrust.

The Princess responded as though not bothered. "You were brought back from the brink of hell. Why should we not return you into that abyss?"

"I no longer have a House," her tone was softer, almost pleading. "I could help increase the number of Common Caste in your House. I am good at recruiting. If you provide protection for me, I will pledge my loyal service." She pushed back her long dark curls, and the gold bangles clinked. Scheherazade looked back over her shoulder at Batu and smiled.

Batu felt repulsed. "She has no honor. This vampiress cares only for herself. She would have helped Alexander behead the Magus to gain power and prestige. Do not let her poison the minds of the Common Caste of our House."

Steve whispered to the Princess, then she spoke. "We will consider your request. You may sleep here today, and we shall discuss our decision tomorrow night. We expect you to be well-mannered and grateful. You will not touch anyone in my house, including the mortals. Do you understand?"

"Yes." She bowed her head, then added, "My servant? May I request he be returned to me?"

Steve responded curtly, "He is now under our protection. He no longer serves you."

"But I need him!" she blurted out, then instantly regretted it.

The Princess nodded to her mortal guards. "They will take you to your room."

Scheherazade was not happy to be separated from her mortal snack. Still, she cooperated and followed the guards to a small room near the kitchen. She was given servants' quarters. She looked at the guards and smiled. "There must be a mistake. Surely there is a more comfortable room."

They were told not to talk with her. They heeded their instructions and merely gestured for her to go inside. Then they locked the door. "Shit!" they heard her yell.

Batu was upset that Scheherazade had been spared, not to mention allowed to stay there. He was silent as he waited for the Princess to speak.

"Sir Batu, what bothers you?" she asked.

He knelt before her. "I fear she will only bring harm to our House. I wish the beheading had been permanent."

The Princess looked at Steve and nodded. "Sir Steve, please tell Sir Batu of our wishes."

"We have heard from Lady Cassandra. She believes you will soon be needed in Rossville. Make preparations for your trip tonight. Do not tell the Baroness or Teri of your journey. Those were the clear directives from Lady Cassandra."

"I don't understand," Batu said.

The Princess smiled. "Neither do we, but I have always found it wise to follow her counsel."

Despite his great desire to see Miranda, he responded, "I do not like to leave you with Scheherazade. She is treachery personified."

"Do not be concerned. We will make good use of her," Steve answered.

"Then I shall leave for the capital city tonight and catch a flight tomorrow evening. Though it has not been a year since my transformation, I promise to represent our House proudly. Thank you!" he bowed and left.

"Let us hope the Baroness will be pleased with him," Steve said.

Chapter 27

Destiny

The basketball game against Mirror Point reminded me of when I was in high school. Two small-town teams, with a lot of the players related to people on the other team. We managed to cheer on the Tigers though they lost by twenty points and never had the lead. The team really missed Tomas. After the game, we went to the Friendly Café, which looked like it had barely changed since the sixties. A plastic paradise with yellowed Formica counters, red stools, a grouchy old cook who loudly yelled, "Order up!" and two young waitresses with attitude.

A waitress with curly brown hair sat at the cash register reading, looked up from her book, and told us, "Sit anywhere." I was glad that at least she liked reading.

We put two tables together. I sat with Teri at one end, and Leif was at the other end between Marie and Des. Jacques stared at Tomas and Ashley, who were almost sharing one chair. The tall and thin waitress with long dark hair and a nose ring came over and stood staring at Leif. "I know you. You're the bass player for Carnage! What brings you here?"

Marie rolled her eyes at the waitress' fawning over Lief. "I'd like a coke and loaded fries." This was the first time I realized Marie had a crush on Leif.

"Yeah, sure." The waitress scribbled on her pad. Then she looked back at Leif. "I'm Amie. I've been backstage a couple of times."

"Well, Amie, I'm sorry if I don't remember you. We get a lot of fans backstage,'" Leif replied with a shrug. "I'd like a chili cheeseburger and coffee."

Jacques stared at her wide-eyed. "I would remember you." Embarrassed, he quickly added, "A grilled cheese and a coke, please."

Des slouching in his chair, said, "Yeah, we're all tight with Henry. Give me fish and chips and root beer, hon."

Amie put her hands on her hips. "No one calls me hon. Ever!"

Des sat up and sheepishly said, "Sorry."

Amie was getting points with me. Tomas and Teri ordered, then she turned to me. "Coffee and blackberry pie a la mode. Thanks." I handed back the menu.

Teri said, "I've never seen you backstage."

Amie's eyes got big. "Oh, you're with Henry. I just hung out with the drummer a couple of times. No one cool ever comes in this place," she said, looking around the diner with obvious disdain.

Amie put in our orders then had an animated but hushed conversation with the other waitress. They both brought our food out. There were only a few other people in the diner, and they seemed like regulars, so I guess our order was a lot for the old cook. The food was just okay, but the pie and the Tillamook ice cream made up for it.

On the way out, I noticed Amie give something to Leif. Marie noticed too. I would have to watch Marie around Leif. I liked him, but he was just too old in many ways. She and Des rode over in Leif's truck but switched with Jacques and came back with us. I noticed Tomas put his arm around Ashley's shoulder in the backseat. I could hear them whispering all the way back, and I was glad to see him so happy. Jacques surprised me when he tried to flirt with the waitress. Shades of Alexander.

Fall in Washington was beautiful, cool, and foggy at times but not freezing yet. In a couple of days, we would be heading to Rossville for Thanksgiving with my mom. I still had time enough to get myself and the kids packed. I grabbed a blueberry muffin, glad that my half-vamp DNA kept me on the thin side and hungry. Batu had complained I needed to gain weight the last time I'd seen him. I wondered what he would think now.

Before I finished my muffin, my cell phone rang. It was Danuta. "Baroness, you have to come home now. It's your mom; she's in the hospital. They say it's her heart. Camo and I are with her at the Catholic Hospital in Urbana."

"Oh my God, how bad is it?" I was stunned.

"She collapsed at the café. She's been unconscious. The doctor said you should get here soon."

"We will!" Tears started falling down my cheeks. "Tell her we're coming!" Even if she was unconscious, I prayed Mom could hear that we were on the way.

"Teri! Kids!" I yelled as I ran upstairs. "Grandma is in the hospital. We're leaving for the airport now."

Shouts and questions filled the air as we stuffed backpacks with essentials and hit the road. My kids were great in an emergency. I called Leif to let him know what was going on. He would take care of Lug and let Guillaume know what had happened. Tristan was still in Seattle, and I got Clive, Tristan's butler, on the phone. I stayed focused on tasks. I would not let myself start to fall apart.

"Clive, we need the Baron's jet. It's my mom. She had a heart attack, and we need to fly there today."

"Baroness, I'm so sorry. Of course! But I will have to find a pilot. The Baron's pilot is away and not expected back for two nights."

"Damn it! Just have someone get the plane ready. I'll find a pilot!" I called Leif again and explained what we needed. Teri broke the speed limit several times as we headed to SeaTac. The kids just stared out the windows, afraid to talk about what was happening.

"Starbucks!" I called out a little too loudly as we got off the highway near the airport. Teri pulled up to the drive-thru. We bought a jug of coffee and cleaned out their supply of pumpkin bread for the flight. Anxiety hung over us like a fine Seattle rain for the rest of the ride to the airport.

We got through security and pulled up to the hanger. As we got out of the car, a guy in mechanics overalls came over and asked, "Are you Baroness Mordecai?"

I nodded, and he told me the jet was fueled and ready, and we could get on board to wait for the pilot. As the kids climbed up the stairs into the plane, they were quiet and subdued. They were very worried about their grandmother. I knew this was as hard on them, as it was on me after losing my dad so recently.

Jacques hugged me. "She's going to be okay, right?"

"I don't know." I looked into his sad eyes. "But she's tough."

"We gotta be strong for grandma," Tomas stated and settled into a seat.

Marie touched my shoulder and handed me a cup of coffee, then she curled up in a seat with a blanket. Des and Teri stowed the food. I went back out and paced in the hangar as we waited for the pilot. I could not conceive of a world without my mom. I had barely started to heal from my dad's death. Thoughts of the things I should have done and things I wished I had told her assailed me. I fought back tears as Leif's car pulled into the hangar.

The passenger door opened, and Cramer got out. I stood staring at him, a little confused.

He walked over to me and said, "Reporting for duty!" and saluted.

"Oh, right! I forgot you were the Magus' pilot. Can you get us to the Urbana airport?"

"I called ahead and filed a flight plan as we drove in. We'll be in the air in about 45 minutes. We were able to get everything arranged so quickly because your ex knows the right people in Seattle."

"You mean bribed the right people? I don't care. When was the last time you flew a jet?"

He gave me a sheepish grin. "A while, but I'm good. As they say, it's like riding a bicycle. Here," he handed me a bag from Taco Time. "The Baron never stocks the fridge."

"Just get us to Illinois!"

Once we were in the air the flight was a little bumpy, but we could still move about the cabin. I shared my cherished brew with Cramer. Tomas was thrilled that he got to sit in the cockpit with him during the flight. Marie read the Tale of Two Cities and said very little. Des played electronic games to keep his anxiety down. Jacques drew pictures of Rossville. I was surprised by the beautiful detail in his art. Teri fell asleep holding her phone. Obviously, she had no photos of Henry to comfort her, so she hoped for a message if he woke during the day. I did not know how Tristan or the other undead would react. I had little energy for them at that moment. I hated to think well of Cramer, but he made a lot of points that day.

Clive arranged to have a limousine pick us up at the Champaign/Urbana airport. We raced to the hospital as the sun was setting over the cornfields. Camo was waiting for us in front of the hospital and led us to the Cardiac Care Unit.

Dr. Midland, a heavyset older woman, came over to me and asked, "Are you her daughter, Miranda Mordecai?" I nodded. She led me a few steps away from everyone. "The emergency has passed, and we are keeping her comfortable. She told us she had several previous episodes but never told anyone or sought treatment. The damage to the heart muscle is beyond repair. I don't know what is keeping her alive. There is also evidence she suffered a few small strokes. She is not a good candidate for a heart transplant, and she signed a DNR form witnessed by your housekeeper. I'm very sorry." As she said that, a nurse called her away.

I turned to the others. "Let me see Mom alone first."

Danuta was sitting by the bed and came over and hugged me when I entered the room. She left me alone with the woman who brought me into this world. Mom looked pale and small in the big white bed. Multiple tubes supplied the drugs that bolstered her failing heart, and a tube under her nose, supplied oxygen. Her usually neat short hair was in disarray. I smoothed her hair like she had done for me a million times. "I'm here Mom," I touched her bruised hand. Mom's eyes flickered. "I love you," I whispered as tears wet my face.

She opened her eyes and coughed a little. "Miranda," she muttered, "water." I helped her take a few sips. She managed a little smile. "It won't be long. You must listen."

"Mom, I can help you. I can get some blood from...."

"No, honey, I will not cheat death." She stared at me. "Always know I'm proud of you. Stay stubborn and headstrong," She stopped and took a breath. "There are letters in my dresser. Please deliver them. There are things that need to be said. Pete is waiting for me. I want to talk to my grandkids. Bring them in now."

It scared me when she mentioned my dad. I called in the kids. They stood two on each side of her bed, trying to hold back tears. "Grandma, you should come to Seattle," Tomas said.

Marie told her, "You can have my room. You can see the river."

Des added, "You can bring Piglet."

Jacques spoke for all of us, "Grandma, please don't die!"

She smiled. "You must be very grown-up for your mom and me. Tomas, you're a wonderful, talented young man. Des, I know you have a kind heart, don't be afraid to let the world see it." She paused and took a breath. "Marie, don't worry about what others think. Free yourself from expectations, live your life." She coughed again and closed her eyes for a minute, and then she looked at Jacques. "Let your quiet strength guide you. You're more than your fathers could ever be." She paused and took a breath. "I love you all! You'll always be in my heart."

They each hugged her despite the tubes and medical equipment. She told them she wanted to talk to me alone again, and they quietly left the room. I could hear muffled crying in the hall where Teri, Camo, and Danuta comforted them.

"Don't worry about Stan. You've made him more human. He'll thank you one night." Her voice was raspy, "Don't let those vampire bastards push you around. They need you more than you need them. I'd tell you to protect the kids, but I know you will. Don't ever trust the Magus." She closed her eyes for a moment.

Tell Batu he was right. He'll understand." She looked at me and whispered, "Tell Omar I have no regrets...."

The monitor started beeping. I cried out, "Mom! Mom!" The nurses ran in and gently moved me out of the room. I huddled with the kids in the hallway. One of the nurses came out and told us that Mom was gone. The staff let us grieve together for a few minutes. I heard someone mention a chapel, but we did not respond.

Doctor Midland made it official and asked if we wanted to sit with her for a little while. I declined for all of us. Our loved one was gone, and I didn't want the kids to remember her as she was now. I took a deep breath. "Kids, please wait for me in the limo. I've got to sign some papers. Camo, can you stay with me?" He nodded. I was afraid I might faint, and I knew he was strong enough to catch me.

As the kids left, Jeanne and Bart arrived. "Ma chère." Jeanne hugged me tightly.

Bart touched my shoulder. "I feel great sadness."

I looked at the only saint I knew. "Jeanne, will you say a prayer before they take her away?" She nodded, always the stoic warrior. "Thank you both. I'll see you back at the house."

They entered the room, and I heard Jeanne softly say a prayer in Latin. My mom would appreciate being attended to by a saint.

A nun came up to me. "Can I be of service to you and your family?"

"Our religious needs have already been taken care of, thank you."

The sister glanced at Camo, taking in the red-haired biker with a mohawk and a black widow tattoo on his neck, standing at my side. She did not know he was one of my guardian angels. He had performed CPR on my mom at the café and had kept her alive until the ambulance arrived.

She nodded. "Of course." and then led us to a small office where a social worker offered grief counseling, which I turned down. Then I signed some official papers that would register the end of my mom's life in some records somewhere and allow the funeral home to take her body. It was the same mortuary that had helped bury my dad.

The young man with the social worker title leaned close to me. He patted my hand as though he knew me. "If you ever find the burden of dealing with the affairs of the deceased becomes difficult, you may always call me here." I think he meant well, but I did not like his patronizing demeanor.

I shot to my feet and, maybe a little too loudly, said, "Deceased was not the right word to use for her. She will never cease. A life force like my mom could only move on to the next adventure. Death is a departure, not a destination. Excuse me." Without another word, I turned and rushed out of the office, followed by Camo.

Camo caught up with me and said, "You were great."

"I'm just being Connie Ortega's daughter. It's clear he never met my mom."

Camo smiled. "I think he just did."

His words stayed with me on the ride back to Rossville. So much of what I was, came from years of watching my parents react to their world. What example did I want to set for my kids? I looked at their somber expressions. More and more, I felt determined to start my own House regardless of the wishes of the Magus or the Haute Caste. I knew my mom would have approved.

At sundown, Clive woke the Baron with the sad news. He was prepared to be yelled at for not waking him earlier, but his boss just appeared to be shocked. "You're certain?" Tristan asked.

"Yes, I'm sure you'll get a message about it soon. Cramer is flying back now and should arrive in a few hours. The Royal family is in Rossville. I imagine they are preparing for the funeral."

"Natural death?" he asked as though the concept was foreign to him.

"Yes, a heart attack, sir."

"Why didn't anyone save her?"

"I don't know any more details, I'm sorry. Perhaps Sir Bart...."

"Leave me!" he said abruptly.

Clive hurried out and heard a cut crystal lamp crash against a wall as he closed the door. It was hard for the butler to imagine the Baron so upset about the death of the woman who often got on his nerves. Connie's lack of personal boundaries always irritated her son-in-law. Clive heard the shower running but decided not to hand him towels. He would wait for the Baron to summon him.

Clive would never imagine that the Baron was crying as the water fell over his body. Tristan's sense of control had taken another grave hit, first, the divorce, and now this. For him, the loss of a human life by natural causes was unnecessary. "We could have saved her," he cried out. The thought that Miranda or his children might one day choose natural death gnawed at the remnants of his soul. He would do anything to prevent that. That was why he had agreed to have Tomas injured so that Kyoto could study his blood. Tristan had not thought about the Magus using it as a weapon. He was only concerned about their longevity. "How can I let any of you perish?" He had not understood love before, and now it consumed him.

"Clive," he bellowed. "I must leave as soon as possible. I won't wait for my jet. Arrange for a plane to Danville."

"Of course." Clive had already made some calls while the Baron still slept. "A pilot and chartered jet will be available in an hour. You'll be flying out of Paine Field in Everett. A friend of Lady Pomp made the arrangements."

"You woke her?" The Baron was surprised by Clive's nerve.

"Yes, and she was most anxious to be helpful to you."

"Send her six dozen pink roses with a card that expresses my gratitude."

"Certainly." Clive had already packed a suitcase. "Please convey my condolences to the family. The car is waiting."

The Baron paused and looked at his old servant. "Thank you, Clive, you've done well."

The butler beamed as Tristan headed out the door. It had been many years since he had heard praise from his benefactor. He straightened his suit and whistled God Save the Queen as he picked up the pieces of the broken lamp. It had been many decades since the Baron had hired Clive and his brother in the UK and brought them back to his California estate. Like most of the faithful long-serving staff of the Haute Caste, they were much older than their apparent age. Periodic infusions of Haute Caste blood kept them youthful and healthy

I was the only one still awake when my ex arrived at the house in Rossville, near dawn. Grief had kept my insomnia company all night. I greeted him when he got to the top of the stairs. He hugged me tightly. His strength gave me some comfort. "Thank you for coming right away."

He followed me into his old bedroom. Camo and Danuta had moved their things out earlier. "I don't understand," he said and sat on the bed. I collapsed in an overstuffed chair in the corner.

"She was ready to die. I think she has been ready since Dad was killed." My voice sounded matter of fact. I was physically and emotionally drained and had no tears left.

"No one offered their blood?" It was clear he could not comprehend her acceptance of death.

"She did not want it. She embraced her mortality. She lived her life fully and had no regrets. She misses my dad and believes she will join him now. I know it is hard for you to comprehend, but try to remember your life before you were transformed. It's dawn. Sleep well. I'll see you tonight." I stood and walked to the door.

"Share my bed," he said softly.

I turned and looked into his blue eyes. For a moment, I could feel his pain join with mine. Then something made me turn away, maybe a premonition that our truce would not last. "No, we'll talk tonight." I went back downstairs and curled up on the couch, realizing that two stabilizing pillars in my life were now gone. Silent tears rolled down my cheeks as I stared into the dying embers of the night's fire. Piglet jumped up on my lap and stared into my eyes as if she shared my grief. I rubbed her little head, and somehow, I fell asleep.

Teri was relieved to get a call from Henry. "Henry, I miss you."

"How is the family? Did Tristan arrive?"

She was a little put off that he got right to the point. But that was Henry. "Yeah, he's here. They're all devastated, even the Baron, which surprised me."

"Most of us are not fond of death, contrary to popular belief."

"I appreciate that. I've never had anyone close to me die. I did not know Connie long, but she was good to me and could always make me laugh with her comments about the grandkids. She was very special, but she could get on the Baron's nerves."

"That's not hard to do. I wish that I had been able to meet her. There are rumors that many will attend the funeral. Some will come to pay respect to the family, and some only to try to curry favor with the Baron, the Baroness, and the Magus. Remember that in our society, there is much plotting and conspiring. It is often hard to know what their true motives are. Protect yourself from their influence my love."

"I'll be fine. I'll stay close to Miranda and the offspring. We'll be back in Granite Falls soon."

"I know. She must return to establish her House. Please tell her I will ask the gods for protection for all of you."

"Sure." Teri wondered upon what ancient Egyptian gods he might be calling. She touched the necklace he had given her. "I love you!"

"I cherish you," he whispered and hung up.

Chapter 28

The Letters

The next day I found three sealed envelopes in the top drawer of Mom's dresser. One was for me, one for Tristan, and the third was for the Magus. It was difficult not to tear them all open, but I respected her request. I took a deep breath and sat on the bed to read my letter. My hands trembled as I ripped it open.

To my darling daughter Miranda,

I wish your life could have been more normal, easier. Your mixed heritage has always been a challenge, but I hope you find strength in it. I can't tell you how much you are loved. I don't know how I will die, but I will be ready when the time comes. That's how much I miss Pete. Every time I have a spell and my heart hurts, I know he is telling me it won't be long.

You must live your life in a way that brings you peace. I knew you would never stay in Rossville. I understand why you divorced Stan. A lot of women would never have had the nerve. I have always been so proud of you. I hope you keep writing, though I have to confess I could never get through your vampire book. Too close to home, I guess.

I have left the café to Danuta and Camo. The house is yours. I hope you keep it for the kids. I want my ceremony simple and no priest, except Grigoryi. He is a pure soul and has been good to me. Please see to it that he will be comfortable for the rest of his life. Also, tell James thanks for taking care of Sally. I never got to visit her. I know you'll take care of Piglet.

The Lithuanians have no idea what you and the kids are capable of. Never be afraid of them. I'm sure you'll each find a way to let them know they are not all that great. I know you will make good choices!

Love you always,
Mom

I smiled while tears ran down my cheeks. I read it over twice more, then put it back in the envelope. Her dying wish ensured I would give the Lithuanians hell. My mom was descended from a Knight Templar, after all. I hoped Tristan would let me read his letter. I had a feeling the Magus would never share his. I was not sure if she meant my Mexican American or Vampire-Mortal heritage, or maybe both. Make good choices? Mom! She did not go to the doctor when she was having heart issues. I never realized how sad she was without my dad. I was glad she expressed faith in me and her grandchildren. One day I would share the letter with them. For now, I had to take care of a million things.

Her funeral would be at sunset tomorrow, which would give the vampires time to get here. I knew many of them would arrive tonight, and daytime sleeping arrangements for all of them would be tricky. To help find room for the "hoards," I sent a message to Reuben to ask if he and his sister, Sarah, could bring their "rock-star" like RV and called the Magus's butler at his Chicago estate, to request he drive down the royal RV In the beginning, I was intimidated by the nocturnals. Now it was getting easier for me to tell them what to do.

I called my best and longtime friend. "Hi, Lolly. I've got sad news."

"What is it? Did something happen to Tristan or the kids?" Lolly asked anxiously and called out to Al, "It's Randie. Something's wrong." She put the call on speakerphone.

I was always a little sorry that they had been pulled into my vampire world. We were lucky they remained mortal and crazy enough to still care about us. "No, it's my mom. She had a heart attack and passed away."

"Hon, your mom was amazing. I'm so sorry. You've had to deal with so much. You can't seem to catch a break."

I started to choke up. "I gotta go. I just wanted you to know we'll talk later."

"Is there anything we can do to help?" Al asked

"Thanks, guys, but I think I have it handled. I'd invite you to the funeral, but I'm going to be overwhelmed by Tristan's side of the family."

"We understand. Call if you need anything or just want to talk. We'll get together when you get back to the coast," Lolly said.

"Give the kids our love," Al said.

"And Tristan," Lolly added.

"Thanks!" I hung up. I was relieved they did not insist on coming to the funeral. I loved my friends, but I would have more company than I could handle the next few nights. I did not call my biological father. I knew he would get the news and come.

My day was filled with making sad arrangements. The funeral home was one of my more manageable tasks. We could bury Mom next to my dad. Not one day went by that I did not appreciate the financial freedom that Tristan had provided. I was grateful that I could make all the arrangements without worrying about finding a way to pay the bills. I hated to think of people burdened by grief and then end up in debt because of funeral expenses.

In the early afternoon, I met with Danuta and Camo in the kitchen. We decided to keep the café closed for a week. When I told them that they would be inheriting the Café, Danuta burst out in tears, and even Camo got a little choked up.

"She was always so good to us. Oh my God, I never thought this would happen." She looked at Camo as she dried her eyes. "That is really too much. We must pay something."

I looked at them and said, "You both took such good care of her. This is what she wanted."

Camo smiled. "She and Pete would always help people out when they needed a meal. We could provide a free meal for people who are struggling. We could have a spot on the wall next to the cash register with meal tickets. We'll call it Connie's Treat."

"She would love that." Now I was getting a little choked up.

Grigoryi walked in and saw us sitting quietly at the table. "Sorry, I didn't mean to interrupt," he turned to go.

"It's okay. Please join us," I said.

"Connie left the café to Danuta and me," Camo told him.

Grigoryi smiled at them. "That is really great. I was wondering what would happen to it."

We spent a few minutes talking about the funeral plans, then sat quietly. Everyone lost in thought.

Finally, Grigori started to get up. "I should pack."

"Where will you go, Greg?" I asked.

"I talked to the owner of the bagel shop in L.A., and he said I could have my old job back."

"Mom didn't forget about you. She made arrangements so that you will never have to worry about having a job."

"I don't understand, you mean I can work at the Café?"

"Not unless you want to. She left you enough money so that you can do what you would like or go anywhere."

He looked at me, stunned.

"Do you have a raincoat?" I asked him. "We would love if you came to Granite Falls with us."

His eyes lit up. "Really? You want me there?"

"Of course. You are part of the family now, and I miss your bread in the morning."

"I don't know what to say."

"Just say yes," I said to him with a smile.

"What about Bart and Jeanne and the horses?" Danuta asked.

"I don't know, and I hadn't thought about that yet. Whatever Bart and Jeanne decide will be fine with me. The kids might want the horses back at home. We have enough land. I won't sell the house, especially with Mom and Dad buried here. You're welcome to live here as long as you like. I'm not sure when we'll ever be back to visit."

Camo said, "I love this place. It felt like home from the moment I sat down in the kitchen that first day. I can't thank you enough. You trusted me to look after you and the kids. Not many people would have done that."

Danuta turned to Camo. "The first time I saw you, all I could think was, "Who

208

is this crazy-ass biker. Now I love you."

"It was my chili that won you over."

"I'm glad you'll take care of this place. Now about the nocturnal visitors. I'm not sure how many will show up, but I'm sure the Magus will be here," I said.

Danuta's eyes got big. I wasn't the only one who wasn't a big fan of the Magus. I'll need you to get the guest rooms ready. I will have the boys bunk together, and Marie will sleep with me. That will free up more space. Don't worry about refreshments. It's BYOB."

"Good thing. I don't think Jeanne and Bart have enough in their blood bank for a party," Camo remarked. Danuta elbowed him. "I mean a funeral. Sorry."

"I have never been around a lot of vampires when they were not fighting," Grigoryi said.

I smiled. "Grigoryi, I can almost guarantee they will be very polite. They like to appear better than they actually are. They believe they are moral, superior beings, but they are just narcissists that follow a messed-up code of ethics. And you know that all of you will be on the No-Bite list."

"That's a relief," Camo said. "It's seriously fucked-up that we need a "No-Bite list."

"Yes, it is. I'm sure most of them will leave right after the funeral. They hate the cornfields. I don't think Mom would approve of them all coming here, but in their weird way, they think they are honoring her."

"The sooner they leave, the better. Just let us know what you want us to do. We'll start getting the rooms ready." Danuta wanted to take action to fight her anxiety and grief.

"Could you help the kids figure out what they'll wear for the funeral?" I had a feeling they would take suggestions better from her. "Greg, Mom wanted you to speak. I'll see if the kids want to say something. She would have wanted a simple ceremony."

He bit his lip, nodded, and looked down at his feet.

Bart and Jeanne found me at sunset, standing by my father's grave at the far end of our property. I was leaning against an old oak tree for support.

"Miranda," Jeanne asked, "How can we be of service?"

Bart added, "I got word that the Magus will be here later tonight."

I walked over to my trusted, undead companions. "Keep Tristan occupied. I just don't have any patience for his self-centered crap right now."

"Of course," Jeanne promised and tried to hide her amusement.

"I have heard that Lady Kananga will be coming as well," Bart told us as we walked back.

"I expected the House of Plows and Arrows, but not the House of Wands."

Jeanne patted my shoulder. "She is very fond of you and the offspring. She is one of the few besides your husband who dares stand up to the Magus."

"Tristan never will. He is the Magus's pet," I replied.

"You're being a bit harsh," Bart commented, "His love for you and his children is his first priority. It causes him great pain."

A windowless van pulled up to the front of the house, and I suddenly felt a familiar presence. "Bart, I think his pain is about to get worse."

As we walked over to the van, a figure stumbled out, looking like he had just woken up.

"Batu!" I ran to him. "You came!"

He picked me up in his arms, and we kissed passionately. When we came up for air, he wiped my cheeks with his sleeve. I hadn't even realized I had been crying. I stared into his chiseled features and felt his now enhanced strength. He looked even more handsome than I remembered. His scent had a hint of spice and musk. "I will miss Connie. She was a wise woman and always kind to me."

"Her dying words were, ''Tell Batu he was right.' What did she mean?"

"She meant you would be okay despite the circumstances of your birth." He smiled, and some of his old warmth returned.

"That isn't all, is it?"

With a tender look, he said, "No, but not now."

Tristan came out of the house and approached us. "Sir Batu, thank you for coming to the funeral. What word from the Princess Khunbish?" His tone was cold.

"Her House is in fine order. Scheherazade arrived the day I left. The Princess and Sir Steve are dealing with that sorry excuse for a vampiress."

"Didn't she try to kill you once? It is probably better you left." Tristan couldn't resist the verbal jab.

Batu's voice had a hostile edge. "Since you've known her intimately, I'll trust your judgment."

They stood staring at each other like two male elk, with full antlers about to fight over a doe. I was not having it!

"Stop it! My mom just died, so stop with your testosterone-charged chest-thumping. Batu, please go see Danuta. She'll fix a room for you." I stood glaring at them until Batu lowered his head and walked away, embarrassed. I headed toward the house and muttered, "Assholes!".

I heard laughter, then applause. The kids were out on the porch. They ran up to greet Batu leaving Tristan standing silently alone.

Marie looked over at me and said, "Nice, Mom!"

None of us mortals got much sleep that night. It was crazy and chaotic enough to push away the grief monster for a while. Ruben arrived in an RV following his sister, Lady Sarah, on her Triumph. Ruben cornered me in the kitchen and asked if Lily would be coming. I had no idea and just shook my head.

"She's back with Kyoto, can you believe that?" he said with wounded pride. "Seriously, she's choosing a dishonored, treacherous, no caste vampire over me!"

"I've got a lot on my mind besides your love life right now," I stated flatly.

"Oh, yeah, sorry about your mother," he managed. It was difficult for him to imagine anyone else's suffering. Did I mention that most of the undead are self-centered, egotistical, twits?

"Why are you here?"

"Everyone is going to be here." He noticed my look of irritation. "And, uh, it's the right thing to do. You know, to honor her."

Fortunately, before I could respond, Jorge and Franco came to the kitchen door, I was relieved to see my old friends, and I waved them in. They dropped their suitcases on the porch and came inside. They wore almost matching silk suits in shades of gray.

Jorge gave me a big hug. "My heart aches for you. First, your dad and now Connie. She was such a remarkable human being. Truly one of my favorite mortals."

I turned to Ruben. "That is what you say when someone's mom has died."

Ruben just walked away, biting his lip. Franco looked at me, shaking his head. "I can just imagine." He ran his fingers through his straight dark hair and looked down at his rumpled suit. "Do you have a steamer?"

Jorge sighed in frustration, "You're almost as bad as Ruben. Don't bother her now with your vanity."

"The Magus' butler drove the RV down if you don't mind using it. Knowing the Magus, it probably has everything you could need."

"Our accommodations should be the least of your concerns my dear," Jorge said.

Franco responded, "I've never slept in the Magus' bed. This should be interesting."

I almost laughed, "Yeah, well, he'll be sleeping in the house. I'm really glad you're here. The ceremony will be a little after sunset tomorrow night."

Marie ran into the kitchen and handed me her phone. "It's Uncle James."

Jorge and Franco left the kitchen to give me some privacy.

Marie and my old friend had stayed in touch over the years. He encouraged her to one day become a veterinarian. "Hi James, I'm sorry I didn't call you about my mom yet." I guessed Marie had told him.

"Hi Miranda, your mom was a kind person. I called Marie because Sally has been acting strange. I have to wonder if the old she-wolf somehow sensed your mom died. Sometimes Marie talks to her on the phone, and it calms down the old girl. Your daughter has a way with critters, but nothing worked tonight."

"Mom loved that wolf. She told me to tell you that she was sorry she never got to visit. Cook Sally a cheeseburger tonight. That's what my mom used to give her."

"I will. She's just lying on the kitchen floor looking sad. I'm gonna put the phone next to her head. Would you mind saying something your mom might have said? I know it sounds crazy. I'm just worried about her."

This was one of the weirder moments in my life, and I'd experienced quite a few. "Sure. Hi honey. Good girl! I have a cheeseburger just for you coming up. That's my girl!"

"She reacted! Sally lifted her head and cocked it to one side. Thanks for not thinking I'd lost it. "

"Sally, being a vamp-wolf, probably understands a lot more than we know," I told him.

"Well, I guess I better start cooking."

"We'd like to stop by to visit on our way back home." Marie smiled at me, nodding.

"I would love that."

"Great! We'll see you in about a week."

I was looking forward to visiting him. He was the most normal person I knew, and I could use that right now. I also thought he could use more human company.

Throughout the night, more nocturnals showed up. A couple of hours before dawn, Anastasia and Omar arrived in a silver Roll's Royce. They would only stay two nights, but the Tsarina had a huge trunk with her "bare necessities." My father just had an overnight bag. The Sheik of the desert, dressed in his traditional robes, looked out of place on the prairie. Anastasia wore a Chanel jacket, pearls, and very tight black pants. She did not quite fit in either.

As Danuta and Camo helped Anastasia get situated, I pulled my father aside and asked if he would join me on the porch so that we could speak privately. When we were alone, I told him, "My mom said to tell you she had no regrets." As I spoke, the scene in the hospital room came back to me, and I started to tear up.

"I don't either," he said quietly. He leaned towards me, touched my hands, and looked at me with soft brown eyes. "She was a lovely woman and a wonderful mother. She kept our secret for so long. I never saw her again after that night. I wish that I could have spoken to her one last time." The sadness in his voice started my waterfall again.

"She's gone!" I wept, and he hugged me tightly.

"Nothing will ever be the same. You are now the head of your family and your House. You will make us all proud."

"You know about that?" I wiped my eyes with my sleeve.

"Sir Henry called me after he heard about Connie. He urged me to support your decision. You should never doubt my loyalty or dedication to you and my grandchildren. Lady Anastasia echoes my sentiments. We will keep your plans secret until you make a formal announcement."

"Thank you," was all I managed to say.

"At first, I was amazed that you won Sir Henry's allegiance. He believes that the vampire world needs you for its evolution and survival. Also, he said that you are not boring. I certainly can agree with that," he said with a smile. "Perhaps our kind is not worthy of you and your offspring. I'm sure Connie would have agreed."

"She pretty much said as much at the end."

We hugged again then walked into the house. The kids, actually young adults now, politely shook his hand. No more pats on the head. Omar spent a few minutes talking with each child like a politician working a crowd. They looked radiant afterward.

Lady Kananga and the Magus arrived together in a limousine. They were here for a funeral, but it looked more like celebrities arriving for the Oscars. Several people scurried to get their luggage.

My kids stayed back as I walked down the porch steps. I gestured for them to join me. "Lady Kananga, thank you for coming," I nodded to her, and she touched my cheek.

"You look well. You must stay strong. You're a lioness like your mother," she kissed my cheek, and whispered, "You have my protection."

I smiled and moved aside for my offspring to greet her.

The Magus looked at me with sympathy, that had I not known better, would seem genuine. "I am sorry such an interesting woman remained a mortal."

I looked him squarely in the eyes. "She wasn't any mere mortal. Excuse me."

Without another word, I turned, walked away, and called to the kids, "Let's walk with Lady Kananga."

I glanced back at the Magus and saw the Haute Caste fawning over him. He did not look upset by my snub. I looked forward to handing him the letter from Mom.

In her RV, Sarah lay back in her queen size bed on top of satin sheets wearing a red silk robe. She arranged a couple of pillows to best display her seductive powers. "Lady Pauline, you look uncomfortable."

Pauline sat on the edge of the bed, full of desire. "I have wished for this moment since you transformed me. You're a hot, sexy bitch." She moved closer. "But I thought you preferred men."

"Why be constrained by the limits of gender when I can find pleasure with both." Sarah reached out and pulled Pauline down beside her. She slowly undressed her.

Pauline was not used to being told what to do during sex, but she enjoyed it in this case. They lay naked, and Sarah gently rubbed a honey-infused lotion slowly over Pauline's shoulders and breasts. It took all of Pauline's self-control not to jump her bones. Sarah handed her the jar. "Your turn."

Pauline obliged with enthusiasm that even surprised Sarah. The honey lotion was an aphrodisiac that Pauline found quite unnecessary. Pauline caressed and kissed every erogenous zone on Sarah's body. The sweet wetness of their bodies was the true love potion. Sarah returned the passionate favor and found her new partner very responsive. Her touch started very gently, but soon she applied more pressure to her clitoris. Pauline cried out as waves of pleasure washed over her. They lay motionless in each other's arms.

Pauline gently rested a hand on Sarah's breast and began to lightly tease a reaction. She pushed Pauline's hand away. "I'm done for now. I have never been with anyone like you. No one has satisfied me like that."

Pauline sat up. "At your service, Lady Sarah."

"Never call me lady when we are being intimate." She kissed her. "Call me hot bitch again."

Pauline's eyes lit up. "Then I take it we're not done, Lady Hot Bitch."

"Don't believe everything I say," she said as she pushed Pauline back down.

Chapter 29

Farewell to Connie

Scheherazade paced in the locked bedroom where she was detained. It was comfortable, but the night called to her. Even through the door, she could smell the mortal guards' blood. She was anxious about how the Haute Caste would deal with her. Surely surviving a beheading should count as time served. She did not have a sense of how the Princess felt towards her. She decided against seducing and feeding on a guard. "They should not have taken my servant away," she muttered. His HH blood had been a treat after so many bland common blood meals.

There was a knock on the door. "Enter."

Chang stood in the doorway. "Your presence is requested by the Princess."

She scolded him as they walked towards the main room. "You act as though we've never met. I transformed you. Have you forgotten so soon?" Chang looked straight ahead and said nothing. "You owe me," she added.

"I never really knew you." He gestured for her to enter the audience chamber.

The Princess wore finery intended to impress and intimidate. A jeweled headdress complimented her elaborately embroidered silk tunic. Sir Steve wearing traditional Mongolian attire, stood on her right side, Kyoto, and Lily on her left, both dressed in Western clothes.

"Well, well," Scheherazade glared at Kyoto. "You've landed on your feet. I sense your powers have been allowed to return to their past glory. And Lady Lily, so you once again subjugate yourself to him. How sad."

"Silence," the Princess warned, "You forget your place!"

The vampiress nodded and looked down, but no one believed she felt any regret.

Sir Steve looked at Scheherazade with scorn. "You attacked Lady Antoinella, and you sided with Alexander when he tried to overthrow the Magus. You sent an assassin to kill Sir Batu when he was mortal, and you gave a poisonous snake to a mad monk to attack the Baroness. Considering your crimes, what did you expect when you came here requesting a place in this House?"

Before she could answer, Kyoto spoke up, "She wanted to kill Batu to find favor with the Baron."

The Princess demanded, "Is that true?"

Scheherazade responded with every bit of charm and tact she could muster. "I have never been fond of Batu and had no problem allowing him to be attacked by a Common Caste vampire in London. Now he is a Haute Caste vampire of your House, which I must respect."

Lily spoke, "With the permission of the Princess, I shall explain your options." Princess Khunbish nodded. Lily moved in front of the prisoner and continued. "You will be a subject in our research concerning the blood of the Baroness, or you will be cast out at noon by our mortal guards."

"You wish me to choose between poison and annihilation by sunlight?" She looked incredulous.

"Yes," the Princess replied. "We know the effect of the Baroness' blood on the Haute Caste, but we are not certain how it will affect the Common Caste."

"If I survive, will I be protected by your House?"

"You shall not be allowed to leave here until we believe you no longer threaten our society. You shall be the responsibility of the House of Cups unless the Magus requests your presence. Those are the conditions agreed upon by the Magus and the Parliament."

Steve added, "We do not lightly jeopardize the existence of one of our kind. Even when they have transgressed our valued traditions and ethics."

"You give me no choice." She looked at Lily. "You really do not know how this will affect me."

"The powers of the Haute Caste are diminished. That is the only noted impact on our kind, and that has been temporary. You should be grateful the Magus has given you this chance. Sir Borgia and Lady Antoinella were quite upset that you managed to keep your head."

A tiny smile came to her lips. "That is comforting. I agree to participate in your research."

One of the guards moved an antique fainting couch to the center of the room. Kyoto set up a saline IV and jabbed her with the needle, with a little more force than was needed. Lily took a syringe out of an ornate brass box and injected Miranda's blood into the IV bag. Within seconds it began to enter Scheherazade's vein. They had feared giving it to her full strength would have been too toxic and ruined any research findings. It was much less than Kyoto, and Alexander had been given. Kyoto was loath to admit he still had feelings for the beautiful vampiress due to liaisons centuries before. His recent transgressions also made him more forgiving of others.

Scheherazade mumbled, "Time, I need more time." She fell back unconscious, and her body began to shake as small seizures erupted. Lily cushioned her head. A baby cobra crawled out of Scheherazade's sari and fell to the floor. A guard stepped forward and sliced it in half. Clumps of her hair began to fall out, and the texture of her once perfect skin became mottled and wrinkled. She foamed at the mouth. Then all movement ceased.

"Does she still exist?" the Princess asked.

Kyoto carefully checked her vital signs. He turned and bowed. "Not as a vampiress."

Lily quickly took a sample of Scheherazade's blood and went over to a small table with some lab equipment. She prepared the sample then looked at it on a slide with a microscope. "Unbelievable!" Lily turned towards the others. "There is no trace of vampire properties. The antigens from the Baroness completely destroyed them. Her blood cells look entirely mortal!"

Steve observed, "She looks 100 years old."

Scheherazade opened her eyes, looking around the room squinting. Her vision was no longer as sharp as it had been, but she retained her mental acuity. "You could not kill me," she uttered in a raspy voice.

Lily picked up a small mirror from the table. "But you are now mortal again." She held it up in front of Scheherazade.

Scheherazade could make out an image of a withered face framed by a few tufts of hair. "No!" she cried out and pushed the mirror away.

"That is all the proof I needed. She has lost her power." Khunbish decreed.

Kyoto added, "We must carefully watch her during the next month. We must be certain that she does not regain her powers as Alexander and I did. May I suggest a vegetarian diet and absolutely no access to blood for now. Her guards must be very careful. She is an old mortal, but she still has all the knowledge and cunning of our kind."

It was almost sunset as I prepared for my mom's funeral. I walked to the spot near my dad's grave and the lightly frozen prairie grass crackled beneath my boots. The final resting place for her was ready. I knew such a small hole could never really contain her. The hearse would arrive soon. I had barely spoken to Batu since his arrival. There were so many visitors, and everyone had wanted a moment with me except the Magus.

After a while, I walked slowly back to the house, enjoying a few minutes alone. I could not wait to leave Rossville. One day I might return and reminisce, but now it felt like it would swallow me up whole. I walked into the house and saw the kids lined up in the foyer like soldiers waiting for inspection. Danuta, dressed in black, stood behind them. Piglet had a black ribbon attached to her collar. They were young adults, ready to engage the world, but they still wanted my approval.

Marie said, "We wanted to wear clothes Grandma liked." She wore a pink sweater and a strand of my mom's pearls, which was not Marie's style at all. The boys all had shirts in pastel shades of blue and lavender and black pants, their hair neatly combed. "Where did you find bow ties?"

"They were Grandpa's. She kept them in a box of his clothes in her room. Danuta gave them to us."

I smiled at our housekeeper and savior. "Thanks, Danuta. You all look great." Camo walked over, wearing a suit and bow tie. "Wow! You even got Camo dressed up. You are a miracle-worker!"

"Danuta threatened me," Camo remarked.

"Mom would have approved. I'm going to get changed." As I closed the door to my room, I realized I was not alone. There was the scent of spice in the air. "Batu!"

He was sitting on my bed. "Miranda, I just want to hold you."

I smiled. "I wish, but I have to get dressed for the funeral."

"Let me help." In an instant, he was off the bed and smothering me in kisses while he pulled off my clothes. It would have been so easy to melt into his embrace. I longed to feel the passion that we had been denied while I was married, and he was my bodyguard.

I reluctantly pushed him away. "Thanks, I can take it from here." I was down to my bra and underwear. I looked into his dark, soft brown eyes. "You're different. Stronger, leaner, colder, but still, I sense your core is the same."

He moved back to the bed and watched me dress. His eyes said it all. "My devotion to you has not changed. I have more to offer you now."

Sadness overcame me, and it was not just the loss of my mom. It was also the loss of his mortal nature. "I was happy with you before. Please, Batu, we'll talk later. Leave me now."

He kissed me gently and left. I collapsed in the chair. "What the fuck! He is like the rest of them now." The vampire world robs everyone of their last ounce of innocence.

I was exhausted, mentally and physically. I pulled on a black cashmere sweater and black pants. Then I insulated myself from the world with a heavy coat. My mom would not like it if I did not dress warmly. From the back of the closet, I pulled out a long plaid scarf she had given me years ago and wrapped it around my neck.

By the time I came downstairs, the Haute Caste were talking quietly with the children. Kananga stood by Marie as though guarding her. The boys were near their father and the Magus, who nodded to me. I didn't respond and headed out the door. Without a word, they followed me out to the gravesite. Dozens of roses in different hues were piled on top of the casket. The scent of their perfume filled the crisp air. The mortuary staff gave everyone a candle to hold. Jeanne, Bart, and Grigoryi lit the candles. Immortals and mortals gathered in a semicircle around the casket. My sweet ex-monk, Grigoryi, looked nervous. I patted his shoulder and said, "You can start at any time." Tristan made a point of standing beside me. He looked so sad, handsome, and lost. The undead have no clue about how to handle the death of someone they cared about. Batu stood in the back with Teri, Camo, and Danuta. When I glanced back, I saw his look of sadness. I smiled to give him hope, but I had no idea if there was a future for us. Light snow began to fall.

Grigoryi cleared his throat, and I took a deep breath. The kids did their best to remain stoic. Jacques tried to keep Piglet quiet.

"We are gathered here...," Grigoryi began.

I heard Franco say, "Is he performing a marriage?" Jorge elbowed him.

"...to honor a life well-lived. Mrs. Connie de Molay Ortega was the kindest, most honest, and generous person I have ever known. She loved her family and friends with all her heart." He paused and sniffled. "She gave strangers a home and a purpose. She fed people who were down on their luck. Connie bravely stood up to anyone she felt was in the wrong, no matter who they were. Everyone lucky enough to know her admired her. She brought out the best in us. God bless this remarkable woman and receive her soul in heaven."

After Grigoryi finished, I looked at the kids, and Tomas nodded. I turned towards the Haute Caste who had attended the funeral either out of respect for my mother or to garner favor with me. "Most of you never really knew her. Never knew what a strong and perceptive woman she was. She pretended to be blissfully ignorant of all of you and our Templar roots. I believed that she didn't know that my biological father was Sir Omar or that vampires even existed. Family to her was most important, and she did everything in her power to protect her husband, my children, and me. My mother was very clever at letting others underestimate her to help her keep her loved ones safe. After my dad, Pete was killed, she told me that she had learned the truth from her mother. When she told me that she had known the truth all along, she felt a sense of relief. She no longer needed to act like all our nocturnal visitors, on liquid diets, were just eccentric, or Lithuanian."

I paused and took a breath, wiping my eyes. "The kids and I will be fine. We will not forget what she has taught us and has done for us. Do not doubt she has taught me well, and I will do the same for my family. Thank you all for coming."

As I finished, a long line of Harleys thundered down the driveway and stopped short of the funeral gathering. The nocturnal guests all stiffened, prepared for a fight. Camo called out, "It's all right! I know them."

A burly man with a heavy beard and a black leather vest came forward. He handed Camo a beautiful heart-shaped wreath with a cross made up of red roses. They spoke no words, merely nodded to each other, and he returned to his motorcycle. The Outlaws left as quickly as they had come. Camo leaned the large wreath against the tree that would shade her grave. The kids and I started crying. She had touched so many hearts.

Wiping our eyes, we headed back to the house and blew out our candles one by one. I looked back and noticed that Batu was the last to leave. He looked as though he was praying beside her casket. Back in the house, the vampires gathered in the living room, and the mortals hung out in the kitchen with the kids and me.

"Thank you, Grigoryi. Your words were beautiful."

He was embarrassed by my praise. "It was all true."

Piglet barked, and I turned to see Tristan in the doorway. "What would you like me to do?"

I grabbed a mug of coffee. "Please tell your side of the family that I have an announcement. I'll be there in a minute." I knew I would have years to feel and adjust to my mother's loss, but now I had to protect the living. I adjusted my emotional armor.

"As you wish." He looked at me with concern and went back to the living room.

I looked at the kids, then turned to Teri, Camo, Danuta, and Grigoryi. "I'm making a power play. Wish me luck."

"Go get 'em, Mom!" Tomas said.

"We got your back," Des added.

"I'm not going to miss this!" Marie asserted, and they all followed behind me.

The room fell silent as I entered. Sir Omar flashed me a knowing smile. He stood beside Anastasia in the back of the room with Jorge and Franco. Batu was off to the side where he had been engaged in conversation with Kananga. The Magus and Tristan were seated on the couch, flanked by Pauline, Sarah, and

Ruben. The House of Plows was always kissing up to the head of the vampire world. At least they were loyal. Jeanne and Bart sat behind the Magus. I had no idea how my announcement would be received.

I took a sip of coffee and placed my mug on the fireplace mantle while they waited. "Thank you all for coming to the funeral. It means a lot to us. My children and I are unique to both the mortal and the vampire world and part of both. Neither world has ever had to deal with the challenges we face. The centuries-old rules and strategies were never designed for our situation. In order to best protect and provide for my family, I'm taking this opportunity when so many Houses are represented to announce the creation of a new House." I paused, and you could have heard an eyelash fall. Tristan looked like he wanted to stop me but said nothing. "I will be the head of the new House of Sun.

Sir Henry and Sir Guillaume will be my Knights, and possibly Alexander. We will stay in our current location near Seattle. We do not wish to upset the House of Plows, so our domain will only encompass Washington state. I have decided that I shall remain mortal, at least for now."

Bart responded first, "One does not lightly start a new House." Jeanne touched his hand as though admonishing him to be quiet.

The Magus stood and declared, "You have not consulted with me and the Parliament. Such a decision must have the approval of the leaders of our society."

I was ready for his challenge. "You mean the leader. No one asked me if I wanted to be the first half-vampire. Yet, I was created for reasons you have yet to explain to me. I don't need anyone's permission to fulfill my destiny or to care for my family." I felt my vampiress DNA kicking in. The kids all moved closer to me. The room felt a little cold and damp, but maybe that was my imagination.

Pauline's eyes got big. Sarah took a deep breath. Jorge smiled and said, "Bravo!"

Ruben exclaimed, "What were the odds?"

Kananga declared, "It is your time, my dear, to claim your heritage. The House of Wands will support you." Then she looked at the Magus. "This is unprecedented, so I believe the normal procedure does not apply, my lord." That was a quick save.

Omar added, "The House of Swords welcomes your House. Dear Magus, I see this as part of the grand evolution of our kind of which you have often spoken."

Tristan finally chimed in, "I have no choice but to offer my protection to the House of Sun." Not a ringing endorsement, but it would do.

Sarah did not offer an opinion for fear of choosing the wrong side. I knew she would support whatever the Magus decided. Her House had looked after me as a child, and I knew this was not easy for her. I hoped she would not see me as a threat.

Batu spoke, "I know that the Princess will never question the wisdom of the Magus on this matter."

"Seriously?" I responded, then wished I had not. I wanted to bitch slap him! A slight grin appeared on Tristan's face as he read the situation. So much for undying Mongolian devotion.

Anastasia walked over to me and touched my shoulder. Her delicate, well-dressed beauty captivated everyone's attention. The Tsarina adjusted her long strands of pearls and turned to the Magus. "My lord, we must adjust to the changing times. Conflicts between the Houses would only threaten our world. Please consider her decision as a way to move our society forward."

The Magus looked like a captain confronted with a mutiny. I could not have been more pleased. He responded, "I will consider all of your opinions. Baroness, I would like to meet with you alone to understand your motivation in this matter better. At your convenience, of course." Always the best manners.

"Thank you. In an hour in my bedroom would work for me."

There was whispering among the vampire elite, but I could not make out what was said. I turned to the children. "I want you to stay with Anastasia and Omar."

They looked at me with new respect. Des said, "Give him hell."

Tomas added, "Don't back down."

Jacques gave me a hug, and Marie said, "We're proud of you."

When I got to my room, my heart was still beating fast as the adrenaline rush started to subside. Tristan entered silently, but I felt his presence and turned around. "I'd like to be alone to prepare."

"Not even Batu," he commented with a satisfied smile.

"Fuck-off!" He was not helping me calm down.

"Don't you want my help with the Magus?"

"I appreciate your offer of protection, but that does not mean you support my decision."

"It's the way you are going about it. You don't just order the most ancient vampire around. He could bring you to your knees with a flick of his wrist." Tristan was clearly worried about me.

"Maybe you would like that. After what the Magus had done to Tomas, it is clear to me that I can no longer allow him to use us as pawns in his twisted scheme."

"Miranda!" He came over to me and lightly touched my cheek. The longing in his deep blue eyes brought me back to the first time he held me in his arms. I succumbed to his kiss like I had a hundred times before. Undaunted, he whispered, "Allow me to stay during the negotiations."

I pushed him away. "So, you can protect me, like you protected Tomas? I'm sorry I allowed you to kiss me. It was a moment of weakness. I can never trust you. Now please leave me alone!"

"Passion is never a weakness," he stated and slammed the bedroom door on his way out.

I stood at my window and looked out at the acres of brown withered remnants from the corn harvest, covered with a light layer of snow. I knew that in the spring, life would return to these fields. My mom would not be here to witness it, and neither would I. It was time to build a new life for our family in the West. It was time I embraced my vampire heritage, but I would never forget that I had come from this small rural town.

I had calmed down by the time the Magus knocked. I opened the door. "Thank you for meeting with me." I gestured to one of the two stuffed chairs that faced each other.

He sat down and began, "Baroness, you have managed to garner support from a majority of the Haute Caste. I have not asked Sir Borgia or Lady Antoinella their opinions, but I do not doubt they would side with you. What makes you so reckless? It is the second time you have openly challenged me in front of others. As fond as I may be of you, I have my limits."

"Before you say anything else, you might want to read this letter from my mother." I handed him the sealed envelope. "I have not read it."

He carefully opened the letter without tearing the envelope. One-on-one with me, he seemed almost human. Maybe that was my effect on him because, until now, he had no reason to fear me. He read the letter quickly, and I saw his face become more serious. He carefully put it back in the envelope and put it in in his suit pocket. It was weird to see him so distressed by the words of a dead mortal.

The Magus looked at me with a somber expression. "You are very much your mother's daughter. I will not share the contents, but she explicitly demanded that I not interfere with you and your family."

I knew he was telling me the general truth of her letter. He considered it dishonorable to lie. "Could you be more specific?" I leaned forward in my chair.

"No. That, my dear, is between your mother and me. Now, tell me why you have decided to create your own House? I assume you felt no need to discuss it with me due to ingratitude and ignorance of our ways."

"So, you're dropping your polite façade. I prefer that." I sat back and stared at him. I felt my body shifting into fight or flight. My vampire nature was rising to the surface. The palms of my hands were moist. I had to stay in control of myself. "I considered the times I was abducted, threatened, and the latest attack on my son. It is clear that either you are unable to control the vampire world, or you're behind my misfortune. It was never easy to have faith in you, but the incident with Tomas has left me suspicious of your every move. I have established my own House to gain the respect of the vampire world and provide for the safety of my family. I will do this with or without your approval."

A little frost had formed on the inside of the windows. He looked around the room like a dog looking for a bone. "Fantastic!" He went to the window and touched the glass. The Magus clapped his hands, a sudden sensation of heat emanated from him, and the dampness disappeared. He smiled in a way that made me want to cringe, but I forced myself not to react. His approval was much scarier than his criticism. "You have found your power. Until this moment, I would have denied your House, but now I sense your power. Lady Cassandra was right. So be it! I will leave for my home in Chicago now."

I was startled by his sudden change in attitude. "Just like that? What about your attack on Tomas? What about my mother's letter? And what did Cassandra say?"

"I'll make no apology for what I do to advance our kind. One night I might share the letter with you or with one of your children. Lady Cassandra told me that she saw your power increasing in a vision months ago, but the outcome was yet to be determined. Good evening. I will send out a decree about the House of Sun. Good night Empress."

He was gone, and the room felt dry and warm. The storm had passed. I had won! Or at least he wanted me to believe that. He had even addressed me by my Tarot card title. Now I had more questions than answers, typical of a conversation with the Magus.

Teri came running in. "What happened? The temperature in the house suddenly went up 15 degrees!"

"Our discussion got a little heated. It's all good now. He agreed to the creation of our House."

Chapter 30

The Baron vs. Sir Batu

I came downstairs to let everyone know that I was fine, and that the Magus had not disintegrated the rebel Baroness. I felt pretty proud of myself until I looked outside and realized there was a ring of melted snow around the house. I hadn't noticed the wave of heat the Magus produced, extended beyond the walls of the house.

Jorge stood by me as we looked out of the living room window. "The Magus was more than a little provoked by your demands," he said with a sly grin. "My dear friend, keep in mind his power comes from the very ground we are standing upon. I don't know what you told him but be grateful you were able to assuage him."

"I gave him the letter from my mom."

Franco stood on my other side and removed his jacket. "It feels almost tropical. I don't recall the last funeral being this entertaining. Your ex and current flame are having words by the barn. Ruben is taking bets."

My eyes got big, and I tore out of the house. Unfortunately, I did not notice the icy patch at the bottom of the porch stairs. I fell backward, hitting my head on the hard, muddy gravel. Sarah and Pauline rushed out of the house and came to my rescue, carefully helping me to my feet. The back of my head ached. Sarah, who had paramedic training, checked my pupils and the back of my head for any injury. "You need to go in the house and lay down. You probably have a mild concussion," she told me.

Before I even turned to go into the house, we heard Batu and Tristan shouting. As I looked over in their direction, Pauline said to me, "They're not worth it!"

"Batu won't stand a chance. He's just a baby vampire." I started to tear up. I think it was a combination of the funeral, the Magus, and the hit on the head.

Sarah said, "I'll handle this! Get her inside!" and she marched off in the direction of the barn.

Pauline tried to steer me into the house, but I was not missing this. Neither were the rest of the Haute Caste or my kids. Batu and Tristan had stripped off their jackets and shirts and were circling each other. Ruben looked at me and shrugged. "Cockfight."

Anastasia and Omar moved beside me. My father said, "You should go inside."

Pauline rolled her eyes. "She slipped and hit her head pretty hard but won't listen to anyone!"

We could hear Tristan yelling at Batu, "You are not worthy of her! How dare you interfere in our relationship!"

"You have no idea what she needs, and you never did!" Batu yelled back. "What are you waiting for? Take your best shot!"

Tristan pointed at Batu, who rose several feet off the ground, then dropped hard on the frozen gravel. Batu's face was scraped and bleeding. He held the palms of his hands up to Tristan, who went flying backward fifty feet. Tristan got to his feet, and bits of dirt and rock were embedded in his back. The hatred in their faces meant the next moves would involve much more blood. I did not want the kids to witness the vampire violence that had shocked me years ago.

Sarah moved between them, but I pushed her aside just as Tristan was about to strike again. "Stop this!" I screamed and collapsed on the ground. Pauline and Sarah carried me to the house with the kids, Omar and Anastasia, in tow.

Kananga looked at my battling suitors. "Look what you've done! If you care for anyone besides yourselves, you'd consider her feelings. Her mother just died, and you act like dogs fighting over a bitch in heat. Do you think, for one minute, that she would desire either of you self-centered idiots now? I cannot wait to get back to the Congo." She turned and headed to the Magus' limousine waiting in the driveway.

The Magus had watched all of this from the back of his limo. When Kananga got into the vehicle, he said, "I hope they heard you, my dear." He leaned over and kissed her cheek. "Our kind would have perished long ago if not for the wisdom and influence of the vampiresses."

As the limo left, Chief Flemming pulled into the drive, responding to a call from a nearby farm reporting a fight.

He walked up the steps to the house, was surprised to be greeted by Omar. It was the first time in his life he had seen someone in Arab garb, other than on TV. The sword made him a bit nervous, but he thought it was only right to withhold judgment. The Chief decided he was probably some international business friend of Miranda's husband.

"Hello, I'm just checking up on a call about a disturbance. Where's Mrs. Mordecai?"

"This way," Omar guided Chief Flemming into the living room where I was lying on the couch. They had not been able to get me upstairs because I started to throw up.

"I am so sorry about your mom. Are you okay?" The Chief stood over me to be sure that no one was trying to influence my response. The tall, gray-haired man looked so normal next to all the beautiful vampires in the room. Some of them scattered, leaving Omar, Anastasia, Bart, and the kids.

"I slipped on the ice and banged my head on the ground. I'm a little dizzy, but Dr. Bart is looking after me. We had a small ceremony earlier. I think it was what my mom wanted."

He smiled. "I'm sure it was fine. She was kind of no-frills. I remember Dr. Bart took good care of you when Jacques was born. I know you're in good hands." He put his hand on Bart's shoulder. Bart looked uncomfortable with the mortal's gesture but managed an awkward smile. "I was called by one of your neighbors. They reported a couple of men fighting and thought I should do a safety check."

"An old grudge, you know how funerals can get people upset, but they worked it out. Sorry if anyone was worried. Tell them thanks." I was doing my best to be Midwest polite. I thought the neighbors must have loved the Outlaws' visit.

"Is there anything I can do? I've got a chicken noodle casserole, and a couple of pies the Methodist women's auxiliary sent in the back seat of my car."

"Thanks, Chief. I know people in town want to do something, but we're fine. There will be a special mass on Sunday in Hoopeston. The kids could go out with you and get the food. Chicken noodle casserole was one of my mom's favorite comfort foods."

"Okay, but don't hesitate to call if there is anything I can do for you. I checked on the café, and it's all locked up. I will make sure that no one will bother it."

The kids followed him out, and I breathed a sigh of relief. My head ached, and I just wanted to sleep. Bart rechecked my pupils and gave me acetaminophen. As long as I did not move, the queasiness stayed away.

"We'll take turns, sitting with you the rest of the night, and the mortals will care for you during the day. I know that your healing ability is enhanced, so rest and whatever nourishment you can tolerate should be enough. I won't give you anything stronger for the pain," Bart told me.

He had delivered Jacques at home when a snowstorm made the roads all but impassable. He had studied surgery at Johns Hopkins. I trusted his medical advice enough not to argue with him. "Thanks, Bart. Will you and Omar do me a favor? Make Batu and Tristan stay in the barn? I don't want to see them again till tomorrow night."

My father replied, "Of course." He and Bart left. Anastasia, Sarah, and Pauline sat around me. If Tristan or Batu somehow got past the others, these ferocious ladies would stop them.

"Lady Kananga berated the Baron and Batu before she left," Anastasia said. "There is no excuse for their behavior. Rest now."

"I hope spending the day sleeping in the barn will be enough to lower their testosterone levels. Assholes!" I mumbled as I faded off. I knew they were struggling with human emotions. Good!

Omar and Bart confronted the supernatural fighters who had moved behind the barn with Ruben when the police car showed up. They had pulled their jackets on over their wounds and pretended the cold did not bother them.

Ruben asked, "Any chance for a rematch?" as he looked at the bets on his phone.

"Fuck you!" Batu exclaimed.

Tristan wisely said nothing.

Omar just shook his head. "Both of you are Haute Caste and should be ashamed of yourselves. You are to sleep in the barn today, by orders of the Baroness. She is resting and does not wish to see either of you."

"How is she?" Batu asked.

Bart replied coldly, "She has a concussion. She will be watched the rest of the night and tomorrow during the day to be on the safe side. No contact with her until I tell you she is recovered enough and desires to speak with either of you." He had never commanded the Baron to do anything, but his concern for Miranda made him bold.

Tristan nodded. "I trust your medical opinion." He looked at Omar. "Your daughter's wishes will be followed."

Batu said, "The barn is fine. I don't mind the smell of horses." He could not help but imagine it would offend Tristan.

"It's not their company that will bother me," Tristan snapped back.

Bart snapped, "Stop it! You'll share my guest room. It has two small but comfortable beds."

Omar added, "That is probably more than you both deserve. If you start fighting again, you'll be sleeping on the ground, in the straw. I can't believe you both would act so selfishly. Have you no regard for Miranda and the children's loss? Excuse me. I must see to my daughter before I retire."

Batu and Tristan followed Bart into his apartment that was built on the side of the barn. The horses whinnied as though they disapproved of the jealous duo as well. As they entered, they began to jockey to be the first to go in. Jeanne watched them from the small living room and called to them, "Mon Dieu! Have you lost your minds?" Which caused Batu to back off and allow Tristan to enter before him. Bart held his laughter. "I've left a cup of O-positive by each of your beds."

"Thanks," they blurted out at the same time.

Batu added, "I'm sorry to have troubled you."

Not to be outdone, Tristan quickly said, "I appreciate your kindness."

Jeanne headed to the bedroom she shared with Bart. It was getting close to dawn. "Good night, gentlemen."

Bart looked at his ancient friend and the young vampire he had known as a mortal. "You are noble vampires who possess the power of air. Please consider all that you have in common. The Baroness is not a prize you could win through violence. You will only drive her farther away with your petty squabbles. Love can drive us mad with longing, but only if we let it. Find a way to coexist in a respectful fashion. You are better than this."

Tristan asked, "You can read her thoughts to some extent. Could you tell us if she has a preference? I swear I will respect it if it is for another."

"I will also agree to respect her choice." Batu was convinced it would be him.

Bart just shook his head and walked away.

They sat on the simple wooden beds with old-fashioned quilts facing each other. A small Victorian-style lamp lit up the room, creating a soft ambiance.

"We blew it," Batu said sadly.

Tristan, who very rarely admitted a mistake, nodded. "I have only seen her that angry once before. It was when she fought a vampiress who had attacked me."

"Good thing she did not come after us," Batu said, and Tristan agreed.

Tristan looked at his competitor in a new light. "I must admit I felt relief as well. She is much like her mother."

"Connie was kind to me. I will miss her." Batu looked sad.

"I never thought I would, but I will miss how she would say the most inappropriate things. She told Miranda she thought I was gay."

"Seriously? She said I was okay for a Mongolian. I never knew what she meant. You have great kids, really great."

With a bit of pride, Tristan replied, "Yes I do."

"I sleep in the nude. I can't stand sleeping with clothes on." Batu started to undress.

"I only dress for going out." Tristan slipped off his clothes and went into the bathroom, where he got a couple of wet towels and handed one to Batu. "You would do well to clean your cuts. They will heal more quickly if you remove the gravel."

Batu appreciated the gesture. "I was impressed by your ability to lift me so high. I don't have that kind of power yet."

Tristan smiled. "I was surprised by how strong you have become."

The two handsome vampire specimens had made peace. Being quite civilized, they avoided looking at each other's private parts. They retired without another word, not wanting to take a chance that their fragile truce might be shattered. Each thought it was unfortunate that the other would have his heart broken by Miranda.

My guardians continued to assess my condition per Bart's orders. At dawn, Sarah and Pauline passed the baton to Danuta and Camo. I heard the kids checking on me at times. Des said, "I've never seen Mom so pissed, and I gave her lots of cause over the years."

Camo said, "Years ago, my mom almost killed me after I wrecked her car. It was a restored classic Corvette. She hasn't spoken to me since. Don't make the same mistake."

"Yeah. I'll be careful when I borrow the Lamborghini," Des tried to assure me.

I opened my eyes. "As long as I live, you're never driving it."

Camo laughed, but Des looked hurt. "Geez, Mom. That's harsh."

It was noon, and my stomach growled. Camo checked my pupils. "You look normal. Want some chicken soup?"

"Yes please, and coffee. I'm going to try to sit up."

"Bart said only decaf after your concussion. Des, ask Danuta to fix a tray. Okay, Baroness, just take it slow." Camo gently helped me into an upright position. My head still hurt, but it was tolerable, and the dizziness seemed to have passed.

"Do you know if anyone besides the Magus and Kananga left last night?" I asked.

"Yeah, Jorge and Franco. They said they would see you in Seattle. You didn't ask about the boys?" he smiled.

"The idiots? I hoped they destroyed each other." I grabbed a pillow and held it over my chest. "Fuckers. Where are they?"

"They're sleeping in Bart's spare room. They buried the hatchet last night after everyone told them they were assholes."

Danuta entered with a tray. A wonderful aroma of garlic, parsley, celery, and other spices came from the soup. "That smells amazing, Danuta. Thank you!"

"I'll watch her now. Come back in half an hour," she said like someone in charge.

"No problem, darlin'." The giant biker politely went to the kitchen.

"He is so in love," I said. She ignored my comment.

I swallowed a spoonful of soup. It stayed down, and my tummy demanded more. "It's good." I managed half a bowl, a few bites of bread, and a little cheese. "Any problems with all the company?"

"No, they all go out of their way to be kind. Especially Omar, he is very considerate."

"Anastasia?"

She looked a little uncomfortable and whispered, "She brought her own sheets. So, I made up their bed with them. I think they're silk."

"She was born that way. I think I'll rest again, then take a shower when I wake up." I still felt pretty beat up. Danuta pulled the throw over me like a mom tucking in a kid. "Thanks," I mumbled and was soon asleep and dreaming.

I was standing in a deep snowdrift, a hooded figure in black approached me, I tried to run away, but the snow kept me from moving. The wind began howling, and soon I was in a white-out and lost sight of the ominous stranger. I raised my arms and tried to shade my eyes to help me see. The hooded figure was right in my face! I screamed, "Leave me alone!" The hood fell back, and light fell on Alexander's face. The storm stopped, and he put his hand on my cheek. It felt warm and comforting.

"Mom! Mom! It's okay," Jacques said as he touched my cheek.

I woke up and took a second to orient myself. "I'm okay. I was just dreaming."

"Sounded like a nightmare," he said, alarmed.

"It started out that way, but then it was fine, confusing, but not bad."

"Whatever you say."

"Tell Danuta I'm awake. Thanks, Alex. I mean Jacques."

He looked at me like I had lost my mind. "Okay, but don't get up till she gets here."

I could feel Alexander using his connection to me. He would be part of my new House. I sent him a text message.

You made an appearance in a very weird dream.
Maybe it was the concussion.
Welcome to the House of Sun.
See you in a couple of weeks.

To my surprise, there was a quick response. He was very late getting to bed.

Wet dream? Concussion? Did you fall?

I replied,

No, weird dream. Yes, but I'll be ok.
I fell but not for you.

Almost immediately he texted back,

Maybe not yet, my Baroness.
I shall go back to sleep.

I felt him again, his presence, his scent, but it quickly faded. I needed to clean up and change. Danuta went upstairs with me and kept watch while I showered. The headache stayed about the same, but the shower helped my mood. I put on comfy sweats and laid on my bed. That little exertion was enough to make me need to nap again. "I'll be fine now."

"I have to check on you every hour. Dr. Bart's orders until he gets up."

I was not alone long when someone knocked on my door. "Come in."

"Mom, we just got back from riding. I miss our horses," Tomas said.

The others followed him in. "That County Sheriff was watching us with binoculars near the east side of the farm. I flipped him off," Marie said.

"Dad once called him a Cossack," Des laughed.

"In his case, it's true. He needs a real crime to solve instead of harassing us."

Jacques asked, "Can we bring the horses to Granite?" He was already referring to home like the locals in Granite Falls. He really liked it there. It felt like home to me now too.

"I'm giving you all a mission. Convince Omar and Bart to move them to our place. It may take a while until we can fence off a pasture and build a stable."

Marie looked at me with a sly smile. "We loved it when you told them about our House. It was really bad-ass."

Des added, "The Magus was pissed."

Tomas asked, "What did you say to him to make him agree to it?"

Taking advantage of the situation so I didn't have to go into details, I said, "I'll tell you another time. Let me rest now."

They each gave me a gentle hug, then closed the door behind them. Peace till sundown.

Chapter 31

Miranda in Charge

I got a phone call in the afternoon from my mom's lawyer. He would draw up the papers, giving the café to Danuta and Camo. The money in her account and whatever we would get from the sale of her house in town would go to a no-kill animal shelter in Hoopeston. I wanted to leave that night, but my head was not about to let me. I made it downstairs and had some coffee and pie as I soaked up the kitchen's ambiance. Memories of the kids growing up flooded my mind along with Tristan's visits, and Mom going on about what a "precious man" he was. She also liked Batu, but she would never come right out and tell me who she preferred. All I knew is that she wanted me and the kids to be happy. I would do everything possible to make that happen despite the machinations of the undead.

Marie wandered in. She grabbed some pie and lamented. "I miss grandma. I sort of expected her to be in here getting dinner ready with Danuta."

"I know hon," I put my arm around her. "Something will always be missing now. I guess there's no reason to come back here."

"Can we celebrate Thanksgiving with Uncle James at his ranch in Montana?"

"Sure, that's a great idea. Why don't you talk to him about it? How is Sally?"

She smiled. "Better, he's giving her a cheeseburger every night."

Tristan and Batu came in the back door.

Marie looked at them and whispered to me, "Fill me in later. Promise!" and left.

Tristan asked, "May we talk?"

I took a sip of coffee and decided to play nice. "Sure, why not."

They each took a chair across the table from me. Batu said, "I'm sorry about last night."

Tristan added, "I truly regret upsetting you."

Tristan's musky forest scent and Batu's cinnamon and clove scent, combined with their handsome features and intense eye contact, were giving me a natural high. I took a breath to tamp down my hormonal response. I wondered if my life would be easier if I were a lesbian. I shook my head and got back to the matter at hand. "You are magnificent vampires, and any woman would welcome your attention, but not me at this moment. As you may recall, my mom just died. I need time to grieve and establish my new life. I can't be bothered with your adolescent jealousy and rivalry. You both suck as superior beings." I immediately regretted saying that.

Batu replied without a hint of humor, "Yes, we do."

"Miranda," Tristan responded in a most adult fashion, "I only wish to help you and our children, to support you in any way I can."

"I feel the same way," Batu added, "Whatever you might want of me, just ask."

A sad smile came to my face. "Tristan, as always, you may visit the kids whenever you like, but I do not want to be part of your interactions with them." I thought that was pretty clear. "Batu, please stay here and help with the transfer of the horses when we have a proper stable and grazing land set up for them in Granite Falls." I looked at their expressions as each calculated what chance they had with me. "My crystal ball broke, so I have no idea about my future, except that I don't want to have either of you try to win me over. Just leave me the fuck alone!"

My head hurt, and a wave of dizziness passed over me, but I kept the pie down. I picked up my mug, went into the living room, found Omar sitting in an armchair, and collapsed on the sofa. I leaned back and closed my eyes. "Jerks," I muttered to myself.

"Indeed," Omar responded. He moved over, sat beside me, and gently took my hand.

"I didn't mean you."

"I know." He smiled. "How are you my dear?"

"Cranky, but better. We'll probably take off for Montana in a couple of days and spend Thanksgiving at James' ranch."

"That will be a good break for you. You should rest until you feel well enough to travel. If you don't need us, we'll depart this evening. You have created quite a stir, and we are eager to quell rumors and set the record straight."

A floral delivery truck pulled up to the house. Danuta went out, then brought in a beautiful arrangement of fragrant lilies, jasmine, and delicate orchids. She handed me the card,

Please accept our deepest sympathy for your loss.
We will support you in all your endeavors. Do not hesitate to ask for our help.

Cesare and Antoinella

I showed the card to Omar.

He read it and said, "The House of Pentacles is behind you. Excellent! Batu's presence testifies to the friendship of Princess Khunbish. This is great news. Lady Cassandra had a vision about your mother and sent a message to the Princess to send Batu a week ago."

With so much going on, I had not thought to question how he had arrived in time for the funeral. "I wish someone would've warned me."

Omar merely shook his head. "Even had you known of her vision, it would not have changed the outcome. Casandra is always concerned that revealing her visions to too many people can have dire consequences." We sat quietly for a moment, then he asked, "What happened with the Magus?"

I sat up and turned towards him. "I discovered the source of my power." I held my hand over his, and in a moment, tiny drops of water began to fall. Then I sat back and closed my eyes. That small act was exhausting.

"Water! Of course. You showed the Magus you have evolved. He must have been pleased."

"I suppose so. He looked smug as always. What is your element?" I asked.

"Fire. I use it to temper my blades." He pointed his hand towards the fireplace. Sparks ignited the wood. Soon there was a pleasant, warm fire.

"Hey! My father is hot." I joked.

He smiled. "In a matter of speaking. Your powers are evolving, yet you are still mortal. Do not be afraid of your power. Respect it. You and the children represent a new reality. You truly exist between two worlds. Your mother would be very proud of how you asserted yourself. If you'll excuse me, I must help Anastasia get ready to depart." He kissed my forehead and left.

I was grateful I still had a parent in this world, even if he was an ancient blood-sucking vampire who could behead people with one swing of his sword. He was nice to the kids and me.

Manny was on his way back to the West Coast when he got an email from Sheriff Fleming that Connie Ortega had died. He decided it might be a rare opportunity to have a look around Granite Falls while the family would be in Rossville. His trip to Illinois had not been helpful. The bizarre story about a mysterious wolf that attacked and killed Pete Ortega's assailants led nowhere. How could a beast like that just disappear into thin air? "Damn it!" He hit the steering wheel. He was not about to start believing in werewolves. He would make a pit stop in Salinas before going to Granite Falls. Molly was worried about him for good reason. He did not want to throw away his career on a hunch about the Pill King's murder. Maybe it was just a rival drug dealer. Manny did not wish to face Miranda Ortega, her ex-husband or Chief Jenkins without hard evidence. His confrontations with them had not gone well. As Manny was leaving Danville heading toward St. Louis, he noticed a biker following him. After about an hour's drive south through the cornfields, the Harley rider turned around. The detective had to admire their security. He found a Hawaiian music channel on Sirius to calm his brain chemistry. There had to be a reasonable explanation for all these weird incidents. He was determined to find out what it was. He had plenty of time to think about it on his long drive home.

When he arrived back home in Salinas, he found Trouble was content with all the TLC Molly provided. However, Molly was not so happy with him as he filled her in on the details of his trip.

"So, Illinois was a bust. You have to let this go! Manny, you don't want to lose your job. What police force will want you if you get fired?" Pots clanged in the sink as she cleaned up after dinner.

He began to load the dishwasher; it was the least he could do. "Molly, I just want to know the truth. If I don't find anything, I promise I'll be back soon."

"You are so stubborn!" She glared at him and wiped her hands with the kitchen towel, then threw it at him.

"Assaulting an officer." He smiled, then gently took her hands. He looked into Molly's blue eyes and pulled her close. Manny loved the way she smiled at him. He realized, perhaps for the first time, how important she was to him. Molly was the person he wanted to spend the rest of his life with.

Their personality issues did not matter anymore.

"What are you waiting for? Kiss me already," she said.

He kissed her lightly at first, but she made it clear that was not enough. He fell back on the kitchen table with her on top of him. They both started laughing when Trouble inserted herself by pawing Manny's cheek.

Molly stood and picked up the fat cat. "She's jealous."

"Of you or me?" Manny asked. He got to his feet, rubbed Trouble's head, and said, "I have to get ready to go. He packed some clean clothes and hugged Molly. At the front door, he turned back and said, "Molly. When I come back, I'm going to ask you to marry me. I just want to warn you."

"Yes. I'll say yes. I just want to warn you!" As he drove away, Molly whispered to Trouble, "Don't worry. If we ever get divorced, I'm keeping you."

I was having a peanut butter and jelly sandwich in the kitchen when Sarah, Ruben, and Pauline came in to check on me and decided I would live. "I could have made a small fortune on that fight," Ruben whined.

I looked at the vampire bookie. "What are the odds on who I'll choose?"

He was surprised by my comment. He grinned. "Two to one that you'll pick your ex. C'mon he's the Baron."

"Baron Asshole," I responded.

Pauline started to laugh, until Sarah glared at her. "They were properly chastised for their unseemly behavior." The head of the House of Plows patted my hand. "I support your plans, with one caveat."

"What is it?" I knew better than to say whatever you want to a vampiress.

"Take Oregon."

"Why would you give me Oregon?"

Ruben merely asked, "Have you ever been to Portland?"

"Not yet, but I've heard Voodoo Donuts is amazing, there is a giant bookstore there and the people are a little eccentric."

"And so are the vampires," Sarah responded like she had tasted something foul, "They don't eat meat, just this weird, clotted blood substitute. Good luck with that."

"Agreed. I'll include Oregon in my House." I was not sure if this would be a good thing.

Pauline said, "We leave for Toronto in an hour. We'll take the chopper that Billy left behind. He texted me he wouldn't be coming back here."

"That's fine." I felt the grief monster tugging at me. "I don't imagine any of you will be coming back here again. I'm not sure I ever will."

They gave me hugs, and Ruben said, "Go Bobcats!"

"Thanks." I thought back about him having attended my high school basketball games. It now seemed pretty hilarious him pretending to be a local to watch over me.

As they loaded up and got ready to leave, suddenly, I felt my mom's death like someone dropping an anvil on my heart. The world was upside down. Everything was different, but the world was going on as if nothing had changed. The kids would go back to school after Thanksgiving break. Over the winter, the farmers would repair their farm equipment for next year. People would make plans to invade the retail world on black Friday. Danuta and Camo would fight back tears when they opened the café without Connie Ortega. I decided we would leave tomorrow and head to Montana for Thanksgiving. A new tradition would be good for all of us.

Teri and I went into Danville and bought an Escalade. The salesman was pretty happy when I agreed to the sticker price and paid cash. Between my new wheels and my old Jeep, we could accommodate everybody and all our stuff for the long drive home.

I gathered the kids in the living room. "Take anything of grandma's that you want to keep and anything else in the house that matters to you. Then be ready to leave tomorrow morning."

"I want the Lamborghini!" Des said.

"I'm giving that back to your father." He looked disappointed.

My little carpet baggers went off to pillage, and I went to my office. I closed the door and unlocked a drawer of my desk. Inside was a pile of valentines from my offspring and a smaller pile from an "anonymous" admirer. Batu had been the sweetest mortal. I worried that my adorable suitor would just be a tender memory now. I collected all of the valentines and put them in an envelope, and I stuck it in a backpack. I added the first printed editions of my ghost book and my vampire romance. After all this time, I had only published two books, but they had sold well. Life, death, and the immortals had gotten in the way of my writing career. Once I established my House, I promised myself I would author another book and dedicate it to my parents. Leaning against the wall was the only photo ever taken of Tristan. On our wedding night, he had put on a latex mask, blue contacts, a wig, and flesh-colored gloves to pose for a photo for my parents. The photographer had stood far enough away that he looked natural. My mom must have put it in my office when she cleaned out her old house. I stared at the picture, and tears began to fall. I had been an innocent virgin, struggling with my feelings for Tristan, yet I looked happy and in love. The Magus had not yet told me that I was half-vampire.

I wrapped the large-framed picture up with a throw and carried it out to the Escalade. I set it carefully in the back. If Tristan saw it, he would only feel encouraged. I would also keep from Batu that I still had his valentines. I had no idea where my fate would take me, and I was not about to make either of them think they were the chosen one. I could not allow myself to shun the past or let it dictate my future.

A few hours later, I called for a meeting with all those that remained. I tried to make the ambiance friendly and safe. My kids would be present so that they could weigh in on our decisions and keep the rivals from getting too heated. I put several shot glasses of O-positive on the living room coffee table with small plates of raw sirloin. Danuta was still squeamish about the vampire snacks. She set out a platter with chocolate chip cookies for the mortals.

Jeanne and Bart arrived first. They were unusual vampires due to their lack of fondness for wealth and their absence of vanity. They were good-looking but not glamorous. They preferred cotton and wool clothing to silk, running shoes to designer footwear. We had not talked much since the funeral. "I appreciate everything you did for my mom."

Bart always looked humorless, but his eyes gave away his soft side. "She was an amazing woman. I shall miss her irrepressible nature. I shall never forget Alexander's face when she told him off and gave his pug to the children."

Jeanne added, "She set limits with Scheherazade as well. She displayed no fear of our kind."

"Yes, I think our kind tends to bring out the strengths and weaknesses in others," I said

We sat down on the couch, and Bart turned towards me. "You said, 'our kind.' I am glad to hear that."

"The kids and I are hybrids."

Jeanne put her hand on my shoulder, and I felt a sudden sense of peace. I turned to her. "What did you do?"

She replied, "That is my gift. It comes from the earth. It is a sense of being at one with everything." Jeanne removed her hand, and the feeling diminished.

I had to know. "What happens when you're mad?"

"Let's just say that I can make people very uncomfortable."

"Good to know."

Just then, the others started coming in. Tristan and Batu stayed at a distance from me in high-backed chairs. Teri and the kids sat next to the coffee table, close to the cookies. Grigoryi brought me a mug of black French Roast, bless his heart. Camo and Danuta sat on the hearth.

I looked around and smiled. "My mom told me many times how you all helped her after Dad died, and now you're helping the kids and me. Thank you. I wanted to let you know that we plan to stay in Granite Falls. Living in Rossville was my parent's dream but not mine. You all know that Camo and Danuta will take over the café. I'd like to move the horses to our new home when we get a stable and pasture completed. Grigoryi will come with us. Jeanne and Bart, you are always welcome. Let me know what you want to do. You could stay here as well. Batu will stay and help with the horses and their transfer to Granite Falls."

Marie added, "We love all of you. You have to come and visit us! Uncle Bart, I've known you all my life."

"You saved my life when I was born," Jacques added.

Des said, "You taught me not to lie."

Tomas replied, "He needs more lessons."

"The point is you're all our weird family. No matter where we go from here, I don't want that to change." I took a drink of coffee.

The vampires helped themselves to shots of blood and bits of meat. I could not help but watch Batu. He was aware I was watching him and seemed uncomfortable with my scrutiny.

It was still strange to see him act like the others.

He raised his glass in a toast to ease the tension. "Bottoms up!"

Des asked Batu, "Do you really like it?"

"Yes. It's an acquired taste."

Marie rolled her eyes. "Whatever." Of all the kids, she was the least impressed or intimidated by the vampires.

Tristan cleared his throat and looked at the kids. "I will tutor you all in the ways of our kind. You are old enough now."

Tomas asked, "Can you teach us to levitate people? That was awesome."

"No! Your father has a gift, and it's not transferable." I did not know if that was true, but I did not want them to have superpowers at this stage of immaturity.

Jeanne jumped in. "We'll care for the horses until you want them at your new home. We do not have any plans yet." She looked at Bart. "We will see where we can be of service." He nodded.

That was not a common vampire sentiment. "Lady Sarah has given Oregon to our House. I think you might like Portland."

Bart said, "Perhaps. You're already thinking like a ruler. You want loyal people in your kingdom."

"I don't know what the fuck I'm doing, but I trust you."

Des suddenly said, "I think the slogan for our House should be, 'What the fuck!'"

Teri started laughing, and the others joined in.

"You'll have to translate that into Latin." I gently nudged Des.

Grigoryi spoke up, "Connie told me to pray for all of you. I will continue to do so."

Tomas smiled. "Only Grandma!" He had the presence of mind, not to mention that praying for the undead was awkward.

Jeanne added, "She called me a saint, but I think she deserved that title."

The room became quiet. The thought of what had brought us all together loomed over us. Jeanne and Bart rose to leave. I stood and hugged them both. "We'll leave in the morning. See you on the coast in a few months."

Batu came over to me and, in front of everyone, announced, "I have waited years. I can wait longer." Then he kissed my forehead before going out to the barn.

The room felt tense. It was emanating from Tristan. The kids grabbed cookies and Tomas said, "We're gonna finish packing."

No one wanted to be around Tristan when he was upset. Teri went with the kids. Danuta and Camo hurriedly gathered up the shot glasses and dishes then went to the kitchen. I wondered if things would fly through the air or if it would start to rain indoors?

Tristan moved over to the couch and sat down beside me. His gaze held pain and wonder. "How can you pretend you could be with anyone else? That's not fair to Batu."

His scent was primal forest. His eyes reminded me of the river when the sun brings out the blue tones of the water. His thick platinum hair framed his haughty cheekbones. I did still love and desire him. I could not be with him now, but I was not sure I could be with anyone else. "Since when did you care about Batu? Tristan, I'm not the virgin you amazed, thrilled, and seduced. She left town with my innocence and patience for your extramarital affairs."

"Now I understand how you felt. Can we move on?"

"This is not about revenge." I touched his hand. "It's about my desire to find my place in this insane world. I won't be overshadowed by you. I've never fit into your idea of a relationship."

He faced me, and his other hand gently rubbed my shoulder. Just enough pressure to remind me of the pleasure of his touch. "I have never asked for a woman's love before."

"Congratulations!" I moved away from him. He just made it easier to turn down a sexual escape to ease my pain. My tolerance to his charm increased by the minute. "Love is not the issue. Get a handle on your emotions! I'm not in charge of making you happy." I got up and went to my room.

Des was right. Our motto should be some form of, "What the fuck!"

Chapter 32

Leaving Rossville

The undead avoided me after our family meeting, except for Jeanne. She found me as I packed up my mom's unclaimed belongings for charity.

"Chere Miranda," she spoke softly with a lovely French accent, "you have du sang-froid like your Templar ancestor. He would be proud of you." Her pale skin, long dark hair, and delicate features disguised her remarkable strength.

"Thanks, I mean merci. Guillaume speaks highly of you."

She smiled. "Give him a kiss on the cheek for me. You will be well-served by his wisdom." She took a gold fleur de lis necklace out of her pocket. "You must wear this as a reminder of your noble heritage. Bart and I decided we will go to Portland. We want to be part of your unorthodox House."

She helped me put the lovely necklace on. "Thank you. I will wear it always." She quickly left without another word. My interaction with her lightened my spirit, but I felt a little sad for Guillaume as she was perfectly happy with Bart. Then I thought about the vampire view of time. Maybe in another hundred years things would change. It might take a century for me to be intimate with Tristan again if I stuck around that long.

It was almost dawn when we loaded up the vehicles. Camo and Danuta gave us hugs and a basket of food for the road. I could smell the fresh baked cookies. Grigoryi, Jacques, and Piglet rode with me in the Jeep. Teri was in the Escalade with the triplets. I caught sight of Tristan watching us leave from his suite upstairs. He would fly back to Los Angeles that night and confer with the Magus about how our House would impact their world. Batu would join us sometime later with the horses. I needed time to search my heart. The Princess was way too generous with her newest vampire stud. I should have been able to figure out why, but I had a lot on my mind. Alexander was playing nice. Way too nice. It was more than a desire to be Dad of the Year. The mind-numbing drive to Montana was quite welcome.

Piglet wore a little harness that we could attach to the seatbelt, which she did not mind at all. Pugs are not the brightest beasts. She never let some twist of fate bother her. All she cared about was a lap and treats. I wished I could go about life with the thought. "It's all good." As we headed out of town, I looked at the farmer's fields covered with patches of snow. Mixed emotions struck me as I wondered if I would ever return.

Jacques yawned. "It's about twenty hours to the ranch."

From the back seat, Grigoryi said, "I got my driver's license two months ago. Connie taught me to drive so I can share the driving with you."

"Good to know." I was not sure I could let Grigoryi put our lives in his hands. He once drove a lawn tractor into the side of the barn. "I'll be okay. We'll stop for a break every couple of hours, and we'll spend the night in Sioux Falls, Iowa."

Jacques looked at his phone. "I've pulled up every Starbucks on our route."

"Bless you!" I took a swig from my travel mug.

"I want to share Piglet with my other dad. I think he misses her."

"Sure." I glanced at him. "You're handling having him in your life well."

"Like you and Grandpa Omar. I decided to see it as a positive, 'cause I can't change who I am. Anyway, you seem to like him."

I could feel Grigoryi staring at me. "You are friends with Alexander the Great?"

"He will be an ally of our House."

Jacques smirked. "A close ally."

I decided to change the subject. "I have two knights, Henry and Guillaume. Alexander might become one as well. They're all gifted, brilliant, and powerful. It might take a minute, but I think you'll get used to them like you did the others you've known."

Jacques added, "And Pompadour! I think she cheats at cards. Des likes her a lot."

"She stays in Seattle." I did not want to say much about her. My House might need her skills and experience. I was also concerned that Jacques or Grigoryi might blurt out some remark I might make about Pompadour to Tristan. Political correctness was not my strong suit, but I had to make an effort.

In the Escalade, the kids grilled Teri. "So, what is Henry really like?" Marie asked as she sat in the front beside her.

"He's really sweet, and...."

"Kind of scary," Des injected from the back seat.

"Not to me."

"He's mysterious," Marie said.

"Is it true about Cleopatra?" Tomas leaned over the seat. "That he had a thing with her?"

Marie shoved him. "Shut up!"

Teri just smiled. "Why don't you ask him?"

Marie found a Sirius XM station that played experimental rock. "I want to do some new stuff. Our own stuff, I wrote a song called Sucking Air, about my life," she told Teri.

"Too easy. I'm letting that go," Des remarked.

"Knock it off!" Teri warned, "Or you'll have to listen to Led Zeppelin for the next two hours."

Tomas said, "Okay, okay, we'll behave! Anyway, I like that song Marie. I think we should call it Sucking Blood."

"Yeah," Des added, "I want to see Dad's face when we play it. You know he'll blame it on Mom."

Teri asked, "What if he likes it?"

"Damn!" Des said.

We pulled into a rest stop outside of Peoria, Illinois, and piled out of our vehicles. I noticed a guy riding a chopper with familiar patches zoom by. I looked at Teri.

She shrugged. "Daylight security."

I knew the dark side of the family would watch out for us. I wondered who would show up tonight. I hoped it was not Pauline. "I texted you the address for the Iowa Holiday Inn."

"Okay. Hey, you want to switch cars? The triplets were arguing about who was going to sit in the front because that person controlled the music."

I chuckled, "No. I'm good." They were older, but the sibling rivalry would never stop.

After eight hours and two more rest-stops, we arrived at the edge of the world, on the outskirts of Sioux City, Iowa. I knew that Starbucks would become fewer and farther between, but I did not panic. I could survive on truck stop coffee if I had to. It was freezing and dark as we pulled into the parking lot. Teri, Grigoryi, and the triplets took our overnight stuff into the hotel. Jacques put a sweater on Piglet, and we waited for her to find the right place to leave her mark on Iowa. She was on a long leash and suddenly ran out in front of a truck. A young guy slammed on his brakes and jumped out.

"You coulda got yer dog killed!" the stranger yelled. "Go back to Mexico where you belong!" The yahoo adjusted his cowboy hat and spat on the ground.

Jacques tried to step in front of me and said, "We were born here."

"Jacques, take Piglet and go inside. Now!"

I heard a familiar voice behind me. "Is there a problem here, Tex?" Ruben moved up next to me. His angry stare alarmed me. I could see the tips of his fangs.

Apparently, Tex decided it might not be the best idea to take on Ruben and said, "Y'all ain't worth my time," and got back in his truck.

Ruben shook his head and said to me, "You do have a knack for getting into trouble."

I decided it best to let it go.

We all went into the hotel and quickly got checked in. Ruben escorted us to our rooms.

"You'll be okay now." Ruben asserted.

"When and how did you get here?" I asked surprised at his appearance.

He smiled. "We have our ways."

"Whatever. Where are you staying?"

"Unfortunately, here. Why couldn't you stay somewhere that has a five-star hotel? Sometimes you can be such a peasant." He pulled back the covers on one of the beds. "Look at this thread count. How will I even sleep on these cheap sheets in the morning?"

"We all have to make sacrifices!" I replied. "Who is going to visit us tomorrow night?"

He collapsed on the only chair. "That's a surprise." He grinned. "I will be on my way back to Toronto and civilization by then. Will you promise to have dinner delivered to your rooms? We don't want another incident."

We had a quiet night, besides the usual arguments about who cheated during the video game. In the morning, we grabbed breakfast burritos at a bar across the street. The triplets decided to stick with Teri, but Tomas rode in the front.

Jacques asked me, "Do you like Alexander?"

Grigoryi, sitting in the back seat, was leaning forward to be sure to catch every word.

"He is fascinating, intelligent, and charming. I have to work at forgiving his deception, but I'm grateful to have you."

Grigoryi butted in, "You like him."

"He has been on his best behavior and promises to support my House, so I guess I do. I won't forget what he did, but forgiveness is in our best interest."

I looked at Grigoryi in the rearview mirror. "What do you think of him? You were both there when he lost his bid to oust the Magus."

Grigoryi said, "I don't trust his motives. I'm sorry Jacques. I can't help but think he only lives to fight and win."

Jacques added, "It's okay, Grigoryi. I think he wants the best for all of our family. He doesn't have an army anymore, just us."

I was blown away by my son's insight. "That's true. I had never thought of it that way."

Jacques smiled. "Now he's part of your army."

Grigoryi added, "But the Baron, whose side is he on?"

"I don't care," I turned on the Spectrum rock station on Sirius.

By chance, the song "Ex's and Oh's" by Elle King came on the radio. Jacques said, "Our band should play that song."

Hours later, we stopped for the night near Deadwood, South Dakota, at a questionable three-star hotel with one-star coffee and iffy Wi-Fi. An old woman with long gray braids and a sweatshirt with Las Vegas spelled out in bling checked us in. The lobby looked kind of tired and smelled a tad musky like old magazines.

We settled into our rooms and ate the burgers and fries we had picked up at a diner next door.

Marie complained, "They really should have a vegetarian alternative on the menu."

"In another ten years, maybe. This is cattle country." I did not dare add that the burgers were delicious.

Teri pulled a bottle of sriracha sauce out of her backpack. "Add this to everything!"

All the guys wandered in, and they hung out slurping sodas and considering the future of their garage band. Des said, "We want to use our music to do more than make us famous."

"That's nice, but you haven't played a gig yet." Harsh reality. I know.

Tomas said, "Henry says we'll be big."

Marie added, "We're going to represent the people who don't fit in. It's who we are."

Teri said, "Henry has faith in your talent, but it will take a lot of self-discipline. You'll have to work together. You can't even play a video game without acting like jerks to each other."

She was the best nanny ever. They became quiet. "Okay, get some sleep, tomorrow we'll see James and Sally!"

Just then, there was a knock on the door. I started to get up, but Teri put out a hand to stop me and stood next to the door. A wicked-looking knife had appeared in her hand.

"Who is it?" I called out.

"Angel."

"What the fuck!" I said as Teri opened the door. "So, you're the surprise. Did you come all the way from L.A.?"

"I'm staying with James. Someone has to check on you troublemakers. You have no idea how upset everyone gets when you're on the road." He sat on the bed next to Jacques and Piglet. "Heard someone got a little rude with you in Iowa." He barely looked at Teri. He knew she was with Henry now.

"Yeah, Ruben showed up. It was nothing."

There was another knock at the door. Teri answered it. The woman from the desk looked concerned. "Is he staying? You'll have to pay extra."

Angel grinned. "I'll be leaving in a few minutes. Just visiting with my old friends."

"Well, all right." She turned away mumbling.

Angel hugged me and said, "I'll be around for a while, keeping an eye out. In a few hours, I'll head back to the ranch. Don't be too loud when you arrive tomorrow. I need my beauty sleep."

Teri looked uncomfortable but said nothing. The guys went back to their rooms, and we settled in, secure in the thought that a dark SoCal Angel was looking out for us.

In Granite Falls, Cesare and Antoinella were checking out the new House of Sun. Guillaume welcomed them and sent a text message to Teri about their arrival.

Henry and Leif walked in just as Guillaume served cups of blood in the living room. Henry said, "Sir Cesare and Lady Antoinella, both of you coming here is an honor. I hope you will be supportive of the Baroness." He kissed the lady's hand,

and she felt his power of seduction but ignored it.

Cesare responded, "We hope we haven't come at a bad time. We thought it better not to attend the funeral, but we did want to express our support for the new House. Like the Magus, we understand that this development is part of the evolution of our kind. We are certain the daylight House will only help to ensure our survival in the future."

Manny was hunkered down in the tree line behind the house and watched the meeting in the living room through binoculars. "Take a look," he handed them to the Granite Falls Police Officer, who agreed to check out his concerns even without an official request from the Salinas PD.

Brandon was not impressed. "So, some people are talking in the living room. Is that a crime in Salinas?"

Before Manny could respond, the Haute Caste vampires followed Leif out to the garage where Cramer was working.

"Did you see that? That's where they're cooking it," Manny exclaimed.

Inside the garage, Cesare and Antoinella were amazed to see an elaborate laboratory where Cramer was working on Tomas's sunscreen formula. The visitors made him a little nervous.

"Hi Cramer," Leif said, "These are some friends of the Baroness. They wanted to see what you're working on."

Cramer looked over at the beautiful and well-dressed undead couple. He knew they had to be Haute Caste, which made him anxious. "Tomas came up with the idea of creating a sunscreen formula that would work with your peculiar sensitivity to sunlight. We've got a long way to go, but I believe it's possible."

"Brilliant! I hate putting on layers of clothing, latex masks, and gloves whenever we fear we might get exposed," Antoinella said.

"We are combining fire retardant chemicals with sunblock formulas," Cramer told them, feeling a bit more at ease. "Tomas is brilliant."

Outside, Manny and Brandon moved closer to the building and were able to see the laboratory through the open doorway.

"Holy shit! You're right! I'm calling this in," Brandon said. They retreated to the line of trees to wait for backup.

Five minutes later, a couple of Sheriff's cars and another Granite Falls patrol car arrived, sirens and lights blazing.

"What the fuck!" Henry exclaimed.

The officers had their weapons out as they approached the garage, ready to take on a drug cartel. Guillaume looked at the others and said, "Cramer, come with me."

They stepped out with their hands up. Guillaume calmly asked, "Officers, how can I help you?"

Manny stepped forward to take charge, which pissed off the locals. "We would like to search the garage. We believe you are making illicit drugs."

Cramer stifled a laugh and put down his hands. "I don't think sunscreen is illegal. Some of you know me. I teach chemistry at the high school. I'm helping Tomas, who is one of my students, with a science project.

"Show us!" Manny demanded.

One of the officers stepped in. "May we take a look inside the garage?"

Leif stepped forward and asked in a hostile tone, "Do you have a search warrant?"

Before the officer could answer, Guillaume said, "It's not a problem. We have nothing to hide. Feel free to look around."

They all went inside. Cesare greeted them, "Good evening. I'm afraid my nephew is not here to answer your questions. His aunt and I are looking after the place as they had to go to Illinois for his grandmother's funeral. Such a silly assumption that something nefarious was going on here."

Antoinella added, "Where is our hospitality? Would any of you like some coffee?"

The local police were feeling her Italian charm. They all wanted a cup of coffee from the alluring, beautiful vampiress but declined her offer. Manny fought it and looked at Henry, recognizing him from the incident at the club. He smiled in a way that made Manny want to hide under a rock.

"Who are you?" asked Brandon

"I'm the nanny's boyfriend. I also play in the band Carnage at a club in Seattle. Then he asked Manny with a smirk, "Didn't I see you there once?"

Brandon looked at Manny with suspicion. He regretted ever listening to the Salinas detective's story. One of the sheriff's deputies who had extensive knowledge of narcotics and synthetic drugs looked at the materials in the lab. "I don't see any evidence of drug manufacturing unless you've found a way to get a buzz from aloe vera and lanolin. Sorry to have bothered you folks." He walked out shaking his head.

Brandon and the other officers followed him back to their cars. Manny faced the elite Haute Caste and felt more humiliated than scared. "Who are you really? Mafia? Cartel?" He looked at Henry. "Voodoo priest?"

"Boo!" Henry yelled.

Manny jumped backward. His audience burst out laughing. "Thank you," Cesare said, "It's been years since I found a mortal so amusing."

Guillaume remarked, "Detective, the Baroness will not be happy with this stunt."

Henry's voice had a threatening tone. "What will it take to get you to leave us alone?"

"The truth," Manny replied.

Guillaume said, "The Baroness told you the truth, and you did not believe her. What lie should I concoct to satisfy you and send you on your way? If you continue to harass our family, your safety cannot be guaranteed."

Henry stared Manny down. "You were already told that we are vampires. If you try to tell anyone, they will not believe you and will question your sanity. We do not take life without careful deliberation. Which is why we have been quite patient with you."

Manny was overwhelmed with information that did not compute. He looked at them and asked, "How is that possible?"

Henry remarked, "You exist. Why can't we?"

Manny shook his head. "I've got nothing. If all you say is right, no one will be held accountable for the murder of the Pill King because you think the law does not apply to you."

"Our code is different," Guillaume asserted, "but we also want justice."

Antoinella stepped towards him. "Our reality is difficult to accept. Very few mortals have ever been allowed to learn about us. We only target those whose behavior harms society and have managed to circumvent prosecution for their crimes. You could even say we are kindred spirits."

What she said almost made sense to Manny. His phone rang, it was Molly. It startled him and broke Antoinella's "spell." "I don't want to believe anything you've said, but I can't find any other explanation."

Manny turned and quickly walked down the drive to where he had parked his car behind some trees. "I've got to get out of here," he muttered to himself. To his surprise, Brandon's patrol car was still there. He walked over to apologize.

"I'm so sorry I dragged you into this. I thought it was...."

"No problem. I'll find a way to live this down at the station. Are you okay?"

Manny was touched by Brandon's concern. "Yeah. They are weird, but we can't arrest anyone for that." He decided against sharing any more details.

"If weird were illegal, half of Granite would be locked up." Brandon slapped Manny on the back, smiled and said, "Detective, maybe you should get your ass back home."

Manny decided to take his advice. He drove south and stopped in Portland, where he loaded up on VooDoo Donuts. Powered by caffeine and sugar, Manny drove straight through and made it to Salinas in thirteen hours. When he got home, he told Molly that he was exhausted and promised he would explain everything after he got some sleep. Molly tucked him in, shook her head, and said, "I'm just glad you are home and safe."

Chapter 33

Thanksgiving in Montana

We arrived at the ranch before sundown. A wolf's howl echoed across the plains as a large wooly creature came around the house in her winter coat. Marie ran to her and hugged the wild creature. The boys followed except for Jacques, who held Piglet. The pug began growling. She was acting like she could tear the vamp-wolf to pieces. Somehow Sally knew the little dog was all bluster and no bite. "Take our little diva into the house," I told Jacques.

James came out of the cabin and hugged us all. The years of living on the plains had given him a rugged, handsome look. There was gray in his light brown hair, but he still had an easy smile and a gentle gaze that held our secrets.

"You look good. Healthy!" I remarked as he helped us bring in our stuff.

Teri gazed out on the desolate surroundings. "This is a great place. You have found the middle of nowhere."

"Rooster is five miles away. It's got two bars, a grocery store, a church, and even a Dairy Queen. It's the capital of nowhere."

"Sally snores, so I decided she needed her own room, and since I have been getting visits from our nocturnal friends, I added onto the house."

"You have been keeping busy." James was the original soft-touch. Sally was lucky. "I was sorry to hear about Gracie. She was the sweetest Dalmatian."

"I miss that girl, but Sally is good company. I never thought a wolf could become so domesticated. I think it started with all the treats your mom left her at night."

We all gathered in the spacious living room on an old leather couch and worn matching chairs. A cozy fire kept the house comfortable. James pulled out a platter of brownies and poured some mugs of coffee. "I like dessert before dinner."

"Uncle James, you rock!" Des declared as he inhaled a brownie.

James smiled and continued, "Angel will be awake soon, then we'll figure out where everyone is gonna sleep. I've enjoyed his company, but I'm not a night owl anymore. He thinks we're all pretty safe now that the rebellion is over."

Grigoryi took a brownie. "Thank God for that."

I put down my mug. "I told the Magus about starting my own House, and at first, he was displeased. Now he seems to have changed his mind. That still concerns me."

"Angel filled me in on your plans. You've got to do whatever you can to set boundaries with these undead fuckers." James's voice had an angry edge.

The kids looked at him with surprise. Angel appeared out of nowhere. "May one of the undead fuckers join you?"

The kids started laughing, which helped ease the tension. "Angel, I wasn't talking about you."

The So Cal vampire sat down beside Teri. "That's okay. It's an honest description."

"Absolutely," Teri said, got up, and went into the kitchen.

James looked at Angel, then towards the kitchen and back at me. I just shook my head. There was no way James should get involved in their issues. He put an arm around Jacque's shoulders and looked at all the kids. "I'm sorry about your grandmother. She was a force to be reckoned with. I know she was proud of the whole family."

Uncharacteristically, they were quiet. "Thanks," I replied for all of us. "Omar came to say goodbye. It felt like some cosmic circle coming together in Rossville, of all places."

Tomas added, "I feel like we've just gone through a rite of passage. I guess we're adults now."

Des agreed, "Yeah! As an adult I need a car."

Marie punched him in the shoulder. "You can be such a jerk. I can't believe I shared a uterus with you."

Jacques grinned. "I didn't have to share."

"Knock it off!" I said.

Angel looked at the kids. "Never a good idea to piss off your mother."

Des replied, "Or Teri!"

"So true," Angel replied and high-fived Des.

James stood up. "I should get dinner on the table."

"I'll help you," Grigoryi said, and we followed James into the kitchen.

Teri was sitting at the table, just staring at her phone. "You're not gonna believe what happened in Granite."

She showed me a long text message from Henry about the "raid" at our house. WTF Manny! I grabbed her phone and called Henry.

"Hi, Henry, sounds like quite a shit show. Thanks for handling that mess. Are the police gone?"

"Good evening Miranda," He was always polite, the opposite of his stage persona. "Yes, much ado about nothing. The detective embarrassed himself, and the local police are not happy with him."

"Will you do me a favor, thank Borgia and Antoinella for checking on things and ask them to keep this quiet? I will deal with the detective myself. I don't want Tristan or the Magus making him a Target when he's just a nuisance."

"Of course. I almost felt sorry for Manny. It was his big bust, and he failed miserably. After everything he has been told and has seen, he still tries to deny we exist."

"We seem to have that effect on people." It was becoming easier for me to identify with the undead. "Thanks again for dealing with everything. I'll give the phone back to Teri. We'll leave for home in a couple of days."

"Wait, I heard about the way you handled the Magus. It made me more comfortable with my decision to align with your House." I felt his charm, even through the phone, but it was a comfort, not a threat.

"I'm not sure I handled anything. My 'gift,' as you call it, decided to come out of the closet. Luckily, he was impressed. Thanks. Bye," I handed the phone back to Teri, who told him they would talk later and hung up.

James gave me a questioning look. "I promise I'll explain later," I told him.

He opened the oven, and a beautiful, roasted turkey made me give up my vegetarian ways for the night. He had all the trimmings. We put bowls of mashed potatoes, stuffing, green beans, cranberries, and corn muffins on the table. Teri made the gravy and, of course, added a touch of siracha. James asked Grigoryi to carve the huge bird.

We gathered around the large old wooden dining table. Marie brought in candles from the fireplace mantle to give a golden glow to our gathering. My heart filled with love and gratitude. For the first time, I truly felt that the kids and I would be all right.

Des started to grab a turkey leg. James tapped his wrist. "Wait a minute junior. Miranda, will you say something?"

"Sure." I looked around at the faces of people I cherished, including the fat pug in Jacque's lap and a lone wolf by my feet. "Thank you, magnificent Creator of the universe!"

"Gratias Tibi ago, as is s in Latin," Grigoryi said,

"Well said, let's eat!" James announced, and we stuffed ourselves.

Angel sipped from a cup, amused by our delight at the huge meal. I filled them in on the details of Manny's botched drug bust between bites.

"I wished I had seen his face when they told him we were cooking sunscreen," Tomas grinned.

"I think he expected *Breaking Bad*. What an idiot," Des shook his head.

Teri added, "Well, now the police have met some of our people."

"Be careful about drawing attention to yourselves. From the moment we are transformed, that's something we are told to avoid. Knowledge of our kind must be protected," Angel explained. "Your daylight tolerant House is breaking all the rules. I worry about the more traditional vampires taking offense. The vampire world survives by having minimal interaction with mortals. Your existence can enhance or threaten the balance of power."

"Haute or Common Caste?" I asked.

"Both," he replied

Marie said, "Most of them think we're freaks."

"We are!" Des remarked and bit into a corn muffin. "Own it," he added, spitting out crumbs.

Tomas took exception. "We're hybrids! No one understands our potential."

"Like Spiderman." Jacques grinned.

"I like Spiderman," Grigoryi said between bites.

"Face it, we're fucked," Des stated.

"You mean gifted," I said.

Tomas threw a corn muffin at Des. "Gifted asshole!"

It was on. Muffins, green beans, and spoonfuls of mashed potatoes flew between the siblings. Teri, James, Angel Grigoryi, and I took cover. Sally was loving the "fallout."

After a couple of minutes, I put a stop to it. "James, I'm sorry."

"They're royal?" Angel muttered.

"Royal pains in the ass," James said. "No problem. Just make them clean it up."

Teri said, "Oh, I will."

We stood and surveyed the battlefield. Stuffing was a poor projectile; it was the only item that remained untouched. The kids looked at me, prepared for harsh words. They wiped food off their clothes and hair.

"Everyone outside!" and I headed toward the door.

"Mom, it's freezing!" Des complained.

One stern look, and they all followed me and assembled under the moonlight on the cold clear night. I stood a dozen feet away from the porch and stretched my arms out. "We are gifted!"

The kids looked at me like I had lost it. The air became heavy with moisture.

Drizzle began to fall and started to freeze. The little pellets of ice stung as it fell on us. They all moved back under the cover of the porch.

Marie yelled, "Mom! Are you doing this?"

Grigoryi uttered, "It's a miracle."

I smiled as the ice turned to small snowflakes falling in an area about twenty feet across. "Yes!"

The kids ran out and hugged me, almost knocking me over. I lowered my arms, and the snow stopped. Angel stood on the porch with the others. He clapped his hands. "Baroness Miranda Orteg- Mordecai has arrived!"

James was astonished. "That's not possible."

"She's not even a vampire," Teri declared.

James responded, "She's something else."

Angel said, "Only a few vampires develop those extraordinary powers, and Batu appears to be one of those. Kyoto and Lady Lily have begun collecting blood samples of all of our kind. No one knows what they are looking for."

James stared at Miranda and the kids as they started to come inside. "I don't think what she has will be found in a test tube."

Teri and Angel began to understand what the Baroness saw in James.

Marie pushed her long dark hair back and announced, "So we're gifted freaks. At least we aren't boring."

Tomas looked at me with thoughtful, intense brown eyes like his grandfather Omar. "Mom, when did you realize you could make that happen?"

"For years, I had dreams about snowstorms, not understanding the meaning. Then recently, I started to be able to concentrate the moisture in the air and even make it rain or snow. Henry and Guillaume helped me focus my new gift."

We went back inside, and Jacques asked, "Can you do that whenever you want?"

I put my hand on his shoulder. I could not help but see a resemblance to Alexander. He had the same wavy hair and handsome yet delicate features. "I am still figuring that out and have no idea how these gifts work, how to control them, or how they will affect all of us."

Des said, "Pie might help us figure that out."

I picked a glob of mashed potatoes out of his curls. "After you clean up the mess!"

"What mess?" Marie asked. We looked around the kitchen, and the food was gone, even the stuffing.

I heard a burp and noticed Sally lying in front of the fire. Teri said, "You owe her. At least wash the dishes."

While the kids were in the kitchen, the adults gathered in front of the fireplace. I took a plaid throw off the back of the couch and threw it around my shoulders. Teri asked, "Are you okay?"

"Yeah, just a little chilled. I'm fine while it's happening, but then, I feel exhausted and cold. I'll be okay soon."

James handed me a mug of coffee. "Do you need anything else?" I could see the concern in his eyes.

I started to tear up. "I'm so lucky to have your friendship, to have all of you in my life." I leaned down and patted Sally's head. I took a deep breath and looked at the fireplace to aid my composure.

Angel smiled. "You don't have a clue about the anxiety you create in our world. You're a mortal with ancient powers." Then he turned to Teri. "I hope we can be friends. You've moved on. I'm okay with it. Are we cool?" He held up his fist.

Teri fist-bumped him but was still a little embarrassed. "I'm still your F.O.V."

"Without benefits!" He grinned. She hit him in the arm. "I wish Sir Henry good luck."

"Henry?" James asked,

I responded, "You'll like him. He's an ancient rogue vampire in Seattle. He fronts a Goth band and is supportive of my decision to start a new House."

"He's amazing. He looks like the Rock. You know, the Scorpion King," Teri sighed.

"Good thing he's on your side!" James remarked. Then changing the subject asked, "Pie anyone?"

I could not blame him for not wanting to know more. He was worried about us enough as it was. While everyone helped themselves to pumpkin pie with heaps of whipped cream, Angel pulled me aside.

"You know I work for the Magus, but I will be careful about what I tell him. I've been hanging out at his place and running errands. He really hates disloyal people, and I like my head where it is. I'm sorry, but it would be better not to say anything around me that you don't want him to know. I wouldn't be able to lie to him and get away with it. This has to stay between us."

Sadness touched my heart. "I'm sorry too."

"We all do what we gotta do to survive."

"Right." I surprised him with a hug. "You're always welcome to join my House, Sir Angel."

"Thanks, but I owe the Magus. One more thing, your ex will do anything to get you back. Be careful."

I felt a sudden chill. "I know. He sees love as a competition. That brilliant, gifted vampire could learn some things from you. Like politely stepping aside and not burning bridges."

Grigoryi came up to us. "This has been the best Thanksgiving ever. Thank you for bringing me. I will do whatever I can to help you and the children."

The Royal offspring had set up a video game on James's television. Insults began to fuel the rivalry. I looked at Grigoryi. "Good luck with that."

Chapter 34

Seeking an Ally

The day after we got back home, a FedEx box arrived from Danuta. My gut told me to open it in private. I went into my room and closed the door. I sat in the red velvet chair to surround my body with comfort and grabbed a box of tissue. The grief monster sat at my feet, ready to pounce. I slowly opened the box and found a card from Danuta and a letter from my mom wrapped in her old butterfly scarf.

Danuta wrote,

Your mom made me promise not to tell you about this letter
and just send it after you got back home. I hope you're not upset
with me. Everyone here is fine.

Hugs,
Danuta

I opened the envelope that had Randie written on the front in a shaky script. My hands trembled. A second letter! The envelope was scented with lavender perfume, her favorite. I inhaled deeply.

My sweet, stubborn, bright child, I love you so much. I just have
a little more to say. My chest hurt worse today, so I gave this to Danuta
in case I don't make it to Thanksgiving. I'm not sure I will get past
the Pearly Gates, I hope Pete helps me sneak in a back door.
I always knew what I was doing. Though my mom kept me from vampires,
I recognized Omar in that hotel bar and went along with it so I could have
a baby. I knew my V-8 juice was being spiked at the café to help
me get pregnant.

It was all worth it to have you! All those years of them visiting our town
made me suspicious that it was more than just looking out for a descendent
of De Molay. I don't know what their grand plan is, but I know
you will be fine. You and the kids are going to surprise them all.

Just stay true to the things and people you love and never trust the Magus.

Big Hugs,
Mom

PS Tristan and Batu are something else. Good luck with that.

Through tears, I had to laugh. "Good luck with that." Really? I was just relieved she had not told me who to choose. She would not have to sneak in. I'm sure some special envoy met her at the gate. So, she had known what they had been up to for years! I wished I had her optimism. The unrest in the vampire world had gone from a blazing fire to smoldering ashes since Alexander's plan failed, but like embers, it could reignite at any moment. I did not want my House to be in the center of any new uprising. I wanted the House of Sun to be a neutral fortress that could protect our unique kind. I needed to know why the Magus was so interested in our blood, and Dr. Kyoto was the only one with answers. I carefully wrapped the letter back in the scarf and placed it in the desk drawer with her other letter.

I sat for a moment thinking, then sent a text message to the Magus and Tristan,

I am willing to give you samples of what you tried to take from us, but only if Dr. Kyoto comes here and answers some questions.

Though direct and straightforward, I knew it would be hours or nights before I got a response. When I went downstairs, Leif and Cramer were waiting for me. "Welcome back!" they both said.

"Thanks for taking care of Lug and the police raid. I hope that detective is back in Salinas now. Any fall-out?"

Leif looked at Cramer, who said, "I thought I should be proactive and met with the Chief of Police on your behalf. His daughter is in my fourth-period class. It went well. I told him that we realized they had no way to know it was just a science project and assured him we would not press charges. I said it was an honest mistake, especially with the history of meth production in the area."

"Nice! You should go into politics."

"Oh, it gets better," Leif said.

Cramer continued, "I volunteered Henry's band to play a charity concert. I thought that might keep us from getting in trouble when the beautiful, cool nocturnal people start showing up to check out the House of Sun or if the kids' band gets too loud."

"You are now officially hired as the public relations officer for our House."

Cramer's face lit up. "Thanks, that will help since the Magus cut me off."

Leif said, "C'mon. I need help with the goats."

"Being in charge of public relations will probably be almost a full-time job, and I've still got school lesson plans. Get the kids to help you. It's good for them," Cramer answered, clearly not pleased with the thought of working with the goats.

"He's right. You can tell them I said they had to do it."

Team House of Sun was coming together. I found Grigoryi in the kitchen baking bread. "Smells great! Where's Teri?"

Grigoryi pulled a loaf out of the oven and set it on a cooling rack with a satisfied expression. "She's getting a pedicure. I believe that means Sir Henry will visit tonight. Should I stay in my room when he comes?"

That was a good question. "Sooner or later, you'll have to meet, so why not just make it brief tonight. It should be fine. Depending on his mood, of course."

"Like the Baron?" Grigoryi looked thoughtful.

"Yes. He's powerful, egotistical, ancient, yada, yada, yada. You know what they're like."

"I wish they were all more like Guillaume and Bart. They have both been very kind to me."

I smiled, "Guillaume is my distant cousin. I'm glad you like him. Are you happy you came here? You know you can leave any time." I filled my mug and grabbed an almond cookie from a batch he made earlier.

"I like it here very much. Should I make lasagna for dinner?"

"If you make lasagna, I'll probably change my mind about ever letting you leave."

In Mongolia, Scheherazade was adjusting from her return to mortal life. Day by day, she was becoming stronger but hid it from the Princess. She was allowed to wander about the royal compound under the watchful eyes of guards. The vain ex-vampiress detested her reflection and silently vowed to return to her once beautiful state again. Her recent source of HH blood was staying with Kyoto and the monks in preparation for his transformation. Sapna, her former servant, had seen her once from a distance and could not believe she had been turned into an old hag. He thought that it served her right.

One evening she was brought before the Princess and Sir Steve. She stood hunched over and stared up at them with undisguised hatred. The Princess ignored her insolence. Steve longed to send a blade into her dark heart to finish Scheherazade once and for all. Kyoto entered with Lily and joined them.

"Arrangements are in place for tomorrow night. We must leave for the airport this evening," Kyoto informed them.

The Princess nodded. "Very well. Scheherazade, you shall be sent to Los Angeles with Drs. Kyoto and Lily, and you will be examined by the Magus. He wishes to see what has become of you. I shall be glad to have you removed from my sight."

Scheherazade responded in a weak voice, "It is not over yet. I gladly go before the Magus." She stood a little straighter.

Two mortal guards would accompany them to keep Scheherazade secure and unable to harm anyone. Within an hour, they were in a van headed for Ulaanbaatar, the Capitol of Mongolia. They took no chances with the prisoner. Handcuffs irritated her aged, fragile skin, but no one was sympathetic. They knew she had arranged the attack on Batu in London and how badly she had treated the mortal servant she had brought with her. Scheherazade took a deep breath. She loved the scent of mortals. A couple of hours into the trip, she was given some bread and mutton. Food no longer caused nausea. She ate to build up her strength, but it did not satisfy her hunger. As the guard took her bowl away, she grabbed his wrist and bit him with all her might.

"Bitch!" he pushed her away and looked at the bite marks that had broken the skin.

Scheherazade grinned and licked her lips. She had felt a rush from the tiny bit of blood she had tasted.

"Sedate her!" Lily ordered. She and one of the guards held down the troublesome prisoner. "You disgust me!"

Kyoto pulled out a syringe and gave her enough sedative to keep her unconscious for the trip to L.A. "If the Magus had not insisted on seeing you, I would have ended your miserable existence."

"I will return to...." Scheherazade slipped into unconsciousness.

Lily tended to the wound on the guard's wrist and gave him a bottle of antibiotics. "I don't want to take any chances." She handed him a syringe. "Here is another dose of tranquilizer. If she starts to wake before we do, use it. Even if it kills her."

The guard was grateful. "Thank you, Lady Lily. I'll stick her the moment she moves."

The kids were still at Leif's place, and I was relaxing on the deck with Lug and Piglet. Alexander arrived an hour after sunset, unannounced. The pug jumped out of my lap and scampered over to her previous owner. He picked her up and kissed her furrowed brow. His features were very masculine yet more delicate than Tristan's or Batu's. His brown hair fell in loose waves to his shoulders. He wore a white dress shirt and dark blue jeans that flattered his fit body. I sometimes forgot how charming Alexander could be, full force.

He pointed at the chair across from me and asked, "May I?" I nodded.

He sat, and Piglet settled into his lap. "Baroness, I extend my sincere condolences for the passing of your mother." His scent was fresh, with a touch of white flowers.

"Thanks. The kids and I are doing the best we can. It helped to spend Thanksgiving with an old friend. Why are you here?"

"I thought you could use a break from the battling suitors who pursue you."

"So, you heard about what happened in Rossville."

"Sir Ruben posted a blog. He was upset that he had to return the bets." Alex tried not to laugh, but I could see the amusement in his polychromatic eyes. "Tell me about your House of Sun," he said in a serious tone.

"The Magus says he is supportive, but I don't trust him." I decided to be honest, as I believed he wanted to protect Jacques. "I have no idea what I'm doing, but Henry and Guillaume have agreed to be my knights. I tried disengaging from the undead world, but that didn't work, so I shall use my Haute Caste status to protect my family."

"I would like to offer my services as your counselor. Like Henry, I understand the ancient culture and politics of our kind. I promise I shall not underestimate the Magus again. My thought of a return to past glory made me careless." He patted the content pug's head.

I felt his energy, strong and sweet like a spoonful of warm honey. "You're back aren't you. I mean your power, abilities, and strength."

He smiled. "Is it that obvious? Yes. I have a suggestion and a proposition."

"Go ahead," I said, a little suspicious.

"Build a guest house for the nocturnal visitors. You'll be expected to entertain members of the Haute Caste at times, and having a second house will help you maintain your privacy and security. No one will expect you to have a palace," he looked around at the rustic setting. "But make them feel comfortable. I would suggest you make peace with Pomp. She can be a formidable enemy or a very effective and powerful ally."

"I'm fine with the vampire bed and breakfast, well, I guess bed and dinner, but Pomp? Let me think about it? What is the proposition?"

"Allow me to be your romantic interest." He paused to let the idea sink in. I stared at him, amazed by his audacity. "They each believe you cannot have affection for another. Do you wish to feed their egos, to allow them to see you that way? Or the rest of the vampire world, for that matter?"

"You and Kyoto got me pregnant without my permission. I have not forgiven either of you," I crossed my arms and stared daggers.

"I understand and shall beg your forgiveness all of my nights, but now you must think strategically as the head of a House."

Unfortunately, I could see the value of his proposition. Tristan and Batu had pissed me off at the funeral. I uncrossed my arms and leaned forward. "Beg for my forgiveness."

Alexander the once Great put Piglet down and got down on his knees. He looked into my eyes and quietly said, "Forgive me Baroness."

Just at that moment, the royal offspring came around the corner of the house. "What the fuck!" Des exclaimed.

Jacque's eyes were huge. "Mom!"

"Don't marry him," Marie cried out.

Tomas just shook his head.

Alexander stood and turned towards them. "I would ask for her hand, but I know that at this time, she would not have me. I was merely offering my support for the House of Sun."

Nice save! Their expressions shifted from confusion and anger to relief.

Tomas said, "Welcome to our House. We seriously need all the help we can get."

I stood and announced, "Sir Alexander will be counselor to our House."

Des said, "More like consigliere."

"That's enough for now. Go set the table for dinner. Grigoryi made lasagna. We'll be in in a minute."

Jacques hugged Alex, which made us all choke up. He looked up at the ancient vampire. "I'm glad you're on our side." Then they went into the house.

Alexander was moved. "That is the first time he hugged me."

"Jacques is a gentle soul. He has a quiet way of bringing out the best in people," I mused out loud.

"I sensed that too. What do you think of my proposition?"

"Alex, this idea of pretending to have an affair won't work. Henry tried it, and Tristan knew it was a lie."

He moved closer to me, into my personal space, and looked into my eyes with desire. "Henry was acting. I am not. Everyone will see that I want you. Most importantly, you will feel it."

I let him pull me into his arms. It was more than his charms. It was the comfort of the flesh. I was hungry for more than dinner, and he knew it. He softly kissed my neck, causing delicate waves of pleasure. Somewhere in my brain, the voice of sanity questioned my behavior. "Alex, not now...." I pushed him away. "What kind of counselor are you?"

"You may always seek my advice and assistance. On all matters."

"Maybe you should be less hands-on," I remarked and started to walk away.

"My proposition?"

"I'll think about it." I was about to go from a love triangle to a square. Maybe I should get to know Pomp. She had a lot of experience with court intrigue and the aristocracy of the vampire world. Alex had given me a lot to consider. "Join us. There's O-positive in the fridge."

Over dinner, the kids told Alex about their trip and Piglet's encounter with Sally at the ranch. Jacques looked at me. "Does he know about you and the snow on command?"

I took a breath. "Well Alex, apparently, my gift is water. I seem to attract moisture, and I can sometimes summon a little rain or snow."

He looked quite serious. "That explains the Magus accepting your claim to a House. Madame, you are the only mortal with rare Haute Caste powers. He must have suspected it all along. What other talents do you possess?"

"I can tune into people, but not their thoughts exactly. Not really read them like Cassandra, but I sense things and can sometimes communicate a little." I knew the kids had suspected I had ESP, but we had never discussed it.

"Me too," Marie said softly.

"We never talked about that." I stared at her.

"When you were kidnapped and being held prisoner in the warehouse in L.A., before the fight in Las Vegas, I had a vision of where you were.

I looked at the others. "Any other unusual talents."

Tomas nudged Des. "Show her."

Des, who usually loved to brag, was hesitant. "I can light candles." He looked at a decorative candle in the middle of the table. After a few seconds, the wick smoldered then ignited.

I smiled. "I can extinguish them." I stared at the candle, and it went out.

"Tomas and Jacques?"

Tomas said he could tell who was a friend and who was a foe. "Even when we attacked your compound Alex, I knew you weren't really bad. I was glad they didn't hurt you permanently. That vampiress, with the snakes, I just saw darkness around her."

Alex replied, "You're a good judge of character. Jacques, what about you?"

"I draw pictures, and then sometimes they happen. I drew Teri with a tall, dark man about a year ago, then well, Henry happened. I don't know if the drawing makes it happen or if it is more like Marie's visions.

"You all have some traces of Haute Caste abilities. Over time mine has been getting stronger. I don't know what abilities you may develop, but you must tell me when it does. Promise me!"

They all mumbled versions of agreement. It got quiet till Marie asked Alex a very pointed question, "So do you enjoy fanging people?"

"Fanging?" I dropped my fork. "Marie!"

"It's fine." He gave her a bemused look. "I have seen mankind inflict many forms of torture over the centuries, often in the name of some particular holy belief. I have never inflicted suffering on anyone. Even in battle, the cut of my sword was quick and lethal." He paused and took a sip of blood. "Like my bite," he added. No one spoke. "Did I pass your test?"

Marie gave him a sly grin. "Yeah. You can be our counselor."

Jacques beamed with pride. "Do you want to watch our fencing lesson?"

"Of course." Alex helped the kids clear off the table. He was doing everything to ingratiate himself into our household, and it was working. He headed out to the barn with the kids. Tristan and Batu could learn a lot from him.

Chapter 35

Vampire History 101

I helped Grigoryi with the dishes to calm my brain down with mundane tasks before Henry arrived. Cleaning counters and loading the dishwasher helped me focus. I was becoming a clean freak for my emotional survival. Tomorrow I would contact a local construction company about a barn and fencing the for pasture. Though I had never been able to ride, the kids had grown up with horses. I would get on one of those enormous creatures and just let them do whatever they wanted. Bart had tried to teach me that I had to take charge of the horse but had soon given up on giving me lessons. The kids took to it quickly and loved riding. A lot of people in the area owned horses, so I was hoping that it might help the kids bond with some of the neighbors. I was worried about their unique, budding powers and their ability to control them. I could not help but wish for more normalcy in their lives.

Teri and Henry sauntered into the kitchen. She had been in Seattle with Henry since we got back from the ranch. So much for Teri not letting their relationship get in the way of being a nanny. Okay, a bodyguard, the kids insisted they were too old for a nanny. Teri was radiant with passion and totally beguiled with her vampire. I remembered those days. At least I had Grigoryi now to help out with the kids.

"Hi!" I poured myself some coffee. "Want anything?"

"No, we're good. We stopped at the Monte Cristo latte stand on the way," Teri said. She already answered for him like a couple who had been together for years.

"That's the best coffee stand around. I love them," I replied.

Henry smiled. "Miranda, may we talk in the living room?"

"Sure." I followed them in and settled in a chair. They sat as close to each other as humanly possible on the couch.

Henry started, "I would like to talk with you about ancient history. It might help you forgive Alexander and trust his motives for the good of your House."

"Okay." I took a sip of coffee to fortify myself.

"As you already know, the Magus was the first of our kind. Once he realized he was the first of a new species, he had to find others to transform. He started with Lena, and together they searched for those that might be worthy. You've met most of the ancients, the originals, Hannibal, Cassandra, Kananga, Omar, Alexander, and me. We all sought to be a favorite of the Magus, but he allowed Lena to remain his second in power. When others were transformed, like Tristan, Sudovian, Borgia, Kyoto, and Jorge, Lena convinced the Magus to let her pick who would be the third most powerful vampire. She picked Tristan because he had great potential, and he expressed gratitude to her for his transformation. The first year of his immortal existence, she periodically gave him some of her blood to fortify him, enhancing his powers and abilities. He is a third-generation but perhaps more powerful than ancients like me."

"And vainer," I added.

Teri said, "When I heard about all this, I told Henry you should know."

"I already knew most of this and that Lena had planned to use Tristan after she took down the Magus. What else?"

"The Magus not only convinced Sir Omar to participate in his plan to orchestrate your conception, but he also wanted to pair you with one of the original ancients. Alexander desired to be chosen for you and pleaded with the Magus. It was a major blow to his pride when the Magus turned him down. Lena intervened, told Tristan of the plan, and persuaded the Magus that he would be the best vampire to court you. She succeeded, and you know the rest."

"Do you know why the Magus decided on Tristan?" I asked.

"Don't you know about his power of electricity?" Henry asked.

"What are you talking about?"

Teri said, "Let me tell her. This is so cool. He can pull electrical energy out of the environment, as you do with water."

Henry continued, "We all tend to keep our gifts hidden. I suppose he had his reasons for not sharing that with you. You know about his levitation ability, but the Baron can also deliver a strong shock. No one knows how powerful he is, but that ability is unique to him. He rarely resorts to it as it weakens him. He has to rest and have nourishment to recover."

"The Magus chose the vampire with the most unique talents. He probably is hoping one of the offspring will inherit that power," I suggested.

Henry nodded. "You are probably right about that.

"So, what does all this have to do with Alexander?" I asked.

"Alexander never forgave Lena or the Magus. That was when his plan to overthrow the Magus became crystallized. He wanted the family that had been denied him. You are in a matter of speaking, his Helen of Troy."

"When Alexander kissed me, I felt more than lust. He felt like a giant chasm seeking to be filled. I could not figure him out till now. Thank you. All this time he kept his distance."

Henry carefully watched my response. "He wanted to offer you a kingdom."

"He knocked me up by proxy, thanks to Kyoto. That takes all the romance out of this fairy tale." I stood and walked to the windows that looked out towards the barn to calm myself.

Teri remarked, "I told you it would be a cold day in hell before she would forgive him."

I turned to face him. "Henry, why are you so interested in Alexander and me? It's not just the House of Sun. I already accepted his offer to be my counselor."

He weighed his words before responding. "Many reasons. I don't relish Tristan or Batu being your consort. They have alliances with the Magus and Princess Khunbish. A vampire owes a debt to the one who transformed them, one that can't ever completely be repaid. You saw with Tomas's accident that even Tristan might choose the Magus over his family. The Princess did not send her favorite young vampire because he longs for you. She must have some motive. I am concerned that you might find yourself used by one or both of them. Alexander owes everything to you. You demanded he and Scheherazade be spared. He is brilliant, gifted, and a natural-born ruler. His recent fiasco humbled him. It has made him wiser and more careful."

"I don't have to have a consort. Queen Elizabeth did just fine alone."

"She was an effective yet miserable queen. I sense your pent-up desire," Henry remarked.

Teri added, "You could do a lot worse than Alexander."

"Are both of you done? I'm tired of other people making decisions about my life!" I walked upstairs to my room and slammed the door. No one was going to tell me who I should fuck. I know Henry and Teri meant well, but seriously, they did not have a clue who I was. "Consort my ass!" I said to no one. I ran a bath to calm me down. I added lavender-scented oil to the water and got into the tub. Henry was right about Princess Khunbish. I had to figure out why she wanted Batu to be with me. I decided to take Alexander's advice and extend an olive branch to Pomp. She understood how to use royal intrigue, which would help me protect my House. My thoughts wandered back to Alexander. I finally understood what his longing was about and why he went to such lengths to have a child by me, but it did not excuse his transgression. The song "Gimme Shelter" by the Rolling Stones played in my head. There would only be one throne in the House of Sun, and that would be mine.

My phone buzzed as I dried off. It was a text from the Magus,

Agreed

That was all it said. At least in part, I knew he had agreed to me creating the House of Sun because he wanted samples of my blood to continue his research. Kyoto owed me just like the others for whom I had demanded mercy. I knew that I still could not trust him. Perhaps Lily would tell me why the Magus wanted blood samples so badly. I pulled on my robe, thinking about my next move to establish my House.

Teri knocked on my door. "Miranda, can I come in?"

"Sure," I called out.

She sat on the bed, and I curled up in my big chair. "I wanted to tell you that Henry is willing to make peace with Pomp for the sake of the House."

"That would be good," I replied. "Also, could you ask him to set up a meeting for me with her for tomorrow night. I think it would be helpful to get some tips on how to manage my House from Pompadour."

"I'm sure he would be happy to. You know, he doesn't get why you don't want to be set up with Alexander, but I do."

"Alexander is very sexy, charming, and brilliant. If I met him at a bookstore, we would have had a chance, but I don't trust him. That's not even the most important point. I will run my own House. Period!"

"I know. I'll support you whatever you decide Great Ruler."

"Hey, counting the kids, I've got a dozen followers."

Teri patted my shoulder. "I got a text from Billy and Robert. They want to know what happened in Rossville. They would like to stay here instead of at Henry's."

The next night Guillaume drove me to Pomp's mansion on the shore of Lake Washington in the middle of Seattle. Over the years, she had built up a vast fortune and now had a place worthy of royalty. We pulled up to the tall ornate gates in front of the palatial-like home. Guillaume identified us to the security guard who passed us through. By comparison, my house looked like servants' quarters. She had decorated her house elegantly with small crystal chandeliers and Persian rugs. The furniture was covered in sky blue silk fabric, and decorative pink pillows, her favorite color, were scattered about. We found her draped across a loveseat under a large painting of men and women frolicking at Versailles. She wore a low-cut red cashmere sweater, a tunic, embroidered slippers, and a large blue sapphire necklace. Her pale blond hair fell in long spirals past her shoulders, and the scent of Chanel N°5 filled the air.

"Bienvenue Baroness. Mon chèri Guillaume! I hope you don't mind my casual attire since this is not a formal affair."

I wore blue jeans, a Levi shirt, and a peacoat. Guillaume wore a fitted black dress shirt, matching slacks, and black boots. Standard vampire attire. "It's fine. Thanks for meeting with us. I'd like us to be on better terms."

She clapped her hands, and Ms. Grisham appeared. I was a little surprised to see she was now working for Pomp. Grisham took my coat and Guillaume's leather jacket. I was glad she wouldn't be back at the high school.

We sat in pale pink velvet chairs around a small ornate marble table.

"Refreshments!" Pomp called out, and Ms. Grisham appeared with a porcelain coffee set and two small cups of blood. She filled my cup with dark roast and never met my gaze.

Whatever. I did not have to let my ex-husband's sexual exploits derail my purpose. I sipped the dark brew. "Good coffee, thanks."

They politely took small sips until their cups were empty. Then she asked, "Why have you come here?"

"Pomp, I'm just starting to understand my power. You know the intrigue of the vampire world and how to negotiate royal court life. I researched you. You went from a mistress to an advisor to one of the leaders of France. I think I could benefit from your years of experience dealing with royalty and the Haute Caste males."

She sat up and smiled. "My relationships, even with the late King and your Baron, have always been about survival and success. I always find a way, though it may not be through the front door."

Guillaume commented, "You deserve the front door."

Pomp smiled again and continued, "I was surprised and relieved when Sir

Henry contacted me and asked that transgressions on both sides be forgiven. Since my voice has been restored thanks to the intervention of the Baron, I agreed. We both understand we have the chance to be part of a new era in the vampire world."

I felt a twinge in my gut. "But you will not forget."

Her smile became icy. "I can put it aside."

"Will you give your word to not plot against my House or anyone in it?" I tried to cover any possible act of revenge.

She looked at me the way the Magus had when I showed him my unique ability. "Baroness, I believe you may be up to this task. Yes, I will agree to that."

"I will demand this of everyone who joins my House. Although, I can't promise the kids won't play tricks on each other."

"They are ruthless," Guillaume added.

"Pomp, I have to ask, how did you manage all those male egos at court?"

"I let them use my ideas and think it was theirs, and I let them think they had seduced me."

I took another sip of coffee. "I won't do that."

She smiled. "Neither will Lady Kananga or Princess Khunbish, but they do respect the men who contribute to their power."

"You did not mention Lily or Sarah?"

"Lady Lily has been under the spell of Kyoto for ages, and Lady Sarah, for all her modern ways, has never disagreed with the Magus. She reminds me of myself when I first arrived at court."

"But you never became Haute Caste," Guillaume commented. "As a mortal, you went from Mademoiselle Poisson to Marquise de Pompadour, but your status as an immortal has not changed."

I got the hint. "I can try to pressure the Magus to give you Haute Caste status. I have royal blood leverage."

Her eyes lit up. "No one has ever offered me that." She leaned forward and touched my hand. "I regret bringing Scheherazade to the club. At court, I often had arrangements with other women, even the Queen, to allow us to get ahead without harming each other. It was one of the reasons I thrived at Versailles. I offer my services to you."

Guillaume asked, "Have you heard any rumors of Haute or Common Caste who are critical of the new House?"

"So far, only curiosity and concern. Lady Cassandra and Sir Hannibal would like to visit. They wish to offer their support and counsel. I think Sir Hannibal misses your children."

"As long as he doesn't lead them into battle again. We did not part on the best terms."

Pomp smiled. "He can be headstrong, but he is a fierce ally. Be content he is supportive. If I can forgive Sir Henry, you might find it in your heart to make peace with Sir Hannibal and Alexander. You need them. The support of the ancients is quite important."

"I'll think about it. My head tells me you're right. Thanks for everything. Just one more request. Please be careful with Des. He has an enormous crush on you, and I don't want him to be hurt."

She nodded. "I'm aware. I would never take such a young lover."

As we said goodbye, Pomp had no idea what a relief that whole conversation had been to me. I had been worried that she would not be so cooperative and helpful after our previous encounters. I had already imagined Des sneaking off in the middle of the night for a rendezvous with her. I could not blame him; she was gorgeous and had flattered his young ego. I was thankful Henry had made peace with her. I would try to be magnanimous with Hannibal. I would need the support and protection of as many of the undead as possible because unknown threats could be around the corner. Since I had married Tristan, there had been numerous plots against my children and me. I feared that another disgruntled vampire might decide to come after us because we were different or more fortunate.

Chapter 36

Fangs

The spring had come and gone, and we made to the end of summer without incident. The stables and guest house were finished, and I had used the time to consolidate support for the House of Sun. I referred to the Marquise as Lady Pomp, though she had not been decreed Haute Caste by the Magus yet. She gave me her support, and I told her she was welcome to Tristan. He often spent time with her when he visited the children. His interactions with me were minimal but polite. Alexander and I had become closer but not intimate. Like Pomp, he was an excellent source of information about how to navigate through the world of the undead.

One night I met Alex in Seattle at Pike's market. We sat at a candlelit table that overlooked the Sound. I sipped espresso while he pretended to enjoy red wine. Underneath our conversations, I felt his desire, but he was the perfect gentleman. His charm and handsome features caused the waitress to linger at our table. He always smelled great. He wore a black cashmere sweater, snug blue jeans, and black boots.

"Jacques is glad that we get along. He wants you to come over when the horses arrive next week."

Alex smiled. "He has found a place in his heart for another father." He took a sip of wine and smiled. His lips reddened from the wine."

A premonition of danger came over me, but I pushed it away.

"Perhaps he inherited his love of horses from me." His gaze was soft and searching. "Are you okay?"

"Yes, just a memory. I'm fine. Omar gave the kids the horses when they were born. I assume the horses are enhanced with nocturnal DNA, so they age slowly."

He reached over and touched my cheek softly. "Like you, dear Miranda."

"I should probably head home." Every time I saw him, I wanted to jump his bones. Luckily, I had been able to control myself so far. I tortured myself with pseudo dates because I missed romance but did not want the complications of an intimate relationship with another vampire. Alexander seemed safe enough.

We left Pike's Market and walked back to my car. As we passed an alley, three scruffy young men started following us. I could hear their footsteps getting closer in the poorly lit side street. Alex was holding my hand, and I felt him tense up.

"Hey! Can you help us?" One of the young men wearing sweats and a baseball cap pulled down over his dirty hair called to us loudly.

We turned, and Alex pushed me behind him. I smelled cigarettes and urine as the other two men moved closer. "I'll pay you to go take showers." I pulled some money out of my purse and threw it on the ground. I hoped it would be enough to distract them. These poor fuckers had no idea the level of rage they might unleash from Alex.

The leader pulled out a gun and pointed it with a shaky hand. "Give us your wallets. Now!"

A second street thug flashed a nasty-looking knife. The third took a bicycle chain from around his neck and leered at me. "Nice piece of ass."

I stepped beside Alex and said to him, "Just give them your wallet." His soft, seductive features had changed to the wild look of a predator. I took a step back.

"Leave now and I will let you live." He stared them down.

"This is bullshit," the leader sneered and aimed his gun in our direction.

I heard the gun go off and cried out as the bullet grazed my arm. Alex pushed me to the ground as he went after our assailants. He broke the neck of the man with the gun and threw him back into the dark alley. A roundhouse kick sent the thug holding the knife against a brick wall so hard his head cracked and left a bloody streak as he crumbled to the ground unconscious. Alex had moved so quickly they never had a chance to run. With one powerful hand, he grabbed the third guy by the throat and lifted him off his feet. His eyes opened wide with terror as he gasped for breath.

"No!" I cried out, "Stop it!"

Alex lowered him to the ground with a grim smile, and with one blow to his chest, the young man collapsed, holding his broken ribs. "My lady has shown you mercy, but I'm not done." He walked over to the ringleader, lifted the moaning man by his hair, and bit his neck with precision. I saw him drink deeply, then pick up the knife lying on the ground and used it to cover the bite marks. It was like the first time I had seen Tristan feed, but I did not throw up this time. I saw the undead savagery behind his polished façade without fear or revulsion. My heart raced, but I managed to stand. "Alex! We need to go."

He rushed to my side and helped me to the car. He said he would drive, and I gave him the keys. He got me seated, pulled the license plates off the Jeep, tossed them in the backseat, then drove away. The attack was over so fast we were able to get to Henry's building before we ever heard sirens. I stared at him as he parked. "Thank you." I could still see his fangs peeking out under his upper lip.

"I'm sorry that you live in a world where such creatures exist," he responded. "It will be safe here." He did not hear the irony of his words. "Your arm needs medical attention."

I stared at my bloody sleeve. "Damn, I liked this jacket! I'm fine. Really!"

"You're in shock, come!" He had moved into an apartment above the club. The tension between him and my ex had caused his relocation. My upper arm throbbed, and I felt light-headed. I was not in the mood to argue. That was rare for me.

266

I leaned against him as we took the elevator to his floor. He stared at me with honest concern. Clearly, he had no idea how seductive that was. The entryway to the apartments had dark red carpet and tapestries of ancient Egypt. Statues of gods and goddesses guarded a hallway that smelled of incense. We came to a door with a bird of prey painted on it, and Alex ushered me in.

"You'll stay here tonight. You're in no condition to go anywhere." Alexander was taking command, and I let him.

"Let Henry and Teri know I'll be staying. The kids are with them at Leif's for band practice."

"Of course." He quickly sent a text.

I slowly sat down on a velvet chaise lounge. His apartment was full of beautiful antiques. Alexander took off my denim jacket, then laid me back and began to take off my blouse. I stopped him.

"I have to dress your wound," he said quietly. I allowed him to slip off my blouse carefully and clean and wrap the wound. His features softened, and his touch was gentle. There was no longer any trace of the lethal maniac who had taken out three criminals. "You won't need stitches, just bandages. You were lucky the bullet just grazed the surface of your lovely arm. How do you feel?"

"Weird," I answered. The room was becoming cool and damp.

"Miranda, please stop."

"Oh, wow, that was me. I didn't even try."

He smiled and sat on the edge of the chaise. One of his hands played with my unruly brown curls. "Perhaps it is our chemistry." He leaned down and kissed me with tempered passion. The hormonal scent from his recent fight ignited my senses. He could feel that my repressed nature was about to be unleashed. The arousal was explosive. I grabbed him with my good arm and pulled his body down on top of me. My vampire DNA was taking over. I no longer felt any pain as I pulled off his sweater, and he removed the rest of our clothes. We were starved and ready for a feast.

I pushed him off of me, and he laid down on the Persian rug. I kissed and teased every pleasure center in his body, and he returned the favor. His lips reached my hardened nipples and I gasped. It was sparks to kindling. The air was thick and warm with the scent of sex. Alex maneuvered on top of me, his eyes full of delight. He entered me with particular attention to my clitoris. My body arched to increase the pressure. I cried out, and he was quietly intense. With all the energy I had left, I pushed him over. I would be on top, damn it! I guided him, and he entered me. Orgasms shook me to the core. I collapsed, exhausted on top of him as he climaxed. We lay with our bodies entwined until our hearts began to slow down.

He gently embraced me then carried my relaxed form to his bed with golden silk sheets. Though exhausted by sex, he checked my bandage before lying down beside me. We fell asleep for about an hour, then I woke with a start, confused as to where I was. He put his arms gently around me. "All is well."

It took a moment for the night's events to play out in my head. "You killed someone."

He looked at me with a touch of pity. "Miranda, he aimed his gun at your heart. I knocked it away at the last second. He may not have been on the list, but he was a Worthy Target. The others will survive though they will not be the fine unwashed specimens of manhood they once were."

I sat up. "What happened, I mean, between us. This was...."

"Rhapsody in blood." He smiled. "That is how we make love after a kill." He laid back and put his arms behind his head. "Your fangs showed."

I ran my fingers over my teeth. They seemed normal. "No way!" I stared at him.

"Rite of passage." He pointed to his shoulder. Two tiny puncture wounds marked his perfect skin. "Blood can trigger it. Though I did not expect you to create a rain forest." He handed me a glass of water. "You must be dehydrated."

I shook my head. "I tasted your blood?"

"Just a tiny amount. Do you desire more?"

"No!" I had a slightly metallic taste in my mouth. I sat up and emptied the glass. "I'm a mess!" I ran my fingers over my neck checking for a bite.

He shook his head. "Madame, I hope never to experience a donation of your blood again. You and the children can be sure no one wants to sample any of you."

I remembered how he had been punished with injections of my blood to diminish his powers temporarily. "It really worked?"

"You have no idea how much the vampire world fears you. "He pulled me down on his chest and played with my hair. "You're the most beautiful freak of nature I have ever encountered. You are worth the wait. A mortal vampiress."

I whispered, "We can never let this happen again," as I fell asleep.

Alexander fell into the deep sleep of the undead, with a smile.

At dawn, I woke from a dream about floating down a river. Alex lay with his hand on my abdomen and a leg over my calf. His thick brown curly mane framed his face like a halo. He looked like a very sexy saint. My arm hurt, but it was manageable. He woke as I tried to untangle myself. "I must rest now, though I envy the sun as it watches over you. Teri and Henry stayed in Granite with the children to give us privacy. You may remain here. When you wish to leave, take one of Henry's cars. Your jeep has been on the news. They're saying it was driven by an invisible man."

"I'm on the news?"

He yawned. "Just the Jeep, you were slumped down in the seat. No plates to identify it, but to be on the safe side, leave the get-away car here for now."

"What did you tell Teri?"

He pulled up texts on his phone and handed it to me.

Miranda is spending the night here.

She had replied,

Seriously? Rock on! We got the Royals.

I dropped the phone. "I need coffee."

"I had the apartment next door set up for you. I had hoped for a morning like this for a very long time. You are more magnificent than I imagined. And I have a great imagination." Though badly in need of rest, he rose from the bed in all his

268

naked beauty and embraced me. His kiss was just enough to tease my senses. He smelled great. "I must sleep now. I have had an apartment prepared for you next door, hoping to bring you here someday. Until the evening my love."

I pushed away. "I'm not your love. I don't understand what happened last night, but it was a big mistake."

"Beautiful liar." He smiled and laid across his bed.

I pulled on my clothes and slammed the door as I left his place. "What the fuck!" I was upset with myself as I had wanted to keep some distance between Alexander and me. I decided that I could blame it on the events of last night, adrenaline, the wine, and elevated hormones.

I found the door to the apartment next door unlocked. I opened the door to Mirandaland! Photos of the kids and I were on the mantle above a small fireplace. On the kitchen counter, there was a bag of Sumatran coffee beans and a grinder. Copies of my books sat alone on a bookshelf by a window seat that overlooked Pioneer Square. A MacBook Air sat on a desk. I opened the closet and found every article of clothing I might need for a weekend, including lime green Converse sneakers, everything in the correct size. He had studied me well, or Teri had helped him. A comfy, dark brown suede couch with brightly embroidered pillows from Mexico added life to the place. A note was on the pine dining table for two.

My dearest Miranda,

You have finally experienced my desire for you. You have always been more than the mother of my son. I have waited to hold you, to share this existence with you for many years. I hope I have not overstepped any boundaries. I long to earn your trust. I will abide by any limitations you impose on me. I will always cherish you, regardless of your status.

Yours,

Alexander

I made a cup of coffee and nibbled on some chocolates. WTF! I had fangs, and I had used them. Even a tiny amount of Alexander's blood would help my arm to heal quickly. Our blood connection would be stronger now. I found myself in the weird position of wanting to tell Alex, "It was just sex. Get over it." I knew it was more than that, and so did he. Had I crossed some point in my half-undead development where it would get more difficult to reign in my special abilities? The tropical storm effect during the fabulous sex was new. I had given myself permission to enjoy his body. I had not been out of control or under the influence. I had let sex get crazy and quite memorable. What would I tell the kids? They would be working on music with Henry and Leif as the club was closed for remodeling. I texted Teri,

I'll be back tonight

I wanted time to quiet my brain. I sat at the window and looked down at Pioneer Square. I saw a woman pushing a stroller with a sleeping baby. She would never have to explain the development of fangs to her kid. I laid down to take a long nap. The shower would have to wait until I recovered from my first experience as a mortal vampiress.

It had been another slow week for Manny. His last bust involved a young dealer from Indianapolis who was sold some chopped-up macadamia nuts, instead of crack. The Hoosier had gone back to the corner where the dealer hung out and raised holy hell, but the nut salesman was long gone. He got busted for disturbing the peace, as it was not against the law to be a dumbass.

His captain had been giving him the worst assignments since he came back from leave. He knew he would never get promoted if he stayed in Salinas. He and Molly were officially engaged and had moved into a larger apartment. Trouble liked the new place and especially chilling on Molly's lap at night. He had lost a cat but gained a life partner who would always have his back. The night before, she found Manny awake at two in the morning, watching a Dracula movie. She made some popcorn and joined him. Miranda Ortega was right. Exposure to whatever her family and associates were into made him second guess reality.

He finished his coffee then checked the police reports in Seattle, his daily routine before going home. "Damn," he muttered, then looked to make sure his captain was not around. No one paid any attention to him as he became engrossed in the latest Pacific Northwest murder. The victim's neck had been broken then, oddly, slashed. The dead man was well known to the cops for rape, burglary, and assaults that never seemed to stick. The other victims had priors and incarcerations for petty crimes. They were hospitalized but expected to recover. They gave no information about their assailants except that it was a man and a woman. They were afraid to identify them. He checked out the location of the incident. It was a few blocks from the club where he had seen the freaks fight months ago. Manny was sure he knew who was responsible. He wished he had not seen this report, but he could not forget it.

He made a plan as he drove home. He would apply to the Seattle P.D. and find a way to convince Molly to move and look for a job there. It was a beautiful, exciting city. He hoped she would be enthusiastic about the idea.

Later that evening, he presented his plan to her. Molly sat wide-eyed across the dining room table. "Are you out of your mind?"

He scratched his chin. "Captain Jenkins will never promote me. There are more opportunities there."

"More crazies! C'mon Manny. I know what this is about. You're still obsessed with the vampire thing. Besides, I've got five years towards my pension."

"Just come up with me, spend a three-day weekend looking around. You know you're underpaid. Just go online and check out the job listings. Okay?"

Molly knew he was miserable since he had returned to work. "Will you promise not to bring this up again for a week while I think about it?"

"Not a word," he grinned. "And I'll do the dishes every night."

"And the cat box!"

Chapter 37

Scheherazade Escapes...Again

Soon after sundown, the Magus was appalled as he first set eyes on Scheherazade. She stood several feet away from him with a vacant stare. Not a trace of the beautiful temptress remained. Even her voice sounded harsh. One dose of Miranda's blood had almost destroyed her.

Kyoto and Lady Lily joined the Magus and Scheherazade in the small, nicely furnished guest house on his property at Paradise Cove, California. The Magus had wrought iron bars installed on the windows and an extra deadbolt added to the door to prevent her escape. Kyoto was glad to be back in L.A., away from the demands of the Princess. He continued to be subservient to Lily and the Magus because of his transgressions. Lady Lilly and the Magus sat in two high-back chairs. Kyoto stood beside the Magus as they stared at the ancient woman who kneeled on the rug.

The Magus finally spoke, "Would you like to die?"

Her eyes lit up. "No," she coughed and continued in a raspy voice, "I want a little HH blood. Just a little. Aren't you curious about how it would affect me?"

"May I venture an opinion?" Kyoto asked.

"Of course," the Magus replied.

"I would try a little Common Caste blood first."

"Lady Lily, what do you think?"

She looked grim. "I would rather she be lit on fire, but for the sake of research, I would agree with trying the Common Caste blood first. A tiny amount."

"Thank you, gracious beings," Scheherazade responded and bowed her head.

"Your performance is nauseating. First, handcuff and shackle her," the Magus instructed Kyoto.

"With pleasure." Kyoto made the bonds tighter than necessary. He then guided her to a wooden chair.

Lily opened a medical bag, produced a vial of Common Caste blood, measured out a small dose into a medicine cup, and handed it to Kyoto. She carefully avoided touching their prisoner. Kyoto held it up to Scheherazade's mouth, and she sucked it in then licked her wrinkled lips. "Delicious."

The Magus said, "We will return in a few hours."

They left her slumped over in the chair, not in the least concerned that she might fall to the floor. They retired to the patio that overlooked a moonlit coast. A servant brought them plates of cubed raw steak. The Magus used a fork while Lily and Kyoto preferred chopsticks. Tristan arrived with apologies for his tardiness.

"I saw a man assaulting a woman in the airport parking lot. I hope you don't mind if I added him to the Worthy Target list, impromptu." His lips were still slightly red.

The Magus simply said, "I trust your judgment in the matter."

Lily could smell his after-kill scent and felt excited. "Dear Baron, you only missed her being given a taste of Common Caste. Due to Scheherazade's decrepit state, it will take a little while for any reaction."

"My ex-wife's blood is that toxic?"

"Would you like to see her?" The Magus inquired.

"Yes. I'm extremely curious about how the mix of royal and mortal blood affects the Common Caste."

When they got to the guesthouse, they found the lock was broken and the door wide-open. A servant was lying on the floor with his throat slashed.

"Impossible!" the Magus exclaimed. "Find her!" He commanded the two servants who had accompanied them.

Kyoto looked at Lily. "Who provided that sample of Common Caste blood?"

"Batu."

He shook his head. "The Princess and I enhanced Batu's transformation with our blood. The Princess continued to give him small amounts of her blood to increase his powers."

"The Houses must be made aware. I imagine she will head for Seattle or London to seek revenge and to recruit followers," the Magus said grimly. "I'm amazed that even diluted, the HH blood could reverse her fragile state so quickly."

Tristan texted Miranda and gave her a quick account of what had happened, then called Henry. "I'm sorry to inform you Scheherazade's whereabouts are unknown. We don't know if she has recovered all of her abilities, but she is well enough to be a concern."

"Damn it!" Henry bellowed. Even Magus and the others heard him as Tristan moved the phone back from his ear. "We will take precautions. Perhaps you should bring Delilah to Miranda's house," Henry suggested.

"Of course. Anything to protect my family. I'll fly up as soon as possible."

Henry hung up the phone. Leif, the kids, and Teri were all in the living room of the goat herder's house. "Don't get alarmed, but Scheherazade escaped from the Magus. She's probably not as powerful as before but may be able to tolerate sunlight. We don't know if she'll come here, but we must take precautions. Leif, you should move your goats if you want to have any left after tomorrow night. The Baron is bringing Delilah to help guard against Scheherazade."

"A panther here? I'll never have to worry about pumas again."

"I don't think Delilah likes dogs," Jacques kissed Piglet's head.

"She likes us. That's about it." Tomas said.

"Maybe we should let Alex keep Piglet at his apartment for a while," Jacques suggested.

"I'll keep Lug here," Leif said. He had heard stories about the Baron's pet. "I've got some friends nearby with goats. I think they'll help me out and take the goats in for a while."

"You don't want Piglet?" Marie giggled.

"If she were a dog, I'd agree. I don't know what she is. Sir Alexander can have her."

Jacques covered Piglet's ears.

Des remarked, "Grandma really did not like Scheherazade."

"We have to tell Mom!" Jacques stood, ready to go home.

Teri tried to sound calm. "I'm sure she knows by now. She'll be back in a few hours."

"You never told us why she stayed in Seattle." Marie tried to read Teri's thoughts. "Alexander?"

"She'll explain what happened when she gets back. Let's go to the house and fix dinner."

They all went to the main house. In the dining room, Henry gave the latest news to Guillaume and Grigoryi. The monk's eyes got big as saucers at the mention of the panther.

"Chill out, Greg. She's just a really big cat," Tomas told him.

"With really big teeth and claws," Grigoryi responded.

Henry asked Marie to speak with him outside and they headed for the back door. Teri told the boys to get cleaned up for dinner.

Henry walked away from Marie and stopped halfway to the river. She was confused by this special attention as he had always treated her the same as the others.

"What's up Henry?"

He looked at the pretty young woman with paternal concern. "I must warn you about someone. I am only telling you so as not to alarm your mother and because I'm not sure of what she would do."

"What are you talking about?"

"Marie, you are the focus of attention of many of my kind. They speculate about...."

"Getting me pregnant," she interrupted. "I can handle myself Henry. Are we done?"

"Marie." He rested a hand on her shoulder. "It's not just that. I know you are not easily swayed by their attention or compliments but someone powerful might...."

"Stop that!" she brushed his hand away. "That was creepy! You're like an uncle to me."

"I'm sorry. You felt me trying to influence you. I barely tried to reach you. I just wanted to give you a warning. Marie, imagine what it might be like if someone loved you and would do anything to have you."

She stared at him, searching for a name. Her developing telepathic ability caught fleeting images of vampires, but one stood out. Then her eyes went wide.

"The Magus!"

"Yes. During a rare unguarded moment, I felt his passion for you. He never reveals feelings for others. When I called him on it, he became angry. You're his Achille's heel. Love can forge our destiny. When Cleopatra died, it was either suicide for me or disappear and become undead."

"I'm sorry you lost her. She must have been amazing."

"Yes, she was." He looked sad for an instant. "But now I have found Teri."

"I hope the Magus finds someone else. He always paid more attention to my brothers. I thought he was sexist and just ignored him."

Henry looked pensive. "He kept at a distance because it would have been unseemly to act before you matured. Your father did not approach your mother until she had graduated from college."

"Maybe I won't go to college. Then I won't have to worry about him. What an asshole. He probably thinks I'll be all grateful that he likes me. I'd rather have sex with Grigoryi."

"Bold talk from a virgin."

"Yeah, well, so is Grigoryi. And he's nice. How did you know?"

"You're all virgins except Tomas. I can read people too."

"Tomas and Ashley?"

Henry displayed a Cheshire grin. "I will never tell."

"Why me?"

"That is complicated. The Magus always has a myriad of reasons for his actions. He could desire to have children by your House to strengthen his position of power. It is possible he truly has feelings for you. Whatever his motives, you do not have to be part of his plan. Teri and I will do whatever we can to protect you from him."

"My mom would kill him. What about my dad?"

"She would certainly try, which is why I am telling you. My best counsel is to keep your distance; he can be very engaging. Since the Baron allowed Tomas to be hurt, I'm not sure he would see the Magus' attention the way we do."

"I still can't believe he was okay with that, but I won't say anything to him. Thanks. Don't ever do that weird touch thing again."

"I won't. Teri suggested I let you know what to expect. She does not care for the Magus either. I am honored to be considered an uncle to all of you."

Upstairs the brothers were gathered in Jacques' room discussing a new video game while they avoided chores. Des looked out the window. "That looks suspicious."

The others saw Marie talking with Henry.

"No way," Jacques said. "Teri knows they are out there."

"Yeah, he probably just told her she's a badass drummer," Des assured them.

Tomas grinned. "Anyway, I know who she likes, and he isn't Lithuanian."

I quietly entered Alex's apartment at sunset.

"Hannibal's elephants make less noise." He yawned and sat up. He gestured for me to join him. It was not easy to decline, but I was on a mission.

I sat in a chair across from him. "I want to meet with you and Pomp tonight. Can you arrange it?"

"Do you mind if I shower first?" he asked as he got up from the bed, I averted my eyes to keep me on task.

"This is serious. Scheherazade may be headed this way. She may try to contact you or Pomp. I need allies."

He put on a dark blue silk robe. "Will you look at me now?"

"Tristan sent me a message about Scheherazade before he retired last night. I read it when I woke up and decided to stay and get your help since you know what she is capable of."

He walked over to me and touched my cheek. His enticing scent was mixed with remnants of our sexual encounter. I felt my heart rate speed up. His gaze was intense. "She is no match for you. I am always at your service, be it in your bed or at your side."

"Great. Let Pomp know, then go take a shower."

"Of course." He picked up his phone, sent off a text then turned back to me. "Care to join me?"

"Seriously? An evil vampiress is about to attack. I'll be next door. I need more coffee." I left before I changed my mind about his invitation.

I made a cup of dark brown wonderfulness and sipped it while I called Teri.

"Hi! Is everything okay?"

"Yeah. How are you? What's up with Alex?"

"I'm weirded out a little, but okay. Alex is, well...Alex. We're going to meet with Pomp, then come home. Tell the kids I said to do whatever they are supposed to do."

"No problem. Hey, Jacques decided to give Piglet to Alex while Delilah is here."

"Delilah is coming?"

"Yeah, Tristan will arrive with her tonight. She will not be a happy cat. She hates flying. Alex can pick up the pug tonight. There's so much going on. I'm afraid Scheherazade can be out in daylight now. Better fill Cramer in. Watch out for snakes, and I don't mean just her!"

"Miranda, we got it! Go meet with Pomp and get back here. I want to hear about Alex."

"You and everyone else, bye."

As Alex and I drove through the city, I felt sorry for Seattle. I wondered how it would be able to support the new influx of the undead. How many Worthy Targets could there be in the Emerald City? Could they find enough blood bank employees to bribe? Guillaume said he was getting his supply from Portland. Even though Alex had his wrists slapped by the Magus, I knew the vampire world was still in awe of him. I glanced at his handsome countenance. I was not proud of myself, but I did not regret last night. There would be life after Tristan.

We arrived at Pomp's home, which had the look of old-world elegance with the latest in electronic surveillance. Special cameras could capture heat signatures to be able to track the undead. Pomp was very clever, and since Henry had attacked her, much more careful. Grisham answered the door. She could not keep her eyes off of Alex, but he ignored her. That got him more points. We walked past her to the living room. Pomp sat in a chair upholstered in her distinct royal pink.

Alex cut right to business. "We have little time this evening for pleasantries. Any news of Scheherazade?"

Pomp replied, "She was seen near Fresno early this evening. There was a report of an attack on a drunken man outside a bar. The attacker was a beautiful woman who got away with his wallet and left him in critical condition."

"Her skills are compromised," Alex said. "In the past, she would never have allowed herself to be spotted or let him live."

"Let's hope," I uttered.

"It didn't take long for her to regain her looks." Pomp observed, "She will need more vampire blood to fight your antigens and maintain her youth. She became ancient and brittle after being given an injection of your blood."

"A single dose of me almost destroyed her?"

No one responded. Apparently, talking about my effect on the undead was not considered polite conversation. My evolution included the development of natural vampire repellant in my blood. Darwin would have loved this. Vampires, not so much.

"Pomp, Tristan will arrive tonight with Delilah, but we won't be ready at my place for her till tomorrow night. Tristan's condo building isn't really panther-friendly. Would you mind accommodating his cat?" I asked.

She smiled. "They will both be quite welcome here."

"Thank you. I think that's it. Don't underestimate Scheherazade. She won't fight or attack like a man. I mean, who hides snakes in their clothes?" I immediately wanted to take back that last remark. Alex and Pomp snickered.

Alex stood up. "We should be going. After you Baroness."

Chapter 38

A Mongol in Granite Falls

When we got to the house, the kids were busy making improvements to our security system. Tomas was on a ladder putting a new camera above the front door. He regarded Alex and me with a look of disapproval. "Where were you last night?"

Alex responded before I had a chance, "Recovering from an attack by street thugs." At that moment, Leif and the other kids came around the corner from the backyard. "A bullet grazed her arm, but it is not serious."

"Mom!" Jacques ran over and hugged me.

Marie asked, "Did you give her First Aid all night?"

Des and Tomas struggled not to laugh. Leif looked away at the river.

"I was in shock. Alex took care of the idiots who attacked us. It was on the news. We hid the Jeep at Henry's building. Alex set me up in an apartment next to his. That's where I stayed all night. We are not discussing this further." I gave them my best shame-inducing maternal glare. You would think the kids would have asked more about the attack

Jacques turned to Alex. "Thanks for keeping Mom safe."

Alex nodded and smiled.

"Where's Henry?" I asked.

"They're all at Guillaume's discussing strategy," Leif responded. "Teri, Cramer, and I will be daytime security, and the nocturnals will take over at night."

Des added, "We told Grigoryi he should just worry about cooking."

Marie nudged Leif. "C'mon, we have three more cameras to put up."

"Alex and I will be with the others," I said.

As we walked away, he whispered, "That was uncomfortable."

"I can't blame them. Tell me about Scheherazade. Who was the idiot that transformed her?"

Alex looked pleased to fill me in. "She caught the Magus' eye. Two hundred years ago, her parents had a Persian rug shop in London, and he was a good customer. She translated because of her gift for languages and charm. The Magus recognized her intelligence and cleverness."

"And cleavage," I added.

"She has AB blood, so he would not transform her. He has always been a snob.

In battle, I have never thought a King's son any more noble than a commoner."

"Alex, who transformed her?" I had this bad feeling in my gut.

"Your ex-husband. He has never had the best judgment when it comes to sharing the gift with a female."

"No wonder she wants his approval so badly."

Alex enjoyed adding, "He used to give her his approval gladly."

"That's not a news flash. What is her real name? What a joke, taking the name of the heroine in the Arabian Nights."

He placed his hand on the door and stopped. "Her parents tried to Anglicize her. She was once called Sybil."

I couldn't help but laugh, thinking how appropriate it was that she had the same name as the multi-personality character from the movie. "I have to ask. Did you ever...?"

"Never. I am very particular about my intimate partners." He leaned into me and lightly kissed my cheek.

"Like Franco and me?"

He pulled back. "Yes. Though very different, you are both exquisite lovers."

"Shut the fuck up." I pushed past him.

As much as I liked Franco, I resented being told I met some standard of his. Just like I hated Tristan putting me in his 'wait for me at home' box. Vampires!

Teri and Henry were waiting with Guillaume in his living room when Alex and I walked in. Teri hugged me and demanded to see the wound. "Later. I'm fine. Alex bandaged me up. So, what's the plan?"

Guillaume pulled up a chair and handed me a cup of black coffee. "Bless you," I said and sipped the caffeinated goodness.

"It has been centuries since anyone said that to me." He looked thoughtful.

Henry got down to business. "We hope she will be picked up by sensors that detect mortals. Dr. Kyoto believes she is enhanced but not fully restored to her former self."

"Lady Lily thinks Scheherazade will deteriorate without additional doses of our blood," Guillaume said. "No one is safe until we find her. She kills with little regard for anyone but herself."

Alex responded, "She may wait until she has accomplices. She may persuade others to help her. Scheherazade had several Common Caste followers in London."

"Damn her! Why would they want to help her?" I grumbled angrily.

Henry touched my hand. I felt his calming vibe slowing down my heart rate. "Breathe. By now, the Common Caste have heard about how your blood almost destroyed Scheherazade. They fear you and the children more than they fear any of us."

"The Magus wants to use us, and Scheherazade wants to get rid of us," I said.

Alexander looked around at the group. "She was corrupted by ambition. She wants power and respect."

"You would know." Everyone ignored my rudeness. "I'm sorry."

Alex continued, "It's true, though her ambition has never been tempered by love."

I asked, "What can we do?"

Guillaume looked at Henry. "Could we offer her something, perhaps negotiate a pardon with the Magus if she leaves the House of Sun alone?"

Alex replied, "She cannot be trusted to keep her word."

Henry added, "We have no way to contact her. For now, our best action is to prepare for an attack, day or night."

"We will be ready to fight if we have to," I declared.

Des came running in and yelled, "Batu is here with the horses from Rossville."

"Great!" I followed Des out.

Batu was helping unload the horses. The kids were in heaven, being reunited with their steeds.

The kids led their horses into the stable, and I approached my old Valentine, Batu, with trepidation. My life was a bizarre romantic square. I was not sure I should pull him in any deeper. He wore jeans, a denim shirt, and a brown leather vest. His long dark hair hung past his shoulders. I found him more physically attractive in every way since his transformation. I walked up to him and smiled. "Welcome, you crazy Mongol bastard. I've missed you."

He pulled me into his arms and kissed me gently. I loved his slightly spicy scent. He whispered, "I forgive you."

I pushed him back. "For what?"

"Whatever you're about to do," he grinned.

I started back towards the house, and Batu followed. Guillaume, Henry, and Teri were in front of the house watching us. Alex and Jacques stood off to the side. As we came up to the group, Henry and Batu stared at each other with the "who is the alpha male" look on their faces. Guillaume tried to ease the tension by shaking Batu's hand. "Welcome Sir Batu of the House of Cups. We prepared a room at the main house for you."

Teri hugged him and turned to Henry. "He watched over the kids for years in Rossville."

Henry extended his hand. "We can always use another trusted friend to protect the royal family."

I was getting a little choked up. All these bizarre powerful nocturnal weirdos really cared about us. As they shook hands, I saw Alex and Jacques head to the barn. Alex did not even look my way. I did not want to hurt his feelings, but rhapsody in blood, or whatever that was, did not mean we were going steady. I did not like being so callous, but you've got to play hardball with vampires.

We all went into the house, and I showed Batu to Teri's room. She had moved all her stuff to Henry's place, and Guillaume had installed dark shades and heavy curtains. Batu moved behind me, quickly closed the door, and pulled me down on the bed. His tender, unrequited passion was killing me. I wanted to give in, but so much had happened and might yet happen. I was still in recovery mode from my tryst with Alexander.

He began to smother me in kisses, but I did not respond. He sat up. "What is

280

wrong?"

"Batu, we have to ease into this. I haven't seen you for months, and now you're a vampire." His dark brown eyes looked confused and hurt. "The kids and I are in danger. Right now is not the time."

His hand ran over the bandage on my arm. "You're hurt!"

"I was mugged last night. Alex saved my life." He looked like a confused puppy. I got up from the bed. "C'mon, I'll fill you in. We have to discuss how to defeat a pissed-off semi-vampiress."

Scheherazade waited at the airport in San Jose. She was afraid the airport in San Francisco might be watched by friends of the Magus. Sophie and Paul descended from the private jet they had leased, unsure what they would find. The message from Scheherazade made them question everything they heard from the Haute Caste. The Common Caste of the House of Pentacles had a secret meeting and sent them as representatives. They were not blind to Scheherazade's ruthless character, but what she claimed had been done to her alarmed them. Sophie had left a message about their plan with the one member of the Haute Caste she could trust to be on the safe side. Sophie and Paul had to find out what was actually going on.

They walked out of the terminal and heard someone call out to them from a white van. Not a vehicle their kind would typically ride in. They walked up to the driver's window. The effect of Batu's blood that had been given her was wearing off. They were shocked to see an old woman with hair that looked like it had been dyed black, speak their names, "Sophie, Paul, get in. We must find a safe place to talk and rest for the day."

"Scheherazade?" Paul looked unsure.

"Yes! The Magus tried to destroy me. Get in!"

Sophie nodded to Paul. She believed they could overpower her if need be. There was a backpack on the front passenger seat and fire extinguishers on the floor, so they climbed into the back seats. The scent of a dead animal mixed with expensive perfume assaulted them. They noticed the corpse of a small pig, with bite wounds, in the cargo area.

"Where are you taking us?"

"A nearby hotel. I've paid for two nights so that we won't be bothered tomorrow."

Sophie noticed a box that held silver steak knives, a couple more fire extinguishers, and guns. She realized the CO_2 in the fire extinguishers would be freezing cold when released and could be used against the undead, and the silver knives could inflict serious wounds on vampires. Sophie slipped one of the knives into her jacket as a precaution.

Paul asked, "Was it the blood of the Baroness? Is that what happened to you?"

Scheherazade glanced at them in the rear-view mirror. "Yes. The Magus had me injected with her blood. It's erased my powers, made me mortal and old. I almost died, but a little Common Caste blood revived me." She drove away.

She turned into a dark street in a warehouse district. Scheherazade sped up, which caused Sophie to brace herself. Then Scheherazade slammed on the breaks and reached for a fire extinguisher. Paul went headfirst over the front seat into the windshield. Sophie had been able to brace herself and barely missed the same fate. "What the fuck are you doing?" Sophie yelled.

Scheherazade turned and sprayed them with the fire extinguisher. Paul was unconscious, but Sophie managed to scramble out of the van. She was struggling to move after being hit with the freezing cold spray. Paul's blood oozed over his face from a head wound. "O-positive!" Scheherazade exclaimed and cut his throat with one of the silver knives, then drank deeply. He moaned, and she drove the knife into his chest. She felt the strength of his blood infuse her with power.

The signs of age were disappearing, and she felt her old abilities returning. She touched her face and felt the youthful firmness in her cheeks begin to return. Her hands were barely wrinkled. "Excellent! Thank you, Paul." She left the silver knife in the wound, knowing it would keep him from healing. In his weakened state, she could feed on him for weeks. She looked for Sophie. She had expected the blue-haired vampiress to be too badly injured to escape but there was no sign of her. Scheherazade put handcuffs on Paul and laid him on the floor in the back of the van. Then she slowly drove through the area, searching for Sophie. It was two hours until sunrise. The latest infusion of blood made her more sensitive to the sun, but she was still mortal.

After half an hour she gave up and went to a cheap hotel near the airport. She would travel north with her food source in the evening. It was time to rest and solidify her plans. It was too bad that Sophie escaped, but she couldn't worry about that now. She never wholly trusted that ambitious member of the Common Caste. In general, Scheherazade never trusted women. She thought men were much easier to manipulate, at least mortal males and the males of the Common Caste. Scheherazade forced a sedative down Paul's throat, then put a knit scarf and hat on him to hide his wounds. She carried him into her room through a back entrance.

Sophie hid behind a dumpster until Scheherazade left the area, then ordered an Uber. "Bitch from hell," she muttered and pulled out a small vial of blood she kept for emergencies. Then she called the only member of the House of Plows she knew she could trust and left a voice message. "Lady Pauline, Scheherazade betrayed us. I escaped. I'll be at the Airport Hilton. Pick me up tonight. Tell the Baroness to be prepared."

Sophie had booked a room for the night they arrived, in case Scheherazade was a no-show. She checked in, went to her room, and put up a do not disturb sign. "Paul, you poor blighter," she sighed. He was not the brightest vampire she had ever known, but he didn't deserve what Scheherazade would do with him. Sophie collapsed on the bed, pissed-off that she had allowed Scheherazade to ambush them.

She got a text message,

See you tonight, Luv.

Sophie managed to smile at the thought of spending time with Pauline again. Her visits to London were never long enough. She hoped the rumors about Pauline and Sarah weren't true. She did not want a jealous Haute Caste vampiress throwing shade.

Just before she fell asleep, Sophie sent a text to the House of Pentacles,

Don't trust Scheherazade.

Chapter 39

Good Golly Miss Molly

"Just a long weekend away. It'll be fun you said," Molly muttered as they made it up the side of a hill of blue spruce trees across from Miranda's home. They were outfitted in rain gear and night goggles. "So romantic."

"Quiet," Manny whispered, not aware his love was close to homicidal. She was about to go back to the car when he said, "Look!"

The Baron got out of his silver Jaguar followed by his black panther. It cautiously sniffed the ground. Molly and Manny froze as it lifted its head and looked in their direction. The kids ran out and hugged their beloved cat. "Oh my God, you were telling the truth."

Manny would have felt satisfaction if not for his fear of being discovered. "It's never good when he shows up. We should go."

They quietly, carefully made it back down the dark hill to their car. Every shadow looked like it concealed a threat. With each crunch of pine needles, Molly's anxiety rose. Manny did not want to press his luck and expose Molly to any more danger. "We'll go back to the hotel." They got in the car and sighed in relief.

A man jumped on the hood and yelled, "Get out!". Molly screamed. The tall figure with long dreadlocks stared down at them. Manny tried to start the car, but it was dead. Henry's eyes blazed with anger. He gave a powerful kick and cracked the windshield.

Manny yelled, "Stop it! We give up! Don't hurt her!"

Teri opened Molly's door and helped her out. She trembled but was okay.

"I would never hurt an innocent woman," Henry said as he walked over and barely touched Molly's hand. She suddenly felt calmer. Manny jumped out of the car and rushed to her side. Henry glared at Manny. "You were warned. I have no qualms about punishing a man who would put someone he loved in peril."

"Let her go. I'll come with you."

"No," Molly grabbed him and looked at Henry. "He just wants to be a good cop. He did find you. Maybe he is too good."

Teri smiled. "Impressive. Well, my curious mortals, you're in luck. The Baroness wants to speak with you."

"Mortals?" Molly blurted out, then regretted it. Leif appeared and popped open the dented hood. He leaned down and reconnected the battery cable, then drove it away. "Wait! My purse!"

Teri said, "You'll get it back. Move it! The Royals are waiting."

They walked in front of their attackers. Molly whispered to Manny, "Your gun."

Henry, from a few feet back, said, "We let him keep it because it is not a threat to my kind."

They walked to the house in silence.

Teri ushered the shaken visitors into the living room, where Tristan, Batu, Guillaume Alexander, and I waited.

"You don't look like vampires," Molly said nervously, not about to wait for them to get the first word in. She hoped they would say it was just a misunderstanding and let them go.

I smiled. "Goth is reserved for special occasions." The look on their faces reminded me of when I first became aware of the undead. She impressed me with her composure.

Tristan added, "Looks can be deceiving. Sit down."

Grigoryi came in with a tray of mugs filled with steaming coffee. "Cream and sugar?"

Manny shook his head, and Molly replied, "Yes, both please." Henry's touch had worn off, and this was pure Molly. She could read people. They might not have appreciated the surprise visit from Salinas, but she could tell they wanted something from them. Manny was amazed by her reaction. "Do you mind if we take off our raincoats?" Molly asked.

Teri took their coats, and Molly loaded her cup with cream and three spoons of sugar. She took a sip. "Good coffee, thanks. I've had months to think about the possibility that vampires existed. I'm relieved to know Manny wasn't losing it. Are you all, uh, night people?"

Manny choked on his black coffee. "Not now Molly." He turned to their captors. "What do you want from me?"

Alexander smiled. "From both of you. We need more daytime security. You shouldn't be so rude to your partner again. She is quite charming."

Molly elbowed Manny. "Thanks."

It was easy for Alex to win her over. Tristan did not like someone else speaking for his family. He added in a serious tone, "The length of your life matters little to me, but if you agree to help us, it will undoubtedly be longer. There is a woman you saw once before. She has a way with snakes. We believe she may desire to harm the Baroness and our children. She could attack during the day, which is why we would like your assistance."

"She was in the parking lot that night."

"Yes." Henry replied, "She is deceitful and quite dangerous."

"We will offer you each a generous amount of money to stay at the house next door and keep watch from sunrise until sunset. We should have the whole affair settled within the week. There is a possibility of long-term employment if you are helpful." Tristan said.

Molly, always the pragmatist, asked, "How generous?"

Tristan smiled and answered, "That depends on how helpful you are."

"Yeah, that's if we survive. I'm a police officer. You want me to be some kind of vigilante? I don't go outside the law."

Tristan's eyes drilled into Manny. "Yes, you do. You faked an illness to take time off to investigate our family and trespassed on our land. Will you still refuse to assist us?"

Batu scoffed, "I don't think anyone so void of insight could be very useful."

"That was rude," Molly said. "How many normal people do you have to help you?"

Henry liked her. "There is the man who took your car, a military veteran, a cook, a bodyguard, the Baroness, and the kids are, all what you would call normal."

Tristan added, "And Delilah, my cat."

Molly looked suspicious. "All that money and all those people to deal with just one pissed-off woman?"

I replied, "She used to be a vampiress. She is a treacherous, jealous bitch who wants her powers back. She has no conscience or respect for life. She is very dangerous, but she can be destroyed. I won't ask you to do anything I wouldn't do myself. I'll be up every day, at dawn with you. No one in this room will harm you. Manny, you wanted to take out a killer. Here's your chance."

Manny looked around the room. "I can't agree to anything until I know more. I'm not sure who to protect and who to arrest."

"I understand. We'll talk more tomorrow morning. The kids and I need to get some rest. If you decide to walk away then, no one will stop you. Deal?"

"You promise not to, uh, change us?" Molly looked concerned.

Guillaume smiled and shook his head. "We are not interested in your blood types."

"That is really creepy," Molly whispered and moved closer to Manny.

"I was bitten by a poisonous snake thanks to this woman, and it could have killed one of our children." I pulled up the leg of my jeans and showed the scar. "That's why I am asking for your help."

Molly looked at Manny and nodded. He turned to me. "Okay, fine. We'll spend the night and talk in the morning."

Teri put her hand on Manny's shoulder. "C'mon, I'll take you over to Leif's place. I'll fill you in on what I know."

As they walked through the trees, Manny said, "Molly, I can't believe you are okay with all this. I thought you'd lose it. You handled them better than I did."

"I'm just relieved that you aren't delusional. I'm also glad they didn't bring that leopard out."

"Black Panther," Teri corrected them. "Her name is Delilah. She probably won't leave the kids' sides while she is here. I will give you both a tiny glass vial with the Baron's blood to wear on a chain. She'll smell it and know you're a friend."

Manny looked at Molly. "You wanted a souvenir of this trip."

When they reached Leif's cabin, Cramer and Leif were eating stew with freshly baked biscuits. After the introductions, they joined them for dinner. Molly watched them eat and said, "So none of you are...."

"Lithuanian," Teri said with a smile. "No."

Molly continued, "I remember that from Miranda's book. I even recognized Tristan, I mean the Baron, from her description. He's hot. But the rest of you weren't in the book. She never mentioned the sexy Jamaican guy, the handsome charmer, or that mysterious Asian guy."

"He's not Jamaican," Teri asserted.

Leif grinned. "But they are all Lithuanian."

Manny took a few mouthfuls of stew before getting down to business. "What are we dealing with? How much of a threat is this woman? What kind of weapons will we need? Do you expect her to be alone?"

"We don't know if she will have company. I'll let the science teacher answer about the weapons," Leif said and bit into another biscuit.

"The undead don't use guns. They consider it beneath them. They are sensitive to silver. It won't kill them, but it does harm them. We filled hollow-point bullets with silver dust and glue for the snakes. She is known to strengthen them with her blood," Cramer explained

"What will they do with the woman?' Molly asked.

"They will probably behead her," Cramer answered.

Molly pushed the bowl of stew away.

Leif smiled and added, "They invented the guillotine."

Molly wondered if she had the stomach for all this violence. She had cried when her hamster died. "This is all really fucked up. It feels like I'm in a sick dream."

Cramer said, "Believe me, the world will be better without Scheherazade. To meet her is to loathe her."

"Scheherazade? That's really her name?" Molly asked, a little wide-eyed.

"Just let it go Molly," Teri said.

"If I help, it will be to apprehend her, to stop her from hurting anyone," Manny said.

"Yeah sure." Leif threw the dog a biscuit. "We have to keep Lug away from Delilah. The panther is okay with most vampires and the horses, but that's it. I keep goats, but a friend is taking care of them until this is over."

Molly patted the Lab's head. "That's a funny name."

Leif said, "C'mon, Lugosi, I'll get you your dinner."

Cramer grinned, "The kids named him. Have you met them yet?"

Manny shook his head. "Just briefly in Salinas."

Cramer took the last biscuit. "They are very bright but a serious handful. The Baroness and the offspring have the vampire world sweating, 'cause no one knows what they will do or how powerful they might become. I would suggest staying on their good side."

Molly picked up her biscuit, hoping it would calm her stomach. "Why does she need us to protect them?"

Leif responded, "The Baroness has her reasons. That's all that matters."

Cramer lowered his voice, "That charming guy you mentioned earlier, that's Alex, he's the father of the youngest kid, Jacques. But don't say anything about it. I'm just telling you, so you know he will do anything to protect his son, you can count on him."

Molly was surprised. "In the book, she was only with the Baron."

Leif said, "It's a long story for another night. We need to get some rest. I took all your stuff out of the car and put it in the spare bedroom."

Manny shook his head. "How did you know we would stay."

Teri responded, "Lithuanians can be very persuasive."

Alexander, holding Piglet, bade me goodnight beside his car. "Dear Miranda, we have a special bond that I do not truly understand. You may ask anything of me except never to see you or Jacques again."

I stood a couple of feet away to avoid a kiss. I knew Batu and Tristan were watching our goodbye. "Just help us all stay safe. I worry that the kids and I will never be able to stop looking over our shoulders."

"You would be wise to be cautious, but I will always look out for you." He bowed to her, then climbed in his car and drove away.

I walked into the kitchen, where the kids were feeding Delilah. They gave her a couple of whole salmon to eat. She made quick work of them. Tomas patted her head, and she rubbed against his knee, almost knocking him over. Marie filled a large bowl with water for her.

Tristan was uncomfortable with everything. He would stay in one of the kid's rooms upstairs until they had dealt with Scheherazade. Tomas and Des would double up because neither wanted to endure Jacque's snoring. Batu and my ex circled each other like fighting cocks whenever they were in the same room. They did not shake hands when Tristan arrived, just barely discernable nods. I was glad Alexander returned to Seattle.

I felt someone behind me and turned. "Tristan, don't sneak up on me!"

He was looked amused. "You were always easy to startle." He stroked my cheek lightly. It was enough to bring a sense of longing to the surface. "Stop that!" I moved away.

The kids looked at us. Tristan said, "I heard about the attack in Seattle. I'm glad Alexander protected you. Is the wound serious?"

"No, he took good care of me."

Des smirked, and I ignored him. Tristan regarded his son with raised eyebrows. "Let's go into the living room. We have more to discuss before you all retire." Tristan muttered, "Alexander? Really?" as he followed behind me.

Batu, Guillaume, Teri, and Henry were engrossed in a serious discussion about the security system. They also had a large first aid kit and several bullet-proof vests on the coffee table.

"I think the detective will stay on," I said and sat on the couch next to Guillaume to avoid getting near Batu or Tristan. My ex remained standing and stared at me intently. He was not going to forget about Alexander. Batu watched us, wondering if it was about his arrival. The room was tense to begin with, but now it felt very uncomfortable.

"We heard she used fire extinguishers against two vamps before heading towards Portland." Teri stopped hanging on Henry to put an arm around my shoulders, and she added. "Leif has Bear spray. He will hand it out tomorrow. If it can stop a grizzly, it should at least slow her and her snakes down."

I looked around at my powerful protectors. "I appreciate all of you. I know she will not win, but I'm afraid of the damage she'll do before we stop her, especially during daylight. The worst part is that my blood may have made it possible for her to be able to attack day or night."

Batu responded, "Her despicable behavior is not your fault. I should have ended her miserable existence in Mongolia."

Tristan cleared his throat. "Regrets are worthless. No one appreciated the threat she posed, not even the Magus."

Teri patted my shoulder. "Manny and Cramer are great with guns. We doctored the ammo with silver."

"We should not sink to her level by using silver," Tristan stated.

Henry countered, "We won't, but the mortals will need every advantage we can give them."

"I don't have a problem with that. What other precautions have you taken?" Tristan asked.

I turned to the kids lurking in the doorway. "Leif is setting up traps by his house, so you guys and Delilah stay away from the line of trees."

Marie looked upset. "No band practice?"

I looked at her. "Not until this is all over. After that, we'll arrange a concert."

"Do we have to go to school?" Des asked.

"Yes!" Tristan and I said in unison. I added, "Cramer will be at the school, and maybe Manny can drive you."

Jacques displayed a self-righteous grin. "Des, I told you that you should've done your homework."

"Go get some sleep. Des, I will wake you early to finish your homework. Tomorrow's Friday, you can get through one day with just a few hours of sleep." Des glared at Jacques and punched him in the arm.

Tomas said, "Don't forget you promised I get a can of bear spray."

I was too tired to argue and mumbled, "Sure." I knew that would probably get me the Mom of the Year Award if we lived in Alaska but I wasn't sure the high school in Granite would see it the same way. "Only use it on bad vampires."

Henry chuckled, but the others remained stoic. Teri kissed him goodnight. "C'mon Miranda. I'm camping out with you until we bag Scheherazade."

Chapter 40

Portland Rebels

Near the Lan Su Chinese Garden in Portland, two figures dressed in black quietly entered an old brick warehouse building that had been converted into sleek modern condos. They dropped their backpacks and pulled back their hoods. Shelly, a Common Caste vampiress with short red hair, brought them small crystal shot glasses of O-positive. "We are honored by your presence here. I'll tell the others to come over now."

"Good," Jeanne said. When the younger vampiress left the room, she whispered to Bart, "Scheherazade may have already contaminated this community."

Bart sat on the gray silk love seat and gestured for Jeanne to join him, but she could not relax enough to sit down. "Something is not right. I feel it. Be prepared."

Jeanne felt her fangs begin to appear. Was there something in the air that made them so uneasy and tired? "No!" she screamed and crashed through a window onto the street. Bart, without a second thought, followed close behind her.

"Aerosolized silver!" Bart coughed.

Jeanne drew a deep breath of fresh air. "We must warn the Baron!"

He was shocked. "That was outlawed by a decree from the Magus. Even Alexander did not resort to such foul play. Scheherazade will pay!"

"As will Shelley!" Jeanne then ran to the alley behind the building and found the treacherous member of Portland's undead getting into a BMW. Jeanne picked up a trash can and hurled it into the windshield. Shelley gunned the engine to run Jeanne down. With incredible speed and agility, the ancient vampiress jumped on top of the car, then leaned down, punched through the cracked windshield, and stuck a knife in Shelley's forehead.

Jeanne jumped off just as the car crashed into the side of the building. Bart had watched from at the entrance to the alley. "You are truly impressive!"

"Let the Portland Common Caste find her. Let's get out of here before someone comes."

"Normally, I would pull her into a building away from the light of dawn, but she sealed her own fate," Bart said and grabbed his backpack. "We have a lot of work to do here. The Portland cousins have been ignored for too long. We don't have much time before sunrise. We need to go."

On their way to the Portland Hilton, Bart called the Magus to inform him of the situation. The Magus took the news calmly.

"Thank you for informing me. Sir Bart, I would like you and Jeanne to stay in Portland. These misguided relatives must be enlightened to the responsibilities and importance of adherence to our code. I will inform the Baron and go to Seattle."

"Of course," Bart responded though he and Jeanne had wished to head to Granite Falls to help protect the Royals. "We shall seek out and take charge of these wayward individuals."

I woke to pounding on my door. "Crap! I just got to sleep!" When I opened the door, Tristan, Batu, and Guillaume were in the hall, and I saw the kids peeking out of their rooms.

Tristan spoke first, "I just heard from the Magus. Scheherazade was in Portland and has convinced some Common Caste to join her."

"How many?"

"Maybe as many as a dozen, maybe less," Guillaume informed me. "They have been cut off from the mainstream community for fifty years. They are sort of communal with no regard for Haute Caste status."

"More rebel vampires? Great!" I said.

"Several Common Caste will be no match for us!' Batu asserted.

"They fight in unconventional ways. They tried to attack Bart and Jeanne with silver gas." Tristan told us.

Guillaume was pissed. "Sacre Bleu! Have they no shame!"

Clearly, I was missing something. Tristan looked at me. "Nanosilver particles can be mixed into a liquid, aerosolized, and sprayed into the air as a mist. It weakens us, and a high enough dose can put us in a coma. The Magus has outlawed it as chemical warfare."

"Are any shorts helping her?" I asked.

"We don't know. Until this is over, we can't send the kids to school," Tristan said.

"Woohoo!' Des yelled and high-fived Tomas.

"I hate Scheherazade so much. When vampires go bad, they are the worst!" I said, and an uncomfortable silence followed.

Guillaume gave me a hug. "I'll let Leif and the others know the kids won't be going to school before I retire."

I looked at the powerful vampires I would have to protect during the day. "We'll keep you safe till sundown." Then I yelled at the kids, "Go back to your rooms and get some sleep!" Like that was going to happen.

The Magus ordered his jet to be prepared immediately and sent a text to Pomp, informing her of the new threat, and that he was coming to Seattle.

Pomp ever the French aristocrat laid down on her pink satin sheets with a smile on her lips. She was thankful to the Baroness and Scheherazade for creating the crisis that was bringing the Magus to her home. After hearing about what happened in Portland and remembering the unwashed masses who had taken down her beloved Royals in France, she had hired three more armed guards to patrol her property, in addition to the electric fence and surveillance equipment. She had encountered the Portland undead a few times and was repulsed by their lack of respect for the Haute Caste and that they thought she would want to join them. She had heard rumors that they maintained a supply of the banned "silver gas." As a precaution, she had gas masks discretely hidden in every room. "Vive le Roi," she muttered. She would entertain the Magus tomorrow night. She could not wait until the vampire world heard about that.

I watched the news the next morning. A bizarre death involving a woman's charred body found in a car in Portland made me wonder. No reports of bodies with slashed throats, so I was not sure if it involved the undead. As Manny, Molly, and Leif wandered in, Delilah lifted her head. The vial of blood Molly wore protected her, but she was still nervous about the panther and sat at the far end of the kitchen. The kids were still asleep.

"It's okay. She won't hurt friends. You can pet her," I said.

Molly declined, but Manny could not resist, and Delilah allowed him to stroke her head. "She is amazing. Your life is unbelievable."

"Right! Living the fucking dream. Do you want coffee? Teri made some cinnamon rolls."

Leif snickered, "And Cramer is at his dream job at school and said he'll cut out early."

Manny looked serious. "I have to know, have you ever killed anyone?" he asked me.

"No! But I cut off a vampire's nose once. He attacked me when I was pregnant." No one said a word. "It would be better if you didn't ask the others that." I knew that what I was hiring Manny to do, went against every cop cell in his body. "You can apprehend all the mortals you want, but don't try and arrest a vampire. It would not end well. You're just a guest in their world."

"No one is above the law," Manny flatly stated.

Leif said, "They are so far beyond our laws. Manny, they are the freakin' undead who have been around for hundreds of years. C'mon man, deal with it!"

Manny shook his head. "I'm trying."

They helped themselves to coffee and cinnamon rolls as we sat around the table. "I'll do what you asked, but Molly does not get involved."

"Yes, she does!" Molly declared. "And don't talk about me like I'm not in the room." She turned to me and asked, "So, what's this all about?"

"It's good you read my book. That should help. Where do I start? The vampire world is divided between the Haute Caste, the elite rulers, and the Common Caste, sort of the working class. Originally, you had to have HH blood to be Haute Caste. But to make a long story short, the Common Caste demanded more, and other blood types were granted Haute Caste status, like Batu. It's too little, too late for some. Scheherazade preys on the discontented vampires and gets them to help her."

Manny asked, "Why are they after you? You're not even one of them."

Leif jumped in, "It's a blood thing. For some reason, Miranda's blood can weaken the Haute Caste and kill the Common Caste. She's half-vampire, and the kids are three-quarters. The Common vamps are afraid that we will use her blood against them. Scheherazade was given a dose as punishment for trying to mutiny against the Magus. It almost killed her."

Molly put down her cinnamon roll and turned to me. "You should have put that in the book. The part about being half-vampire and your blood thing."

"I wanted it to be believable." I took a sip of coffee. "I want you all to carry bear spray at all times and wear your bullet-proof vests. Teri is proficient with a number of weapons as well as martial arts. That should be enough to take care of any daytime hired thugs. Manny, you are free to handcuff and arrest them if you want. At night we'll have plenty of protection."

Leif added, "Manny, Cramer, and I will also have guns, you know, for snakes."

"No guns for me or the kids. Molly, I would like you to help with surveillance and computer searches. I want to know of any suspicious, unexplained killings between Portland and Seattle." I pointed to the flat screens set up in the kitchen. "You can help monitor the grounds and I'll give you a laptop for the online work."

"Sure, I love to research crimes," Molly excitedly replied.

Teri entered, carrying bulletproof vests and a bag with cans of bear spray. She dumped them on the table. "Help yourselves!"

Manny and Leif decided to do a patrol of the grounds.

Molly said, "It's beautiful here, living on the river. I mean, if you weren't afraid of a mutant vampire attack."

I started laughing, and she joined in. "Welcome to the asylum," I said and drank some more coffee. "I'm sorry you and Manny got involved. It's not easy for regular people to know about this secret world and not be able to talk about it to anyone besides us."

"I thought Manny was going to get fired. He would not let go of that murder in Salinas that got him interested in you. To tell the truth, he's been unhappy about his job for a while." Molly played with her engagement ring. "He's been talking about us moving to Seattle."

My eyes lit up. "I hope you do. I mean, when we have dealt with all this, I could use more normal people in my life." I liked talking to someone who was just a regular person. She wasn't model skinny, and her long brown hair was pretty but not perfectly styled. She had freckles, and her teeth had a tiny gap in the front. It was a comfort to have a normal person around, unlike the vampires whose dark natures hid behind a façade of physical beauty.

A FedEx delivery truck pulled up, and Des went out for the package. It was snake antivenom courtesy of Dr. Al.

Molly asked, "Look, I know this situation is serious, don't get me wrong, but who are you with now?"

I shook my head. "Don't confuse my book with reality. My life is much more complicated. Some day when we've got a few hours, maybe we can talk about it, but for now, nobody."

She gave me a look that said bullshit. "Really?"

"Batu has been waiting for me for years. Alexander, the same deal. Tristan does not believe I could really walk away from him for good. I can't deal with any of them right now, so, for the moment, nobody."

Luckily Manny and Leif returned. "We're ready for whatever they bring," Manny said.

"Have any of you ever give any shots?" I asked, looking at the FedEx package.

Chapter 41

The Attack

Friday was quiet. Molly helped monitor the surveillance cameras. Manny, Leif, and Cramer made hourly inspections of the grounds surrounding the House of Sun. In case any outsiders came around, they wore jackets over their vests and carried their bear spray in small backpacks. It felt anticlimactic as the mortal crew met for dinner at Leif's place.

"You've got to try this. Omega makes great pizza. Thin crust heaven." Cramer put two large pizzas down on the kitchen table.

Molly took a bite of a pepperoni-mushroom slice. "It's good, but I like deep-dish. The best pizza I ever had was in Chicago."

Leif laughed, "Cramer is from New York. You don't want to go there."

Cramer looked at Manny. "How much did you sell your soul for?"

"I didn't sell out. I agreed to help protect the kids." He put down his pizza. If he weren't so hungry, he would have left the table.

Molly smiled, "Miranda might want us to move here."

"Bingo!" Cramer took a big bite, grabbed a beer and continued. "It's not so easy to walk away once you're in their world. There's one guy, an old friend of the Baroness, who got in deep, but he moved to a godforsaken corner of Montana to get away from the craziness. The Lithuanians don't like remote areas with small populations."

"That's the guy in the book that was a lawyer."

"He actually is a dentist," Cramer shrugged.

Molly took another slice. "In the end, the heroine goes to Alaska to get away from everyone."

Manny gave Lug a piece of crust. "Maybe we should do that."

I was hunkered down in the kitchen, watching the security screens and drinking my eighth cup of coffee. It's bad when you start keeping track. The kids were battling aliens in Tomas' room. Robert and Billy were out on the back porch. I could hear Robert singing a beautiful blues song, harmonizing with the outlaw's harmonica. I had to smile. They played "House of the Rising Sun."

Grigoryi had made ravioli for dinner, and the kitchen smelled great. Teri put a bowl of salad on the table and said, "That should be your House anthem."

"Maybe." I stretched. "Thanks for making dinner guys."

Greg smiled. "I'll get the kids."

Teri pulled some warm baguettes out of the oven. We decided not to use garlic due to all the extra undead company in the house. She remarked, "At least we don't have to cook for the night crew."

Later, Tristan, Guillaume, Henry, Billy, Robert, and Batu were sitting in a circle of chairs in the fencing barn sipping dinner, discussing the situation. Delilah was at Tristan's side.

Henry looked grim. "We do not know where all the Portland Common Caste are. Several are missing. They probably have silver weapons as they are not respectful of the code."

Batu added, "Scheherazade has poisoned them against us."

Tristan stood. "I am going to walk the perimeter with Delilah."

Guillaume reminded Tristan, "Remember the traps in the tree line between the houses. Leif rubbed goat dung on them to mark their location."

"We shall stay clear of the trees." He patted Delilah's head. "It will be difficult to show mercy, but I fear the Baroness will insist on it."

Henry rubbed his hands. "We should allow them to survive to warn others never to harm the Royal family."

"She never said we could not severely damage them." Batu asked Tristan, "May I go with you?"

"Of course."

After they left, Guillaume turned to Henry. "Where is Alexander?"

"Probably stuck in traffic after taking care of that damned Pug."

Alexander had hated hearing Piglet's cries as he walked away from his apartment. One of Henry's waiters would take her for a walk later. Alexander was complicated. He could not stand to see an animal in pain, but taking the life of an enemy never caused him a second of remorse. Alex still mourned the death of his beloved steed Bucephalus, killed in battle two millennia ago. Yet, he had dispatched the mugger who attacked Miranda to the next world without a second thought. The list of those he cared about was a short one. Alexander would do anything and everything to protect them. He had bought a Jeep Wrangler Rubicon because he knew Miranda liked Jeeps and he wanted a vehicle that could handle the mountain roads. Sitting in traffic as the sky darkened made him wish for centuries past when he would ride his horse free of constraints. Perhaps he would buy a home in the country near Granite Falls. He could not get there soon enough tonight.

As the kids loaded their plates, I announced, "No one leaves the house tonight. Do you understand me?"

"We need to practice with Leif," Des protested.

"That has to wait. Leif and the others are tired from looking out for us all day." I noticed Marie checking her phone. "And I do mean no one!"

Marie sighed. "I hope we get this over with soon."

Des wondered out loud, "How much of a threat could these strange rangers from Portland be?"

"They're not even Haute Caste. They don't have a chance," Jacques asserted.

"We don't know much about them. Never underestimate a Lithuanian," Tomas proclaimed.

Teri and I looked at each other, and she agreed, "Truth Tomas! Henry and the others are treating this seriously."

We finished dinner without further protests. When Tristan and Batu came in, I returned to watching the security cams. I was glad to see them getting along better. I poured my ninth cup of coffee and vowed it would be my last. At least for a few hours. The kids headed to the game room, and Delilah followed them. Tristan sat beside me, and Batu went out on the deck with Teri.

"How is it possible for the infra-red cameras to detect the undead?" I stared at the images and tried not to pay attention to how good he smelled.

"They are not ordinary infra-red cameras. The Magus had them specially developed to be able to pick up our kind. It is a technology that we don't particularly like. Still, mortals will never realize it is possible because they don't believe we exist."

"I don't think you have to worry about Manny and Molly telling anyone. I still feel sorry they got caught up in this mess."

He patted my hand. "You warned him. It is his own fault."

"Poor fucker," I muttered. "Hey, look at that!" I pointed to the weathervane on the roof of the fencing barn. "Snakes on the vane!"

Tristan leaned in and stared. "Unbelievable!

I could see their glistening, writhing bodies cascading down from the roof. "Fuck! Tell Teri and Henry and have them call Leif. I'll warn Guillaume and Henry."

I messaged them. Then I ran upstairs to tell the kids to stay put with Delilah. I came back down to watch the cameras.

Outside, Tristan, Billy, Robert, Batu, and Teri formed a line and walked towards the barn. Their flashlights lit up the damp, dark grass. A silent army of slithering rattlesnakes moved quickly towards them. Dozens of snakes hissed and began to attack. Across the yard, Henry stood in the doorway of the barn sending little balls of fire to fry them. Guillaume skewered several with his sword. The mortals came through the trees from Leif's house. Even with the doors and windows closed I could hear them yelling warnings and encouragement to each other. I watched Manny begin shooting at the snakes while Cramer went at them with a machete. Leif raced to protect us, but before he could reach the house, I saw him fall. I thought he had been bitten by one of the snakes but to my relief, seconds later, he got up and made it into the kitchen. I let out a breath I didn't even realized I had been holding.

"I'm okay! I just tripped," he told me as he entered.

I breathed deeply in relief. "The kids are upstairs!" Before he closed the door, a snake slithered into the kitchen. "Go! I got this." I grabbed a butcher knife and whacked off its head. He saw I had things under control and ran upstairs to look after the kids.

Alexander pulled into the driveway, jumped out of his car, and ran to the far side of the house. "Do you have a death wish?" he yelled as he grabbed a hooded figure that was trying to climb up the side of the house.

I had been so focused on the snakes I did not notice the other invaders. On one of the security screens, I watched the blurry image that was Alex, throw the would-be invader to the ground with such force that I was sure it broke his ribs. Then he stomped on his leg and kicked him in the head. I flew up the stairs to check on the kids.

In the game room, Delilah let loose a blood-curdling snarl. With all his strength, Leif was holding her back. He nodded at a bloodied male and female vampire standing in a corner. "They made it in through the window but Delilah stopped them."

The female looking very pissed off, yelled, "Get that beast away from me!"

"Where are the others?" I demanded.

The male said, "Fuck you, mortal trash." He leaned over and grabbed his side.

"Let go of Delilah," I said to Leif. His eyes got big. The panther growled and batted a wooden chair, knocking it over.

"The goat herder's house," the female cried out.

"How many are there?" I asked.

"He's alone," she answered.

I pulled out my phone and called Guillaume, "Get to Leif's house! There is another one there."

I called Tristan, and he arrived with lightning speed. When the undead saw him, they cowered. "A guillotine would be too noble a demise for traitors like you. How dare you attack my family." Tristan snarled.

I responded loudly, "Don't destroy them."

The invaders looked at me, then at each other.

"Scheherazade lied to us," was all the female said. She pulled back her hood and revealed spiked purple hair, which made her resemble an anime character.

The male did the same. He had dirty red hair and lots of piercings. "She said you would poison all the Common Caste just like you did to her. She told us you had no honor."

I noticed the female's wounds had begun to heal, but not the male who was bleeding through his shirt. "You're mortal," I said.

He looked at the floor as though ashamed. "I can't help it. They won't transform me."

"Take them downstairs," I told Leif, "And hand-cuff them."

Tristan looked at them. "Will that be necessary?"

The female shook her head. "No. We submit and beg for your mercy."

In Leif's kitchen, Molly stared at the disheveled blond man dressed in black. Her back was up against the wall. "You're one of the bad ones."

"My goodness, we're judgy. You wouldn't by chance know where the goat herder is?"

He crossed the room in a second and stared into her eyes. She pushed against his chest and screamed, then stabbed his arm with a fork.

He didn't react except to say, "Ouch."

"What do you want?" she cried.

"Not O negative, thank you very much. Where is Leif?"

"Why? He's mortal. He can't hurt you!"

"That isn't your concern." He touched her cheek, and she felt aroused despite her fear.

Guillaume burst through the door, followed by Manny, Henry, Batu, Billy, and Robert. Manny grabbed Molly's arm and pulled her away from the intruder. Batu quickly came to their aid and restrained the rogue vampire.

Manny stared at Molly's neck. "Are you okay?"

She threw her arms around him. "Yes! He didn't bite me." Molly glanced at the blond vampire held by Batu who merely smiled back.

Henry stepped over to him. "You're Haute Caste."

"Yes, but I never use that ridiculous title." He stared at Henry. "I believe we have the same benefactor. She got tired of me in Istanbul, and I wandered around until I found a home in Portland."

"Lena?" Henry was astounded. "You must be Raf!"

"At your service. It appears our plan has run amok. Scheherazade failed to tell us about the interest of the vampire world in these mortals." He smiled at Molly. She turned away, embarrassed by her attraction to him.

Batu shoved him against a wall. "You threatened the lives of the Royal family."

Raf straightened up. "Ah, the Mongol horde speaks."

"Raf, just curious, why did you put the snakes on the roof of the barn?" Robert asked.

"We hoped that they would find their way into the vents and go after anyone inside."

"Another genius plan! And you were in charge of this sorry gang," Billy scoffed, shaking his head.

"Let's go back to the house," Guillaume said. "Your fate is in the hands of the Baroness. Manny and Molly, you're welcome to stay here with Cramer. The threat has passed. Leif will be back to fill you in."

As they walked back, Henry noticed Raf had a slight limp. "Who injured you?"

Raf replied, "The goat scented trap, crude but effective."

As they approached the house, charred snakes crunched under their boots.

We left Delilah upstairs as we brought the two prisoners down. Alexander was sitting in the living room with his feet resting on the broken body of a sniveling Common Caste rebel. "This sorry specimen is Jeremiah," Alex said, shaking his head. "He is sorry for staining your rug with his blood."

He had dark hair and a scraggly beard. Damn! These vampires needed makeovers. "Go stand by your friends. Help him sit up."

Batu and Guillaume brought Raf in, and the female said, "Raf, this was a shit show. Scheherazade set us up."

I looked at Raf. "Were you in charge?"

"At times. You must be the Baroness. I fear that our loyalty might have been misplaced. Perhaps I owe you an apology."

"Is this your whole gang of misfits?" I asked.

"Yes, that's everyone, but you are not seeing us at our best," Raf replied.

"Where is Scheherazade?" Tristan demanded.

Raf shrugged. "I have no idea."

I stared at Raf for a moment. "I can't deal with any of you right now. Guillaume, will you please lock them up in the barn till tomorrow night when we can meet and discuss what to do with their sorry asses?"

Tristan looked at Raf. "How the arrogant have fallen. Tomorrow the Magus will be arriving, and I will go apprise him of what has happened here." He turned to Batu and asked, "Would you accompany Miranda and me tomorrow to Lady Pompadour's home to meet with the Magus.?"

Batu nodded then he and Guillaume took the attackers away. They had to assist the badly injured vamp, but I knew he would be in better shape by tomorrow night. Leif stood next to Marie. I was disturbed by the darkness in her eyes. "Why would they go after Leif?" Marie demanded.

"I don't know. Is everyone safe?" I suddenly realized someone was missing. "Where's Grigoryi?"

"Crap!" Teri took off out the back door.

We followed her outside. Grigoryi was on the ground unconscious, foam on his lips. "Help me get him in the house!" I yelled.

Grigoryi had a nasty snake bite on his arm. He started to have a seizure as Des and Tomas laid him on the couch. He was deathly pale and breathing shallowly. Henry took charge. His outrage changed to compassion. "Poor innocent soul! Take off his shirt!" I got the antivenom kit out of the fridge. I held back tears as I touched Grigoryi's cool, trembling hand.

Henry quickly gave Grigoryi an injection to counter the effects of the venom. Then to my surprise, he had Teri tie up his arm and fill a syringe with his own blood, which he injected into Grigoryi's uninjured arm. The thought of poor sweet Grigoryi dying overwhelmed me. I took a deep breath and turned away for a minute. When I looked back, Grigoryi's color began to improve and he was breathing more normally. He had refused to drink vampire blood in the past. Now the Haute Caste's vital fluid had saved him.

My faithful monk opened his eyes. "Thanks," he muttered, then fell asleep.

Teri gently cleaned and bandaged his wound.

Henry displayed a grim smile. "He'll recover, but it will take a few days.

Someone should stay with him."

"Marie, get some blankets. It's better not to move him. I'll watch over him." I looked at my people and felt a wave of love and pride. "Thank you all. You have been so brave! I think the threat has passed for now. Everyone should try and get some rest.

"We will after we make one more sweep of the yard for snakes," Teri said.

Grigoryi mumbled, "I hate snakes."

Henry added, "Since the Garden of Eden."

Chapter 42

Scheherazade by Any Other Name

Alexander returned home and had rested well after helping the Royals stop the attack. The following evening, he left Piglet with a bowl of food, water, and a chew toy. "I shall never call you a pig. Be good Lady Penelope." He was expected at Pomp's place for a meeting with the Magus to discuss Scheherazade before returning to Granite Falls. He had not spent time with the founder of the vampire world since the Magus had punished him for trying to unseat him. Alexander reminded himself that had he not been defeated in his coup attempt, he never would have been accepted into the Baroness' House, nor would he have experienced "rhapsody in blood" with her. That night of intimacy made his fall from grace more bearable.

He wore a Toscana sheepskin coat over a black turtleneck cashmere sweater and black jeans. He had taken particular care to look attractive to Miranda, including cologne from a parfumerie in Paris.

Alexander drove to Pomp's mansion, hoping the meeting would not take up too much of his evening. As he approached the gate at the end of the narrow street, Alex sensed something was wrong. He pulled over behind a large pickup truck and turned off the headlights. His sixth sense had always protected him from harm in battle. Alexander got out of the car and quietly approached Pomp's home, staying behind the tall bushes that lined the edge of the property. He quickly climbed over the fence and almost landed on the body of a guard, whose throat had been slit. There were tiny bite marks above the slash. Alex knew it had to be either a young vampire or an old one who had lost their powers. Either would be dangerous because of their carelessness. He thought that it must have been Scheherazade.

The body was already cold. The guard had been killed during the day! Fear was a rare emotion for Alex, but it stirred within him. He silently made his way around the house to the glass doors that looked out on the deck. He stayed behind a column as he peered into the living room. All the lights were on as though expecting guests. The room was empty. He wished he knew where Pomp slept, but he had refused her flirtations. He went around to the kitchen entrance, finding the door unlocked. Alex entered and quickly moved into the hallway. Thick rugs and beautiful renaissance paintings decorated every inch of her home. He went past the library and started up the stairs. The odor of mortal blood combined with that of rotting flesh assaulted him.

"Good evening Alexander. I wanted to visit you today, but Henry's security system stopped me."

He turned to see Scheherazade come out from behind the library door. "Where's Pomp?" he demanded.

Alex was shocked by her condition. White roots gave away her dyed hair, and wrinkles testified to her withering state. She wore all black except for a red silk scarf that partially covered the scars from her beheading. She would have merited pity if she had not been such a foul, nasty creature. She had left Paul behind near death. Now the contamination from Miranda's blood was counteracting the rejuvenating effect of Batu's blood given to her in Mongolia, causing her body to decay. She needed Haute Caste blood.

He ran up the stairs looking in every room until he found Pomp's suite. Her pink sheets were stained red. She was laid out perfectly with her severed head a foot above her shoulders, a look of horror frozen on her face. A very sharp long knife lay on the floor.

"Why did you betray me?" Scheherazade stood in the doorway. "I helped you escape. I offered myself to you, served you, and you cast me aside for the Baroness!"

"You have never been worthy of my attention." He went to the bed and moved Pomp's head so it rested on her shoulders.

Scheherazade was on him in a second. She raised her hand, holding a can of aerosolized silver, and sprayed it in his face. He fell backward, gasping. Alexander's hand grabbed the silver knife in Scheherazade's sari. His fingers burned as he tried to plunge it into the mutant vampiress. She jumped out of his way and cackled. "The Great Alexander defeated again!"

He threw the knife into her shoulder. "Bastard!" she sprayed him again. He fell to the ground, his lungs burning. She removed the knife; blood made her dark clothing glisten. In his weakened state, she was able to grab his wrist and bit him. She drank deeply, then moved to the window. "May you burn in hell!" She took a lighter out of her pocket and lit the drapes.

Tristan, Batu, and I arrived at Pomp's home for the meeting with the Magus. After getting no answer when I rang the doorbell, I tried the door and found it unlocked. As I opened it, we all smelled smoke and blood.

Tristan looked around for a couple of seconds and said, "It's coming from upstairs!" He raced up the stairs, followed by Batu and me. We ran into Pomp's bedroom and saw the draperies engulfed in flames, and Alexander motionless on the floor. I summoned rain, which doused the flames, Batu opened the window, and the air began to clear. Tristan looked over and saw Pomp's remains on the bed. He went to her side to see what he could do to save her. Batu tore down the remaining burning curtains and stomped the flames out. Alexander looked lifeless, and I kneeled beside him and began chest compressions. After a few seconds, he coughed, and I saw a flicker of life in his eyes. Suddenly, Scheherazade bolted from behind an antique dressing screen and ran across the room, trying to get past me. I grabbed her by the leg, but with strength fueled by Alexander's blood, she stayed on her feet and dragged me into the hall. I lost my grip on her leg and jumped to my feet, yelling, "Sybil! Do you want more of my blood?"

She turned back to me, shocked to hear her real name. She snarled, "You and your children must die!" She jumped on me and wrapped her bloody fingers around my neck. I felt the pressure against my windpipe and started to lose consciousness. I gathered my remaining strength and kicked her so hard she flew back across the hall. Batu caught her, and she pulled a silver dagger from her waistband and tried to stick it in his throat. He tried to block the knife, but she stabbed him in the hand, and got free.

A powerful voice from the bedroom made us all turn and look. "Enough! It's over!" The Magus entered the bedroom through a hidden door behind Pomp's bed and watched us from the doorway. "You've had a lovely, though short, reign of terror, dear Scheherazade. Now you must stop."

Scheherazade ran to the Magus and threw herself at his feet. I hated her, but her groveling made me lose any remnants of respect I might have had for her. I looked over at Batu and saw his hand still impaled with the knife. I managed to remove the dagger without throwing up. He grimaced but said nothing. His beautiful dark eyes searched my face. "I have to take care of Alexander," I said. I went to Alex, knelt next to him, grabbed a throw from a chaise lounge, and wiped the silver residue from his face and hair. I could sense his life force returning. He opened his eyes. "A little blood please, to cleanse my palate," he whispered.

I looked up to see Tristan working on Pomp, though she did not seem responsive. On the bed next to her was a vampire "first aid kit." It contained, among other things, surgical supplies to sew severed parts back on. I saw a mini-fridge next to the bed, went over, opened it, grabbed a bag of O-positive, and brought it to Alex. Sybil was still groveling at the feet of the Magus. What a shit show. "What will you do with her?" I asked the Magus.

"Bind her hands and feet," he threw handcuffs and rope to Batu. "She is important to us, if only for research."

I glared at him. "You let her escape. You allowed all of this to happen. All this pain, fear, damage, and death just for your sick experiment!"

Tristan glared at the Magus. "You put my family in grave danger!"

I had never seen Tristan show anger towards the Magus before.

The Magus responded calmly. "She escaped sooner than expected, but I trusted that you would apprehend her."

I was filled with anger at the Magus. Before I said something I might later regret, I turned back to Alexander and helped him sit up. "Try to take a deep breath."

He inhaled deeply, then said, "Thank you!"

I looked around the room at the havoc caused by another of the Magus' plans. I turned to him and said, "I can never forgive you for endangering my children!"

The Magus asked, "Were they harmed in any way?"

My look should have made him burst into flames, but instead, the room suddenly felt very cold. "No, they weren't. No thanks to you, they will be fine. Leif

304

and Delilah kept two of the rogue vampires from hurting them. You have them to thank that my children are safe."

The ancient vampire, characteristically stoic, amid the chaos simply said, "Perhaps. What have you done with the other Portland intruders?"

Tristan responded, "They are injured and waiting for an audience with the Baroness and me."

I heard Sybil chuckle. "My snakes will disappear back into the woods."

Batu tightened her handcuffs and shoved her to the floor. "We killed them all and left their bodies for the scavengers.

"My beautiful snakes," she shrieked.

"Quiet!" Batu snapped and then kicked her.

Tristan, still tending to Pomp, said, "She is breathing." Her lips were stained red with the blood from the minifridge and fortified with some of his. She was finally getting the attention she craved from the Haute Caste. I hoped Tristan would treat her well now. Her neck looked like Dr. Frankenstein had stitched her up. A shiver went down my spine. I don't know if I would ever get used to being part of the undead world.

The Magus went over to the bed and gently touched Pomp's cheek. "You have served me well. The Baroness wishes you to be Haute Caste. I agree." Her eyes opened for the first time. All I could think was that they deserved each other.

Alexander whispered to me, "She has suffered much at the hands of the Haute Caste. Pomp will recover and use what happened today to enhance her reputation." He slowly got to his feet. "Please excuse me. I must shower and get the rest of the silver off." He went into the bathroom but left the door open. He was not shy.

The Magus ordered Batu to take the bound Sybil to his car and dispose of the security guard's body. Batu threw her over his strong shoulders and quickly carried her off, but not before closing the bathroom door.

The Magus gave one more look around the room and said, "Excuse me for such a short visit, but I must take the prisoner back to L.A."

"Fuck You!" I spat at him.

He shook his head and disappeared the way he had come. Tristan turned to me and asked, "Will you help clean her up? She must not be moved until tomorrow evening for the neck wound to heal properly."

I grabbed some pink linens from a hallway closet. They smelled of roses and lavender. As I put the clean sheets on the bed, I noticed how carefully Tristan washed the red stains from her skin and hair. He had the same look of concern I had seen when he had revealed his undead nature, and I had fainted years ago. The tender side of Tristan was very attractive. He had no idea how much more powerful that was than his vampire abilities. Pomp, still unable to talk, mouthed, "Merci."

I found a black silk and lace nightgown in an armoire. Tristan helped me change her. Not once did his eyes rest on any particular aspect of her anatomy. He was the perfect gentleman.

After we had gotten her settled, my thoughts returned to the Magus. Once again, I was filled with anger at everything his plotting had caused.

Through clenched teeth, I growled, "I really hate him."

Tristan looked at me for a moment as if not sure how to respond, then simply said, "He has his reasons."

"He always has his reasons, but they're always diabolical. Our children could have been hurt. Or worse! Our mortal friends could have died protecting us, and it could have been the end of Alexander and Pomp. And poor Grigoryi almost died from a snake bite."

"The Magus would have saved Lady Pomp," Tristan responded with a slight smile.

"He is not welcome in my home. I cannot ban him from visiting Seattle, but I never want him to set foot on my property."

Tristan looked at me with compassion. "You will always be part of his world, even though you reject and curse him. All of this is to help us understand the effect of your blood on our kind. The consequences could be disastrous if we do not study and understand the effects. Don't you see, your blood allowed a Common Caste to attack during the day. Lady Pompadour's mortal security guards were useless."

"And what about their lives?"

"We will compensate the families of any that were killed."

"Do you think money will make it all better? Whenever I start to remember why I ever married you, reality stomps on my heart. You and the Magus are the most arrogant, cold, self-centered creatures on the planet!"

Alexander came out of the bathroom, looking like a male model. He had recovered from the loss of blood and silver spray. "Am I interrupting anything?" He appeared quite upbeat, considering the horror he had just survived.

"No, I'm done here." I said flatly, "Let's go."

He gave Tristan a Cheshire grin and followed me out of the bedroom.

We passed Batu in the hallway. "We'll take Alex's car. See you back at the house."

Batu simply nodded. When he got back in the bedroom, he punched the wall, making a large hole.

Tristan said, "We have been fools. Alex has been our rival all along."

"What does she see in him? After what he did! I hate him!"

"I think they had sex after she witnessed Alex eliminate the street thug in Seattle. Do not blame her for being driven by her nocturnal nature. Alex was aware that when he protected her, he would reap the benefits. Be patient. She is awakened. Miranda caused the mist, the shift in room temperature, and she is still mortal." Tristan could not hide his admiration. "It is why the Magus is so lenient with her."

"I thought by the time I transformed and came here she would be past the divorce and...."

Tristan shook his head. "You just might be more clueless about women than I am. The Magus, Lady Kananga, Lady Sarah, and Lady Lily have all tried to reason with me. Only recently have I begun to understand that women view the world differently than we do. Do not take women for granted. Do not try to predict how they will react."

"Never assume," Pomp whispered hoarsely.

Tristan brought her hand to his lips. "I shall not, my lady."

By the time Alex and I got back home, the dawn was fast approaching. Grigoryi was still tucked in on the couch in the living room. Cramer and Leif could walk, though Leif was limping. There were cheers and gasps as Alex described the attack and takedown of Sybil at Pomp's mansion.

Des asked, "You're sure Pomp will be okay?"

I ignored him. "What did you do with the Portland idiots?"

Guillaume spoke up. "They have been given nourishment. They can stay where they are until you are ready to speak with them."

Tomas was pissed. "So, the Magus knew?"

Alex was tactful. "He strongly suspected what would happen. I don't believe he quite expected Scheherazade to cause so much damage. She is still more mortal than immortal."

Marie shook her head. "We're just lab rats to him. I hate him!"

Henry put his arm around her, and in a soothing voice, said, "No one can contain or control you, Marie."

Manny grabbed Molly's hand. "Thanks for the unforgettable weekend, but I think we should head back to Salinas now."

"I've already made a deposit into your bank account. You both certainly earned it."

Manny looked at me puzzled. "How could you know...?"

I laughed. "We have our ways. If you get bored or decide you want a less normal job, we could use both of you here."

"We'll think about it." Molly hugged me, and they headed to their car.

Cramer walked with them. "You should get the windshield fixed before you head home. I've got a friend in Granite who can do it for you."

It was too close to sunrise for the undead to return to Seattle. Henry and Teri would take a bedroom at Leif's house, and Alex would stay in a guest room. Since Batu had not returned yet, I guessed he would remain at Pomp's with Tristan.

Chapter 43

The Portlandians and the House of Sun

I was standing in the middle of a sunny cornfield when a light rain started to fall. Dark clouds appeared on the horizon and quickly devoured the summer sky. The wind howled as the rain began to pour down on me. I put my arms out like a scarecrow as I tried to command the storm. The wind gusts battered me. I fell on my knees and clutched my chest. "Tristan!" I cried out.

"Mom, wake up!" I felt Jacques shaking me. "You're dreaming."

Lug jumped up and licked my face. It took a moment for reality to set in. I had fallen asleep in a stuffed chair. I looked around. "Where's Grigoryi? How is he?"

"He's a little better. Leif and Cramer helped him lay down in his room. He ate some soup."

"What time is it?"

"Three o'clock. I would've let you sleep, but you yelled Dad's name. I think you were having a nightmare."

"I was. It's weird when I have a bad dream. I always call out to him." I sat up and put the throw on the back of the chair. "It's okay. I'm fine now. Where is everyone?"

"Cleaning up. Mom, can I ask you a personal question?"

"That sounds serious. Let me get a cup of coffee first."

We headed into the kitchen. I turned on the coffee maker and looked out at the river. Leif and Marie stood a foot apart, talking as the sun was starting to set. Several yards away, at the fire pit, Tomas and Des were making sure they burned the remains of every last snake. They all were young adults now. They had been through so much. It was time to treat them as adults. I poured the coffee and took a sip. Heaven! Jacques sat at the kitchen table with Lug at his feet. "So, what did you want to ask?"

"Are you dating Alex now? Is Batu just a friend? Or are you getting back together with Dad."

"No to everything at the moment." I sat down and took a slow drink. "It's complicated." My kids would know if I lied, so I considered what might be the most appropriate version of the truth. "I'm not in a relationship with anyone. I may spend time with someone, but that does not mean anything serious is going on. Got it?"

"I guess so," he looked a little sad.

"Why do you want to know?" I wondered if he wanted me to be with Alex.

He looked sheepish. "Des is taking bets. I wanted to win for once."

"Jacques Omar Ortega-Mordecai, go tell your brother if I hear of him making bets about my love-life again, he'll be cleaning out the horse stalls for a year. All by himself!"

"No problem! I'll tell him the bets are off." He ran out of the door. I had to reconsider that adult thing.

I looked out and saw Jacques talking to Des, then watched as Des started waving his arms, cussing, and kicking at the fire. I think it was one of my finer moments as a mother. I grabbed some cookies. My body needed fuel. Soon I would have to talk with Marie and Leif about their relationship. I was not ready for any more drama. A bath would give me time to consider how to deal with that.

I was a little sore from my encounter with Sybil as I climbed the stairs. I peeled off my clothes and ran a hot bath with jasmine-scented bubble bath. I sank into the tub and closed my eyes. The water was a healing balm to my sore muscles and nerves. The immediate threat was gone, but now I had to figure out how to protect my loved ones and govern my small vampire House. Deciding what to do about Alex and Batu weighed on my heart but was not a priority at the moment.

"Did I come at a bad time?" A man's voice disturbed my thoughts.

"Who the fuck...."

Raf stood in the bedroom and stared at me. "Good afternoon Baroness."

I grabbed a towel and managed to cover myself up as I stood. I glanced at the window and saw the sun had not fully set. "How is it possible? It's not night yet."

"I've always been able to tolerate fading sunlight."

"Have you never heard of knocking?" I moved out of his line of sight, put on a robe, and then walked into the bedroom. "Where are the others?" He wore the same dirty clothes and had a little too much vampire and goat scent. I kept my distance.

"Waiting for the night and permission. My speed and stealth allowed me to get past your offspring. It's one of the advantages of being Haute Caste. My nickname is Flash."

"What do you want?" I moved beside my night table, where I kept a dagger.

"To serve the House of Sun. I mean you no harm. It is obvious you have the support of the ancient ones. Scheherazade did not tell us that. She said you wanted to destroy the Common Caste. I now know that isn't true. I throw myself on your mercy." He bowed.

Teri ran into the room with nunchucks in her hands and stood between us. "Are you okay?"

"Yeah, I'm fine. He won't hurt me." My head and gut said he was telling the truth. "He could have attacked me while I was in the tub. He just wants forgiveness."

"And a shower. Dude, you stink!" Teri added.

"I assure you I'm not usually offensive to females. If you could give me some clean clothes and a place to bathe, I would be in your debt."

I had to smile. "Let him use Batu's bathroom. You can grab some clothes from Tristan's suitcase."

"The Baron's threads? Thank you!" He walked into the hallway.

"Teri, please pass on to everyone that we'll meet in the barn in a couple of hours."

She raised her eyebrows. "Does he need supervision?"

"No. Portland will swear loyalty tonight." I surprised myself by how assured I sounded.

Raf was an arrogant prick, and I was feeling sorry for Bart and Jeanne. Dealing with Portland was going to be a challenge. At the moment, I had to attend to another matter. So I got dressed and went to the river to talk with the love birds.

"Hi Baroness." Leif smiled, but Marie looked like I was annoying her.

"I'm worried about you two." I hated to meddle, but it was time to be a protective matriarch.

"Mom, we're just good friends. You don't need to tell us anything, and I can take care of myself. I not a kid anymore." She stared at me, hoping I would just turn around and go back to the house.

"It's clear you care for each other. For now, it has to stay just friends. You might think about giving each other a little space." I tried to be as tactful as possible.

"Like you and Alex?" She glared at me.

"Marie," Leif intervened. "It's okay. Your mom is right. We gotta be chill."

"Thanks, Leif. I'll see you in the barn in a couple of hours. Portland is going to join us." I turned and walked back to the house before saying something to my daughter I would later regret. I was worried about why someone was targeting Leif. I assumed it was because of Marie's growing fondness for him and some ambitious vampire who wanted to eliminate possible competition. I sat on the deck to process everything that had been happening and what I still had to do.

A while later, I helped Teri get a pot of vegetarian chili going, which smelled great. I checked on Grigoryi. He was sitting up reading my vampire book. "I didn't know you had written about me. Was I really such a silly vampire hunter?"

I smiled. "With a heart of gold who changed his ways. You're a hero at the end."

"I hope so. I'm sore, but I feel better." He bit into a baguette. "The store bread is not that tasty. I better bake tomorrow."

"If you're up to it. We'll have a meeting in the barn tonight. I'll ask Guillaume to fill you in later. I'm going to pardon the visitors from Oregon."

"Pardon the people, but not the snakes."

"Of course." I smiled.

When I returned to the kitchen, a tall blond man with a charming smile greeted me. I recognized Tristan's black silk shirt and jeans. "Raf? You clean up well."

Alexander walked in shirtless, looking very fit. "Good evening." He reached into the refrigerator for a small container of O-positive and poured some into an espresso cup. "Ah, cold but refreshing." He looked at Raf. "Would you like some?"

Raf just shook his head and stared. "Alexander the Great! It has been centuries since we last spoke."

"He has his moments," I said. Alex merely smiled.

A car pulled up, and Batu entered the kitchen with a suit bag and laid it over a chair. "Alexander, here are the clothes you asked for." He looked at Alex parading around half-nude and said, "I guess we are going casual." Batu took off his shirt and displayed his incredibly muscular shoulders and chest. Raf, not to be left out, started to remove his shirt.

Leif, Marie, and her brothers came in for dinner. Marie looked at me and rolled her eyes.

"Tickets for the Gun Show?" Teri commented as she walked into the kitchen.

"All of you put your clothes on. Idiots!" I went up to my room. The House of Sun was a dumpster fire.

I sat on the bed, my head in my hands. There was a soft knock on the door. "Come in."

Batu entered, still shirtless, carrying a bowl of Chili and some cornbread. "You need to eat."

I remembered him making Mongolian dumplings for me in Rossville. He was worried that I had lost too much weight after my dad died. I started to tear up, my bottom lip quivered.

He shut the door and sat down beside me. "Eat." I grabbed the cornbread and almost got the whole piece in my mouth. Crumbs fell on my lap. "Nice!" he commented with a smile.

"Comfort food," I mumbled. I started on the bowl of chili like I had not eaten for a week, and it was gone in no time.

"You've been under a lot of stress. You have to take better care of yourself." His scent reminded me of a spice shop. I put down my bowl and leaned against Batu, who turned to me and ran a hand through my hair and down my back. His touch was gentle but effective. If I had been a cat, I would have purred. "Do you wish me to stay?"

"At this moment, very much, but I don't know what will happen next." I looked into his eyes and put my hand on his smooth, hard chest. He bent down and kissed me. I responded with the yearning and desire I had kept hidden for years. We were wrapped in each other's arms as the bowl and spoon clattered to the floor. I let him stay on top of me as we quickly shed our clothes. "Batu," I whispered.

His lips found my every erogenous zone, and my nipples became hard as his mouth and tongue caressed them. My back arched as his hands slipped under my bottom. His eyes never left mine as he entered me. Every thrust went deeper. I wrapped my legs around him. The pressure on my clitoris elicited soft moans. Our eyes closed. The passion so long denied caused waves of tension to be released. We were lost in the moment. Then he lifted me up, and we rocked together while orgasms claimed us. "You're amazing," I said breathlessly. That had to be the quickest orgasm on record. He kept his arms around me as we collapsed on the bed.

Batu whispered, "You are everything I imagined."

Teri yelled from the hallway, "The meeting is about to start!"

"I'll be there in a few," I called out. "Crap!" I muttered.

I ran into the bathroom, took a quick shower, and pulled my clothes on. I did not want my intimate activity to be obvious. Vampires have an amazing sense of smell. I tried not to think of how, in one week, I had been with more males than in my entire life. Batu sat up and grinned. "Miranda, you should zip your jeans."

I looked down. My pink undies showed through the zipper. I could not believe I almost went downstairs looking like a guy who just came out of the john. "Anything else?"

"No, you're perfect."

I was not proud of myself as I looked at the magnificent man in my bed. "No expectations."

"None," He tried to look serious, but a grin appeared.

"Please get cleaned up before you come to the meeting. And put on a shirt!" I left quickly.

Cramer was in a surly mood. He cornered me as I walked into the barn. "You can't trust anyone from Portland. They would have let those snakes bite us and step over our writhing bodies."

"Who said I do? I will give them all a chance to prove they are sorry and admit they should not have believed Scheherazade, I mean Sybil." From now on, that's what I would call her. "Cramer, I gave you a second chance too."

He did not like the comparison but did not argue. I walked to the center of the barn. Batu entered, fully dressed, and stood next to Alex, who had put on a cashmere sweater and nicely pressed slacks. I could swear Alex sniffed Batu discretely. It was probably my paranoia.

The Southern invaders huddled together, and Raf was speaking softly to them. Purple girl had a permanent frown. The injured vamp with dark curls to his shoulders glared at Alex. The mortal grimaced due to a shoulder injury from Delilah.

Leif and the kids stood with Guillaume staring at their attackers. Teri joined them as Henry walked over to stand by my side. Just as I was about to speak, Tristan arrived with Delilah on a leash. She snarled at the Portland contingent. They cringed in unison, except for Raf.

Tristan said, "Delilah, we are amongst friends now," and patted her head. She sat majestically beside him.

"We are the House of Sun." I made eye contact with everyone before I went on. "I would have liked a different way of coming together, but perhaps a clash before reconciliation was inevitable." Guillaume smiled at my words. I felt encouraged. "Though some of us walk in daylight, we are not enemies of the nocturnal folk. We all share bloodlines and secrets that the mortal world is not ready to acknowledge, and we must protect each other to survive."

"Well said!" Raf said. Purple girl jabbed him in the ribs.

"Scheherazade, Sybil, misled you to get your help. We only hurt you in self-defense. We offer you a chance to join our House and be forgiven for your transgressions." I knew Grigoryi would appreciate that.

The vampiress spoke up, "I'm Mathilda. The Haute Caste have never respected us. Will you? Will you keep your word?"

312

Cramer responded, "They forgave me after I harmed one of the royal offspring, and I'm just a short."

The room fell silent. Henry touched my shoulder. "I have agreed to serve as a Knight to the House of Sun."

The dark-haired vampire with the piercing stare reacted, "I can't believe Sir Henry, the legendary Haute Caste rebel, has joined a House!"

Tristan said, "The House of Sun is governed by the Baroness. She has three knights, Sir Henry, Sir Alexander, and Sir Guillaume." Everyone stared at the second most powerful vampire as he kept a tight hold on his panther. "If anyone should cause this House any difficulties, they will also have to deal with my displeasure."

Tomas, his siblings at his side, stood with his arms crossed. "And ours!" I was proud of my kids.

I needed a little display of my power, so they would not think I required the Baron's back-up. "Showtime!" I held my hands palms up and closed my eyes. The moisture in the room became a fine mist and then formed tiny droplets.

Mathilda cried out, "She can manipulate water! She's not even one of us yet."

"Stop it Mom!" Marie cried out. She hated getting her hair wet.

I put down my arms and it stopped. Delilah shook herself. The contingent from Oregon all bowed their heads, and Raf spoke for them, "We will be honored to serve your House. Please allow us the privilege."

Des said, "You didn't apologize yet."

Raf raised his head. "We are sorry for believing lies about you and for attacking your House and ask forgiveness." The others from Portland all nodded in agreement.

Alex stepped forward; the room fell quiet. The ancients had a way of commanding respect. "I am the father of Jacques, so never even consider lifting a hand against him or any member of our House."

Batu smiled. "Princess Khunbish, of the House of Cups, also extends her protection to the House of Sun."

"I will give you all a chance to prove your loyalty." I couldn't believe that I actually said that. "Sir Guillaume, please allow them to clean up and provide them with clothing."

Guillaume smiled. "I like being called, 'Sir.'"

Teri looked at Mathilda. "I've got something that will probably fit her."

Guillaume took the newbies back to his home. The rest headed for the big house to dry off, but I stayed behind to think. The dampness comforted me. I sat in a wooden chair on the side of the room and considered the last few days. Thoughts of Alex, the mugging, the snake attack, the Magus' betrayal, Batu, and confronting the Portland undead caused my brain to overload. I had almost forgotten about poor Manny and Molly. After the past few days, they would never be the same. I hoped I would hear from them again. "What the fuck am I going to do with my life?" I said out loud.

"You've come a long way from the naive writer I married." Tristan stood in the doorway. "You're even more beautiful." Delilah ran over to me and licked my hands. I kissed her smooth head. In an instant, he was standing before me. Show-off!

"Yeah, fucking gorgeous." I pulled at my damp, unruly curls.

"I was going to stay with Pomp, but I heard you calling for me."

"This afternoon, in a dream, more of a nightmare, really. It's strange that I still do that." I looked at his proud face, perfectly chiseled features, and killer blue eyes. His blond hair fell around his strong shoulders like Thor. How could I have divorced him? How could I have ever married him? My tangled emotions were choking me.

He could sense my distress. "Miranda, you don't have to make any decisions about us or any other relationship now."

I looked at him wide-eyed. "When did you become a therapist?"

"When I had to come to terms with our divorce." He held out his hand. "We have much to discuss. I have news from Sir Bart and Lady Jeanne."

I held his hand for a second, then let go. "Are they still in Portland?"

We began to walk back to the house. "Yes. They found Paul, the other member of the House of Pentacles. Scheherazade had almost drained him dry. Fortunately, they were able to save him. She tricked them into helping her. It should not be hard now for Lady Jeanne and Sir Bart to convince the other Common Caste to be loyal to your new House. Lady Pauline and Sophie are on their way back to London with Paul, the injured Common Caste. They will assist Sir Borgia, Lady Antoinella, your father, and Lady Anastasia as they educate the members of the House of Pentacles."

"They will need to reach out to the Common Caste everywhere to stop another uprising and quell the rumors," I added.

He stopped in the moonlight, and I turned to face him. "What is it?" I asked.

"Why don't we start another rumor." With lightning speed he pulled me into his arms, and we kissed. He released me and bowed his head. "Just a reminder of what you could have."

"Or what I don't want. You asshole. You knew that the others would see us." I saw a few faces looking out the window.

"I must be getting back to check on Pomp. If you don't want me, stop calling me in your dreams."

Chapter 44

Surprise!

We had a few weeks of relative calm. I was keeping my distance from Alexander and Batu. The rogue vampires had gone back to Portland and were trying their best to make a favorable impression on Jeanne and Bart. The Magus had taken Sybil back to L.A. where she agreed to help Kyoto in his research as a condition of her survival. I disliked her, but I could understand her desire to be respected by the Haute Caste. Her inability to have compassion for others made it impossible for her to earn that respect. Pomp was also ambitious, but she was not heartless, and after the details of having survived Sybil's attack, she was gaining status. I was consolidating my new House and the ability to protect my family. I was not envious of the powers that others possessed and did not care if the Magus could cause the ground to shake. He had better not threaten my loved ones again. My sole motivation for engaging with powerful vampires was to keep them from ruining our lives.

To make things more complicated, I was weeks late! I managed to secretly buy a pregnancy test kit while grocery shopping with Grigoryi. I waited till Teri was in Seattle and the kids were at school to take the test. I locked my bedroom door and went into the bathroom. After Jacques was born, I had my tubes tied. I recalled when Tristan had warned me that there were vampires that would try to garner power and prestige by seducing me and getting me pregnant. I thought he was just being jealous and trying to keep others away from me. I had sex once with Alex and once with Batu; that was it. That had been a weird week, and I had not pursued physical contact with either of them since then. I was not ready to have another male making assumptions and expecting more than I was willing to give.

I sat on the edge of the toilet seat and waited for the test result. A bathroom seemed like a sad place to find out if you were knocked up. After what seemed like an eternity, the test confirmed what I already knew, but hadn't been ready to accept. Finding out I had been pregnant with Jacques had been a shock. But this was a lightning bolt. I laid down on the bed and rested my hands on my belly. I did not know who the baby daddy was. "Welcome to the House of Sun," I mumbled. I vowed never even to kiss another man.

This meant eight months of decaf. My mind was spinning. What was I going to tell the kids? This was not planned; this was life unfolding in its own mysterious way. Sometimes all you can do is just fasten your seatbelt and hold on. I told Alexa to play Green Day and I stayed in my room until Grigoryi brought the kids home from school.

The kids headed to the game room and heard the music.

Des looked concerned. "The last time she blasted Green Day was when they got divorced."

Tomas turned to Marie. "You go check on her. Maybe it's...well, you know."

"Hormones?" she shoved him. "Ass hat!"

Jacques decided to take one for the team. "I'll talk to her." He knocked on the door.

I called out, "Come in, all of you." I told Alexa to stop the music, and they gathered around me. "I guess you could say it is a bit hormonal." They looked at each other surprised I had heard their conversation.

Tomas said, "See!" Marie glared at him.

"After Jacques was born, I had a tubal ligation." The boys stared at me, looking a little confused.

Marie blurted out, "You're pregnant."

Jacques' eyes got big. "Is Alex the...."

"I don't know if it's Alex or Batu. I'm not proud of this, but you're old enough to understand that these things happen."

Tomas looked at me. "Maybe you should have paid more attention when you talked to us about sex." The others glared at him. "Just saying," he shrugged.

"You're the first to know." I got choked up. "I'll tell Batu and Alex next."

They all crowded around and hugged me. Marie said, "Maybe I'll get a little sister this time."

"Mom, we got your back. You know that," Tomas said.

"I know. Now promise me you won't say anything to anyone till I tell you it's okay." They all nodded or grunted that they would keep my secret. "So, go act normal. You know, play video games instead of doing your homework."

Des said, "I'm not changing diapers," as he went out the door.

The house was unusually quiet as sundown approached. I went down to the kitchen and found Jacques helping Grigoryi with dinner. I found a bag of decaf and made a pot. Jacques did not make eye contact with me. "Smells good Grigoryi, mac n' cheese?"

"Yes, with three kinds of Tillamook cheese." He smiled as he pulled the baked cheddar masterpiece out of the oven.

I was anxious but not overwhelmed. I had felt this way before. I began to focus on the new tiny being that had been created from lust. I had to admit, it had been great sex. Both times.

Grigoryi put a large bowl of tossed greens on the table. He looked at me with concern. "Are you okay?"

"Not really, but I will be." I looked at Jacques. "We all will be."

Jacques hugged me. The others came into the kitchen, called by the aroma of Grigoryi's cooking. Our culinary monk smiled. "Mangia bene!"

We dug in. I needed comfort food. Des asked, "Are you gonna be a carnivore again?"

Marie kicked him under the table. Grigoryi looked confused, and I tried to smooth over the awkward moment and said, "I'm a little anemic again, so I'll go back to eating meat. Whatever you decide to cook will be fine."

"Maybe a roast for tomorrow night?"

"That would be fine Grigoryi. Thanks."

After dinner, the kids helped with the dishes. I turned to Marie. "Tell Batu I'll be in the fencing barn."

"Sure, Mom. Don't take any shit." She high-fived me. Did I mention that I loved my kids?

I went out to the fencing barn and sat on a wooden bench beneath the display of swords, hoping I would not feel like using one. It was funny how this place had become like my throne room. Maybe I would get a special chair.

Batu came in. "What's up? Is everything okay?"

"Close the door and sit down." He pulled up a chair and sat way too close to me.

"What is it?" He started to reach over to take my hand, but I waved him off.

In a calm voice, I said, "I'm pregnant." His eyes lit up. "I'm not sure who the father is."

"Me! It has to be...."

"Or it could be Alexander." I decided to stay with the cold truth.

"Miranda, how can you not know?" He stood up so quickly the chair fell over, and he began pacing. Unfiltered pain and anger poured out of him. "Alexander? After what he did? I can't believe you would treat me this way. I waited years for you!"

When his tirade petered out, I shook my head and snapped, "What a selfish bastard. I expected more from you, but I should have known better." Without waiting for a reply, I stormed out, leaving him looking confused.

As I left the barn, I saw Tomas and Des run around the building and back to the house. They had seen and heard everything. I walked through the house and grabbed my purse and jacket off the coat rack. I yelled to whoever could hear. "I'm going to see Alex. I don't need a bodyguard."

I texted Alex to meet me at my favorite Pike's Place Market café. After Batu's outburst, I wanted to be in a public place for my next confrontation. I was numb from my encounter with my Mongol lover. I could not begin to process what I was feeling. I turned on the radio and jacked up the volume for the ride into the city. "You're the size of a pea," I said out loud, "and look at all the havoc you've created. You're definitely one of us."

Alex was waiting for me at a table, with a great view of the lights reflected on the dark water. He was dressed in Ralph Lauren casual, and as always, a little on the tight side. I took a breath as he stood and embraced me. "You smell great," I muttered.

"I always wear this fragrance for you." He stared as we sat down. "I can sense that something is not right."

Before I could respond, the waiter appeared and asked for our orders. "Decaf cappuccino and blackberry pie a la mode. Thanks."

"Cabernet." He reached across the table and gently covered my hand. His touch was comforting and erotic at the same time. I leaned back and gently pulled away. "What is it? How can I help?" he asked.

"Please don't get too excited." I looked at his handsome face. "I'm pregnant, and I don't know if you or Batu is the father." I carefully watched his response.

With a look of concern and a hint of a smile, he asked, "You and the baby are well?" I nodded. "I hope with all my heart that I am the father, of course, but that does not matter."

He was great, really great. Maybe the centuries had granted him the emotional maturity and tact that Batu lacked. I let out a breath I hadn't realized I had been holding. "Thank you."

The waiter brought my coffee and pie. I took a sip of my cappuccino to help compose myself and wiped the froth from my lips.

Alex smiled. "I take it Batu did not have the same reaction."

"No. He was an ass."

"Fool! Do you want me to talk with him? Stress is not good for a woman with child."

"No. I appreciate your offer, but he's got to figure this out himself." I dug into the pie. It was delicious.

"I will, of course, always protect all of your children. I have seen how they stand up for each other. It has not been easy for any of you, and I deeply admire what a great mother you are."

I dabbed my eyes with the napkin. "You said all the right things. And more."

The waiter came over. "Is everything okay?"

Alex smiled. "Yes, we just found out that she's expecting."

"Congratulations! Can I get you anything else?"

Alex said, "No thank you. We're about to leave."

"Have a great night." the waiter said and walked away.

I shook my head. "Damn you! I did not want to like you. Now I'm grateful to have you in my corner."

"Any night, my lady." His expression became serious. "Have you told the Baron?"

I took the last bite of pie. "No, he's coming over tonight. I'm not looking forward to that conversation."

"Do you want me there?"

"You're smart enough to ask, not demand. Thanks, but I can handle Tristan."

He just nodded. We headed out of the restaurant, and he walked me back to my car. We embraced for a long minute. He looked into my eyes. "I will always have time for you. I will always defend you. You have but to ask."

As I got in the car, I said, "Thanks for restoring my faith in your kind." It was hard to drive away.

A Rolls was parked in the driveway when I got back home. I'm sure everyone noticed Tristan's new ride go through town. Way to keep a low profile. When I walked in, Grigoryi was alone in the kitchen, making cookies. "Kind of late for you. What is it?"

He looked sheepish. "The Baron saw the bag of decaf coffee beans, and it seemed to upset him. He's in the fencing barn with the kids."

When I got to the barn, Guillaume and my ex had the kids lined up for a lecture on appropriate conduct while fencing. Tristan stated loudly, "You will not strike while your opponent is suiting up. Is that clear?" They all nodded. I noticed Des had a tear in his sleeve.

I took over. "That's enough for tonight. Take off your gear and go back to the house. I want to talk with your dad."

Guillaume nodded and left without a word. The kids looked relieved to have the lecture cut short. Des mouthed at me, "Thanks."

Tristan stood with his back to me, running his hand over the hilt of an antique sword on the table. I walked to the other side and stared at him.

I could see the cold resentment in his eyes. "Who is the father?"

I swallowed. "I'm not sure. It could be Alex or Batu." I was not about to let my unfaithful ex shame me. "It was not planned, but I welcome this child."

He gripped the handle of the sword. "I warned you!"

I met his angry stare. "Yes, you did. Do you know why my tubal ligation failed?"

He let go of the sword and leaned on the table with both hands. "Your vampire DNA saw the surgery as an injury and healed you." His voice became softer, "I suspected that could happen."

"Why didn't you say something?"

"I hoped it would occur while we were still together."

I saw the pain in his eyes, but it did not lessen my resentment. "Did the Magus know about this? Was this one of his schemes?"

"He hoped you would have more children. As did I but I had hoped it would be with me."

"Well, now I'm making his dreams come true." It was difficult to look at the vampire I had once loved so deeply and completely. "This changes nothing! I won't let the Magus run our lives. He can't order us around like he did to you, to let Tomas be hurt for his research."

He replied, "I did that for you. It was not easy for me."

"You have a funny way of showing affection. Would you go against the Magus to protect us?"

His expression was grim. "I hope that it will never come to that. Am I the last to know about your pregnancy?"

"I told the kids, Batu, Alexander, and now you. I'm sure it will be the talk of the vampire world by tomorrow night. Ruben will be taking bets soon." I walked out, and he at least knew better than to try to stop me.

Chapter 45

Bucephalus II

Not only were my hormone levels affected by the pregnancy, but my pregnancy also affected the vampires involved. I had never imagined the degree of the feather preening, muscle-flexing, and masculinity battles that would take place.

Alexander and Batu prided themselves on their horsemanship. Every evening Batu would practice perfecting his ability to ride and fire arrows with great accuracy. A few weeks after the big announcement, Alexander arrived with a horse transport. When Jacques was born, the triplets already each had a horse. My father, Omar, wanted to give one to him at the time, but since it would be a while until he would be old enough to ride, we decided to wait. The kids had been sharing the three horses. Jacques ran out of the house, very excited. "Alex! My horse!"

I followed Jacques to the corral where Alex was unloading a high-spirited, magnificent black stallion. He turned to me. "I consulted with Sir Omar to find the perfect horse for Jacques."

"He's very handsome," I said.

Alex smiled, and I swear the horse glanced at me when I said that. "His bloodlines go back to the Thessalian breed." Jacques threw his arms around the horse's massive neck.

Batu came out of the barn to examine the new arrival. He looked at Alex. "He's been enhanced."

"Yes. With a little of my blood for longevity, strength, and stamina." He stared Batu down. There was no love lost between them.

Alex smiled at Jacques, who was staring wide-eyed at the horse, and said, "I named him Bucephalus after the horse that I lost in the Battle of the Hydasp."

I knew that Alexander had loved his steed, Bucephalus, and sorely grieved for him. He had even erected a statue of the horse at his Las Vegas compound. Alex handed Jacques a carrot for the horse.

As Jacques gingerly gave the carrot to Bucephalus, he quietly asked, "He looks like your old horse, the one in the paintings. Would it be okay if I called him Bruce for short?" Alex smiled and nodded. Jacques broke out in a huge grin. I was glad to see him so happy. Being the youngest Mordecai had its challenges.

"Can I ride him now?" Jacques asked, looking at me then at Alex.

I looked over to Alexander and deferred to him. Alex replied, "Of course but with my assistance. Bucephalus, well, Bruce will need a little time to get to know you. Though having my scent helps."

The other kids had gathered around Batu, watching their younger sibling. Batu said to them, "We'll have to get your horses accustomed to Bruce. We should bring them outside." They all headed into the barn.

As I watched Jacques giving Bruce another carrot, I began to have a feeling that something wasn't right. I couldn't put my finger on what it was, and decided it was just my normal paranoia when it came to the kids.

Jacques swung up into the saddle while Alex softly spoke to the horse. Bruce rubbed his massive head against Alex's chest. Clearly, they were bonded. I hoped that the great beast would feel the same affection for my youngest. Alex walked beside them out into the corral. It was a touching scene. The love of horses was Jacque's birthright from his grandfather Omar and his biological father.

Alex stepped back, and Jacques began guiding Bruce around the corral. The kids brought the other horses out and stood with them next to the corral, where they could see their new friend. Bruce's ears went forward, and he whinnied at them. They had a similar reaction, and the kids calmly spoke to the horses to keep the situation friendly. I pulled out my phone to take a pic of Jacques to share with Omar.

Suddenly, Bruce started to buck. The other horses neighed and showed signs of distress. In a blur, Alex was next to Bruce, pulling Jacques down. He put him safely on the ground and pushed him toward the barn. Then I saw what had been causing my unease. A large cougar, crouched down at the tree line, was watching us. It broke into a run in a flash, leaped the corral fence, and closed in on the horse. The horse, wide-eyed, tried to escape but had nowhere to go. The muscular cat leaped over the fence then launched itself at Bruce. Alex turned and intercepted it midair. The cougar's claws raked the side of Alex's face. Alex wrapped his powerful hands around the cat's neck, holding it off, its jaws inches from his face. Blood covered them both as they rolled on the ground. The great cat's growls filled the air. Jacques grabbed a pitchfork that was leaning on the fence and started toward Alex and the cougar. I ran towards them without a clue of how to help. Suddenly a whooshing sound went past my head, and I saw the cat go limp. An arrow was embedded in the middle of the cat's forehead.

The kids climbed over the fence and ran to us. Alex pushed the dead predator off him. Jacques and I tried to help Alex up, but he waved us off and got to his feet. Bruce came over, reared up, and brought his front hooves down on the cougar's remains. We all stood silent for a few seconds trying to absorb what just happened. Alex went over to Bruce, stroked his neck, and said, "You will serve my son well. Jacques, take him into the barn."

Jacques led Bruce to the barn, and the other kids followed him with their horses. For the first time, I noticed Batu standing next to the corral with a bow in his hand. Alex walked over to Batu and did something much more difficult for him than fighting a cougar. He said to Batu, "Thank you! Your shot was extraordinary."

Batu gave a small nod and smiled. "Not that extraordinary for a Mongol."

I shot Batu a "What the fuck!" look, shaking my head.

Batu turned and headed into the barn to help the kids get their horses settled.

I looked up at Alex, his face had deep cuts, and his shoulder was bloody. I was starting to tear up, thinking about what might have happened. "Thank you for saving Jacques, but you are hurt."

Alex simply shrugged, touched my cheek, and said, "I'll be fine. Please excuse me while I go clean up," and turned toward the house.

We walked back to the house in silence. Once inside, I took Alex to my room, and he asked if I had a first aid kit so he could take care of his wounds. Of course, he was going to do it himself. "First, take a shower, then let me help you damn it!" I said in frustration.

He looked surprised by my attitude. "As you wish."

His natural scent, combined with the smell of his blood, was affecting me, but I tried my best to ignore it. I helped him take off his shirt. There were three long gashes in his shoulder, just under the small scar from my bite. Though he was in pain, his gaze suggested he was in "the mood." He put a hand on my neck and slid it slowly down until it rested on my breast. I pushed his hand away. "Knock it off! Get in the shower."

Alex headed to the bathroom and said, "I always had sex after a battle."

"No wonder we've had so many damn wars," I responded.

There was a gentle knock on the bedroom door, and Marie quietly said, "Mom?"

I went over to the bathroom and closed the door. "Come in."

Marie came in carrying a load of clothes and a jar of salve. "Guillaume said to bring these for Alex. He wanted to know if you need anything else." She put the pile on the bed, then looked around for the wounded warrior.

"He's in the shower getting cleaned up. He's got some bad cuts, but he'll heal quickly. I think that's all we need right now."

Alex came out of the bathroom with only a towel wrapped around his hips. "Tell Guillaume I appreciate his concern."

Marie tried not to stare. "Sure. Hope you're okay." She left quickly, looking a little embarrassed.

"Seriously? You had to come out just wearing a towel?" I shook my head. "Sit down."

He sat on the edge of the bed, but I motioned to the chair. Reluctantly he moved.

I got the first aid kit from the bathroom, went over to Alex, and put Guillaume's salve on his wounds. It smelled like eucalyptus and lavender. "Ah, that helps," Alex sighed with relief. "Perhaps it is just your gentle touch."

"Whatever." I started to put the bandage on his shoulder and felt his hands rest on my hips. I stepped away. "You can finish up without my healing touch. You just saved Jacques for the second time, thank you, but no warrior sex. I'll be downstairs."

"I did not mean to offend."

"That's the problem. I'm not offended." I left to check on the others. I know my response was confusing, but I did not have any energy to spare right now.

The kids, under the direction of Guillaume, were burying the carcass of the cougar. Even though it had attacked us, I felt sad about its death. Its kind had lived in these woods long before man. We were trespassing on its hunting grounds.

When they finished, I walked over and put my arm around Jacques. "Alex will be fine."

"He took on a cougar for me. I'll go check on him." He walked to the house.

I moved next to Batu. "You always take care of us. My debt to you has increased."

"Alex probably would have killed it eventually. I was just showing off." He smiled and turned towards me. He looked so handsome in the moonlight. "I will always be there for you. Alex lives to conquer and rule. I just want to serve you." He leaned down to kiss me, but I stepped away. "What is it?" He looked confused.

"I'm still conflicted about you, Alex, the baby, and my feelings." I stayed a few feet away and stared into the woods.

Grigoryi came out on the back deck and called out, "Dinner!"

We were all starving. We gathered in the dining room just as Teri, Henry, and Leif arrived from Seattle. The kids filled them in on what happened. Alex sat down with the wounds on his cheek left uncovered. Teri exclaimed, "I don't believe you guys! We leave you alone for a couple of hours, and this happens? Those cuts on your face could use stitches."

"It's really nothing. I will heal in a few nights. What news of Portland?"

Grigoryi handed Alex and the other undead shot glasses of blood. He was handing the whole bloody meals thing better now. The rest of us helped ourselves to grilled salmon, sweet potatoes, and coleslaw. Of course, there was a loaf of freshly baked bread. I was ravenous. Fortunately, I was not plagued with nausea like during my other pregnancies. Batu watched me load up my plate and smiled.

Henry leaned forward. "Sir Bart and Jeanne are still in Oregon and have contacted the community there. So far, they are cooperating under their supervision. Sir Bart said they had not encountered any hostility from the Common Caste. He reported they were very appreciative of you not beheading them."

"Good call Mom," Des declared.

"Way to make friends," Tomas remarked.

Marie wanted to talk about anything but vampires and cougar attacks. "So, the big news is we got a gig."

Henry looked proud. "They're playing a set in the park in Arlington."

Leif added, "As long as it doesn't rain."

Everyone looked at me for approval. "Great. When?"

"A week from Saturday. It's a local battle of the bands and wannabe stoner fest," Jacques answered.

"Will you be ready?" I had not heard more than a couple of tries at "Highway to Hell."

Tomas looked offended. "Of course, and we even have Cringe T-shirts."

Des grinned. "Our name came from the expression on Leif's face the first time we attempted a death metal song."

"Cool name," I said, which, from the expressions on their faces, made me think they now wanted to change it. "It kind of goes with Carnage. Maybe you'll open for them someday."

Teri touched Henry's hand. "He said the same thing last week."

Alex looked at Jacques. "May I hear you practice?"

"Sure," he smiled. "C'mon guys, let's go to Leif's."

They all agreed practice would help them get over the cougar attack, and they needed to go over some of the songs. Leif, Henry, Teri, Alex, and the kids, left and went to Leif's house. Batu and Guillaume excused themselves to check on the horses. I sat blissfully alone in the dining room when Grigoryi entered with a forlorn expression and a slice of cherry pie a la mode.

As he handed me the pie, I said, "Thanks! Please sit down."

Grigoryi sat across from me and anxiously drummed his fingers.

"What is it? The cougar?" I asked. "I think we'll all be more careful from now on."

"I miss the Baron. When he is around, I feel like things go better. Especially with Sir Batu and Sir Alex going at it. Maybe his presence would help keep them in line. Also, remember how he made the other cougar back off and leave the property." He paused, looked down, then added, "I'm sorry if I've said too much."

I took a bite of pie and considered my response. "Grigoryi, you never say too much. I don't need Tristan to be in charge, but you're right about him. His presence might help achieve a certain balance, make them behave better. I know it would be good for the kids. You're very smart. Thank you. I will think about it."

He blushed and looked down at the table. "Anytime." Then he quickly went back to the kitchen.

After a while, I got out my phone and texted His Highness, who was back in L.A.

Kids are OK. Puma attack. Alex hurt, Batu killed it.
Grigoryi says we could use your help.

Within minutes he replied,

Tomorrow night.

Protection was big for vampires. They hated it when anyone messed with their world. Be it beast or human. I knew he would love a chance to show his status, intelligence, and strengths to everyone in the House of Sun. Hopefully, it would give me a chance to focus on my pregnancy, my family, and my writing like a normal person. I could dream, right?

Chapter 46

Great Balls of Fire

Just as Grigoryi predicted, with Tristan back, things calmed down. One weeknight, while the kids were at band practice, Teri gave me a ride into Seattle to visit Pomp. She dropped me off inside the front gates. "Let me know if you need a ride home."

"I'm meeting Tristan here. He will take me home."

Because the Common Caste did not have the same healing ability as the Haute Caste, Pomp's neck would always have a gruesome scar. She hid the scar with a black lace choker and looked beautiful as ever.

Tristan was already there, sipping on a cup of his favorite beverage and snacking on a few chunks of raw sirloin. For some reason, the only time I felt at all queasy, was around raw meat. I kissed Pomp's cheek then sat on the far side of the sofa away from them.

Pomp smiled. "You look well, ma chère. You have caused such a fuss in the vampire world again with your pregnancy. You would not believe the bets being placed." A servant in a maid's uniform brought in a coffee set and macarons. "It's decaf," Pomp told me." Please help yourself."

"I can believe it. Ruben is incorrigible. He has finally stopped trying to get me to guess the paternity." I poured a cup of coffee and took two of the delicious French cookies.

Tristan was getting irritated by the talk about Ruben. "The children's band will play at a concert in Arlington tomorrow night. Would you be my guest?" he asked Pomp.

"Thank you, dear Baron, but after years of hearing Sir Henry's band blast uncivil, rude songs, I shall stick to the Baroque period. I wish the children well. I'm sure they are incomparable musicians."

I was surprised she was turning down an invitation from Tristan. "How are you doing?" I asked.

"Sleep is improving, but I would like more daytime help. Perhaps Leif could be persuaded to look after my security detail to make sure they are performing their duties properly."

"We can ask him, but he is pretty busy. There must be someone we can get to help."

Tristan interrupted me. "I will talk to him and explain the importance of keeping you safe."

With a look of satisfaction, she said, "Thank you."

Despite the yummy cookies, my gut registered a warning about the talk of sending Leif to stay with Pomp. "I'm sure Cramer would gladly give up his teaching job to keep an eye on things here."

"I would prefer he stay at the school to safeguard the kids." Tristan looked at me. "We should go. I want to spend time with the children tonight, and I want to talk to Leif."

I decided to let it go for now. We said goodbye and headed for Granite Falls. I liked riding in his Lamborghini. It brought back memories of some of our early years. I sat back and tried to relax, but I could not shake the feeling Pomp was up to something. "Who is her sugar vampire now?"

"What are you talking about?"

"I try to like her, give her the benefit of the doubt, but she just turned down your invitation. She has wanted your attention forever. She must have someone else to kiss up to. Someone very powerful. It could only be the Magus."

"After he let Sybil behead her? Miranda, you're being ridiculous. "

"The Magus apologized to Pomp and told her that wasn't supposed to have happened. Now she blames Sybil, not him."

"She has always wanted to be close to the seat of power. What I don't get is how does poor Leif figure into this? I don't want him near Pomp. I am sure she is up to something."

After a moment, Tristan responded, "If what you're saying is true, the only way to find out is to have him be your spy. Welcome to the world of courtly intrigue. You wanted to be the head of a House."

"Okay then, but you get to tell Marie." We were both quiet the rest of the drive.

When we arrived home, the kids were back from band practice and in the game room with Leif. Tristan went right in, but I stayed in the kitchen. I was always hungry, and I did not want to be near the coming storm. I feasted on a baguette and Brie. After a few minutes, I could hear Marie yelling at Tristan. It was apparent that things were not going well.

"No way! You can't make him! You're just trying to keep us apart!" Marie ran to her room and slammed the door.

A minute later, Tristan entered the kitchen with Leif. "I'm sorry for her outburst. This will only be temporary. You will be well compensated."

Leif looked unsure. "I gotta talk with Henry first about the club. I appreciate your confidence in me, but I'm also expecting some new goats." He looked to me for support.

"Talk to Henry, but I like having you here."

"I should go. Please tell Marie I'll see her tomorrow. Good night."

"Thanks Leif!"

Tristan merely nodded. When the door closed, he sat beside me. "I don't know how to deal with Marie. She does not accept my advice or trust my judgment. The boys are more reasonable."

I laughed, "The boys seem like they go along with you but rarely do what you say once you are not watching them. Marie just tells you to your face."

"Why does she care about him. He's rather average. She wants to be with a goat farmer? Any number of Haute Caste would love her attention."

"Did the Magus tell you to separate them? You obviously want to send Leif away too."

I turned towards him and looked into his deep blue eyes. He gently touched my hand. "No, he didn't. I'm not blind to any of those who are interested in Marie. He has not confided in me his feelings for her. I would have told you about that honor."

I knew it was a painful charade. "Honor?" I threw my hands up in the air. "I thought you might be more protective of your children. So, you are okay handing one over to the ringleader of the nocturnal, self-centered, blood-sucking maniac circus. What is wrong with you?"

I heard applause in the hall and saw my sons. They quickly ran up the stairs.

"You're half-vampire my love. They are three-quarters. You insult all of us when you carry on with a barrage of mortal inspired insults." He stood. "I'll be at the concert because I care about my children. Good night." He quickly left.

I hated to have the kids believe he was such an asshole.

Marie stood in the doorway, wiping her eyes. "Thanks Mom. They told me what you said to Dad."

"You're welcome. No one in the world can get me more pissed-off than your dad and the Magus." At least that was true.

She came over and gave me a hug. "Wait till you hear us tomorrow. That concert will be a game-changer." Marie went back upstairs, and I felt a vague, unexplained, feeling of unease.

Leif drove into Seattle to talk with Henry and Teri. He was always uncomfortable around Pomp. Even when she and Henry had been on good terms, Leif did not like how she treated mortals. He found them sitting in the main room of the club discussing renovations.

"Hey lover boy, how's it going?" Teri teased.

"I'm staying out of the fast lane with the little Baroness. I'm not stupid." He sat down beside them. "The place is looking good." The shiny metal fixtures and chandeliers had been replaced with antique bronze lights from the 1930s. The bar and tables were all old wood with little gashes and scratches that had been polished over. "Al Capone and Dillinger would've liked this place."

Henry leaned towards him. "What is troubling you?"

"The Baron wants me to provide daytime security for Pomp. I don't want to do it. I get my goats back this week, and I hate that bitch."

Henry looked amused. "They want to keep you away from Marie. What did you tell them?"

"That I'd talk to you first. I can't refuse, but you could. I will really owe you."

Teri appealed to Henry, "You can't put him in her house. Who knows what she might do to please the Magus?"

"I'll send a message to the Baron and tell him that you're too important to my operation and can't be spared." He paused and took one of his rings off. "Take this." He handed Leif a gold ring, with a symbol of the Eye of Horus, inlaid with a blue sapphire. "Wear this at all times. All of our kind will recognize it and know you are under my protection. You cannot be too careful. It's the Magus who dislikes your relationship with Marie."

"Fuck! The Magus? Why couldn't it have been anyone else," Leif said, slipping on the ring.

Teri reached into her backpack and pulled out a knife in a leather sheath. "Keep it in your boot. Practice reaching for it."

"Thanks, I will. I care about Marie, but I'm not ready to die for her. Does that sound chicken shit?"

"It makes you sound wise. We'll make sure you won't have to." Henry displayed a sly grin. "The Magus has let his emotions get the better of him. This has never happened before. Too bad Shakespeare did not live to see this." He frowned and touched Leif's arm. "Don't trust anyone except Miranda and the kids. The Magus has a lot of spies."

"The concert's tomorrow. I've got to help them set up. What should I do?"

"No problem," Teri replied confidently. "We'll be there."

Leif put the knife in his boot and practiced pulling it out quickly. "Take care of goats, look after the Baroness's place, dream job." He shook his head. "What a nightmare."

Teri sent me a text,

Tell Marie not to worry about Leif.

Before I went to bed, I knocked on Marie's door.

"What?" Marie called out, sounding very unhappy.

I opened the door and found her throwing a dagger into a pillow sitting against the wall. Every hit was dead center. "Your aim is good, but maybe you could find something else to use for a target. Teri said Leif would be okay."

"I know. I just talked to my goat-man. Henry has his back. Sometimes I wish Henry was my dad, and sometimes I wish Alex was. They both stood up to the Magus."

"It's complicated for your dad. I'm afraid one day he will have to stand up to the Magus too. Goodnight hon."

I closed the door but still heard a few thumps as she continued to practice. I was not looking forward to a confrontation between Tristan and the Magus. Maybe I would google a Black Panther versus a Komodo Dragon video. On second thought, maybe not.

My bed was a soft sanctuary of peace and quiet. I nestled under the covers in my comfy flannel nightgown. I felt satisfaction knowing Tristan hated it when I wore clothes to bed. Just as I started to drift off, Lug started barking. I looked out my window and saw Guillaume walking towards the back of the house. Then Batu went running outside.

"Mom!" Des called.

"What is going on?" I opened my door to find Des and Jacques looking worried.

"Tomas got dumped by Ashley. He's out in the yard with an ax." Des and Jacques were breaking the "Never Tell Mom" code.

I grabbed my robe, and we all went outside. Lug ran ahead to find Tomas. He was already talking to Guillaume and Batu. The ax was stuck in a log. "It's not my fault. She should have known I was going to ask her! She should have waited!"

"Before you kill any more trees, why don't you tell me what's going on," I said.

Lug jumped up on Tomas, but he was so upset he pushed him away. "Ashley is going to the prom with that quarterback jerk. He has the IQ of a horse turd."

"Why is she going with her?" Batu prodded him.

His eyes flashed hurt and anger. "He asked her first. I am so fucked!"

Guillaume spoke softly, "If it's meant to be, she'll come back to you."

"Chicks fuckin' love rock stars." Des proclaimed. "You'll see, she'll be at the concert."

"You know what Henry says, 'Play angry!'" Jacques asserted.

"Let's go back inside," I suggested, "I'm getting cold."

As we were walking back, Tomas asked me, "How could she choose him over me?"

"I think she felt taken for granted. She didn't like waiting for you to ask her. Guillaume is right. You have to let it go for now and see what happens. You might tell her you're sorry for not asking her sooner."

Batu whispered to me, "I don't mind being taken for granted." I shot him a "burst into flames" look.

Tomas was lost in self-pity. "She should apologize, not me!"

Shades of his father. I didn't know about anyone else, but I could not wait for the concert. I could use the distraction.

The concert was at the park in Arlington on Olympic Boulevard, the main street in the old part of town. The kids started setting up for their performance. Henry and Leif were good at calming their nerves. They could afford great equipment for a garage band, and they definitely would be heard. I just hoped they did not blow out the windows of the hardware store across the street.

Teri was in charge of the band wardrobe. Torn black jeans, T-shirts with skulls, voodoo dolls, and devils. Jacques was the exception. He wore a shirt that had a picture of a pug with a spiked collar. They were all wearing black eyeliner. Their hair had lots of product, and Marie's had red streaks. I had never seen them look so cool, sort of evil, and adult.

Cramer, keeping to the shadows, came up behind the stage and caught Tomas' attention. Tomas set his guitar down and went to the back edge of the stage. Irritated, Tomas demanded, "What do you want? We go on in a few minutes."

Cramer looked around to make sure no one was close enough to overhear and said quietly, "I have decided it would be in my best interests for me to leave, but I didn't want to go without telling you."

"Why are you leaving?"

"After working with all of you against the Magus, I want to get as much distance as I can from him and his minions. I am heading to Costa Rica, but please keep it to yourself. I can trust you to be discrete. I am proud of the progress you have made on the sunscreen, but the only way to keep it safe from the Magus is to make sure the only place the formula and process exist in here." He reached up and tapped Tomas lightly on the head.

"Will we ever see you again?"

"I doubt it, but I will try to find a way to let you know I am safe. I have two regrets. One that I ever took part in the Magus' plan to injure you. The other is that I won't get to see the House of Sun kick the Magus' ass." With that, Cramer turned and disappeared into the night.

Tristan appeared next to me. "All is well?"

"Not really. Brace yourself. Ashley broke up with Tomas."

"So, he ended it."

"No, she did it because he waited too long to ask her to the prom." I discreetly pointed to an area on the far side of the stage. "There she is."

Ashley stood with a small group of friends, including a couple of kids on the football team. She tried to look as though she had not noticed Tomas, but I saw her glance at him a couple of times.

"She is not worthy of him." Tristan turned so she would not be in his line of vision.

"They're still kids. They're allowed a learning curve. I don't know if they'll get back together or just be a high school memory. Lighten up. She was pretty nice to him when he got hurt."

I noticed a young woman talking to Jacques. It took a minute before I realized she was the waitress from the café in Mirror Point. Teri, Batu, and Guillaume joined us. I turned to Teri and pointed. "Remember her?"

"Yeah, the groupie waitress. Jacques is enjoying the attention. Good for him. At least she's not bugging Henry."

Maybe she was right. Amie was a few years older, but Jacques looked happy. Probably nothing to be concerned about. Leif and Henry were doing last-minute sound checks. Teri looked excited. "They're almost ready." She handed me earplugs and offered them to the others. "Trust me." We all put them in.

Des walked to the front of the stage and grabbed the mike. "Hello Arlington!

We'll let our music speak for us."

Tomas hit a cord that was so loud it made a few people flinch. Des started thumping a bass line, and the drums erupted like thunder. Jacques played a rhythmic melody while Des screamed, "Crash and burn baby! All night long! We'll stay together, baby, right or wrong!"

They were amazing! I hadn't realized how good they had become in such a short time. I could see the astonished looks on the faces in the crowd. Leif was off to the side selling 'Cringe' T-shirts. Henry stood on the side of the stage with a satisfied smile. Ashley had moved closer to the stage and stared at Tomas. He stayed focused on his music and never acknowledged her. A sure way to keep her attention. Des was playing to the adulation of the audience. Jacques kept glancing at Amie. So much was happening.

They played two of Henry's songs, one by Slayer and one by Metallica. A metal version of "Light My Fire" had the audience singing and dancing. Des did a great Jim Morrison tribute. Then Des announced the finale. "For my grandma, bless her soul."

Ashley walked closer to the stage until she was a few feet away from Tomas. A guy grabbed her arm and started to pull her back. Tomas started to jump down, but Ashley pushed the guy back and smiled at Tomas. Teri started towards the quarterback, but he turned away and disappeared into the crowd. Tomas played to his high school sweetheart. I breathed a sigh of relief and hoped Teri did not hurt anyone.

At the end of the song, Jacques thanked the crowd, waved, and left the stage. The other kids were soaking in the cheering of the crowd. A few seconds later, there was a flash of light behind the stage. We all thought it was part of the show, but then I saw Marie throw down her drumsticks and run off the stage. I turned to Tristan and yelled, "Follow Marie, something's wrong!"

Tristan ran after Marie, followed by Teri and Batu. Guillaume and I were close behind. As we came around the back of the stage, there was another flash of light. I saw Henry throw a fireball at two people in black hoodies, knocking them down. Marie was kneeling on the ground next to Leif. She turned to us. "He's hurt! Help him!"

The singed guys in the hoodies smelled of charred Common Caste. They scrambled to their feet and disappeared into the night. Batu and Guillaume carried Leif to the Jeep, with Marie following them. He was unconscious and beaten but no apparent serious wounds. I asked Teri to get the other kids home. Batu and Guillaume laid Leif in the back of the Jeep, and Marie climbed in beside him. Tristan drove, I got in next to him, and we took off for the hospital.

Later I found out that Alexander had also come to the concert. He had caught the attackers and locked them up in Leif's garage. I did not even know Alex had been at the there. Vampires! Teri told me the next day that it had taken half an hour to find Jacques. They had started to panic when they couldn't find him anywhere. Guillaume suggested they search the parking lot. They found Jacques and Amie in the back seat of her Mustang! At the end of the last song, they had gone to her car, unaware of the attack on Leif.

Chapter 47

The Magus is Watching

Leif was checked out at the hospital and had a slight concussion but would be fine. After a couple of hours, he was discharged, and we brought him back to the house. I assured Tristan that I could take care of Leif and convinced him to go back to his Seattle condo. The poor goat herder suffered a lot of physical abuse, trying to keep us safe. I was afraid it would continue as long as he was with Marie. I got Leif settled, had Teri keep an eye on him, and went up to my room to think about how best to protect Leif from further harm. I realized that the only one that had anything to gain from harming Leif was the Magus. I knew he had designs on Marie and would stop at nothing. After deciding what to do, I laid down and slept till late afternoon.

That evening I went to talk to Guillaume about what I had in mind to protect Leif. After hearing my plan, he agreed that it was the best way to keep Leif safe and said he would help arrange the details. That was the easy part. I was worried my daughter would hate me for what I was about to do, but I had to keep the young man from further harm. I called a meeting of the House of Sun at midnight. Henry, Guillaume, Batu, and Alex were the only vampires I included. I had to control who knew about what I was planning. That almighty asshole the Magus would find out eventually, but the later, the better.

At midnight we gathered in the living room.

"What's this all about?" Marie looked suspicious.

"I was concerned that the Magus might have compromised our security," Alex explained. I ordered replacements for all of our electronics.

Batu started handing out new phones to everyone.

Des said, "Sweet! This is better than my old phone." He immediately began downloading apps.

Alex cleared his throat. "Everyone! There's more. I've upgraded security measures after consulting with Guillaume. After the attack on Leif, he did a complete sweep of the grounds and found listening devices and hidden cameras. No doubt placed by order of the Magus, but there is no way to tell how long they had been in place. Besides the new phones, new tablets and computers are also in order." He looked over to me and said, "I would also like to do regular sweeps of the property. The offspring can assist." I nodded my approval. I knew it was difficult for him not to be in charge. "Good. I have new electronics for everyone."

I stood up. "Okay guys, go get all your old stuff!"

The kids ran upstairs to get their electronics. Alex opened a large box he had brought in earlier. He had made some salesman at Best Buy very happy. He started stacking new tablets and laptops on the coffee table. I knew it would not take long for the Mordecai siblings to get us connected again. From now on, we would be extremely careful about who we contacted in the vampire world.

A few minutes later, the kids brought down all their electronics, and Alex exchanged everything for the new equipment, then said, "To be on the safe side, I have also taken the liberty to replace the internet router with a more secure model." He placed a card on the table and added, "Here is the new password."

It didn't take long for the kids to finish setting everything up. Alex asked if it would be a good time to show them how to sweep the house for any cameras and listening devices. I told him to go for it. He and the kids went off to check every room in the house.

Two hours later, they produced a dozen pieces of spy equipment. Alex looked amused by their findings. "I believe we got everything. The Magus only had the hallways and common rooms bugged, not the bedrooms or bathrooms. He is a bit of a prude."

"That was decent not to watch us in our bedrooms," I said sarcastically and plopped down on the couch.

Marie scoffed, "Prude and decent? He's a dickwad."

Alex noted, "He thinks he is morally superior."

I looked over at Marie. "Now that we have that taken care of, we have to talk about something else. This was a difficult decision, and you won't like it, but it's the best way to keep Leif safe." Marie grabbed his hand. "Guillaume and I arranged for Hann to take Leif to the refuge until we know it is safe for him to come back here."

"No!" Marie cried. "Fuck the Magus!"

Leif turned to Marie. "From what you told me about Hann and the sanctuary, that might be a good idea. You know the Magus doesn't give up easily. It will only be for a little while."

Guillaume looked at Marie. "We are not ready to challenge him openly, but that night will come. Be grateful Sir Hann has promised to protect him."

Henry explained, "The ancient vampires do not challenge the Magus lightly. They believe it is their honorable duty to protect him." He paused then continued, "I was supposed to keep this secret, but now I think it is important for you all to hear this. Lady Cassandra told me that Leif has a special role in the future of our House. She didn't explain exactly what that role is, but I have learned never to question her visions."

Leif looked confused. "Lady Cassandra?"

Tomas replied, "She can see into the future. She was an oracle at Delphi."

"No shit," Leif scratched his head. "I always thought that those stories were just myths." He smiled at Marie. "You didn't know I was so special."

She dried her eyes and tried to smile. Marie trusted Hann and Cassie. "I hate to be apart from you, but it would be worse if you were hurt again." She squeezed his hand and sighed deeply. "I guess you have to go." She looked over at me and asked, "When is Hann coming to get him?"

"He should be here tomorrow night."

Chapter 48

Hannibal Ante Portas!

The vampires the Magus sent to attack Leif were still locked up at Leif's house. Guillaume and Henry, and I went to interrogate the prisoners. I told the kids to stay at our place. They were still pissed at Leif's attackers. If the four of them ever united against someone, I didn't know if I could stop them.

When we arrived, Batu was guarding the pair.

This was the first time I had gotten a good look at either of them. "Angel, I expected better of you."

"I'm sorry, Baroness, I had no choice."

I shook my head. "You always have a choice."

Carmen looked me over like she was disappointed and said with a sneer, "You're the Baroness?"

"And you're the Common Caste idiot who attacked a member of my House?"

She shot back. "I thought he was just a mortal the Magus wanted us to dispose of."

Angel shoved her. "Shut up!"

She shoved him back and displayed her fangs.

Guillaume was between them in an instant. "Show respect for the Baroness. She has allowed you to keep your heads. So far."

Angel continued, "The Magus sent us. You can't just make us disappear."

Henry's gaze was as cold as ice. "If you disappeared, do you think he would care what became of you?"

Carmen lowered her head and muttered, "We're fucked."

"Why Leif?" I focused on them, trying to get a glimpse of their thoughts.

Angel shrugged. "He didn't tell us."

Carmen looked at Henry. "I think he's jealous. Weird huh?"

"Shut up!" Angel was scared, but I could not tell if he was more afraid of the Magus or us.

I stared at him. "Let her speak."

Carmen grinned. Vampires loved gossip. "There are rumors that the Magus has a thing for your daughter. He's told everyone to leave her alone, so we figured when she's older, well, you know."

"I was afraid of that." I turned away and took a deep breath.

Guillaume asked, "What shall we do with them?"

"I don't want any more violence, but I don't want them here either." I turned back and looked at the pair. "I don't trust them. I want their deceitful asses sent back to L.A."

Henry said, "Very well. We shall allow you to continue to exist. Do not take this mercy as weakness. You may report to the Magus that you chased the young mortal away. That might help you stay on his good side."

Angel responded, "We can't do that. He will know we are lying."

"Then just tell the Magus you don't know what became of him. That is the truth." I went on, "Angel, you are only being spared because I once thought of you as a friend, but you betrayed me. I won't make that mistake again."

Angel looked down and said, "We are in your debt." Carmen stayed silent.

Guillaume drove them back to their car at the park in Arlington. Henry and I walked back to the house.

"It sucks that Angel did that. Do you think I was right to let them go?"

Henry gently patted my shoulder. "It was a clever move. If they had not gone back to the Magus, he would have grown suspicious. Also, Carmen will spread rumors about how you spared them. The Common Caste will appreciate that."

"The number of vampires I can trust keeps getting smaller. The L.A. undead will all stick with the Magus. Sarah, Ruben, and Pauline will never break with him."

We stopped on the back deck before going into the house. Henry turned to me. "You have earned the support of several ancients like Alexander, Omar, Cassandra, and me. A few others have yet to reveal their loyalty. I believe that the Magus will be careful in how he acts towards your house."

"Thanks. I got a sense of Angel's thoughts, and he was truly conflicted. I know there are others that feel the same way." I did not mention that Tristan was one of them, but Henry must have figured that out already.

We walked into the house and sat with Teri at the kitchen table. The pungent smell of kimchi filled the room. I took a forkful. "Yum. You're lucky."

"Because I eat kimchi?"

"This stuff smells awful but tastes like hot pickled heaven." I took another taste. "No, because you've got Henry." I turned to him. "I know I was suspicious of you at first, but I don't think my House of dumpster fire would've survived without you."

"Henry the Great!" Teri beamed.

Alexander walked in, rolling his eyes, having heard Teri's last comment. Batu and the kids followed him. Des sat down and heaped kimchi on top of a plate of noodles and fish. The others were not as keen on the spicy cabbage.

Batu looked at me. "Is that good for the baby? Wouldn't a mild diet be better?"

"I ate barbacoa tacos three times a week during my other pregnancies. Don't try and tell me what I can or can't eat." I loaded up a plate.

Alex grinned. "Since I have never experienced your condition, I defer to your judgment in all decisions regarding your current state."

Batu left in a huff. I ignored them both. The noodles were just what I needed to soothe my soul. "Teri, if you ever go to the dark side, you still have to cook for us!"

"Sure, just like Guillaume does," she replied.

Des snickered. "She would be the only vampire who likes the smell of garlic."

Teri looked around the room. "Wow! No one said don't transform. Does that mean you're all okay with it?"

Henry stood behind Teri and lightly rubbed her shoulders.

Marie, barely touching her food, said to Teri, "It's the only way you and Henry can be together."

Jacques looked at Henry. "Who are we to judge."

Tomas added, "Yeah, we're already 75% there."

Des grinned. "Just promise you'll have some regular food at the party afterward."

I frowned. "They don't party afterward. They go to a vampire ICU."

Undaunted, Des smiled. "Our House. Our traditions." He had a point.

Guillaume returned from dropping Angel and Carmen in Arlington and joined us in the living room. Batu came back in from wherever he had been sulking.

"Stop pouting," I told him.

Batu stared at me. "Should I return to Mongolia?"

I shook my head. "No! Get over yourself. We found out the Magus has been spying on us. I want you to stay, but you have to promise to run anything you might tell Princess Khunbish by me first. She can't know the truth about Leif. She is way too invested in kissing up to the Magus. Can you do that?" I knew I was putting him in a bad situation.

"I hate to choose, but my heart will never allow me to be disloyal to you." The puppy dog look of sadness combined with his sexual appeal was getting to me.

I searched his mind. "No matter who fathered my baby?"

"Yes!"

I could sense he was sincere. "Welcome to the House of Sun."

When we finished eating, I asked the brothers to do the dishes and said to Marie, Let's talk." We went out on the deck to give us a little privacy.

She pulled her hoodie up and sank in a chair. "Life sucks!"

"I know." I sat in a chair beside her. We both looked out at the river.

"The Magus is an evil, insane genius. He should hook up with Lady Sarah or some bitch who can't wait to fang him. I hate him! I can't even watch the bat houses anymore because he gave them to me. Fuck him! I hate that Leif has to leave here."

"I'm sorry I did not realize how much you and Leif care for each other."

She glanced at me. "You should know I wanted to have sex, but he said to wait."

"I like him even more now."

"Do you think Hann will be able to keep him safe?"

"The Barbarian? Not to mention Cassandra and a herd of elephants. Yes, absolutely!"

"What about Dad?"

"I think he'll do the right thing in the end." I hoped to reassure her and maybe myself too.

"He better!" She crossed her arms.

"Pulling all the surveillance equipment will send the Magus a message. Now let's go in and help your brothers."

The next night, sometime after midnight, a deluxe RV, with an elephant painted on the side, pulled into our driveway. The kids jumped up and yelled, "Hannibal ante portas!" The Carthaginian had arrived. Since their memorable stay at his sanctuary a few years ago, the kids had stayed in touch with him. After the "Battle of Vegas," I slapped and berated him for bringing the kids to the fight, riding his elephants. This was not going to be easy.

He appeared ten years older than most of the undead because the Magus had made an exception to the age rule and transformed the cunning and mighty warrior later in life. The burly vampire stepped down from the RV, followed by Dr. Mayi. The kids immediately ambushed Hann.

He looked them over. "You cannot be the scrawny troop I led into battle. You're tall and strong. What have you done with those unruly children?"

Marie laughed, "How is Leif?"

I was confused. Why was she asking Hann? He displayed a sly smile. "He is fine. His wounds have healed well."

Tomas whispered to me, "It's the name she gave the elephant that the Magus rescued when he was in Africa."

"Nice," I commented. Then I turned to our guest. "Welcome, Sir Hann. Thank you for coming."

He regarded me without warmth. "I believe you still owe me an apology."

I knew this was coming. We were both incredibly stubborn. I took a deep breath and said, "I'm sorry I slapped you." It took all my self-control not to add that I still thought he was wrong for bringing the kids into a battle.

"I understand that you were concerned for your children. I made peace with Sir Alexander after his defeat, so I can forgive you as well."

The kids stared at me to see if my head was going to explode.

I turned to present our goat herder. "This is the other Leif."

Leif shook Hann's hand "I owe you. I will be glad to help out at the refuge any way I can."

The old warrior nodded. "I'm sure you will."

Henry said, "Leif, we arranged for your goats to be taken to the refuge."

Tears welled up in Leif's eyes. "Everyone, I can't thank you enough for doing all this!"

Hann introduced Leif to Dr. Mayi and added, "Though he is a veterinarian, he can also look after any injuries from your recent attack."

Leif shook the doctor's hand. "Have you ever taken care of goats?"

Dr. Mayi nodded. "Yes, they are delightful creatures."

Marie shook her head. "You'll have your goats, so you won't even miss me."

He grabbed her in his arms and kissed her. It was the sweetest moment till Des said, "Get a room."

Batu loaded Leif's duffle bag into the RV They had to leave soon. We did not

338

want to take the chance that there still might be minions of the Magus spying on us.

I said my goodbye to Leif. "You deserve a good life. I'll do what I can to make that happen."

He just said, "You gave birth to Marie. She's all I want, well besides my goats."

Hann went over to Alexander and walked away with him to be out of earshot of the others. "Miranda and the offspring's births changed everything. The Magus is responsible for the challenges he now faces. I appreciate that you have respected the code even when its creator has not."

Alexander replied, "Speaking of the code, when will the Baroness get a copy?"

"Soon."

"Is it true you do not know if the child is yours?"

"I suggested that Miranda could consult with Lady Cassandra, but she declined. How much did you bet?" Alexander asked with a smile.

"You should have asked who I bet on. I put my money on Batu!"

Alexander shook his head. "One defeat was not enough for you?"

Just before dawn, Hann, Leif, and Dr. Mayi said their final goodbyes, got into the RV, and headed off to the refuge.

At three in the morning, the next day the RV arrived at Hann's sanctuary. Dr. Mayi woke up Leif. He stumbled out in front of the ranch house and heard a rumbling sound, then trumpeting as he looked about his new home. A woman in a Raiders jacket and black jeans came around the building's side, leading one of the massive creatures. He had been told about the elephants but seeing them up close was a remarkable sight.

She came up to the overwhelmed young man. "Welcome to our home. I am Cassandra, and this," she said, patting the elephant's trunk, "is also Leif."

Hann and Dr. Mayi joined them. "All is well?" The warrior kissed her cheek.

"Of course. I thought he might like to meet his namesake."

Dr. Mayi asked, "The students took good care of my friends?"

"Yes. They also helped with the goats when they arrived." She turned to Leif. "Your goats are in that fenced-in area behind that building." She pointed to Hann's museum.

He started to go towards them. Cassandra grabbed an arm. "The goats can wait until the morning. Now you must rest." She touched his forehead. The softness of her hand was soothing. She smelled of fresh lavender. "Your concussion has not healed fully. I will make you some tea and show you to your room."

It was the first time Leif had felt a vampire make suggestions to him that felt irresistible. "Sure, I'm pretty tired."

"You are named after a noble explorer." She led him into the kitchen and poured a cup of tea, and said, "You have a rich heritage."

He inhaled the scent of mint in the tea before taking a sip. It was sweetened with honey, and it soothed him. "I was a neglected foster kid. The best thing that ever happened to me was when Henry helped me get clean and off the street. I'm not special."

"We will see about that." Lady Cassandra smiled, and Leif felt like someone unlocked a door to a hidden part of his being.

"You're different, weird." He stared at her. "But in a good way."

"Help yourself to whatever you would like. There's mortal sustenance in the fridge and cupboards. Your room is the last one on the right down the hallway. Get some rest young Viking. I must confer with Hann."

Leif finished his tea. The only Vikings he knew anything about played football in Minnesota. Leif grabbed a box of cookies out of the cupboard and went off to find his room. Having been a foster child made it a little easier to accept being uprooted, but he would miss Marie and his home. "At least my goats are here."

Chapter 49

Betrayal

After a period of chaos, the vampire world quieted down. Word had been conveyed to the Common Caste that I had no desire to harm or destroy them. I tried not to consider what the Magus might be up to as I settled into my pregnancy. Everyone made an effort to play nice to lower my stress. I grew plump and focused on setting up a nursery. I loved the dull, quiet days and nights.

The Portland undead were responsive to Bart and Jeanne's guidance, giving them a pipeline to the larger Common Caste underground. They let it be known how merciful I had been.

Sybil was being kept in a small, locked house on the Magus' estate. In her weakened state, she appeared to be 90 years old. She was cooperating, giving blood samples and acting repentant, probably hoping for a pardon.

As the months went by, Tomas and Des spent most of their time in the garage lab working on the super sunscreen. Tomas had told me to keep the formula secure, and that he had not kept any of his research on a laptop or tablet. He went old school and wrote it out in notebooks. Tomas took Cramer's departing words to heart and burned the notebooks the day after Cramer had gone off the vampire grid. Cramer had played both sides, no doubt incurring the ire of the Magus, and I hoped he would be able to stay hidden. Lucky bastard! I wondered if Tomas and Des would ever successfully develop an effective undead sunscreen without his former chemistry teacher. I saw no harm in their experiments and was glad to see the brothers getting along so well.

The triplets had turned eighteen, and thankfully the graduation ceremony was during the day, so we didn't have to deal with a horde of the "night crew." Teri and I were tearful, not quite ready to see the kids, now young adults, move on to the next phase of their lives. The basketball coach was sorry to lose Tomas, his star player. Ashley and Tomas had finally broken up, but he took it in stride. Marie had been accepted to Harvard, and Des had an offer from Stanford. They both had decided to go to the University of Washington in Seattle along with Tomas. They would not admit it, but they were protective of me and wanted to stay close.

Jacques would miss his siblings, who were going off to college, but I hoped it would give him a chance to blossom. The band was on hold for the time being, with school and Leif still at the elephant sanctuary. The Magus's obsession with Marie still lurked in the background, but I hoped we wouldn't have to deal with it until at least after the baby was born.

Jacques had continued to see Amie, and one day asked if she could come over for dinner. He was seventeen, and I knew that trying to stop his relationship with this young woman would only drive it underground. I wanted to know more about her, so I agreed and asked Guillaume to make his fabulous stew for the occasion.

I looked in the mirror and smiled at the signs of aging that greeted me. For some reason, this baby was suppressing my vampire DNA and allowing my body to age. I had tiny wrinkles and a little sag to my jawline. Most women would have been slapping on the anti-aging cream, but not me. I was starting to look my age of forty-one, and I hoped it would continue after the birth, a month away. The long sunny days of summer had reduced the amount of time spent with the undead, but fall would be here soon. Alex and Batu made few demands on me, yet always let me know they were available. Teri watched over me like a hawk.

It was difficult getting into and out of chairs, but it did not seem as bad as my previous pregnancies. I put on a blouse that resembled a small tent and slowly pulled on super stretchy leggings, then went down to the big dinner with Amie. Jacques had invited Alexander and Tristan, which I thought was a bit much, but I realized he just wanted to impress them with his older girlfriend.

Tristan found me in the kitchen and whispered, "You look radiant."

"I feel like a stuffed turkey, but thanks."

"What do you think of this Amie? First the goat herder and now a waitress? Not to mention the pizza delivery girl. What is it with their taste in companions?"

"You forget I used to be a waitress in my folk's café!" I hated it when he acted like a snob. Wisely he didn't respond.

There was a knock on the door, and Jacques ran to get it. As Amie walked in, I looked at her bulging middle and blurted out, a little too loudly, "You're pregnant!" Then, I sniffed the air. "and you've got HH blood!"

Her mischievous grin put us all on guard except for Jacques. "So are you, and so do you," Amie retorted. She was not at all intimidated by us. "In case you are wondering, Jacques is the father."

"Interesting social skills," Alexander commented.

I glared and took a step toward her. "Did the Magus put you up to this?"

Tristan held me back. "Calm down."

Marie looked her over. "You're sure it was my bro? You must've been the last virgin in Mirror Point."

Amie's eyes flashed anger. "Do DNA testing if you want."

Alexander, always calm in a crisis, said, "Let us discuss this surprising turn of events over dinner."

I felt sorry for Jacques. He tried to hold Amie's hand as we walked into the dining room, but she would not have it. She sat down, looked at Alex, and said, "You're his biological father. I want you to know that I'm honored to carry your grandbaby." Alex stared at her but said nothing.

"Who put you up to this?" I exclaimed. I was sorry to crush Jacque's dream of true love, but we needed some answers. I was also amazed he had been able to keep this secret for so many months. This was not the kind of blossoming I had in mind.

"I'm starving. I'll tell you while we eat." Amie said.

I decided to humor her because she was pregnant. "Sure, why not."

Grigoryi and Guillaume filled the bowls of the mortals, and glasses of O-positive for the nocturnals. The vampires had stopped eating raw meat around me as it made me queasy.

She glanced at Jacques, then stared at Tristan and me. "Nothing personal. You are right. I have HH blood, and I've been promised to be transformed after the baby is born. I hung around the Funeral Pyre for months, and none of you paid any attention to me till I met Angel. He set this up with the Magus. I'm under the Magus' protection now. He is taking care of all the expenses and will take care of me after I give birth."

That explained her attitude.

Jacques tried his best to keep from tearing up. "You don't care about me at all?"

Tristan leaned forward. "Why did you come here tonight?" His voice was cold, and so was his gaze.

She bristled. "To meet the family."

Batu did not hide his disgust. "I am sure the Magus wants Jacques' family to care for the infant. It was clear that Amie is devoid of maternal instinct. I would make a better mother."

Des looked at her. "What a bitch."

"I don't care what you think of me. I'll be Haute Caste after I hand over this kid." She took a spoonful of stew. "Needs a little salt."

That was the last straw for Guillaume. "You are not only a scheming opportunist but ill-mannered as well."

She just rolled her eyes.

I had a long list of stronger insults for her but thought of my grandbaby. "Have you had good maternity care?"

"Yeah, Lily has been giving me check-ups and says the baby and I are fine. Jacques' son will be here in about six weeks."

"Son?" several voices asked.

"It's a boy," she looked over at Jacques and said, "you can name him. I never talk to my parents, so no one I used to know has any idea about this. I'm ready to start a new existence after I give birth. Jacques, you may no longer have a girlfriend, but you'll have a son." There was a tiny hint of sympathy in her voice.

Jacques stormed out of the room. My heart broke for him. "Amie, we will raise Jacque's son. You will not be allowed any contact with our family after the birth. You threw away the chance to have a relationship with a decent, intelligent, and kind young man of means. I cannot feel sorry for you, not after what you've done. You should leave now! I don't want to hear from you again until you go into labor."

"I hope he looks like Jacques," Marie snarled.

Amie gave Marie a dirty look and said, "I guess it's time to leave and headed for the door.

Alexander rose. "I'll walk you out."

Tristan touched my hand and said, "I support your decision."

Though I didn't need his support, I did appreciate it.

Des chimed in, "Jacques, that little fucker! Am I the only virgin left in this house?"

Guillaume replied, "The world is grateful for your restraint."

Marie fumed, "Jacques and the baby deserve better."

Tristan cleared his throat, then announced, "I have something to tell you all." Everyone fell silent and turned to Tristan. "Miranda, Lady Cassandra prophesized this. I asked her who might be the father of your child. She told me that Batu's and Alexander's bloodlines would continue. Until now I did not understand. Since Alexander is Jacques' father, Batu, that means you also will be a father."

Batu's face softened. "I knew it! Fate has at last been kind."

I touched my cheek and thought about my aging skin. "This baby does not have HH blood. That is why the pregnancy is normalizing me." I looked at Batu. "I'm carrying your baby! You should let Princess Khunbish know. I need a few minutes alone to think. I'll be down by the river. Someone, please check on Jacques."

Outside Alex and Amie stood beside her Mustang. Jacques watched them from an upstairs window.

"Look, I didn't mean to hurt Jacques. I just saw my chance and had to take it." She hoped to get on the good side of the powerful ancient.

"The damage is done. I am grateful my lineage will continue, and Jacques will recover. He is stronger than you realize." Alex looked into her eyes and saw a predator. "Contact me when you are going into labor, and I will let the Baroness and Jacques know to prepare. I have known ambitious women like you throughout the centuries. They were not often adept at choosing the victorious side. I hope you make better choices in the future."

"I wish I could know you better," she tried to kiss him, but he quickly pushed her aside and walked back into the house.

Jacques trembled with anger as he watched them and clenched his fists. "Vampires! I hate them all! My son will never be like them."

Tristan and Alexander had gone to speak with Jacques. It was near midnight as I walked down to the river. I could hear a coyote in the distance and the sound of the river rushing towards the Sound. I put my hand on my extended abdomen and felt the little Mongol move inside me. I had not missed the drama during the summer, but now it was back, only without snakes. I could swear Amie took lessons from Sybil in manipulation and treachery. The Magus had been keeping a close watch on us and those around us. I knew he had a database of people with HH blood, which enabled him to find someone with the rare blood type to mate with one of my sons. Jacques had been the most susceptible to her charm and never had a chance. Amie had not been charismatic tonight, but she could pour it on when she needed to. My dad once told me that girls are just little women, but men can't seem to help acting like boys.

Batu joined me at the riverbank. "May I touch you?"

Even in the darkness, I saw the glimmer of sweet joy in his eyes. "Sure. The baby has been moving around a lot."

He rested his hand on my belly and said something in Mongolian. The baby kicked, and Batu beamed.

"What did you say?"

"That I would buy the child a fine horse." I stared at him thinking it was an odd thing to say. He smiled and added, "it's a Mongolian custom." He pulled me into his arms, and his kisses did not disappoint.

As Alex and Tristan approached Jacques' bedroom, they heard a loud thud. Tristan opened the door without knocking. "Jacques, we wish to speak with you."

Jacques was cradling his bloody right hand next to a hole in the wall. Alex went into the bathroom, got a small towel, and handed it to him. "I appreciate the fact that you hit a wall instead of Amie."

His eyes got big. "I would never hit a woman!"

Tristan said, "Mortals, yes, but no one would ever be critical of you if you had to fight off a vampiress."

Alex gestured for him to sit on the bed. Alex and Tristan pulled up chairs facing him. "Jacques, I'm sorry your first experience has given you a bleak view of females."

Tristan shook his head. "You did nothing wrong. She took advantage of you."

Jacques looked at Alex. "I saw her try and kiss you outside! How could I have been so stupid."

"She is very ambitious. Amie wants to be close to a powerful vampire." Alex enjoyed saying that in front of Tristan. "I told her to inform me when she is in labor. I do not want her to contact you or your mother directly."

"Attention from the Magus must have gone to her head, foolish mortal. He would not have considered her to bear your child if not for her blood type." Tristan looked angry. "I'm sorry I did not see this coming."

Alexander patted Jacques' shoulder. "We will rejoice when your son is born."

At times Tristan wished that he had the emotional control and empathy of Alexander. He would never admit that to anyone, and even then, only rarely to himself. "You should be the one to tell your Grandfather Omar."

"Maybe tomorrow night. I just can't right now."

"As you wish," Tristan said, and they both left their son alone to lick his wounds.

It did not take long for his siblings to invade his room.

Des told him, "We would take her out, but she's pregnant." He sat on the bed next to Jacques.

"Yeah, that crossed my mind too," Jacques said quietly.

"Harsh, little Bro," Tomas said. "But seriously, we have to be careful about the blood types of people we fuck."

Marie sat in one of the chairs. "Leif is O-positive."

"Pomp has Common Caste blood," Des mentioned.

Marie rolled her eyes. "You have worse taste than Jacques. No offense Jacques."

Tomas looked out the window, then turned back to them. "Mom and Batu have made up. I kind of felt sorry for him. I guess it's only right he finally gets to be happy."

Jacques said, "I hate her! But I will love my son."

Tomas nodded. "We all will!"

Then they had a group hug causing Des to lose his balance and fall on the floor. Somehow, he made Marie push against Tomas and knock him on his ass. Jacques laughed and said, "Team Mordecai!"

Chapter 50

Upheaval

I avoided the medical world whenever I could, due to the physical peculiarities of our family. Lady Cassandra assured me she was an adept midwife. The kids, Teri and I went to the Sanctuary to prepare for our newest member's arrival. I had Dr. Mayi as a daytime backup if needed. It was a chance for Marie to see Leif again. I had given strict orders through Tristan that the Magus was not allowed to be anywhere near us. My father and Anastasia had also helped convince the Magus to stay away.

We had flown down to the Twentynine Palms tiny airport, where Dr. Mayi picked us up. I had a week to go and handled the flight okay. At times I could not tell if I felt turbulence from the plane or the baby. We pulled into the refuge, and I teared up as Marie ran to Leif. They looked so happy to be together once more. Leif looked like he had recovered and was healthy again. The shadow of the vampire world felt minimal, here amongst the elephants. I hoped it stayed that way.

The bros high-fived their band manager. I had to admit, for a mortal, he fit in well. I think Leif would have hugged me, but it would have been hard for him to put his arms around me in my current condition. "How is it going?" I patted his shoulder.

"I'm fine, and Dr. Mayi has taken good care of my goats. Improved their feed...."

Des interrupted, "You're hanging with Cassandra the Oracle, Hannibal the Barbarian, and his elephants, and you're excited about farm animals? Fuckin' goat herder." He shook his head.

"I've got to lay down." They all looked at me with apprehension. "It's not time, and I just need a nap. Will one of you bring my suitcase in?"

Jacques grabbed it and followed me into the quiet, luxurious ranch house. The room I had shared with Tristan on the last visit was waiting for me. Fresh lavender scented the air, and I laid on the bed. Jacques left and I started to drift off.

An hour later, I woke as painful tremors gripped my body. I grabbed my phone and called Tomas and told him to get Dr. Mayi.

The kids rushed into my room with Dr. Mayi, asking questions all at once and looking concerned. I waved them to silence and told them to wake Cassie hoping it was close enough to sunset for her to be safely up and about.

Without another word, the kids began closing all the drapes and turning on the lights. Dr. Mayi sat beside me as another pain ripped into me. "May I examine you?" he asked.

"Yes, and this is not the time to be fuckin' polite!"

The kids began taking commands from the vet. He told them to wash their hands and arms then bring clean towels, ice chips, and damp washcloths. I lay on my back, propped up on pillows waiting for my water to break. I was trying not to yell bloody hell when the pain hit. Batu and Tristan were not due until later tonight, so there was no one here to cuss out.

Dr. Mayi gently removed my leggings and undergarments and pulled a sheet over me as he examined me. I bet he was more comfortable with elephants. "You're dilated, but you've got a way to go."

Just then, my water broke. "Damn it!"

"I guess I was wrong, maybe not that long now," Dr. Mayi said and told the kids to get some clean sheets.

Cassandra came in wearing purple scrubs and carrying a stick of rose-scented incense. "Good evening," she said calmly. We all just stared at her. She placed the incense in a holder, then took over. "Change the damp bedding and place two thick bath towels under her." My minions got to work. "Mayi, cleanse the birth area with this soap." She handed him a mud-colored chunk of something that smelled like a pine forest. "Jacques, open a window but not the drapes." Everyone did as she commanded.

I winced as the contractions began coming closer together. "Fuck that hurt!" My body was operating on its own. Everything tensed up as a wave of excruciating pain would hit, then it would ease, and I would be able to take a deep breath. I trusted my body to do what women had been doing since the beginning of time. I tried to focus on the new life I would soon hold in my arms, but another contraction hit me. "Damn!"

Cassandra stood over me and whispered in some ancient tongue, then smiled and put her hands on my forehead. "Soon. Everything takes less time for you. Your daughter of the House of Sun is ready."

"Let's get this baby delivered!"

Cassandra smiled and replied, "Of course."

Like my other pregnancies, I felt like I was about to give birth to a baby the size of a Sound Ferry. My body was trying its best to launch its latest creation. Dr. Mayi repeatedly took my vitals, trying to be helpful and looking worried. I clenched the sheets with white knuckles.

What seemed like hours went by with Cassandra keeping a constant watch on me. Marie gave me ice chips, and Des held a cool washcloth on my forehead. Tomas was handling communications as I wasn't in any mood to talk to anyone. Jacques was acting as a nurse's aide, getting whatever Casandra requested.

The contractions started coming right on top of each other. This kid was ready.

"She's coming!" I screamed as Batu burst into the room, followed by Tristan and Hannibal.

"Dr. Mayi pulled back the sheet, and the biggest contractions yet racked my body. After a couple more, Cassandra said, "Keep pushing, you are almost there."

A sudden cry broke the tension in the room, and Cassandra held up our

348

daughter like the scene from the Lion King. She spoke an ancient blessing and laid her in my waiting arms. Everyone was crying tears of joy. Batu bravely came over and kissed my forehead while he touched the baby's cheek. "I'm sorry I did not get here sooner. She is so beautiful." The love in his soft brown eyes was killing me.

"You saw her arrival! Let the Princess know. She will be called River Khunbish Ortega-Mordecai."

"I approve," he pronounced in a serious tone.

I glared at him. "Seriously?"

Batu smiled and said, "I'm kidding. You can name her anything you want after what you've been through."

Des opened another window. "I'm gonna call her stinky."

Hann smiled at me. "You have created your own army."

I wiped my eyes and kissed my little one's forehead. "You arrived so quickly." That was my shortest labor. Just when I was getting good at this, I knew I was done. "This will be my last baby."

Dr. Mayi cut the umbilical cord and cleaned up the after birth. The kids were getting queasy. Cassandra began washing River and asked everyone to leave except Dr. Mayi. Tristan nodded. "Well done." His gaze gave away his affection for me. He guided Batu out the door.

I held River on my chest and closed my eyes. When Dr. Mayi stitched me up, I barely felt a thing. He was a gifted surgeon. Cassandra checked the baby over and said, "Your infant is healthy in every way. You had little blood loss."

The word blood got my attention. "I don't want any samples of our blood to end up in the hands of the Magus. But I want to know her blood type."

Cassandra gave a reassuring smile. "Of course. Use your gifts. What do you detect?"

I sniffed my little one's tiny head. "AB like her father." Cassandra nodded. "I'm glad for her." The ancient vampire touched my hand, and I felt a sensation of comfort wash over me.

"I want to thank you and Hann for taking care of me and for keeping Leif safe."

Cassandra nodded and said, "He has untapped, unrecognized potential. That Viking comes from a long line of warriors. I am quite impressed by Marie's choice."

I was amused, thinking about him taking care of his goats. "Whatever you say."

River and I were cleaned up and carefully examined one more time by our veterinarian and Cassie. They declared that only two people at a time could visit for short intervals so as not to overtax us. No one argued with Cassie, ever! I asked to see Batu alone first. He came in and stared at us with puppy dog eyes. "I'll sleep in here tonight to watch over you and get you anything you want. This is not debatable."

"No problem Sir Batu."

"Smartass." He kissed me. "She's going to be just like you, isn't she?"

"You better hope so. I would love some coffee!"

"Sure, but you're still on decaf. Tristan will be in next. There is some Haute Caste bullshit going on. You can tell him to leave at any time."

We both knew he didn't need to tell me that. My heart hurt for Batu. "It's okay. Send him in."

Tristan politely allowed Batu to exit, then he came in and closed the door. He carried a small leather-bound book. His faint scent of primal forest reminded me of past encounters. He sat on the edge of the bed, and a faint smile came to his lips. "You look well, all things considered."

"I was run over by the happy truck, and this spilled out the back," I said as I kissed River's head.

"I will look after her, just as I have cared for her siblings. In my eyes, they are all Mordecai."

"Ortega-Mordecai. I think it's important they all share the royal name. Thank you for understanding." I looked into his handsome countenance and deep blue eyes. "We have a lot to talk about when we get back to Granite Falls."

"I know." He kissed my forehead. Then he handed me the book. "You asked about the code. This is it. Blood Discipline: The Book of Vampires. Every House has a copy translated into their native language."

"Only you would think now is a good time for that," I said, shaking my head as Batu entered with my coffee.

"Sir Batu, you should read this as well. All Haute Caste should know its contents," Tristan told him.

Batu nodded, and Tristan said, "I'll leave you now." I traded the tome for the coffee. "I'm so tired I can't read. Will you read it to me?"

"Sure." He sat on the edge of the bed and eagerly opened the book, holding it so I could see it. The large decorative script reminded him of medieval illustrated manuscripts. It had an intricate moon adorning the first page. Each succeeding page had one law. He began reading "The Immortal Vampire Book of Laws." I took a sip of the decaffeinated brown fluid and laid back on my pillows. "Our kind has been given abilities and powers unknown to the rest of creation, to watch over lesser mortals. Those with the gift must develop the discipline to control it."

"This reeks of the Magus," I observed.

"I. It is prohibited to take the life of an innocent mortal."

II. After consultation with the Head of a House and notification of the Magus, a Worthy Target may be designated and removed from society.

III. Vital sustenance may be taken from any mortal, as needed, as long as they are not bled dry."

I interrupted. "How considerate." Batu ignored my comment. He was like a Boy Scout trying to figure out how to get his blood-sucking merit badges.

"IV. The criteria for a deserving mortal to be transformed shall include intelligence, a personal code, unusual talent, undeveloped potential, aspirations about to be cut short, reverence for our kind, passion, the courage to take a life when necessary, and an intense desire to become a vampire. The individual may be deemed acceptable if they have an exceptional ability to contribute to vampire society.

V. The transformation ceremony shall be carried out by The Magus or the Head of a House when all requirements have been met.

VI. Any transgressions of the code will be judged by the Magus and the

Parliament. Punishments will be meted out by the Head of the House of the transgressor."

He looked up at me. "So that makes you the designated executioner."

"Keep going. The Magus and the Parliament will not make decisions for my House.

"VII. The survival of our kind depends on loyalty and secrecy. A life may be taken without prior permission if an immediate threat to an immortal or our society is posed.

VIII. All will obey the decrees of the Magus and the Parliament."

"That's enough!" I told him before he could go any further. "Give me that book." I took it with my free arm and threw it against the wall, missing the trash can.

"Miranda, you can't do that."

"You can keep it. I never want to see it again. Please leave us alone for now and tell everyone we need to rest."

He went over, picked up the book, and left without an argument. It was hard to see him so conflicted trying to be the perfect nocturnal soldier. I fell asleep, cuddling River, thinking of how I would protect her from the insanity of the vampire society.

The Magus received a phone call from Tristan. "Excellent news. Give my congratulations to the Baroness and Sir Batu. I know Princess Khunbish will be quite pleased. I should like to see them."

Tristan cleared his throat. "She does not wish to have any other visitors. I must insist you respect her wishes for the well-being of the Baroness and the infant."

"Surely, you can understand the importance of our world knowing of my acceptance of another royal child, especially since she has a common blood type."

"I hope that you will forgo a visit at this time. I will communicate your concern and protection for now. I would insist that you allow the Baroness to meet with you at a later date in Seattle. Good evening dear Magus." Tristan hung up before he got a response.

The next day River and I slept, ate, and slept some more. Finally, in the late afternoon, I let Dr. Mayi supervise the siblings with the baby, and I took a heavenly shower. I insisted on one cup of caffeinated nirvana to help me take life on. Jacques spent the most time holding River. I think he was preparing for the arrival of his son. Henry and Teri stayed in Granite Falls to monitor the situation with Amie. So far, all I'd heard was that she was healthy and eager to get past the pregnancy and give us the child. It would be like raising twins. After raising triplets, I told myself it would be a piece of cake. Grigoryi and Guillaume were busy getting the nursery ready. I could not wait to get back home to my refuge. I fed my daughter then fell asleep while waiting for the night people to rise.

A few hours later, Marie was in the massive barn that held the most recent rescue from the Congo. She had no fear of the great beast as she reached up to pet him. "Gentle giant," she muttered.

"Yes, he is magnificent." Startled, Marie turned, saw the Magus, and prepared to run. "I'm fond of this Leif." He wore a pale blue silk shirt and black jeans. His dark straight hair fell across his forehead. For the first time, Marie realized she was beginning to catch up in terms of his apparent age. She fought the effects of his charm.

"You should not be here. My mother and I don't want to see you or talk to you."

"Marie, we could have a fascinating discussion about your destiny."

"You orchestrated my brother's injury and the attack on Leif and Amie's pregnancy." Defiance shone in her dark blue eyes. "There's nothing I want to discuss with you."

"There are so many secrets I would love to reveal." The Magus' gaze was intense and slightly creepy despite his handsome features.

She stared at him, sizing up her opponent. "Leave me, my family, and our friends alone." Then she boldly walked past him. Once outside, she paused, turned, and added, "I'm not interested in anyone old as dirt." Then Marie ran to the house.

The Magus looked at the mighty bull elephant. He walked over and rubbed his trunk. The magnificent beast remembered that he had helped rescue him. He touched the Magus gently with his trunk. "You understand gratitude. I fear the Royals will have to learn to appreciate and respect me the hard way. So be it!"

Marie sensed a tremor as she entered the house and warned the others.

Chapter 51

The Showdown

Through the window, I watched Tristan, facing the Magus, raising his arms to call up his powers to try and stop the more powerful ancient being. The Haute Caste stood in a line behind Tristan to shield the kids who refused to stay in the house. Cassandra and Batu were with me as I cradled my newborn.

A tremor rattled the house. "Fuckin' Magus," I muttered. "It's time." Cassandra nodded. We both knew what I must do, though we had never discussed it. I turned, and Batu grabbed my arm to hold me back. "I have to do this. Please keep her safe." I gently handed him our sleeping infant. He stood ready to sacrifice himself for our baby and me. "Stay here! I must confront the Magus for my family and all of the House of Sun!'"

Cassandra gently put her hand on Batu's arm and said, "Batu, she must do this. Trust her power."

He acquiesced and sheltered River in his strong arms. I went out in the yard and stood next to Tristan, facing the Magus. I could feel a great amount of energy building up in my ex-husband. "Don't my love," I said to Tristan. I stared at the Magus. "Listen to me." The low rumble ceased as the preeminent vampire looked at me coldly. Omar started to come between us, but I yelled, "Stop! Stop it all of you." I knew the Magus could cause great harm.

It was as if the Magus was seeing me for the first time. "You believe a mortal can thwart my plans? Keep me from my destiny with Marie?"

Leif and the brothers held Marie back, but I could still hear her say, "Fuck your ancient ass!"

Alexander, Anastasia, Jeanne, Bart, Hann, and Omar stepped up and formed a semi-circle, with Tristan and me in the middle facing the Magus. There was an eerie silence. Even the elephants in their barns were quiet. Then a tremor began to rumble again.

Leif ran out and stood several feet from the Magus. "Destroy me and be done with it. Spare them!"

Alexander pushed Leif aside. "Leif, sacrificing yourself will solve nothing. This is not about you. If you try that again, you won't have to worry about the Magus. I'll kill you myself."

The rumbling resumed and I cried out, "No more! Do not turn everyone against you!"

"They won't dare oppose me!. You all will respect my station and power." He coldly stared at the Haute Caste, who had my back. "I demand loyalty and gratitude!"

Tristan fired first. He threw a wave of energy that left the Magus on his back. "Leave here!" Tristan shouted.

As the Magus scrambled to his feet, he pointed at Tristan. Blood began to run down Tristan's chest. He grabbed his throat and fell to his knees. Sir Bart came to his aid and pulled him out of harm's way.

Lady Anastasia let out a short, piercing scream directed at the Magus. He covered his ears in pain, and we all shuddered. The rest of the Haute Caste closed ranks beside me, staring defiantly at the Magus.

The Magus glared at the undead and growled, "How could you all turn against me?" His look of shock gave me the chance I needed.

The image of my pink-cheeked newborn flashed in my mind as I stared at the Magus. "You had no idea what you started when you arranged for my birth. Without my mother, none of your plans would have come to fruition." My voice became more forceful, and the air became heavy with moisture. "You can cause death and destruction and call it a night, but my body can give life. In fact, it has produced several amazing, brilliant, gifted human beings. For all your power and dark abilities, my powers are greater. Any mortal woman is more powerful than you. Remember, your mother protected you from your father. You have always depended on women."

The Magus stared at me for a moment, incredulous. Then without another word, he raised both arms. A wave of fear rushed over us, and the dull roar of the ground shaking got worse. I almost lost my balance. "You should all remember your place. I am the source of your immortality. Without me and what I have done over the centuries, our society would not exist. None of you would exist. You must all stop this and obey me."

"Look at how you treat us. You wound the Baron, threaten us all, and then demand respect?" I took a deep breath then stared at the Magus with a steely gaze. "You broke the first law of the code, causing harm to an innocent mortal when you sent others to hurt Leif, not to mention Tomas! You have lost your claim on all of us. Do you realize how impotent you appear when you try to use your abilities to force yourself on Marie? You dishonor all vampires." I knew that had to hurt.

Alexander added, "In another time, I would have had you chained to an oar."

Hann crossed his arms. "I concur."

The Magus was not ready for a full mutiny. This was the first time that this many of the undead dared to stand against him. "You all owe me your existence!"

He still did not seem to grasp that if he continued to try to force me into submission, it would further unite the Haute Caste against him.

Omar touched my arm. "May I?" I nodded.

"Old friend," his voice was soft as an Arabian lullaby. "This is a natural consequence of the actions you set in motion when you gave me the honor of fathering Miranda. This social evolution is of your own making. To think of controlling or manipulating these young people, who try to respect our ways while they build new lives, is against all of our best interests."

For the first time in his existence, the Magus had been confronted with a weapon against which he had no defense. Truth. The Magus looked away to save face. He might be the oldest and most powerful vampire, but he now realized that he could not win if the other ancients stood together against him. It must have been a shock to him, for the first time, to have his authority successfully challenged. I suddenly sensed the fight dissipating in all of us. I turned to Tristan and saw the wound in his throat beginning to close, and tears filled my eyes.

Sir Bart, still tending to Tristan, looked up at me and said, "The Baron will be fine."

Sir Hann spoke, "We are all better for the mortals that share our world. Many of our old ways must change, and they can help us adapt to the modern world."

Alexander came to my side and whispered, "You are the victor. I wish I had a laurel crown for your lovely head."

Suddenly a limousine came flying down the driveway and stopped next to the house. Only a friend would have the access code to the gate of the refuge. Lady Kananga stepped out, dressed in an Armani suit, looking ready for business negotiations. "What are you thinking Magus? I felt the tremors driving thru the desert. Where is the infant?"

Batu came out of the house with River and Lady Cassandra. Our newborn was wrapped in one of Cassie's purple shawls. I went and stood beside Batu to present our daughter to Kananga. "This is River. She is of many Houses."

Lady Kananga cooed over her, and I sensed everyone, but the Magus, was relieved that the drama seemed to be over. The kids circled around us. Hann and Alexander stayed between the ruler of the night and us. The Magus stood alone, having difficulty grasping how he had possibly lost to me. Lost to life.

Cassandra used all her persuasive power to encourage everyone to honor the newest Royal. She approached the Magus, took his arm, and kissed his cheek. We had disarmed the most powerful vampire in existence. It was over. For now. In time he would recover, but after so many of the Haute Caste stood united against him, he would never be the same. As we walked inside, I overheard Kananga say to the Magus, "You always thought you understood women, but you have never really appreciated our unique powers. You believe that brute force and exercising power are the ultimate weapons, but forget that water dripping on a stone will wear it down. You still need to learn that at times not using your power can result in more success than trying to crush an opponent."

Once we were all back inside, I went over to Kananga and whispered, "Thank you!" She gave me a gracious smile. After everything that had just gone happened, all the undead were acting as if everything was "normal."

Leif came over to me. He was clearly shaken. "What just happened?"

I lowered my voice, "I'll explain it another time. Now please, take the kids and go out to Hann's artifacts building. Stay there till the Magus is gone."

Tomas put his arm around my shoulders. "I'll stay."

Des and Jacques nodded. I was so proud of them for so many reasons. "Please, all of you, go and keep Leif out of sight. I'll be fine." Tomas let go reluctantly.

Marie hugged me. "You kicked ass." They quickly disappeared.

I noticed the Magus look in the kid's direction as they left, but continued to talk with Omar and Cassandra. My father was a supreme diplomat for which I would be forever grateful.

A Tesla raced up to the house, Jorge and Franco jumped out and ran inside. Hann greeted them, and by his gestures, I could tell he was describing the tempest of the past half-hour. Batu stood beside me, holding our daughter tightly. Jorge and Franco came over with looks of disbelief.

Jorge gently pulled back the shawl covering River. "Preciosa." He looked at me. "Your mama just turned our world upside down. A bloodless coup, hereto unknown to our kind. Today will be a legend told in our world as long as it exists."

"I had help." I stared at the faces of my two oldest vampire friends.

"Not that much. She put him in his place in epic fashion," Batu explained.

Franco tried not to show too much admiration. "Naughty girl. So, what did you name this one? Please tell me it isn't Sunny or Stoker-ella."

"Stokerella?" Only Franco could make me chuckle after just avoiding war. "River, her name is River Khunbish Ortega-Mordecai. I want them to all have the same last name."

"Thank the night," Franco gently touched her cheek. His expression became unusually serious. "Jorge and I will go back to L.A. with the Magus. We will always watch out for your best interests."

I gave them hugs. "You're two of my most favorite nocturnal maniacs."

Jorge smiled. "You might consider how many of you we have to look out for before you add to the population. We heard Jacques has taken up your hobby."

Batu told them, "Ruben lost a lot of money on that bet. He called it the Royal Sibling Procreation Derby. He had placed his money on Des."

"You all are assholes betting on my kids."

Batu held a finger to his lips. "Shhh." He looked down at River.

We both knew she would grow up hearing much worse. Vampires tended to be polite but provoke very uncivil reactions from mortals.

Jorge and Franco went to pay their respects to the Magus. My old friend, the sun, would arrive in a few hours ending this night's drama. The Magus, the ruler of the night, was not welcome here, so he had to head back to L.A. Just before he stepped outside, the Magus looked at me, and in my mind, I heard, "Well played, Empress. The night may be coming to an end, but I don't believe we are finished."

I silently countered, "You have no idea all that has happened tonight, but you will."

He then turned and left with Jorge and Franco.

Batu said he had to change River's diaper, and then he'd bring her back to me to nurse. He would be a wonderful father. I was relieved he had not heard the mental exchange between the Magus and me. This was a fragile truce, and knowing the Magus, I knew it would not last forever. He should never have threatened my family and pissed off my children. I knew they would become much more powerful than I would ever be.

I politely asked Anastasia if she would tell the kids they could join us now. You never tell the Tsarina to do anything. Exhaustion was creeping in as the adrenaline from the confrontation wore off, not to mention recently having given birth. Jeanne and Bart came over to me. Their lips bore the slight red stain of their favorite beverage. I never quite got used to that.

"Shall I call you general now?" Jeanne added, "I wish I had a sword to give you."

I touched the Fleur de Lys necklace she had given me. Bart spoke before I could, "That has never been her way." He looked into my soul as only my philosophical brooding vampire monk could. "You have made the decision."

"Yes. Please keep it between us until I can tell Tristan."

"Of course." He leaned over and kissed my cheek. "We will head back to Portland tomorrow night Baroness."

"You delivered Jacques in a blizzard, and you risked the Magus's wrath to care for Tristan. How many times do I have to tell you to call me Miranda? Good luck with my eccentric Oregon nocturnal minions. Thank you both for agreeing to work with them. I treasure your friendship."

Jeanne was amused. "I cannot remember the last time I was called a friend. Merci." She kissed both my cheeks, and they went to their room.

Having so many ancient vampires in such close proximity during a crisis was overwhelming even for the undead.

Batu brought River back to me. I think it was hard for him to put her down, even for feeding. Soon I'd let him take care of her overnight. I looked down as she began to scrunch up her face. "I'll just take her into the kitchen."

He understood I wanted a little alone time with River. "Sure, if you need anything let me, just call me."

"This is my fifth kid, and I think I can handle it. We'll be fine. Please go to bed and get a good day's sleep. I'll let you take over when you rise." I turned so I would not see his look of disappointment. As I walked to the kitchen, I noticed Omar and Anastasia huddled with the siblings in the corner of the living room. Tomas was showing them something on his phone. I would have loved to hear that discussion, but I had to deal with a more pressing matter.

Kitchens had long been my refuge. The undead might grab some liquid sustenance from the fridge, but they never stuck around very long. I pulled a cushioned oak chair back from the table. "River, you just gotta suck." I managed to position my nipple against her tiny mouth so that she could drink and still breathe. After a couple of unsuccessful tries, she did it! "I hope you'll be more chill than your father and I."

I felt someone behind me and recognized the scent, which gave me comfort. I turned towards Tristan and saw a small cut with stitches at the base of his neck. "Miranda, may we talk?"

"Pull up a chair." Anyone else I would have asked to wait.

Concern showed in his handsome face. "You were magnificent. How can I help you and the children?"

The years of discord, petty fights, and jealousy melted away as I looked into his serious blue eyes. "Tristan, when we return home, I'll let you know my decision."

He held a glimmer of hope. "You called me, 'my love.'"

"Not now. We'll talk when we get back home." He understood how emotionally and physically drained I felt. "It's hard to tell the kids what to do anymore, but could you make sure they get some sleep before you retire?"

He softly kissed my forehead. "You've always been a superb mother. I wish the sun could not keep me from you." He used vampire speed to disappear and do my bidding.

My heart was so full. I had so much to discuss with the three vampires who had fathered my children. It would all have to wait till we got back to Granite Falls. River nursed for several more minutes till she fell asleep. I felt a surreal peace in this weird world of the undead and rescued elephants. I said a little prayer to the power that is somewhere. Omar and Anastasia silently entered. I was getting used to it after being around assassins for years.

They pulled up chairs facing me. My father looked quite pleased. "The children have something to tell you."

Anastasia quickly added, "They are remarkable and brilliant like their parents."

"I'm too exhausted to try and get it out of you now. Thanks."

Anastasia reached over and touched River's cheek. "Precious. What your mother accomplished tonight, forcing the Magus to back down, will make the world better for everyone."

"I did not sense the Magus would retaliate, at least any time soon." I looked at Omar for validation of my intuition and saw him nod.

"He has lost face, but it will not take long for him to begin to see how it will be advantageous for vampires to adjust our social structure to better survive the modern world. You and your children represent our evolution."

As Marie would say, 'Fuck the Patriarchy.' No offense," I said.

Omar chuckled, "No offense taken. I think our world is becoming more balanced."

Anastasia smiled. "Hail the Matriarchy!"

"It's been overdue," Omar added. Anastasia stood, and Omar followed her lead. They each gave me a gentle hug, careful not to disturb River. "Whatever you and the children need, you have only to ask." I nodded, and they retired for the day. It had been quite a long night for the undead.

By the time River and I headed to my room, the house was quiet. The rising sun was casting a strange gray aura across the desert. Tristan had managed to get the kids to retire as well. I was tired to the bone but not weary. My sense that all would be well comforted me as I got my little one ready for bed. I hoped her full tummy and clean diaper would let her sleep for a while. Batu had succumbed to the sleep of the dead on a couch.

I pulled back the covers and lying across my pillows was a piece of barn wood. It looked like the sign in Hann's museum. Someone had carefully painted in red. "Miranda Ante Portas!"

Chapter 52

Written in the Cards

A few days later, we were all back in Granite Falls. My Haute Caste allies assured me they would talk to the Magus about a more civil and fair way to interact with the House of Sun. I focused on the newest member of our family. River adjusted quickly to her new home and was a happy, sweet baby. Grigoryi and Teri were helpful during the day, and at night Guillaume fussed over her as much as Batu. I was able to get more sleep than when her siblings were babies, but I worried this kid was going to be spoiled. Luckily her nephew would arrive soon and share the spotlight. Jacques had picked out his son's name, Alejandro Omar Ortega-Mordecai, to honor his fathers and grandfathers. We had three weeks before the newest addition to the family would arrive.

Alexander bought the house and acreage on the other side of Leif's property. I was not sure Granite Falls needed any more vampires, but it did make me feel more secure. Tristan moved his L.A. staff to the mansion he had bought from Pomp, who had decided to return to France. A secure garden was being built for Delilah by a zoo architect. We all did our best to put the crazy confrontation at the refuge behind us.

Leif was happy when his beloved goats returned from the sanctuary. The siblings took care of their horses and had band practice at Leif's or fencing with Guillaume in the evening. A new normal was setting in. Marie, Tomas, and Des had decided to commute for the first year at the University of Washington with some overnights at Henry's place or Tristan's mansion. They wanted to be around Jacques, the two newest Mordecai kids, and their horses. I knew Marie wanted to be close to Leif. They were a darling couple. He was encouraging her to become a veterinarian. Des was all about computers and artificial intelligence. He would probably hack into the Magus's computer one day. Despite his interest in chemistry, Tomas wanted to study law. I thought it would probably be good to have an attorney in the family. Tomas still kept in touch with Ashley and told us that she had enlisted in the Navy and was stationed nearby in Everett. I did not know Ashley well, but I wondered if she and Tomas would ever be content with anyone else.

In the divorce, Tristan insisted that I get a very generous settlement but that each of the kids would receive small fortunes when they became adults. I wanted them to begin to learn how to handle their own finances, so I had each of them open their own bank accounts. Although I provided the money, they had to figure out their own budgets. I would pay their tuition, but each would have to deal with everything else. I had to chuckle when Des complained about the price of textbooks. He never seemed to be concerned about the price of anything before. Their choices of vehicles were telling. Marie purchased a Prius because it got 50 miles to the gallon. Des, not as concerned about the environment, bought a used bright red Porsche. Tomas bought my Escalade to haul around band equipment. Jacques, thinking of his soon-to-be-born son, bought a Volvo because of the crash safety test results and a baby seat.

As the summer slipped by, things were coming together for the House of Sun. Robert and Billy formally joined us; I loved having them close by, so I wanted them to move into the guest house as our resident musicians, but they preferred to live in Henry's building above the club. They swore to kick anyone's ass that bothered any member of our House.

In a month, the kids' band, Cringe, would open for Carnage at the Funeral Pyre. Batu reported that Princess Khunbish and Steve would arrive in two weeks to see River. I was glad to have their support as it would add to the prestige of our House. Sarah and Ruben sent apologies for not visiting the new arrival yet but would visit soon. James, Lolly, and Al would come for a week in late summer when the weather was beautiful, and River and Jacques' baby would be a little older. I even got a congratulations card from Molly and Manny. They said they had decided to stay in Salinas. After their last, dramatic weekend here, Salinas had become more attractive. Kyoto and Lily had sent me a beautiful tiny silk kimono for River. I was not yet ready to extend an olive branch to Kyoto, but perhaps in time.

The kids asked me to meet them at Guillaume's place an hour before sunset. I hoped they had not interrupted our cousin's rest.

They were waiting for me in front of Guillaume's house. "What's up?" I asked.

Tomas smiled and said, "Open the door."

I wasn't sure what was going on, but I played along and pulled the door open. To my surprise, Guillaume walked out wearing a short-sleeved shirt and jeans. He wore sunglasses, a ball cap and smelled of chemicals. "Are you okay?" I asked him.

He merely smiled and walked past me into the fading sunlight. "No!" I shrieked. Des was capturing everything on his phone. I watched, stunned, as Guillaume stood in the fading sunlight for a few minutes before going back inside. We followed him back into the house.

He held up his arms. "I had a bit of a reaction."

I looked at his arms, which appeared pink, a little sunburnt. "I can't believe it! Tomas, you did it!"

"It works, but I have to make it more effective."

Marie grabbed some cool, wet towels and began wiping Guillaume's arms and face. "Tomas sent a video to the Magus yesterday. The sunblock also makes vamps show up on camera."

"I figured that he would find out eventually, so I told him I was perfecting vampire sunblock. I also let him know that I finished it alone, and only I know the formula and the process."

"Have you showed the video to anyone else?" I asked.

"Just Omar and Anastasia, he was skeptical, but he tried it on one arm and was impressed." Tomas was proud of himself. "Anastasia said it needed a little lavender."

"Or rose water," Guillaume smiled. "Each version is better than the last."

Des laughed, "Way better than bursting into flames."

Jacques put his arm around his brother's shoulders. "Tomas told the Magus that if he ever wants to get a sample of the sunblock, he has to leave the House of Sun alone for at least a year."

"Did the Magus respond?" I asked.

Jacques grinned. "He sent a text with one word. 'Agreed'."

"You're kidding." The Magus had been taken down, at least for now, by a 1-2 punch, and he wasn't even arguing with the referee. I was reasonably sure that he was biding his time, and we weren't through with him yet. He is probably secretly proud of the Royals standing up to him. "Do you have any idea where Cramer is?" I asked Tomas.

"Costa Rica. He's off the grid, but I got this postcard."

He pulled a folded, beat-up card out of his jeans pocket. It was a picture of beautiful women hanging out on the beach in Panama. It just had five words on it with no name or return address. I read it out loud, "Don't let the fucker win!"

"He told me where he was going but sent this from Panama just in case it fell into the wrong hands. Cramer's all right." He took the postcard back. "I'll shred it now."

"I don't know what to say. This is amazing!" It was not easy to think well of double-dealing Cramer, but he had helped us in the end. I hugged Guillaume, kissed Tomas's cheek, and went back to the house. I had to speak with Batu about some decisions I had made.

I sat in the kitchen hugging a mug of decaf and munching on some oatmeal and raisin cookies Grigoryi had made this morning. Since I got pregnant, he had been on a health kick and continued after the baby was born. Now even his baguettes were whole wheat. That's just not right!

Teri came in with River and handed her to me. "She loved her bath, but now she's hungry. She tried to suck on the washcloth."

"Thanks." I smiled at my wide-eyed little girl then looked at Teri. "Did you know about the sunblock?"

She replied with a sheepish grin, "They told me a couple of weeks ago but asked me to keep it a secret 'cause you had a lot going on. I'm glad they finally told you.

Poor Guillaume had been using rice powder to hide his pink skin."

"Anything else I should know?"

She grabbed a cookie. "I'm going to miss these. My transformation is scheduled for early next year, if you, as the Head of the House, aka the Great Magus ass-kicker, approve."

"You mean you don't want to spend the rest of your life raising my kids?"

"It will be hard to give up living the dream."

"Is it what you want? You're not just doing this 'cause of Henry?"

"I sincerely want to be an immortal. Henry is a bonus. It's what I wanted long before I met Henry. I always want to know what the future will bring, and after being transformed, I will be able to see a lot of it. I also love that I won't have to worry about disease or my body wearing out when I get old. Can you imagine my martial arts skills after I've transformed? It's who I was always meant to be." She gave me a hug. "Have you made a decision about Tristan, Alexander, and Batu?"

When I said nothing, she continued, "Whatever you decide we're cool. I know you will make the right decision for yourself and the kids. Now I'm off to play with Henry."

We both got a little choked up as she left. When we first met several years ago, I had never imagined she would want to be a vampire. I wondered if I knew what the hell I was doing. I wished that I could be sure I was making the right decision. I had never been good at looking at things as black or white. To be or not to be a vampire presented only one option to the inescapable death of mortals.

My thoughts were interrupted when Batu came in fresh from a shower. His spicy vampire scent was intoxicating. He kissed my forehead and asked, "How is River?" He watched her nuzzle my breast.

"Hungry and darling." His adoring gaze made it more difficult to give it to him straight. "Can we talk about us?"

"Sure." He pulled up a chair. "Am I going to like this?"

"I'm going to tell you what I already told Alexander."

"You told him first?" He stared at me liked I'd slapped him.

"I'm not going to be with either of you. I welcome your commitment to raising our daughter, but that is all. You're a great father. I think we were meant to have a beautiful child together. I'm grateful for all you've done, all the times you protected us. I don't see more for us than friendship."

"What happened? What did I do? Is it postpartum depression?" He looked lost.

"It's just who we are, who we have chosen to be. All those years in Rossville, we secretly dreamed of being together after my divorce. It was just a romantic fantasy. I will always keep your Valentine's Day cards and cherish you as one of my dearest, closest friends. Your affection helped me get through some dark times."

"But without benefits?" He remarked with a wry smile.

I appreciated his unvarnished honesty. "Exactly." River fell asleep while nursing, and I handed her over to him. She looked so tiny in his muscular arms.

"We created someone very special together. There will be times in the years to come that you'll probably say she is stubborn like me. I know you'll be able to handle it."

362

He gently cradled her. "So, what's your final decision?"

"Tristan will be here tonight, and I'll tell him. Then everyone will know."

"I hope you'll be a magnificent vampiress."

"I can't tell you that yet." He looked sad and defeated. "I imagine the female night dwellers will be glad you're available. You're one hot vampire."

He managed to smile. "That's what Lily said."

"Seriously?"

He nodded. "It was part of my training."

"That makes this a little easier. I think River will sleep for a couple of hours. I've got to meet with Tristan soon."

"He was always the one."

"Alexander said the same thing." I walked out to spend a little time alone by the river.

I stood at the riverbank, preparing myself for what I knew would be an important conversation with Tristan. The murmur of the water splashing over the rocks and the occasional calls of owls were the only sounds. The light of a full moon reflected off the river and illuminated the tall fir and pine trees.

Without having made a sound, as only the undead can do, Tristan was standing beside me. Everyone at the house knew to leave us alone, but I suspected they were trying to peek through the windows. In the bright moonlight, his platinum mane framed his handsome face. I looked up into his intense gaze, and before he could say a word, I said, "Please just hold me." His strong arms gently wrapped around me. I rested my head against his cool chest. At times I had detested him, yet it was easy to find refuge in his embrace.

He finally spoke, "What have you decided?"

I moved a foot away. "Damn it! I love you too much." Tears welled in my eyes.

I saw sadness creep into his expression. "This causes you pain?"

"We won't have eternity together. I won't transform, but I won't be quite mortal either." The air became damp.

"You love me so much you choose to leave me? Not quite mortal?"

I wiped my eyes with my sleeve. He handed me a handkerchief with his earthy scent, and I started crying. "I need your help with that."

He pulled my trembling body back into his embrace. He whispered. "Miranda, I don't understand."

If he were only angry, I could deal with that, but his pain was overwhelming. I calmed myself and looked up. "Our goodbye will be slow. I want to live a very long life to see all the children find their way as adults. You saved my life when I was a child after Lena staged the accident that nearly killed me. You've always shared your gift of blood with me. I might ask you for a little blood from time to time to slow down my aging. I want only your blood. I don't want any more influence from Alexander, Batu, or any other Haute Caste." A light rain began to fall. "You've watched over me all my life, and I suppose I should thank you."

"Why start now?" He smiled then gazed at me longingly. "I could never refuse you." He leaned down and kissed me passionately. If I had not so recently given birth, it might have gone further. "You're certain that you want this? I could always transform you later."

I gently pushed against his chest and looked up at his face. "I won't become a vampire, but I'll have a very long life because of my rare blood and some help from yours. In time you'll see me age more, wrinkles, gray hair and all. We won't marry again; we're better this way, and I'll eventually accept if you're with someone else. Love with no strings attached."

He looked surprised. "Now you become reasonable about sex?"

"Do you really want to go there?"

He displayed a faint grin. "No. I always lose to you. The other women always lose by comparison to you." He brushed my unruly curls back out of my face. "Could you stop the drizzle?"

"Sorry." I had not even realized I was causing the weather change. I took a deep breath. I dried my eyes, and it began to let up. "I now realize that I still want you in my life. You risked your existence to keep us safe when you went against the Magus. I understand that you tried to stay within his inner circle to keep us safe. Tomas forgave you and trusted your motives after he got hurt. It's been harder for me, but then I keep calling out to you in my sleep. I thought we were done, but I was wrong."

His expression became serious. "I will always cherish you. I will always be here when you need me. Just remember you may ask me for immortality at any time." I shook my head. "When your time comes to leave this world," his voice cracked a little. "I promise, that though it will break my heart, I will allow it. I've had years to prepare for your decision. You are my beautiful, stubborn Achille's heel and the only one to have my heart. Our love was in the cards, my dear Empress." He pulled a Tarot card out of his jacket and handed it to me. "Lady Kananga gave me this card when I thought I'd lost you. She told me to learn patience."

"The Lovers," I said. "Perhaps we're mature enough now to truly understand what that means. No deceptions and no attempts to control each other."

"Miranda," he whispered and kissed me. It was the most perfect, tender, passionate kiss.

I came up for air. "You're gonna need condoms. Really effective condoms. Or you can forget about what the cards say."

He looked into my big brown eyes. "Remind me why I love you."

Three weeks later, darling Alejandro arrived, and I began writing about the lives of my children and grandchild. We all know stories never end, especially if they involve vampires.

More writings by Susan Old

About the Author

Susan is from Southern California and was a Peace Corps volunteer in Zaire in the late '70s. She went on to earn her master's in psychology and started in the field of Mental Health/Ad- dictions at a street emergency shelter. She worked several years at County Mental Health, a University Medical Center, and at Cedars-Sinai Medical Center. She and her family moved to the cornfields of Illinois (like Miranda), and she became a therapist at a V.A. Medical Center. Over her career, she heard about the struggles of celebrities, bikers, walking wounded Veterans, nurses, felons, farmers, prostitutes, athletes, professors, and musicians. Being a therapist gave her insight into many diverse lives, from a housewife with insomnia to a strange ranger who walked the streets with a suitcase full of Barbie dolls. Writing became her outlet for the emotional stress of her job. In her writing, she created a hidden world that keeps the true nature of the inhabit- ants, secret.

She first considered herself a writer when her late mother- in-law, an author of English historical fiction, said she liked her writing. The manuscript of her first book was lost when lightning struck a power line and wiped out everything on her computer. Rather than take it as a sign to stop writing, she took it as a lesson to back up everything on the Cloud. It took her years to rewrite the book from her notes, but fortunately, she never gave up.

She became a widow at a young age, battled Lupus, and is a two-time breast cancer survivor. Her children, family and friends always encouraged her to pursue her dreams. She believes there is a Miranda in each of us struggling to make sense of an insane world while sipping coffee.

She married a widower who accepts her obsession with shoes and helps with the technical stuff. They live north of Seattle on the banks of the Stillaguamish River with two rescued tabbies, a Black Lab Retriever with criminal instincts, and a Pug who has a very high opinion of herself. She is a volunteer at an animal shelter, and the Unity Museum in Seattle. She loves Barbacoa tacos and consumes an inordinate amount of coffee.

Follow Susan and the continuing adventures of Miranda and her offspring at:
zairesue@susanold.com
Twitter @zairesue
Instagram @zairesuewrites
Facebook book.com/zairesue/

Novels by Susan Old

The Miranda Chronicles: Book I

Rare Blood

Available at Amazon and Barnes and Noble

The Miranda Chronicles: Book II

Rhapsody in Blood

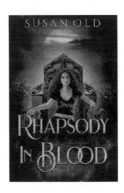

Made in the USA
Middletown, DE
24 July 2021